A DRAGON'S FATE

BOOK FIVE OF THE REMEMBERED WAR

ROBERT VANE

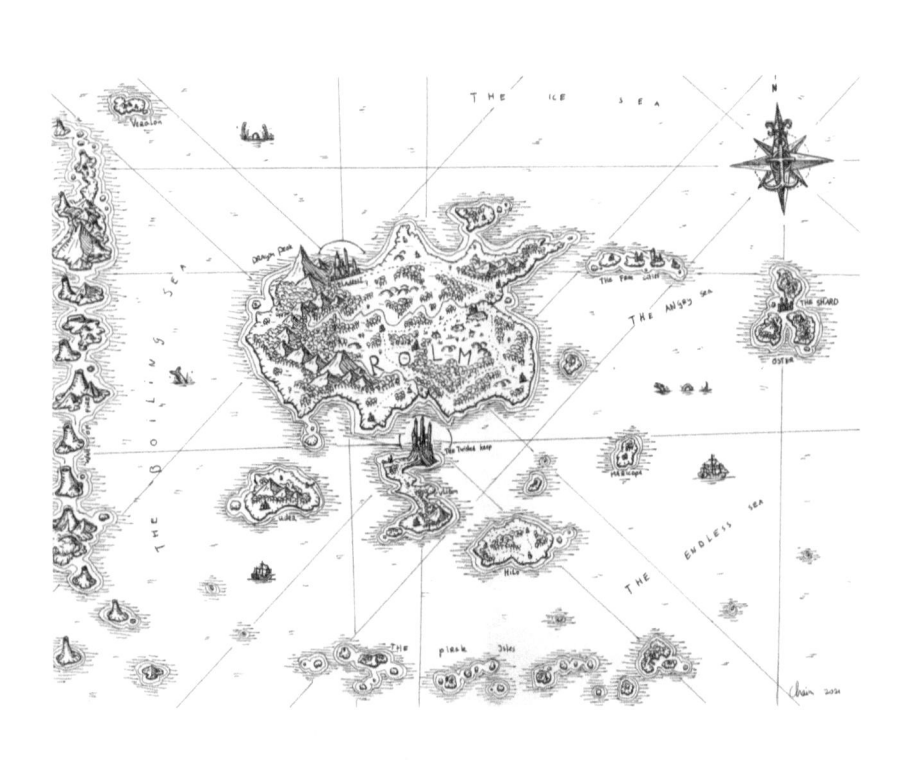

ONE

I left chaos in my wake.

Behind me was the rust, a dangerous wizard, a land in turmoil, and the last of the free dragons in the world. Inexplicably, I flew away from those things, with a human on my back and uncertainty in every beat of my wings. My sister, Kiata, was among those who I'd abandoned. Yet I didn't stop.

For days I flew across the skies, resting and hunting only when I needed, as Harlan and I traversed the vastness of Ni-Yota. We had crossed the Pillar Mountains two days past, entering the former domain of Elasu, she who had torn this land asunder. Beneath me was the late dragon queen's legacy: great keeps of stone blackened by fire, fields and villages reduced to ash, massive pyres of dead humans that looked and smelled as if they each held hundreds of corpses. Not all the blame was Elasu's, of course. Gia had not been gentle to the inhabitants of this land. Of his mysterious enemy, the fiendish tigris, there was no sign from my vantage, but I didn't doubt they lurked in the shadows. I wondered if Legao would have any more success dealing with this foe than the prior Protector. More likely, her desperate attempt to halt the rust's advance across eastern Ni-Yota would consume her energies. The fighting on this side of the mountains would fester, but even that tragedy would not matter in the end if I didn't find a way to defeat the rust.

I flew into the night, the broken form of the moon, Rima, dangling in the sky just beyond my mortal reach. A dearth of clouds made the cracked moon appear even more ominous than usual. A chill wind blew beneath the muddled glow of Rima's strange light. It seemed impossible to believe this object was the source of magic, yet that was what Oracle claimed. How was a creation of such power made? Even more remarkable, what power had damaged it so? The Cataclysm must have been an unimaginably terrible conflict. A conflict caused by humans, I had no doubt.

Harlan shared my brooding mood. "There is an ill omen in the air. We children of the sea call it a wafting—a sign that fate seeks an opportunity to turn for the worse."

I scoffed. "I don't believe in such superstition."

"You should."

Despite my protests of indifference to the strange gusts sweeping across the dark sky, I didn't argue with Harlan when he suggested we find a place to land for the night, nor did I object the unnecessarily large fire the human lit, claiming it would keep the chill off of us. He had conjured the blaze using only his hands and two sticks of wood. It was suitably warm, but the comfort of the fire didn't dispel the doubts gnawing within me.

"I should not have left Kiata," I said. "Or Rinxia. The rust is dangerous. Legao may be dangerous. This land is tearing itself apart as its doom advances. I've only to look down from the sky to see the truth of that."

Harlan didn't look up as he pecked at a haunch of charred rabbit as if he were a bird rather than a man (I had eaten mine some time ago in a single gulp). "Your sister made her desires clear. Don't underestimate her. The time when she needed your protection has passed. And without Kiata and Rinxia, there will be no Ni-Yota to save.

Legao and her human magic isn't enough. Together they may win us time to find a way to defeat the rust."

Harlan seeming nonchalant at my turmoil irked me. It wasn't that I doubted Kiata's abilities. It was just that I could handle Legao's machinations better than she—which sounded similar to doubting my sister, but was altogether different. I'd spent more time with humans than Kiata. I knew how devious and dangerous they were. Harlan was annoying me by telling me otherwise.

"You are formed of contradictions. How is it that you are able to regard a threat to all the world with the same indifference with which you eat that rabbit, yet still you devote a lifetime at sea to a near-endless quest?" Harlan kept picking at his food, pretending my question didn't bother him. "You must have visited many fine lands to retire, to relax, and enjoy whatever it is you enjoy." It certainly wasn't food.

"Home is a ship and crew and my wife. I've lost the first two, and perhaps even the last as well, it's been so long." Harlan looked up to stare again at Rima. "Failure makes you numb on the outside, the way a blacksmith's hands thicken with calluses. But that does not mean the fire he works is any less dangerous for him. I live for my quest for aurathorn and the pledge I've made, but I've had more time to grow calluses around my heart, for I've experienced much more disappointment than you."

For Harlan's sake, I hoped he was exaggerating. I'd known plenty of disappointment.

I slept that night, but not as well as I would've hoped. I kept thinking about the rust seeping onto the ground beneath me. I woke several times to find Harlan tossing about nearby, instead of his usual snoring. Perhaps he shared my uneasy dreams. We set off before dawn in near silence.

In the days that followed, we traversed the turmoil of the vast land of Ni-Yota. Its expanse would've been unimaginable to an inhabitant of Rolm, where the greatest island was little more than a grand farm in Ni-Yota. Little wonder the dragons who ruled this land thought it (and themselves) the divine center of the world. The problem with such a vast space meant there were countless places for the tigris to hide. I bid Ni-Yota a final, silent farewell as the eastern sea finally neared.

It had been many long weeks since I'd arrived in Ni-Yota, flying across the same open sea that now beckoned before me, but it seemed like I'd lived an entire lifetime here—and in some sense, that was true. Much of my free existence had been spent in Ni-Yota. In Rolm I'd been a slave, a warrior, and briefly, a son who had found his mother. In Ni-Yota I'd lived so much more: the lure of Elasu, the warmth (and enigma) of Rinxia, the maturing of Kiata, the hate of Gia. I was a very different dragon than I'd been when I had last crossed the Wall of Fire.

If Harlan felt any lingering ties to Ni-Yota, his tone of indifference hid the sentiments. "I can see the ash of the burning mountains. I can smell it." He spoke as if he knew the wall of infernos, but as far as I knew, only the waveships of Ni-Yota could pass through the boundary. Still, when it came to the sea, I didn't put anything past Harlan.

"It is the journey to Rolm after we cross that will be the most difficult," I said. "Best to fill our bellies and rest before then."

I sensed an unusual impatience in Harlan as he gazed eastward, but he didn't protest my decision to eat and rest. Of course, I was the only one of us with wings, so there wasn't anything to discuss.

I woke before dawn and helped myself to a penned sheep. It was hardly fair to the sheep, but I was in a hurry to eat and get going. The sun was still new in the sky when I left Ni-Yota behind. The land faded in my wake like a distant memory.

Soon, waves appeared beneath me. "That is where you found me, making my last stand on that very shoal as ghastrays sought their next meal," Harlan said. "My crew met their end in that place. May the sea embrace them."

I gazed down at the jagged rocks poking out of the water. One shoal looked the same as any other to me, but I had no doubt Harlan knew well the sight of his last stand against the ghastrays on the day we had first met. "Never have I seen a human fight with such determination in a situation so utterly hopeless," I told him.

"There is always hope."

I gurgled my skepticism. "You were alone, the water at your knees, surrounded by ghastrays, yet you claim to have had hope. As those venomous stingers swirled at you, did you actually expect a dragon to take pity on you and swoop out of the air to rescue you?"

"Well, not a dragon, no. That was unexpected. But I hadn't traveled so far, for so long, to end my days in a ghastray's belly. Each time I swung my sword, I became more convinced of that. I could feel my wife's presence beside me. I know she is waiting for me still, impatient for me to complete my quest. Then, like destiny, there you were, snatching me from the sky, aiding me on the next stage of my journey. I never imagined our course from that day till today, but it seems like fate now."

I mulled his words, quickly deciding Harlan's interpretation was ridiculous. "I snatched you up because I wanted your assistance. You were convenient."

"You could've found another human on land."

"Not one as desperate as you." I beat my wings faster. "Perhaps I felt a little pity as well—for the ghastrays, I mean. I'm sure you taste terrible."

Harlan chuckled warmly. I turned my attention to what lay ahead. Although still impossibly distant, the smoke from the perpetually-erupting mountains grew quickly. At this great distance, it appeared like a blanket of billowing soot pulled from the water below by some great force from the sky—the greatest wall ever created on all of Inkra. Its uncanny expanse extended in both directions, beyond even the ability of my dragon eyes to peer to the end. Perhaps there was none.

I summoned a tailwind, manipulating the Latticework to produce steady gusts that would allow me to fly ever faster with less physical effort. Harlan sang some old sailor songs along the way. His voice grated, but I didn't force him to stop. What Harlan lacked in tone, melody, and grace, he somehow made up for in raw emotion. When he sang of a lonely sea, I had no doubt that he didn't merely babble the words to some old melody, but instead had lived in the moments of which the song spoke. When Harlan unleashed a ballad of love lost to distance, I could feel a small measure of his despair escape his lips.

"You are a long time from those you care about," I said to him.

"Aye, dragon. Aye."

It unnerved me when Harlan turned serious. I let the subject drop.

The sun was about to leave the sky when we came upon the shattered remains of the raft-island on which I had landed after my initial crossing into this part of the world. Somehow, it was in even worse condition than when I'd last seen it. I would have expected Elasu or Aragor to have repaired the place, but instead it looked as if it had been through a terrible storm, its hull shattered on two sides. No life stirred aboard it. So much the better for me—no humans to speak to when I landed to rest. It was a terrible distance to Rolm once I crossed the Wall of Fire. I'd barely made it the last time, although I'd been flying straight from battle then, and I didn't have magic to aid me.

I dropped closer to the floating island, angling my wings to catch the air and slow my descent. Harlan seemed surprised. "What are you doing?"

"Landing. I will rest my wings. I suggest you rest while you can as well."

Harlan shifted on my back, uneasy. "Look at that floating platform. It looks to have been made of direwood, same as the ships of my people. It's tough stuff, but it has been torn to shreds."

I made a closer inspection. The thick wood was cracked, the edges frayed by massive teeth. Only the jaws of a leviathan could've inflicted such damage. Those marks were new. It wasn't that this place had never been repaired since I had last seen it. Rather, it had been attacked again, perhaps recently.

"I see the damage," I assured Harlan, even though I hadn't until after he'd spoken. "Still, I sense no danger at the moment. We need not linger through the night, but it is worth the risk to give my wings some rest." It might have been my imagination, but I still sensed disapproval from the human on my back. I growled at him. "I made this journey without a human on my back last time. If you can carry me across the Wall of Fire, then you can complain."

Harlan didn't cower at my petulance. "There is still blood lingering in the waves." I looked, but saw nothing; I sniffed, but smelled nothing. However, Harlan seemed sure of himself. "Whatever happened here occurred within the last shift of the tide. Danger may still lurk."

He might've been correct, but he didn't have wings burning with fatigue. I had no patience for dissent. "Doesn't danger always find us?" I set down on the damaged barge, but far more warily than I would've without Harlan's warning. I sniffed the wrecked platform thoroughly. "Humans were here recently. Their scent is still fresh." That explained the blood. "Eat what supplies we have, stretch your legs, and do whatever else you must. We won't linger."

I ate the paltry fare that remained from our journey over land in several giant gulps, saving but a few morsels for when we crossed the Wall of Fire. There was little to savor about old animal flesh and brackish water, but I now had enough in my stomach to sustain me for days if necessary. I folded my wings, grateful for a respite, even an uneasy one.

The ominous, smoky plumes from the Wall of Fire loomed ahead of me. The sight commanded my gaze—a jagged array of sinister mountains peeking above the water line, arising with the seemingly singular purpose of spewing putrid smoke toward Haven above. The rocky beasts did their deeds in unnatural silence, rumbling only occasionally despite the continuous eruptions polluting the sky, as if they were nothing more than an elaborate tapestry hung from the sky. I wondered at the origins of the bizarre wall of mountain and fire and smoke, for I had come to recognize that this was no natural phenomena. The Wall was a work of tremendous magic, one with the deliberate purpose of separating Ni-Yota from the islands in the east (or was it Rolm that had been separated?).

When I'd last flown beyond this place, I had known nothing of the Latticework of power that enabled magic to influence the mundane world. Equipped with this knowledge, I could now at least imagine how a work such as this might be formed, although it was far beyond anything I, or any contemporary master of magic, might even dream of accomplishing. A creation of such awesome power could only have been the work of those humans who had lived before the Cataclysm, those artificers who could shape the very fabric of the world (and, being human, had used such power to destroy that same world.) Yet, I could not guess their purpose in conjuring the Wall of Fire, apart from the obvious goal of preventing the crossing of the boundary. I wondered if it had something to do with the rust. Or had the inhabitants on one land feared some other threat that might come by sea?

As I rested my wings and contemplated the imposing fire of the horizon, Harlan prowled the edges of the floating platform, pausing to sniff and study the murky water lapping beneath us. I had better vision, but Harlan knew the sea. I left him to his musings while I closed my eyes to rest, my thoughts lingering on unpleasant memories of the putrid smoke of the Wall of Fire. I sat contentedly in the late light of the day, until Harlan interrupted me.

"The sea stirs." His voice made it clear this wasn't a good thing.

I forced open an eye which I focused crossly at Harlan. "The sea always moves. It is as ceaseless as your pacing and chattering."

"This is the stirring of battle—a great battle, nearby."

That got both my eyes to open wide. I craned my neck upward, surveying the expanse in all directions. "I see not a single ship riding the waves, not in any direction."

"It is not a battle of men and ships," Harlan said. "Creatures of the sea fight each other. The water rumbles, the tide hesitates."

"Where?"

Harlan stared toward the inferno beyond us. Slowly, he raised a hand, a single finger extended to the east. "Far, but not too far. Leviathans—a large number."

"Leviathans don't hunt in packs. Nor do they fight each other—except over a bit of prey perhaps."

"I'm aware of normal leviathan behavior," Harlan replied in a chillingly mild voice. "Yet there are indeed many out there if I can feel the effect on the sea from so far."

I released a long breath from my snout. I'd intended to rest my wings only a short while, but having started my break, I wasn't anxious to end it. Indeed, I had been considering waiting until the morning to continue onward. Harlan was ruining my drowsy plans.

"Leviathans are beasts of the sea. I fly in the air. Does it really matter if they chose to squabble?"

Harlan's brows furrowed in disapproval. "Leviathans engage in battle here, beside the Wall of Fire, as the rust invades Ni-Yota to the west. As you said, leviathans don't usually fight each other. The ghastray warned you that the leviathan that attacked us at Silla was different from others. You cannot truly believe that this has nothing to do with us?"

I answered by stretching my wings. "I hope you fed yourself. It is a long, desolate way to Rolm. Nor will passing through the gas spewed by those mountains be easy. The air will be poison."

"Now you are worried about me?" Harlan barked a skeptical laugh.

I lowered myself enough so he might climb onto my back with a minimum of difficulty. Once the human was with me, I extended my wings, letting the breeze surge beneath me as I felt for the currents of the sky. I launched upwards with a push of my hind legs and a beat of my wings. The wind swirled in an unruly torrent—the sea and the Wall of Fire made for unique flying conditions. I headed in the direction Harlan had indicated for the supposed leviathan battle. It didn't take long to find. Once airborne, I quickly spotted the tumult of white water erupting upwards, punctuated occasionally by a dorsal fin. Even the sea air couldn't cloak the stink of blood as I drew near. A brutal melee of giants.

An area of the sea the size of a mid-sized Ni-Yota farm had become a cauldron of carnage. Chunks of mutilated leviathan floated away from the center of the battle, while massive dorsal fins rose and fell, often entangled with wicked tentacles of adversaries.

"Ghastrays," Harlan said unnecessarily.

I had reached the same conclusion, because the remains of dozens of the creatures intermingled with the erratic waves and leviathan debris on the surface of the battle area. Swarms of ghastrays appeared fleetingly on the surface, their nearly translucent bodies glinting in the exhausted daylight, before vanishing again into the chaotic waves.

I swept in a slow circle around the infected area. We were close enough to the Wall that I felt the heat from the mountain furnaces and the burning stink of the noxious gas they belched. "So many leviathans ... it's a stew of killers."

"They shouldn't be here." Harlan sounded dismayed. "I've never seen so many leviathans in one place. Nor so many ghastrays either. They've been drawn here by something."

I kept circling, also shocked at the sheer number of aquatic predators in such a small area. From the events at the Tayo, I knew the ghastrays to be intelligent creatures, capable of acting with purpose. If many had gathered here, there was indeed a reason. Most of the battle was invisible to me from above, and the blood-infested water stirred chaotically, but the formations of ghastrays betrayed a deeper pattern amid the fighting and carnage. At sea or land, armies behaved in a similar manner.

"There is not anything particular that draws both the leviathans and ghastrays to this place," I told Harlan. "They each have their own purposes. For the ghastrays it is obvious in the way they move—

charging into the battle like cavalry harrying an army on the march. They have come to kill leviathans."

Harlan didn't answer for a while. We both merely gaped at the glimpses of deadly battle unfolding in an erratic dance of sudden carnage and deceptive peacefulness. One moment, there would be nothing but waves; in the next, a tentacle or jaw would flash to the surface. A white cresting wave would suddenly discolor with creeping red; a smooth patch of water would be polluted by dismembered corpses from below.

"I think these leviathans seek to cross the Wall. The ghastrays fight to stop them," I concluded.

"Aye, I think you have the right of it. The ghastrays are trying to defend the barrier. That is their purpose. It's always been their purpose. Just like they did at the river, the ghastrays are fighting where they must. Because those leviathans—they are hollowings."

TWO

The pattern became obvious.

The melee in the sea wasn't a clash of opposing armies. It was an attempt to stop the advancing leviathans before they could cross the Wall of Fire. Presumably they were headed toward Rolm, as we were. That could not be a coincidence.

From what I could make out from the air, the ghastrays came in packs of three, at least near the surface. When a leviathan poked above the waves, the ghastrays struck, attaching themselves to their massive adversaries. There would be more fighting below. Harlan had come to the same conclusion.

"There must be ghastrays deeper in the sea. They are targeting individual leviathans, driving them to the surface, where their fellows attack."

Judging by the mutilated leviathan corpses, the tactic seemed to be working. "They kill well, but how many leviathans are there?"

Harlan didn't answer, because there was no way for either of us to know. Those creatures weren't the leviathans we knew; they were hollowings, their behavior driven by some dark purpose that I didn't fully understand. "The hollowings must have used those ships we saw in Illium. They need only infect one leviathan, who could spread the taint to others. They must have managed to infect a significant number before the ghastrays could attack."

I stretched my claws, wishing for *sai* to make my strikes even deadlier. Still, I would make do. I spotted a leviathan breaking the surface and angled myself accordingly.

"What are you doing?" Harlan shouted, alarm ringing in his voice.

Annoyed at the interruption, I broke out of my dive. "Killing hollowings."

"This isn't our fight. The ghastrays will stop them. Or they won't. In any case, you have told me repeatedly of the long distance to land once we cross that inferno. Save your strength. We can't have you injured in combat now."

I snarled my disapproval at Harlan's sound logic. Ghastrays were vastly superior sea fighters, and they could go where I could not. They didn't need my assistance, and I doubted they desired it. I didn't like ditching a fight, but that wasn't the problem, either. The notion of hollowing leviathans prowling the waters of Rolm rankled. The humans who dwelled there were slavers of the worst sort, yet it was also my home. While not as vast or grandiose as Ni-Yota, the rust didn't threaten it, and I wanted to keep it that way. But I couldn't do that from the air. I banked into a turn, heading toward the Wall of Fire.

The dense plumes of noxious gas pumped upwards, surging from the open peaks in a seemingly endless flow. If shaojiu poured forth in such quantities, the world would be a happier place. Instead, we were stuck with putrid soot from the bowels of the world. I filled my lungs with an infusion of relatively clean air, and advised Harlan to do the same before I increased my speed. Best to get the crossing over with as quickly as I dared.

The dizzying fumes came for me. Even without inhaling, the gas clawed at my eyes and burned at the edges of my nostrils. I beat my wings with purpose. As a dragon, I remembered precisely where I'd previously emerged from the wall on my last trip, even if the smoke plumes had inevitably shifted. In that place, the gas wasn't real. In that place, I could cross, just as the Mizu waveships did.

The next flap of my wings propelled me into the midst of the fumes. Even as I told myself that the gas around me was an illusion, my head shook violently. The sky vanished; I forgot from where I'd come and what direction I sought. For a creature of the air, accustomed to almost constant assurance of my location, it was a frightening feeling. I had lost control. I was like a human, fumbling in fog. I willed my hearts to slow their beating and I commanded my wings to keep me moving. My course had been correct when I'd entered the smoke. I just needed to keep going. The other side had to be near.

The smoke thickened, or at least I perceived that. There was no point in even opening my eyes—I was in a void. Harlan gasped for breath on my back. There wasn't anything I could do for him except to keep going. I forced another hesitant flap of my wings. Each motion was a struggle, as if I'd forgotten even the instinct of flight. The power that created this phenomenon was beyond anything I could even speculate duplicating. Those who deluded themselves, luxuriating in their supposed power, were ants compared to those who came before us.

My chest burned from lack of air. My instinct was to refill my lungs, but I didn't want to do that unless I had no other choice. Harlan could breathe the contaminated air if he had to—he wasn't the one flying. I needed to keep my wits. So I flew on, wings extended. I imagined a giant roasted goat waiting ahead of me. It was the one thing I missed about Rolm. And perhaps my former ryder Bethy Rann as well, if she still lived.

A blast of comparatively fresh air tickled my nostrils. I sucked greedily before I stopped myself, unsure if it was an illusion. But the sweet breeze gliding through my snout into my chest didn't lie. I peered ahead. There was light. My head steadied. I beat my wings toward more welcoming skies. I had successfully traversed the Wall of Fire, again. Harlan was still alive as well, so definitely a success.

Beyond the inferno, endless seas beckoned under a starlit sky, betraying no hint that land might lurk far to the east. The sound of the waves mixed with the low grumbling of the volcanos in an odd symphony. I had the sky to myself apart from the lingering smoke from the infernos in my wake.

"Here is the Sea of the Lost Serpent," Harlan whispered from my back. "Here I am in this place where none before me have gone." I wasn't sure if he realized I could hear him.

"What's that you're saying?"

"Nothing."

I would've questioned him further, but an unexpected tumult in the waters ahead drew my attention. Among the waves, I spotted what might have been a leviathan's tail break the surface. I swooped down to investigate, ready to attack if necessary, but the creature had disappeared by the time I arrived. I banked into a circle, gliding gingerly above the water's surface, searching, but it didn't reappear. There was no sign of ghastrays either. If the leviathan had been one of those I'd seen in Ni-Yota, it appeared to have eluded its pursuers.

"It might've been a regular leviathan," Harlan offered.

"Perhaps, but these aren't their usual waters. They prefer the warmer areas south, as well as the channels between the great islands of Rolm that are laden with sea traffic and tasty morsels such as humans."

"Searching the sea for a leviathan that doesn't want to be found is like trying to sail across a desert—both will leave us unhappy, dead, or both."

I snorted. "A poetic way of telling me to get moving." I lifted us away from the water, hunting for a suitable gust to ride eastward. We had a long flight ahead. The currents didn't cooperate, of course, so I relied more on my own sweat than I'd wanted. When I tired, I arranged a few gusts using the power of the Latticework. I hadn't flown a hundred leagues before Harlan asked his first annoying question.

"Where are we going?"

The sudden and offhand manner in which he asked it implied I didn't know our destination, or at least hadn't given it sufficient thought. I had given it plenty of thought—I just hadn't reached a decision. It was a question of gut versus mind. The reasoned portion of me advised me to return to the island of Maricopa—that was where my mother had made her temporary refuge, where she had birthed Kiata. I had learned precious little about the humans who inhabited that place from Bethy Rann in the short time we had together. The secrets I sought might well be there, or at least it was a logical place to start looking. My gut didn't care about these things—my hearts just wanted to return to Rolm. There awaited my brethren, enslaved and broken. Bethy Rann might even be there. Although if she still lived, she had probably long since fled. Visions of sending the inhabitants of King Mendakas' citadel fleeing danced in my head. My blood heated as I pictured that righteous battle.

"You aren't answering," Harlan pointed out, drawing me away from my tempting delusions.

"We go to Maricopa," I said with dismissive certainty. "My mother was there; she chose to give birth to my sister there. It is an ... unusual place. That's where we may find answers."

My mother had gone to that island with a purpose. I was relatively certain it had to do with destroying the rust. I was connected to that as well. I just needed to understand why she was there. But that wasn't my only task. Even though I had chosen to fly to Maricopa, I had not forgotten my promise to my brothers and sisters living as slaves on DragonPeak. Somehow, I would find a way to free them. Before I returned to Ni-Yota, no dragon would remain a slave.

THREE

The safest route to Maricopa wasn't the shortest.

I opted to fly along the coasts of the Rolman islands of Uder and Hilo, rather than pass too close to the great island of Harcourt. While I was still in Rolman waters, I decided that even if I was spotted by some humans on land or a ship at sea, they would likely think me one of King Mendakas' slave dragons and leave me alone. The king's dragons went wherever they wanted and no one questioned them.

I flew beyond the long, sandy beaches of Uder's south shore before heading northwest, traversing the great channel north of Hilo's soaring black-faced cliffs. Harlan noticed the great watchtower of Kell on Hilo's north tip as we approached.

"That looks to be the highest point for leagues in any direction. We are certain to be seen by the sentries posted in that soaring spire."

I didn't bother to look. I had seen the tower often enough. I knew there were supposed to be humans on post inside its upper chambers, supposedly alert for raiders or others approaching the southern underbelly of Rolm. I tried to put Harlan's concern to rest. "Dragons in this part of the world serve the king. There are no others. Those soldiers aren't going to waste a precious messenger pigeon to report a loyal ryder out on patrol."

"I don't look like a ryder of Rolm," Harlan reminded me.

"We're too distant for anyone to realize that. I doubt they'd look carefully anyway. The winds rip over those cliffs with a cold, angry fury. The soldiers inside the tower most likely took note of my passage, then returned to their fire and their ale."

"Even if that is so, why fly so close to the shore?"

"Better to be closer to Hilo's deserted cliffs, with its lonely tower, than the busy shipping lane filled with merchants that ply the waters off Ulibon's coast. Royal ships patrol those seas, and sailors love to gossip and boast, as you know. They are more likely to spread word of a dragon in the sky than a few isolated soldiers in a desolate tower huddled around a brazier. This is the best route. Once we are beyond Hilo, there is little but open sea between us and Maricopa—no inhabited islands, no busy shipping lanes."

Harlan kept quiet until Hilo was far enough behind us that even my dragon eyes could no longer make out the shape of the spire at Kell in our wake. I congratulated myself for my wise choice of flight path several moments before I spotted a ship—a lone three-mast clipper out where it had no reason to be. The wind was brisk, but the vessel barely moved in the sea. Indeed, it looked to be drifting more than sailing. I didn't think Harlan had spotted it yet. I considered merely raising our altitude toward the clouds to avoid possible detection, before I saw a leviathan break the surface behind the vessel.

I snorted in annoyance as the distinctive fin of a killer closed in on the ship. The leviathan wasn't coming to visit, but even if I'd been inclined to intervene, there was no way I could reach the ill-fated vessel in time to do any good. The sound of a hull cracking echoed loud enough to draw Harlan's attention to the melee beneath us. He offered a choice sailor's curse. No seaman liked to see others suffer.

"That sounded like her keel," Harlan said. "That monster knew exactly where to hit."

To Harlan, the cracking of a keel sounded different than other wood being snapped. To me it was the sound of a lost ship. To the leviathan, it must've been a dinner bell. "I spotted the ship just a moment ago. It didn't even try to escape."

Harlan leaned over my side, trying to get a better look. "Her masts are still intact, albeit with untethered sails, but her rudder might've been destroyed. If her keel has snapped, there's no hope of escape."

As if to put a point to Harlan's morbid conclusion, the leviathan reemerged from the sea's depths, leaping jaws first into the stern of the doomed ship. With a single snap of its teeth, half of the ship disappeared.

"Dive now, Bayloo," Harlan pleaded.

"I can't save that ship. Earlier you urged me to keep clear of unnecessary leviathan battles. We don't even know if that creature is one of the tainted from Ni-Yota."

"This isn't about leviathans." His voice was pained. "Men will die in the water if we do nothing."

I scanned the scene below, dubious of getting involved. The sea was well on its way to consuming that portion of the ship that hadn't already been claimed by the leviathan's jaws. I saw no activity on deck, heard no frantic screams of doomed humans. Harlan was being too emotional. "If there are still any survivors, they are as good as dead already."

His next words had the uncomfortable sound of prophecy to them. "Withhold your hand for a drowning man, and fate shall pull you under in turn."

Displeasure rumbled in my throat. "Dragons don't have hands. Your threat doesn't apply to us." I said the words, but I still tucked my head down and dove toward the sea. I didn't need to give fate any excuse to rally against me.

I came down fast, but as I predicted, not fast enough. The leviathan made a final assault, ramming its head into what remained of the ship's hull. The wood shattered like glass dropped from a tower. The beast swam through the debris, hurling the remnants of its masts into the air. There wasn't going to be anyone to save from this slaughter.

Harlan disagreed. "There! Floating by that bit of the bow. Grab him!"

The "him" that Harlan referred to was a corpse; the unfortunate sailor was face down in the waves. Unless this variety of human had gills, there was no way that the man still lived.

"He's dead, Harlan. They all are."

The leviathan surfaced north of the wreck, sliding across the surface as it scooped inert bodies from the waves before disappearing again under the surface. For the moment, it stayed below, invisible and dangerous. I slowed my dive and prepared to level myself off rather than plunge too close to the water. Harlan barked, but I wasn't going to listen. I had a healthy respect for the wrath of fate, but I absolutely knew a leviathan's teeth would be lethal if I came too close. Though, if it was bothering to eat the humans, this leviathan probably wasn't a hollowing.

I angled my wings, ending our descent, but just before I started to change direction for more altitude, I heard a splash. A little one, not made by a hungry leviathan. One of the sailors still lived, at least enough to kick a leg. I spotted him to my left, grabbing onto a piece of debris. He clutched another of his fellow sailors by the arm, desperately yanking the other human toward his precarious raft. Such camaraderie. Unfortunately, trying to save the probably-dead crewman had been noisy and therefore stupid. The leviathan could hear as well as I, if not better. I twisted awkwardly, diving through wind even as I struggled to get a decent angle to try to snatch the survivor with my claws.

I was fast, but so was the leviathan. We reached the survivor simultaneously; I got the top half of him, the leviathan got the bottom half. My portion might've been slightly bigger. I'm not claiming that it mattered, though.

Harlan gasped in agony, as if he'd been the one torn into sections. To make him feel a bit better (and to not take any chances with fate), I snatched up another face-down floater along my flight path so I held one and a half humans in my clutches. Let no human or deity claim I hadn't tried to save those I could.

I beat my wings to take us away from the leviathan and the sea of death. Only once I was satisfied I was far out of reach of any sea creature did I refocus on the human parts that I held in my claws.

The half-person was unmistakably dead. The other was intact, but didn't seem to be moving or breathing.

"How are they?" Harlan called from my back. He didn't have the benefit of a decent view of my foreclaws.

"I hope your gods of the sea appreciate effort."

Gloom clouded Harlan's voice. "They are dead?"

"Almost definitely."

"Almost?" The false hope was palpable.

"I'm no healer and it's a bit hard to be certain with the whole human clutched in my claw. The other is certainly dead, as I was able to save only half of him."

"If there is a chance we can save a life, we should land."

I stifled a groan of displeasure. Just because I'd flown away from that leviathan didn't mean there wasn't other danger lurking. I didn't like the sea. I couldn't see or smell what was beneath its waves. "Land where?"

Harlan paused only for a moment. We were close enough to the water that his human eyes still had an expansive view of the surrounding sea. "It looks like there are a pair of atolls ahead of us."

The first time I looked, I didn't see anything. Maybe I didn't want to see the grubby collection of black rocks poking through the waves around them. They looked like a leviathan had swallowed the battlements of an entire castle, then emptied its rock-clogged bowels out in the middle of the sea. Landing there would be no treat, but more than that it would be useless. The humans I carried were dead as dead could be. Harlan sensed my reluctance.

"Please, Bayloo." His pleas somehow rose over the howl of the wind. "You are not a sailor. In the lore of my people, to be swallowed by the water is the worst of all possible deaths, but to save a fellow from such a fate is the greatest of blessings, a portent of good fortune. And we have need of some good fortune."

His words didn't persuade me. The fatigue in my wings did. I was tired. I'd leave Harlan's humans on those rocks if it made him and any gods happier. At the same time, I would get rest. Let all be satisfied. I changed course again, targeting the lonely collection of rocks. As I neared, I spotted three more of the so-called islands. If I imagined a line between them, it would've formed part of a circle. I realized that the isolated atolls were not really islands.

"We are about to set down on the very top of an underwater inferno mountain," I informed Harlan, calmly. "The rest of its bulk is hidden beneath the waves. There is no telling how far down it goes. It's probably not active. Probably."

Harlan paid me no mind. I laid the corpses onto the rocks as gently as I could manage, which wasn't particularly gentle. Neither twitched. A wave splashed through the rocks of the atoll, collapsing cold water atop both bodies. Again, nothing from the dead. At least some carnivorous fish would soon be happy at its good fortune. Harlan slid from my back anyway, wisely keeping one hand on my torso for balance, as the water waded through this collection of rocks.

"I don't like it here," I growled, meaning it. This place made me feel like I was standing in the middle of the sea. Dragons weren't meant for water. I kept my wings spread, up as high as they could go, lest they get soaked. "A great wave may appear at any moment. We've done our best for those men. More than any other human or dragon would've done in our place. I'm grateful for a bit of rest, but this place is more dangerous than restful. We must go."

Instead, Harlan waded onto the precarious rock of the atoll. Seeing the ship destroyed must have temporarily damaged his mind. My anger flashed and I gave my wings a flap—I didn't need to stay here if I didn't want to. I presumed Harlan realized another dragon wouldn't be flying past to fetch him anytime soon.

He yelled over the din of the sea, "Fortune may yet smile upon us for our deed."

I almost lifted off, just to teach Harlan a lesson. I might have, but for what he said next.

"This one wears a sealed messenger's pouch." He knelt down beside the more intact of the two corpses. The man did have a leather strap slung around his chest over a bit of what had once been finely-embroidered jerkin.

Harlan yanked the bag's strap, pulling it from the corpse to show me. An oiled leather cylinder was attached. Markings had been carved into the container. "Those would be the sigils of the lord he served," I confirmed. "Perhaps we may learn of some noble's future marriage plans. Or maybe that cylinder contains fish bones. In any case, we should not open it here. I'm leaving. You are invited to accompany me."

Harlan scrambled onto my back. I flapped my wings as a wave burst on the rocks beside me, spraying Harlan and I with freezing, salty water that burned in my nostrils. With a snorting exhale, I left the rock and the corpses. I could hear Harlan fiddling with the pouch on my back. I kept my altitude steady.

"A sealed missive," Harlan proclaimed. "The symbol on the wax looks a bit like a giant fish."

"Humans love their little pictures on their messages. I know that only King Mendakas uses the dragon symbol. I never paid attention to the rest, although the little lords always seemed to enjoy carrying their flags and painting their armor. A bunch of them have fish on them. I promise I won't tell anyone you opened it. Just grip the parchment tightly with those useful fingers you have, so the wind doesn't take it from you."

The sounds of paper rustling followed, then silence.

I got annoyed at the delay. I'd risked my life for that message. "Well?"

"It's gibberish."

I snorted a good, long snort. "You don't understand Rolmish."

"Aye, you have it. The letters are the same as Korithian, where I spent a year long ago. I can read the sounds, but I've no idea what the words mean."

This made me more pleased than it should have. It seemed I liked being the first to know things. I was still finding things out about my free self. "Do your best. I'll translate."

Harlan read out some mangled sounds. Very mangled.

"You sound like you are imitating a rooster. Try again. Go slower."

He tried again. It still sounded mostly like nonsense, like a single garbled word. Something like: "Tarhas-return."

"Try again. Slow. I believe you are supposed to pause when you see a space between the letters."

Harlan grumbled, but he did as I asked.

This time I got the meaning. "It says 'the heir has returned,'" I proclaimed in Avian.

"What does that mean to you?"

I considered the implications of the cryptic message. Perhaps it had been part of an ongoing correspondence. It was also strange that it was sent by ship rather than pigeon. Humans sent message by sea when the writing was too voluminous for bird, or when the skies weren't safe for their messenger birds. It must be the latter case here. I was far from an expert on the politics of Rolm. But I had heard of the heir previously.

"I think it means trouble in Ulibon. That fish symbol may belong to the Lord of the Twisted Keep, the great citadel that dominates that island," I said. "That message means that Rolm is at war."

FOUR

We reached Maricopa.

From a distance, the island appeared an inconsequential speck in a vast sea. Its stature improved little as I neared. Maricopa was a landscape of devastated sand and rock, windswept and inhospitable even to most vegetation. Its overseer was a stern, towering inferno mountain known as the Kraken that loomed over its tiny domain. This goliath was the only place on the island where greenery flourished. The rest of the rock was desolate, but for me the barren shores were laden with memories of the harshest sort. The pain I had experienced in this place pushed all else from my thoughts. I reduced my speed as I approached. I told myself it was fatigue that kept me from pushing harder to my destination. I did need rest, but that wasn't what caused me to slow. I was wary.

I circled the island, tracing its shoreline from above, searching both the sea for danger and the land for any sign of human activity. I found nothing.

"This place is as empty as a docked ship after the seahands get paid." Harlan sounded disappointed.

I scanned the island, my eyes passing over rocky hills and lifeless plains. Only around the great peak of the Kraken did thick growth disrupt my scouting. "It is empty because this isn't a place most humans would want to live. It has nothing, it is near nothing. The only source of fresh water is the rain and the lake atop the mountain."

"But some chose to live here anyway." Harlan said it as if he knew more than I did about the villagers who once dwelled here. The people had been slaughtered by the Mizu who had hunted my sister —the Mizu and the magi, Drasu.

The fishing village seemed the right place to begin my search. I wasn't ready to return to the crater, to that place where my mother had died. My memories of that day were black, cold, and painful. I would go there only when I must.

I set us down beside the restless waves of the sea, near Maricopa's only navigable harbor. I stood not far from the spot I'd occupied when I'd last visited this isle. Back then, the brutal mind of Brindisi had sought to command me. I shuddered at the memory, my mane prickling up with anger. I practically shook Harlan off my back. He deftly obliged, sliding onto the ground and immediately gliding into what remained of the village that had once stood in this place.

I tucked in my weary wings as I examined the runes. There had been so much here to begin with, but now no structure was left standing. The wooden dwellings that had been ransacked by the Mizu had been burned.

"Very thorough," Harlan remarked of the damage. "Even the blood raiders of Orn are not so complete in their destruction."

I wasn't interested in Harlan's stories. "This was done by dragon fire. The scorch marks on the gravel give it away."

Harlan bent down, rubbing the blackened grains through his fingers. He sniffed at the debris. "This happened weeks ago, at least."

"Around the time I fled Rolm." I thought back to the conversation in my cave on DragonPeak with King Mendakas and his minions. "This place was already a ruin the last time I was here. After I was brought back to Rolm near death, King Mendakas sent ryders to investigate this island. Some among his advisors suspected the heir of Ulibon might have been hiding here. I didn't think so. But ryders searched this place on the king's orders. Whatever they found, the king decided to get rid of the remains afterward."

Harlan tilted his head. "Ulibon?" He placed a hand on the messenger's pouch that he'd slung over his shoulder. "This is the same heir that is spoken about on the parchment we found?"

"I thought you were the most worldly human on Inkra. You do not know the conquest of the Ulibon and the lingering whispers of the lost heir?"

Harlan sniffed. "Few have ever heard of Rolm, both because of its distance from other great lands and because of its inaccessibility. Most of what is known is gleaned secondhand from Ni-Yota, for only their waveships ply these waters—and as you know, my people are not welcome in the land of dragons. So as far as I've traveled, as many strange conversations as I've had, I do not know of Ulibon, much less of its fall. But you clearly do know the story quite well. Were you a part of it, perhaps?"

"In Rolm, humans celebrate victories, but it was dragons who actually earned them. The capture of the Twisted Keep of Ulibon was no different in that regard." I let go of a sigh laden with memories of the fallen. "In Ulibon, there were humans known as enchanters— in Ni-Yota perhaps they would've been called magi, although their powers were more specialized." I closed my eyes, remembering the haze of my past life, recalling experiences that were only partially my own. "I didn't understand magic then. I think the enchanters were humans who had learned enough to manipulate magic in a very particular, specialized way. In any case, they were deadly. Their ruler, the so-called Highstar, even more so."

"A great, glorious victory when they were defeated then, eh?" Harlan prodded.

I recalled the humans of King Mendakas' army embracing, celebrating after the great keep had fallen. I saw a young king luxuriating in the triumph, I remembered the joyous shouts and boisterous laughing. We dragons took no part in celebrations. We merely obeyed, although there was satisfaction in having pleased our masters. "Men died on both sides in the battle. Dragons died as well. All over control of large tracts of dirt on a mid-sized island. All so some humans could have more grain, more metal, more of whatever made them feel big and important."

Harlan sensed my changing mood. His own tone turned somber. "The past can look very different when seen by those living in the present." He hesitated, his lips pursed, before pressing on. "I surmise that the ruler of Ulibon—the Highstar, as you say he was known—was killed in the battle. Why did your king think this heir survived, and why would he believe that this escaped son would come to a barren island like this?"

"The boy who was the only son of the Highstar—Alon—his body was never found. Well, a body was found, but none could be sure if it was the boy. But that isn't surprising, given that he and his mother supposedly leapt into the sea to avoid capture. That always seemed to me to be a strange way to attempt an escape for a species without wings, but humans are strange. As to why Mendakas later suspected this boy might've come to Maricopa—I can only guess as to the twisted logic of men. I supposed the first is fear—a king like Mendakas always fears the loss of his precious power. More simply, Mendakas knew the old Highstar could wield magic. Mendakas didn't understand the nature of the magic of enchantment, but his human advisors with their small heads and hairless ears came to suspect that the seemingly backward villagers of Maricopa had also secretly possessed the same power. A logical link for a simple mind to make—the Highstar could do magic, the villagers of Maricopa could do magic. Besides, Mendakas is the kind of human who believes that everything that happens is about him. Perhaps you know the type."

Harlan's voice bristled. "Would I?"

I ignored his protest of the obvious. "A man like Mendakas would assume anything so grandly unexpected such as finding enchanters on a backwater isle was some kind of conspiracy against him."

"But that is not what you believe?"

I flicked my tail at the dust of the destroyed settlement. "There were enchanters here, sure enough. Refugees from Ni-Yota who fled to Ulibon, then this place. Brindisi and I searched the scarred remains of the village. I was more ignorant than a new babe then, my free will still fresh. Yet I remember what we found—ingots of gold, a white sand so fine it was nearly dust, precision tools like none ever seen in Rolm. But I also knew two of the inhabitants of that village well. Indeed, they freed me. Bethy Rann saved my life." *She saved it and I left her behind to die at Mendakas' hand.* "She never spoke of the Highstar, or of some secret heir hiding among her people."

"Did you ask her?" Harlan asked. "It's not the kind of thing one mentions unbidden."

I let a low growl rumble up my neck. "The story of the Heir of Ulibon hiding here is a king's paranoia." I paused for a moment. "And if it was otherwise ... Drasu and his raiders were thorough in their slaughter. Everyone in this village is dead. Even if the mysterious heir somehow escaped the Mizu raiders, there was no way off the island. Mendakas' ryders would've found any survivor and finished what Drasu started."

Harlan nodded slowly, as if reluctant to accept the clear facts I presented to him. "What did these refugees of Ni-Yota—these enchanters—want with aurathorn?"

"They helped my mother use aurathorn to free me." At least that's what Bethy Rann had told me. And that there was no more of that precious vine. No more I could use to free the other dragons.

"How?" Harlan pressed. "How was it used to break the runes that bound you?"

These were details I had not been focused upon at the time. All that had mattered was that I was free. I had known nothing of magic.

Once Bethy Rann told me there was no more, it didn't matter. Embarrassed, I realized that I knew only the barest details. "My old ryder apparently fed it to me in a potion of some kind, specially treated with my mother's magic. But I also drank quite a bit of ale."

"Ale?" The sailor's eyes surged open. "And you *ate* aurathorn?"

"Apparently. It is a vine, is it not? Humans eat lots of stuff that grows from the ground. Do not alchemists use flowers and herbs in their medicines?"

Harlan merely shook his head in disbelief. "A group of human magic users—these so-called enchanters—somehow obtained the rarest of substances, something I and my people have been searching for through generations, and they *fed* it to you." The judgment in his voice was harsh.

"I am an ember dragon," I reminded him, my voice deepening. "I am worth it."

Harlan huffed indignantly. "And you dare say that I am the type who believes everything is about me."

I snarled at Harlan's doubts about how my freedom had been achieved, but at the same time, uncertainty about the full plans of my mother and the dead inhabitants of this island remained. I had assumed the purpose of aurathorn was to help me and my kind. I assumed that was why my mother had come to this place. Maybe it was true. But Bethy Rann's people could have obtained aurathorn for other reasons as well.

A hardening concern had come to Harlan's eyes. "How did they get it? Where did it come from?" He looked around the barren scruff of the island. "It could not have merely been growing in this place, despite the history you shared with me."

"Bethy Rann told me that the inhabitants traded for it."

"Traded?" Harlan pressed. "Who would trade aurathorn?" Harlan seemed to be having trouble breathing due to his shock.

"I don't know." Even Bethy Rann hadn't known—or at least she had not shared the information with me. Harlan digested my answer like it was stone. For once, he stopped talking.

I began to pick my way through the burnt ground of the village. I sniffed and prodded and scratched through the top layer of hardened ash with my claws. I had not searched long before Harlan found his tongue again.

"Aurathorn isn't in the burnt village. It is time to look elsewhere."

I kept ignoring his whining, moving deliberately to the spot where the storeroom for the village's most precious materials had once stood. There was no obvious sign of the gold or specialized sand or other instruments that had once been hidden here, of course. Anything Rolm's ryders hadn't burned had been sent back to Eladrell. Still, I dug at the ravaged ground. Human eyes might miss something that could be located by a dragon's nose.

The potent scent of ash born from dragon fire wafted into my nostrils as my claws disturbed its resting place. I pushed the dust around, slow and careful, my eyes and nose searching. The longer I took, the closer Harlan came to the location where I dug. I tapped the tip of my claw against hard bits that lay beneath the surface.

"What have you found?"

"Come see for yourself. You'll have to get those pretty fingers dirty, though."

Harlan didn't hesitate. He sank to his knees and dug out the small shards I'd discovered from the packed ground far better than my giant claws could've managed. "Glass," he concluded, holding a fragment of dubious treasure between two of his fleshy digits. I said nothing; Harlan kept peering at his find. "It glows ... violet, like a fine burgundy held up against the sun on a summer day." The sailor licked his lips. "The taste of new summer."

I got the meaning, even if I didn't understand all the words. "Violet sand makes violet glass when heated in a furnace. Or if blasted by dragon fire, which is similar to a furnace."

"I have heard of such a thing. The red sand of Doloon is much the same." Harlan placed the shard between his teeth as if he intended to bite, then jerked it out, surprised. "It is still warm."

"Some sands are always warm."

Harlan arched both brows. "That is something I haven't experienced, and I've lain on plenty of beaches."

"The sands of Proving Shore on the Isle of Oster are said to never cool. Each time the cold sea waves wash over them they heat themselves anew, as if each contained a small furnace. Nothing can live on that beach. To spend too much time in the sand is to invite a horrid sickness that often leads to death."

Harlan's eyes grew wide. "The people here had contact with Oster, then?"

"Or at least they acquired the sand from the Proving Shore to use in their enchantments."

"What does it do?"

"I have no idea." Harlan looked disappointed at my answer. "The art of enchantment is more alchemy than true magic. It is done by instruments, from what I gather. It is a human discipline, unknown to me."

Harlan dipped his chin as if he understood. "Is there anything else unusual you smell here?"

I made one more cursory sniff. "You need a bath."

Harlan turned his gaze away from me, his chin pointed upwards at the Kraken. "Then we must look elsewhere for answers."

I didn't look. I knew all about the Kraken. The memories of that place were a sharp blade in my belly, cutting everywhere.

Harlan didn't have sympathy. "There is nothing else on this island but what awaits up there." When I didn't move, he added, "You've traveled a great distance to be here. Why hesitate now?"

"Evil was spawned in that place," I said, ashamed at the childish fear of my own words.

I expected a mocking reply, but to my surprise, Harlan grunted with understanding. "A marked place."

It wasn't a term I'd heard before. "Marked?"

"Where the blackest of deeds have been done. A happening so terrible, it impresses itself on the fabric of the world. Aye, and to return to it is to dance on the edge of the Abyss."

I locked my gaze on the mountain. Something inside me quivered. "A marked place indeed."

Harlan showed his teeth, the humorless smile of a snarling wolf. It was a look I'd not seen on him before. "Then we are in agreement on both the danger and what must be done." That ugly grin widened. "In the darkness hides the greatest secrets."

FIVE

I didn't fly quickly.

It wasn't just the fatigue of the flight from Ni-Yota that still burdened me. The closer I came to returning to the site of my mother's death, the tighter my hearts beat inside me. If I didn't know better, I would've thought that I was (a bit) afraid.

I spiraled upward toward the summit, flying in elongated circles that gave me a view of every side of the mountain. Koa trees clung to the steep sides, their dense leaves clustering together as if they embraced. Based on my past experience fighting the Mizu, the trees made for effective cover, even from the peering eyes of a dragon. I detected no movement beneath the canopy, but on the far side of the Kraken, on the sloping face that gazed out over the sea, there was the unmistakable sign of clear-cutting. The trail was wide enough that even Harlan spotted the hacked vegetation.

"Someone ascended from there," Harlan said with mastery of the obvious. "The trail begins near the mountain base, at the edge of the sea."

I adjusted my flight path, gliding over the site of fallen trees and underbrush.

Harlan leaned to the side to give himself a better view of the sea that lapped against the mountain's base. "There's no harbor on this side of the mountain. No seafaring ship could dock next to that shoreline."

"This island has but one harbor for ships," I confirmed.

"Can you get me closer?"

I swooped downward, tickling the top of the cresting waves with my hindlegs as the water rolled against the hard face of the Kraken's base. I let the water splash on my claws before pulling into a gentle ascent.

"That water is no deeper than my knees," Harlan said. "With jagged rock beneath it that would slice through a hull like a blade through tender flesh."

I caught a gust and let it lift me toward the summit. "So someone swam ashore?"

Harlan leaned over to take another look at the sea. "Those are rough, cold waters. Even a hearty swimmer couldn't get far with those currents. Look at that trail through the trees—it took more than one person to cut it: a group more concerned with speed than stealth. To even access the mountain, a large vessel must've moored offshore, then a smaller craft had to row ashore to pass through those shallow, dangerous waters. Not something to be attempted lightly."

Sharp gusts began to whip out from the east as I flew above the mountaintop. I could've peered into the crater, but I didn't for some reason that I didn't want to examine. Not yet. "Rolmans wouldn't have bothered with such inconveniences as boats and climbing—they'd have come by dragon."

Harlan agreed. "Whoever did this came for the specific purposes of scaling the peak. I want to know why."

I knew I had to return to the crater. I forced myself to turn toward the lush interior of the hollowed mountain, to the place of my haunting defeat and the grave of my mother. I pushed a breath of air from my chest before flapping my wings for speed. I crossed the threshold of the crater's top ring. Reluctantly, I gazed down. My neck tightened with dread at what I saw.

The lake was gone.

Or more precisely, it had been maimed into merely a collection of puddles interspersed with mudflats. The once-pristine shoreline had receded like the hair of a middle-aged human; the remaining water of the lake was choked with the fog of debris. Seemingly random chunks of the blackened beach jutted into what remained of the lake like spears.

I landed near the water, but not too close. I'd involuntarily learned to swim in that lake—if you could call it learning—and I remained instinctively wary of it. I'd also dragged my mother's corpse there. Did her bones lie somewhere in the mud? I pushed the image from my mind. Dead was dead. "If the water was a juicy haunch of meat, this looks as if some predator tore at the choicest ends before being driven off by a still more formidable contender."

Harlan slid off my back. "Let us hope any more formidable contender has departed."

I sniffed my agreement. Devastation had been visited upon this place; I remembered it as lush, a secret garden hidden on an island of barren desolation. That wasn't the case anymore. Trees and other vegetation had been brutally hacked, the ground ripped asunder as if a behemoth had run rampant. Even the rock of the crater walls hadn't been spared. Deep gashes marked the crater's stone. Misshapen chunks of dislodged rock lay on the ground, where something far more vicious than a pickaxe had pounded with vengeance. A trio of wolf-eagles watched us from high above, each one perched on a cliff tree that clung to the rock beyond where the interlopers had managed to venture. I wondered if they were the same birds who had witnessed my mother's death. Probably.

Looking at the ugly mess, I pronounced the obvious conclusion. "No single human did this. I'm not even sure how many it would have taken to tear up the shore like that, and rip the rock from the mountain. Even with magic, I'm not sure a lake that size could be depleted in such a manner."

Harlan had already made his way to the muddy edge of the water. I followed, picking my steps carefully on violently-trodden ground. Harlan placed a hand in the water, feeling around the bottom with no obvious result. "It's shallow. Much of the water is gone. Somehow." He strode to different parts of the lake repeating the process, while I watched with my teeth clenched. I kept expecting him to yank up one of my mother's bones. Perhaps that was better than her remains having been defiled by whoever had destroyed the lake.

On the fourth attempt, Harlan kneeled beside a sandbar-like salient that extended into the polluted water, and stuck his arm further down until only his shoulder was visible. When his hand emerged, he clutched a chunk of aquatic vegetation that resembled a cross between seaweed and a leafless bramble. It seemed unremarkable to me, but Harlan's eyes widened, then narrowed. As we both looked at the fragment, it withered like a burning ember in the sun's light. In three blinks of my eyes, it was gone but for a bit of ash drifting in the wind.

"What was that?" I asked.

Harlan rubbed his fingers against the palm of his hand, smearing the last residue of the strange bramble. "I think it is ... was hrakar."

"So you've heard of seaweed bushes that turn to ash in the air?" I huffed. "Even in Ni-Yota there isn't such a thing."

He dipped his hand in the water, presumably to wash off the residue. "Even if you flew far and wide, it's rare enough to find."

"What does it do?"

Harlan stood and indicated the lake, to the violently-altered shoreline and the pockets of water that had once been a lake deep enough for me to nearly drown in. "Well, I think someone used it to do that."

"That scrawny little bramble that couldn't survive in the open air ravaged this lake?" I flared my nostrils.

"Hrakar can be used as a kind of living sea wall. There are dozens of settlements, and even entire nations that battle the encroaching seas. To them, hrakar is more precious than gold. It can absorb vast amounts of water, altering it using a process that is far beyond my understanding. As long as it remains submerged, the plant grows quickly, feasting on the water, then converting itself to a thick sludge that sticks together as if it was mortar. But unlike conventional mortar, hrakar can be laid beneath the sea, forming a barrier to hold the waves at bay. At least for a while." He pointed at the mud formations that cut into the lake. "See the damage to the shoreline? That's what the hrakar did."

I studied the remains of the lake's shore. "Why use it here on this lake?"

Harlan surveyed the inside of the crater, and I noticed tension around his eyes as he did so. "There was no settlement to save here, true enough. No rising tides." He pursed his lips. "But hrakar might have been useful to someone who wanted to search the lake quickly. Someone who was looking for something that might grow deep in its waters."

The conclusion was obvious. "Aurathorn, then. You believe someone came for it."

Harlan's gaze continued to flicker to the walls of the mountain that surrounded us. "The people that did this didn't know where the aurathorn might be hidden. They searched the water, they searched the rocks, everywhere. Speed. Thoroughness." More quietly, he added, "Someone else wants aurathorn very badly."

"They drained much of the lake using this hrakar. Would that not destroy it?"

"Hrakar wouldn't harm aurathorn, even if it disturbed the bed on which it nested." Harlan surveyed the muddied waters. "I wonder if they found it."

I snapped my tail. "As I said before, Bethy Rann told me it was gone. She wouldn't lie to me." I said it with certainty.

"So trusting of humans, Bayloo. Not like you at all."

I snorted, but the words stung. Unlike my other ryders, I had no magical bond with Bethy Rann. I couldn't truly know her mind the way I did the others. I trusted her because she was Jona's sister. And she had saved my life. Was that naive? It wasn't so long ago, but that version of me was fresh to the world. I tried to imagine myself being wrong. It was hard, of course. I didn't think I was wrong about Rann. I didn't believe aurathorn was here, only a clue where to find it. "The people who did this spent a great deal of effort ransacking this place. They wouldn't have bothered if they had found it."

"Aye," Harlan conceded, finally. "There was no aurathorn here."

"Tell me then, why has no one in Ni-Yota heard of this hrakar?"

Harlan shrugged without a care. "Ni-Yota is a vast continent, perhaps the largest landmass on Inkra. Its cities are mostly unthreatened by rising tides, unlike many other places. But hrakar is bred in dark caves or in special barrels and traded to those places that desperately desire it. Some in Ni-Yota may know it, but it has little use there, and no one has a reason to pay the high price to obtain it."

"But it could have been bought by some lord in Ni-Yota?" I pressed. "A resourceful man like Jinu, the Master of Shadows, perhaps?" I suggested.

Harlan arched a brow. "He might know of hrakar, if any in that land would."

"Yet you still sound doubtful."

"We have been across Ni-Yota. The most powerful living wizard there is Legao, and she knows nothing of the potential of aurathorn. Even the Protector, Aragor, seemed ignorant of its potential. I do not think that whoever did this was from Ni-Yota."

"Then who?"

Harlan walked away from me, toward the ravaged walls of the crater. As he took his third step, he said, "I don't know."

There was something off in his voice. "But you have your suspicions. Strong ones."

"Aye," Harlan whispered, but I still heard his displeasure clearly.

He kept walking away. That wasn't really a problem. I had no trouble projecting my voice.

"Stop there, little human," I commanded. "I brought you here, carried you on my back across this world so you might aid me and continue your own quest. You will answer my questions as I've answered yours, or you'll remain on this island."

Wisely, Harlan turned to face me. He wore as troubled an expression as I'd seen on his face, his lips curled in a tense line. Harlan's distress jarred something inside me. This was more than a mystery he was trying to solve, more than a quest. He'd learned something new and unexpected when he discovered this hrakar. My mane pricked up with suspicion.

"This plant, this hrakar, it is a rather remarkable thing," I mused with suspicion. "Something like that, it reminds me of the glasswings of Ni-Yota—a living thing that has been shaped by outside forces. The kind of power possessed by people who are long since dead and gone."

Harlan's chin dipped and rose. "Aye."

I asked the question to which I'd already guessed the answer. "Who created the hrakar, Harlan?"

"What people wanted to hold back the sea more than any other?" he replied. "The children of islands. The seas around Farlight were rising well before the Cataclysm. My ancestors were resourceful and powerful, and they could change things, as they did themselves. So yes, according to our lore, it was my people who created hrakar."

SIX

"Your people are here?"

"I didn't say that." Harlan sounded like he was trying to convince himself of his own words. "Remember, my people are few, scattered throughout the world, and not many even know of Rolm. Even in Ni-Yota, the islands beyond the Wall of Fire are mostly myth. To reach these waters from elsewhere, to avoid the infernos, is near impossible. As I said, hrakar was created centuries ago. Many other people now possess it. Some merchants have learned the secrets of growing it themselves. As you suggest, it could've been a waveship from Ni-Yota in service of Jinu that came here, or even one of Rolm's rival kingdoms of which you have spoken, who traded for the hrakar."

"But we do know someone else is searching for aurathorn," I observed. "Who would even know about it, but even more, who would know to value it?"

Harlan seemed surprised at the question. "In the legends, aurathorn has many uses. I do not pretend to know them all. Different people have different stories about it." He pointed at my maimed chest. "It freed you when nothing else could. I've chased countless legends of aurathorn in my searches, along with more tales of its uses than you have scales: aphrodisiac, messenger of Haven, restorer of life. Some of them may even be true. I have learned enough of aurathorn to know that a unique power is infused within it."

"Power," I grumbled. "Humans will hunger for it, then."

Harlan's eyes swept back toward the rock walls enclosing us. "Your mother too came here for a reason. Perhaps the now-dead enchanters of this island helped her, but I think she too came for aurathorn. Finding it is the key to my quest, but it's also essential to understanding what your mother sought to do here."

"She died here." The words seemed to tumble from me without conscious will. "I dragged her remains into the lake."

Harlan looked sharply at the muddy pools. There was no sign of my mother's bones.

"We could search," Harlan offered. "Build her a proper pyre this time."

I appreciated the offer. "She wouldn't care about what happened to her bones. She was a follower of the Way. She would not want me to waste time on such a task. Her *jing* is already with me. No body needs to be burned."

"Then let us search the rest of this place for whatever else we might learn."

I didn't move. Dragons don't really do searching the way humans do. Harlan prowled about the place, through cut foliage, scanning the rocks. He found the cave where my sister had hatched, although nothing had been left there. I searched by smelling, by watching, and thinking. Whoever had come here had been very thorough. They'd drained the lake. There was little chance they had missed anything accessible to them. But they were humans, and not all of this place could be reached, even by the most resourceful.

The wolf-eagles gave me the idea. They had been present when I was here last, when my mother had died. They were here now, watching warily; perhaps they hungered for meat but were far too intelligent to take on a dragon. The lake was also the only source of fresh water on the island. Likely, the wolf-eagles' nest was within this valley. I studied the birds. My stare seemed to unnerve them. They took flight, circling in the sky above, unwilling to engage but also not wanting to leave.

"What are you protecting?" I mumbled quietly.

Harlan turned, mistakenly believing I'd said something to him. Humans always thought they should be the supreme object of attention even though they couldn't fly without help.

I lifted myself into the air, flying in a gentle arc that kept me within the bowels of the mountain crater. I inspected the walls of rock and their innumerable crevices and nooks, slapping the rock occasionally with my tail. I found nothing of interest the first time around. Fatigue and impatience might have made me give up on my hunch, except for the wolf-eagles. They'd dropped their altitude, coming far closer to me than they should. I now counted five birds, all of them making low, squawking threats in my direction. That meant desperation. They knew I searched for their nest.

I found it on the second pass. A sprawling, multi-level collection of sticks assembled over two natural rock shelves hidden within a nearly-invisible pocket in the crater wall. The nest was accessible only through a crevice no wider than two of my foreclaws. I locked myself precariously onto the stone outside the entrance to peer through an opening that was far too narrow for my head. The wolf-eagles' den reminded me of one of the elaborate four-story serving platters that the great chefs of Ni-Yota used to display some of their most delectable creations. Except this dish was made up entirely of eggs—probably a dozen.

I twisted my neck up and down, trying to get a better look within. I had no real idea what living aurathorn looked like, but I presumed I would know it when I saw it. But inside the nest was nothing that resembled any vine or flower. I scratched at the crevice opening with a claw as I tried to shove my snout closer to the interior. A glint of something that didn't come from a tree caught my eyes. A dagger, perhaps? Something like that could be easily mistaken as a stick by nesting birds. I pushed my claw against the opening. That didn't quite work. I grabbed the opening with a second claw and applied dragon strength. The rock of the crater wall cracked, then a chunk broke away, falling to the ground. The sound echoed through the crater. I shoved my neck through the enhanced opening.

The first thing I noticed was that wolf-eagle eggs were different colors. The top portion facing the sun was off-white, while the bottom was a deep black. I'd never eaten a multi-color egg, but that wasn't what I had come here to find. Peering uncomfortably through the gap I'd made, I found the piece of metal that had caught my eye earlier, but it was located on the far side of the nest. My claws couldn't reach so far into the opening. I was considering how to solve that little problem when the wolf-eagles struck.

Their talons gouged at my eyes—at least six of them, which seemed like a lot until I realized more than one bird attacked me. The bird pack must've realized the danger in going after a dragon, but the urge to protect their eggs was stronger even than the self-preservation instinct. I flailed my neck and tail, trying to drive off the harrying birds. It was annoying to have to fight over a misunderstanding. I probably wouldn't have eaten their little double-color morsels. Probably.

I heard Harlan's excited voice shouting from down in the valley. I couldn't make out the words, but I assumed he was telling me what I already knew: the wolf-eagles that weren't attacking my face were slicing at my back. I smashed my tail into the rock face of the crater twice. More stone crumbled, creating a larger opening. I shoved my neck inside, taking a bite of the nest. My teeth grabbed the metal object as well as some sticks and a couple of eggs (the eggs were mostly by accident).

The wolf-eagles went into a frenzy of screeching, scratching, and biting. A talon plunged into my face, not far from a nostril; another landed on the thin scale between my eyes. I wriggled my head as I curled my neck downward, trying to shield my eyes and nostrils as I shoved off the water wall with the nest chunk in my mouth. The birds pressed their attack. They were stronger than blood raptors, their talons sharper. The pointed ends of the talons made a horrid screeching sound as they scraped on my scale armor. The vibration shook my bones. I twisted in the air, spreading my wings as I made my way away from the nest. I hoped that my retreat would satisfy the wolf-eagles. They'd defended their home, after all. But these birds didn't abandon prey—and they were too stupid to realize that I wasn't prey. Two of the wolf-eagles clung dangerously to my head, while another latched onto my belly.

I flew straight upwards, spinning in a violent spiral even as I swung my neck wildly. The birds weren't impressed. One of them found a ripped scale on my neck, already bloody from pulling myself too recklessly from the nest, and sank its long, thin teeth into me. The pain surged through me like liquid iron being poured down my throat. I almost swallowed the nest piece held in my jaw. Instead, I spat the contents of my mouth into the air, expelling nest debris, a small chunk of metal, and two intact wolf-eagle eggs. The birds reacted more swiftly than I dared hope. The entire flock broke off their pursuit, every one of them soaring after the eggs as they plunged toward the ground. The feathered predators moved with blurring speed, and even more impressive precision. They snatched the eggs out of the air one after the other, grabbing the falling globes with talons ill-suited for the task. As near as I could tell, the eggs were still unbroken, but I stayed well clear so I couldn't be sure. I swept down toward Harlan. He was sprinting on his little legs, making his way from one end of the valley to the other. It took me a moment before I spotted his quarry: the shiny object I'd vomited out with the eggs was lying on the upturned dirt. I flew over Harlan low enough to graze the top of his head with my tail before landing at the place he was huffing toward. I craned my achy neck down to examine the trinket I'd gone through so much trouble to obtain. Disappointment kicked my teeth. It was just a coin. The round little circles of shiny metal that humans traded with each other.

Harlan finally caught up to me. His face was flush and he was sucking in wind with considerable distress. I searched the sky for the wolf-eagles as I waited for Harlan to calm himself. The birds seemed to have retreated to their lair, but I didn't trust that this respite would last.

"It is time to leave," I said to Harlan. "I'm bigger than those birds, but the pack now believes that I'm a threat to them. They'll be back, whatever the cost to them. I could kill them, but I prefer not to."

"Compassion, Bayloo?"

"I'm being sensible. Their talons are extremely sharp."

Harlan barked a laugh. "You stirred up a hornet's nest of trouble up there. What were you doing?"

"The humans that came to this island searched everywhere that humans could. I thought we might find something useful—maybe even aurathorn—hiding where they could not go. But all I ended up with were some angry birds and a single silver coin."

Harlan picked up the trinket. It was filthy, but he spat on it and rubbed, revealing a bit more detail. "It looks to have been there quite a while. It's battered and faded, but there is enough silver in this coin that it didn't rust."

He held it out in his open palm. I wasn't an expert, but I'd seen humans trade often enough during my slave years. "It isn't a coin of Rolm. They all have dragons on them. This one doesn't. I can't tell what it is, actually."

"It's been damaged." Harlan flipped the coin to the other side. "This looks like a star rising over a mountain."

I looked back again at the wolf-eagle nest. Two of the birds had emerged from the shattered crevice of their lair. For now, they only watched. "The symbol of Ulibon, perhaps. Given what we know of the connection between the villagers and that place, it makes sense such a thing might be here."

Harlan grunted in agreement. "A lost coin picked up by a mommy eagle building her nest. It was a fine thought searching where others could not." He squeezed the coin. "Does it mean anything?"

"It's a human coin." I was annoyed. I'd gotten real wounds for that thing. "More pain, for nothing."

"Aurathorn has eluded me for more years than I care to count. Every time I thought it was close, it has left me only with tears and emptiness. It did not want to be found. But I have a feeling that this time, at last, aurathorn wants to be found."

I didn't want to hear more about fate. I had come to this place to find a way to free the dragons and to understand my mother's plan to defeat the rust. Harlan was too accustomed to failure.

He unclenched his hand and flipped the coin. "You mother used aurathorn to free you, yes?"

"That's what I was told. I have no reason to doubt it."

"Aurathorn can do what nothing else in this world can. That is why my people have sought it for centuries. Your mother sought it to do what no other magic could. Its power is not in doubt." Harlan rubbed a finger under his chin as he thought. "You told me the dead ruler of Ulibon, he was a powerful enchanter."

"Yes, the enchanted artifacts of Ulibon had no equal." I would never forget the brutality of the battle for the Twisted Keep. "Even now, with my knowledge of magic, I do not fully understand how these items were made. Few artifacts survived the battle. The enchanters destroyed many of their own creations rather than have them fall to their enemy in Rolm."

"Do you not find it strange that this long-rumored lost Heir of Ulibon apparently returns as the island of Maricopa is ransacked by someone looking for aurathorn?" Harlan didn't wait for me to answer. "If his father was a powerful enchanter, it seems logical that this heir would be as well."

"You believe that the Heir of Ulibon did this? That he is using aurathorn for his revolt?"

Harlan flipped the coin again. "It does fit. Maybe this coin is not so useless. It lets us know that there is a connection between Ulibon and the people who lived on this island. Money means trade. Ulibon traded here."

I considered Harlan's theory. "The people here came from Ulibon. They were the same tribe. You believe we should go to Ulibon?"

"Where else?" He shrugged unhappily. "Perhaps the heir seeks to turn Rolm's dragons against their slave master. That would be a compelling reason to hunt for aurathorn. I confess I prefer the theory that aurathorn is in Ulibon—or connected to that place—over the possibility that Farlighters did this. If my people were here, they are long gone with whatever they found. If it is in Ulibon, it gives us someplace to search."

"Ulibon may hold some answers," I agreed. "And I can think of no better place to look. The way is not far."

The decision to leave became even easier when the first of the wolf-eagles launched itself into the air, wings fluttering. Harlan didn't need to be told what to do. He was on my back in an instant.

I launched myself out of the crater. The rest of the wolf-eagles emerged from their hidden nest, spreading themselves out across the sky in a wide arc. If a bird can be said to snarl, these were making really nasty snarls. I didn't think they had cause to be so vindictive. I'd already spat their eggs back at them. Still, diplomacy wasn't going to work. The birds came at me at varying speeds, the eagles on the end moving fastest, attempting to encircle me. I was impressed with their speed, but feathered fliers couldn't match me. I pushed on my wings, gaining altitude as I headed west, five wolf-eagles in my wake. Let them think I fled. I knew I gave them mercy.

I rode the wind, and the world shifted around me. Maricopa faded in the distance and I said a silent goodbye to my mother once again.

I flew toward Ulibon to discover the secret of a mysterious lost heir, and hopefully finally find aurathorn.

SEVEN

The wolf-eagles wisely ended the chase.

Whatever hateful instinct drove them, it didn't sustain the birds across the long expanse of open sea between Maricopa and Ulibon. By the time the sky turned dark, I had sole dominance of the sky, save for a collection of stars poking through the velvet sheeting of Haven above. The return of relative calm reminded me that I was hungry. I should've eaten those eggs. I wondered if the top part tasted different than the darker bottom. I'd never know, but that didn't mean I couldn't fill my belly and rest. I changed my course slightly to account for my new desires.

Harlan, ever the navigator, noticed. "Why do you shift to the south?"

"Unlike you, I haven't slept or eaten since we left Ni-Yota ... Food will help to heal this gash in my neck."

"Why is south better than north for that?" As if he could feel my annoyance, Harlan hastily added, "I agree we should rest and eat. I'm just curious."

"Ulibon is heavily populated, including along its southern coast, and I don't want to be seen," I huffed, as if Harlan could have known that before I told him. "Hilo's coast is sparsely populated, but mountain elk still roam the highlands. I can hunt and sleep with a fully belly without being disturbed if we take the southern route." Just saying the words gave me the strength to increase my speed. "I'll keep well clear of the great watchtower. And even if they see me, we'll be gone by morning."

I thought Harlan was going to say something else, but he thought better of it at the last moment. Somehow, that annoyed me even more.

I shot through the night, riding a steady tailwind until I could make out the shape of Hilo's coastline in the far distance. I dropped down close enough to feel the cool breeze coming off the waves of the dark sea below, far too low to be spotted by any human eyes no matter how high their watchtower. Unless there was magic involved, of course.

Six powerful flaps of my wings brought us over the coast. I swept up over the soaring cliff face that formed something like a wall on Hilo's coast before turning on the windswept plateau. I actually had no idea if there were mountain elk in this area. I'd heard some humans speaking about the elk of Hilo many years ago, but I had no notion of where they lived. I just didn't like the way Harlan was questioning me earlier.

I hugged the flat terrain, peering into the occasional ravine. I could feel Harlan twitching with some innocent question about the supposed elk herds. He kept his mouth shut for longer than I anticipated, but inevitably his tongue wagged out its noises.

"I think I saw some rabbits," he offered. "Their coats caught a bit of the starlight. If I missed the elk, it's because my eyes aren't as keen as yours."

I flew a few more futile circles across the barren landscape before giving up. Tired beat hungry; at least the emptiness of this area offered an opportunity to sleep. When Harlan had the nerve to try to slide next to my huge, warm body to escape the plateau's continuous winds, I made a point of blowing some wet snorts in his direction.

Honor sufficiently satisfied, I slept deeply. In the morning I woke to find two dead rabbits laid out on the ground next to me. Harlan had his back to me, pretending to admire the sunrise.

My belly rumbled at even the modest offering. "Are these mine?"

Harlan turned toward me innocently. "They're both yours. I don't want to risk a fire on the plateau. Even though you chose a spot with a small bit of cover, a keen watchman might spot the smoke even at this distance."

I ate his rabbits without feeling guilty. It wasn't my fault if humans insisted on cooking their meat. The rabbits were scrawny, but I savored every morsel, bones and all. Unfortunately, the morning got worse from there.

We left with the sun still new in the sky. I chose an elongated route to avoid the great watchtower at Kell, retracing my flight from the previous night to the east before making a long loop to the northwest, toward the east coast of Ulibon. The first sign of trouble was on the water below—ships. Too many had set off into the seas for no obvious purpose. I counted four craft of varying sizes on disparate eastbound routes, none of which obviously led to any desirable destination.

"One of those is a coastal fishing boat," Harlan noted. "It has no business on the open sea."

"Where are they going?" I wondered aloud.

Harlan was quick to the heart of the matter. "Away from Ulibon."

I flew on to find smoke rising from the landmass ahead of me. It was the brown-tinted smoke of fields on fire. I'd seen it often enough.

"I don't know about this heir, but war has come to Ulibon." Harlan's tone became solemn. "From one side of Inkra to the other, whatever the cause, there are always fires to go along with the killing."

I flew onward. Harlan was correct about both the fires and the killing. Only the amount of each was in question. I rose higher for a better view. Ulibon was claw-shaped, with several narrow choke points as one moved on land from the southern reaches to its northern tip, where its once-proud capital stood. I should've been able to see clear across the island, but there was enough slow-rising smoke hanging above the land to obstruct my view. I could see that several uncontrolled fires raged, one scorching the wheat fields on the south of the island, and another further north.

Harlan summed up the view. "There is no shortage of destruction to watch. Destroying a lake is barely worth mentioning compared to ravaging an island the size of this one."

Without answering, I began our descent. The Twisted Keep was far to the north. Ultimately, any rebellion would end there, but I wanted to know more before I flew toward the formidable fortress of the dead enchanters who once ruled here. I flew over the smoldering fields of south Ulibon and over seemingly deserted coastal villages. A few had been burned, but most merely looked empty.

"The freshest smoke rises further west," Harlan told me, as if I didn't know.

"To the west, sitting on a lonely hill, we will find the keep at Ular. The humans call it Iron Warden, because it guards the passage to the ore mines of the Lartra Hills."

"No army wants to leave a fortress at their back as they march. I suspect the fate of this keep will let us know how successful this rebellion has been."

I inhaled more smoke than I ever wanted while flying across southern Ulibon. Along the way, caravans of refugees clogged the roads, mostly moving toward coastal ports. If their intention was to flee the island, I suspected they would be disappointed when they finally reached their destination—I spotted no boats still at dock. Those who could leave already had done so, at least in the south.

I sensed Harlan's mind at work as he surveyed the torn land below. "Do the people of this island truly long for the return of the lost ruler's dominion?"

"One of my human ryders once commented that commoner people—dirtfolk, as he called them—were basically sheep, except it was much more trouble to shave their hides. Human lords often had the same attitude. There is nothing like the Burden of Haven among the rulers of Rolm, particularly those that serve King Mendakas. Perhaps Ulibon was different, but I never heard such a thing spoken about. I suspect the people here just want to live their lives."

Harlan gave a knowing grunt. "It is much the same elsewhere, with only a few fleeting exceptions. It seems the dragon protectors of Trishan did a better service to their subjects than any human ruler."

"You speak as if that surprises you. I would expect nothing less. Dragons follow the Way. We dragons have two hearts, your kind has but one."

Harlan kept quiet after that, until we reached the keep of Iron Warden. The castle didn't compare to the imposing size of the Fist of Eladrell, nor could it compare in proud elegance to the Twisted Keep. Instead, Iron Warden was a decidedly functional fortress, consisting of a double square curtain wall capped by imposing towers at each corner. The inner perimeter was built higher than the outer wall to allow bowmen to cut down any attacker brave enough to assault the fortress. It had no moat, but needed none, given its placement atop a steep hilltop. None of those defensive measures mattered against dragons, but I'd never contemplated that a human army could successfully overrun Iron Warden. I was wrong.

A gaping hole had been smashed through the southern section of the outer curtain. The corresponding section of the inner wall had been partially toppled. Broken siege ladders lay scattered on the ground between the two barriers. I expected that the battle had been bloody, but no bodies littered the ground. In the central courtyard, the structure which had been the great hall of the resident lord still spewed tendrils of gray smoke.

"That was vindictive," Harlan said of the burning building. "The walls had been breached. They didn't touch the towers, except to tear down the banners. Only the great hall was put to the flame."

I flew closer, sniffing the filthy air, my eyes searching. "There is a head hoisted atop one of the towers, flying in place of those colored cloths you humans enjoy so much. Perhaps it is the former lord himself."

"An apt symbol for a rebel to leave behind."

I flew several slow circles, but the disembodied head was the closest I found to any sign of life in the keep. Warily, I set down within the inner yard.

"What do you hope to find here?" Harlan asked.

"Mendakas built this keep after he conquered Ulibon. Three hundred soldiers held these walls. It would've taken ten times that number to successfully assault this place. The outer wall was thicker than the length of a human arm. It's been smashed to pieces. I want to know how."

"What clues do you hope to find in this ruin?"

I answered with my own question. "Where are the other bodies?" Harlan went to dismount, but I stopped him. "Stay seated and safe. We may need to leave quickly."

I ambled warily over to the blackened husk that had been the largest structure in the inner ward. A mélange of terrible smells poured from the smolder, stinging my nostrils. The roof had mostly collapsed, but a layer of blackened tiles still prevented me from seeing clearly inside. The ruin looked precarious. Rather than picking apart the roof, I poked at the blackened stone wall that faced the courtyard with a claw. The entire building groaned in protest.

"Opening the door seems more prudent than pushing down the wall." Harlan leapt from my back despite my prior admonishment to stay put. The entryway to the structure was a pair of oversized (by human standards) wooden doors wrapped in so many strips of iron the portals were practically coated in metal. Each had a large ring of the same iron attached to its center. Harlan yanked at each door with futility. Then he shoved his shoulder into them. He winced in pain and still the doors didn't move.

He rubbed his shoulder. "I think they've been barred from the inside."

I snorted. "Stand aside."

Without waiting for him to move, I whipped my tail against the twin portals. To my surprise, they didn't collapse inward. I hit them again. They held, but one fell off its hinges. Harlan pried an opening wide enough for him to fit through. He only stuck himself halfway inside before returning to the courtyard. My nostrils suspected what he confirmed.

"It's filled with people, many still in armor. The doors were barred from the inside. Perhaps they made a last stand here." The corners of Harlan's mouth turned downward. "The attackers burned them alive."

"The Heir of Ulibon isn't one for mercy." I gazed up at the head propped up on the tower above. "This is the human who seeks aurathorn."

Harlan looked back at the devastation of the great hall. "Aye, someone who would do this would also seek even more effective ways to kill. Aurathorn offers that. We'll be sailing with a careful eye out."

EIGHT

I flew to find a killer.

Destroying Iron Warden was a grand achievement for any rebel, but no would-be conqueror controlled Ulibon until they could gaze out from the pinnacle of the Twisted Keep on the north tip of the island. From the deep, protected harbor outside that castle, the sea lanes at the heart of Rolm's commerce would be vulnerable. I had little doubt the paramount fortress of Ulibon was the rebel's ultimate goal. I was less certain why King Mendakas had not yet responded to the threat. Whatever kind of military leader this heir might be, he was a human. He had to march places using feet, since there were no horses in this part of the world. Even if the heir was an enchanter, I didn't see how he could match Rolm's slave dragons on his own. Unless he already had aurathorn. The empty skies over Ulibon told me that I was missing crucial information.

It was afternoon by the time we reached the Clutch, so named because it was the narrowest point on Ulibon. Here, the landmass of the island was squeezed between the seas on either side. A series of forts had been erected across the expanse, each connected to the other by a disjointed series of barriers that ranged from stone walls near the center to poorly-maintained wooden palisades toward the edges. The great road of Ulibon ran through the center of the Clutch. I saw that the vassal lords of Ulibon had neglected the defenses during the years since I had last been here. Likely, none had believed that the forts would ever be necessary during the reign of Mendakas and his slave dragons. The result of their complacency was a crumbling ruin of a wall, dilapidated forts, and inevitable defeat. Toppled stones and the plentiful stink of human waste wafting into the air provided me with pungent evidence that the rebel army had made camp here.

"Most of the forts are untouched," Harlan commented as I dropped closer to investigate.

"The army marched up the main road, attacking where the physical defenses were strongest." I spotted a fallen tower, but no sign of siege equipment that might've brought it down. Another spire displayed a typically grisly message from the rebellion: a hanging corpse.

I flew just a bit closer to the hanging body to make certain of what I saw. "It is unclear where the head went."

Flies, maggots, and other tiny scavengers ravaged the decapitated remains. A banner had been shoved through the man's chest—the dragon banner of the King of Rolm.

I flew off. I'd seen and smelled enough.

"That is a crude display. The Heir of Ulibon is either a particularly cruel sort, or he is daring the king to come," Harlan reasoned.

"That is the oddest part of this war. There have been uprisings on Ulibon before—mostly in the years following the conquest. They were all put down, quickly and brutally. Any village where a rebel came from was burned as well. Mendakas is not a man of mercy. The rebellions stopped once people realized that fighting dragons was hopeless."

"Apparently they are no longer hopeless. This rebel seems to be doing quite well."

"This uprising isn't new. Humans don't move quickly on their feet. The fighting must've been going on for weeks at least. Word must've reached the king in Eladrell by now—either by pigeon or ship. There is too much commerce between Ulibon and the rest of the kingdom for this to stay a secret. Yet something has kept King Mendakas from responding to this particular uprising."

"Is it possible this rebel is so powerful that the king bides his time on his own island?" Harlan wondered. "Or that he realizes he must come with an army. Dragons and ryders can fly, but a large force must travel by ship, which takes far longer."

I grunted. None of those possibilities sounded correct. Yet I didn't have a better answer. Why didn't the king's slave dragons fly here to turn this heir and his followers to ash?

"Shall we look further?" Harlan asked.

I peered as far as my eyes would let me, scanning the Clutch from sea to sea. Any soldiers who had been garrisoned here had likely fled days ago, or longer. It was the smoke to the north that caught and held my interest. The plumes had grown since this morning. The battles at Iron Warden and the Clutch had been decided days ago, but to the north, war still raged fresh.

I made a last circle in the sky. "There is nothing more to be learned in this place. If we are to make the site of the next battle before darkness comes, we should depart."

I flew across the northern portion of Ulibon under clouds tinged by darkness. When I flew low enough to survey the land below, I saw people, but not many. Only a few stragglers braved the roads; villages looked empty; fields were mostly burnt to ash. The food situation throughout Rolm hadn't been pleasant before I left. I couldn't imagine it was better now, certainly not for the people of Ulibon. Herd animals were scarcer than people.

The afternoon wore on. I searched for danger, but also for food. The rabbit from this morning wasn't exactly filling. I found no living creature worth eating (I wasn't nearly desperate enough to snack on a human), but on the ledge of a small, rocky hill that seemed to rise without reason beside a muddy stream, I spied the bones of already-devoured sheep. That was a veritable treasure in this desolate land. I wondered who had enjoyed it.

"Even if we find the Heir of Ulibon, what does that accomplish?" Harlan asked as the day faded and the smoke of battle grew nearer. "Do you think he's really going to welcome the chance to speak to you and me—a dragon and foreigner—in the middle of his rebellion?"

"I can be very pervasive," I assured Harlan as I displayed my teeth.

"You plan to pluck him out from the midst of his army to have a chat?" He laughed at the thought, but I didn't think it was funny. Indeed, that was basically my plan. "He'll think you are a slave dragon. One of the king's servants. It could get ugly."

"I can pluck him if I wish. That's the tradeoff of wings over fingers—dragons can't pick our noses, but we can fly."

"The rebel has managed to conquer most of this island and somehow keep the king's dragons away. Don't underestimate what you don't fully understand, Bayloo. He is likely a wielder of magic. Perhaps he even has the power of aurathorn to call upon."

I heard the warning, but in all of this world, the only human who had bested me was Drasu. But that had been before I knew my own nature. I understood magic now. I feared no human. If this Heir of Ulibon had answers that I needed, then I would get those answers from him, one way or another. If he had aurathorn, I would get that from him as well. This heir seemed to enjoy killing. I, too, understood death, and fear as well. The rebels had done well against their fellow humans, but contending with a dragon would be another matter.

The stink of massed humanity became awful just before the sun dropped below the western horizon. The smell was similar to that of a human city, but far more intense. In cities, the humans at least made an effort to dispose of their waste and keep themselves clean. I knew I smelled the odor of an army encampment.

"They are near," I said. "A short flight and we shall be upon the rebel host. The Twisted Keep lies on the other side of the Cut Hills, directly north."

"Then why are you flying in a circle?"

"Because it's a lot harder to spot me at night. By waiting, I can scout their army and perhaps avoid being seen, which, as you pointed out, will likely set off a panic, because they will all assume I'm one of King Mendakas' dragons sent to roast them all alive. We need to be subtle."

Harlan chuckled softly.

"What is funny?"

"I can't recall a single instance of you being subtle, Bayloo."

I chose a charred field where we could rest while I waited for the last of the day's light to fade. It wasn't an ideal defensive location, but there was no cover in the vicinity. If anyone approached, I'd have plenty of warning.

Harlan used the respite to do more musing. "I've seen my share of fighting, of killing. War between kingdoms is brutal, but revolts are the bloodiest. Nothing is so deadly as a fight with your family."

I wouldn't know much about family, but his words reminded me of Rinxia. What was she to me? I didn't answer, so Harlan eventually got around to his point.

"Even by those standards, this revolt is ugly."

"How is that?" I wondered.

"The burning. Castles, those I understand. But setting fields alight is senseless. Win or lose, people need to eat. Destroying what you have when food is already scarce ..."

I had no answer for him other than my usual refrain. "I've not always seen humans behave rationally."

I was impatient for the night to deepen, urging the clouds to blot out the starlight. For once, the conditions cooperated with my desires. Harlan and I took to the air against a backdrop of near black. I flew over the Cut Hills—mounds that had once been grander in height but now were little more than a collection of bizarre lumps and interspersed chasms that had been extensively quarried and mined over centuries. Soon, I was flying onto the plains that led to the Twisted

Keep itself. Once across the hills, I gazed down upon the rebel army. I wasn't impressed.

Judging by the campfires, the host was large but disorganized. The tight lines and evenly spaced distribution of troops that I expected from a Mizu army were absent. Instead, this host had formed itself into uneven clusters. Its perimeter looked largely undefended, making them vulnerable to ambush or rapid strike. Even with my dragon eyes, details of what their few supply wagons contained were difficult to discern, but there seemed far too little food for a force so large. I couldn't locate an obvious command tent, but a huge bonfire exposed the army in the darkness. It appeared to be the source of the smoke I'd seen lingering in the sky earlier in the day. Creating such a fire seemed a stupid thing for an army to do, unless they wanted the defenders of the Twisted Keep to know how close they were.

"How did they ever get this far?" Harlan wondered. "A dozen well-trained horsemen would slice them to bits and burn their supplies."

"Except Rolm lacks horses," I reminded him.

"Do you see any siege equipment?"

"No," I confirmed.

"Yet that rabble broke through the stone wall at Iron Warden."

Harlan didn't say that the rebels had to have some sort of magic at their command, but we both thought that. I wanted to have a conversation with the Heir of Ulibon, but it wasn't clear where he might be keeping himself. There wasn't even an organized center to the sprawling host.

I had seen enough for now. "Let's take a look at how the defenders intend to deal with the assault to come."

I didn't have to fly far beyond the rebel host to find their enemy. To the north, no more than half a day of casual marching from the rebel host's encampment stood the imposing form of the Twisted Keep. When I'd last fought here as a slave dragon, it had just been another castle to conquer; I'd not appreciated its terrible magnificence. Now, I gazed upon the fortress with more seasoned eyes, and I understood the danger of this place. Maybe I even feared it.

Fires burned atop the citadel's towers and along its battlements, providing enough of an outline of the structure to elicit a gasp from Harlan. "By the Waves of Ula, what is that?"

The keep deserved his awe.

The fortress resembled a coiled snake squeezing its prey as its walls, towers, and edifices wrapped around a misshaped mountain that rose from the ground seemingly without purpose other than to serve as the spine of the citadel. Upon closer inspection, the peak's deformities resembled those of the Cut Hills to the south, except starker, with grander proportions. According to the stories, before the Cataclysm, these mountains had held precious ores. The ancients had mined it thoroughly, leaving only the misshapen skeletal remains, but the ridges of the remaining rock provided an excellent framework for the spiraling fortress.

"The early rulers of Ulibon found this mountain and recognized its potential as a symbol of power. The enchanters forged its marble walls and towers and turned it into a fortress meant to deter any attack. The harbor on the far side is deep and sheltered from all but the greatest storms. From here, a small navy can command the most important sea lanes in Rolm."

"Even in the darkness, it dazzles." Harlan, as jaded as he was by his journey to countless lands, was impressed.

"It is the work of enchanters," I reminded him, knowingly. "Only the Shard of Oster is more formidable."

"I cannot gauge its proportion in the darkness. How many soldiers defend its walls?"

I thought back to my last battle here. "Easily a thousand. The interior of the mountain is hollow, the caves inside cool and ideal for storage. Water is captured on the pinnacle of the mountain above the fortress and stored in a reservoir within. If the provisions have been properly maintained, the keep cannot be taken by siege. Even for my brethren and I, it was a difficult and desperate battle to capture this place."

I heard Harlan chew on his lip as he thought. "It takes no master tactician to see this castle is near-impenetrable. Attacking here is like a captain sailing his ship into a cliff. What is this heir planning to do with his host against it?"

"That army appears motley. It must be that he commands some form of magic, although the walls of this place too are riddled with enchantment. If I plucked the heir from the midst of his army, I may be doing him a favor if he intends to attack the Twisted Keep with that ragged force. Thousands of lives may be saved." It pleased me to think of my forthcoming act of abduction as a benevolent service. "I've seen enough. Let's return to the host to see if we might locate the leader of the rebels."

I dipped a wing toward the ground, changing my direction with a wide-arc turn, confident the darkness cloaked my flight. The wind had just a hint of chill. My neck still stung, but my scales were well on their way to being fully healed. I was ready to fight if I must.

As I punched through the night back toward the Cut Hills and the rebel host, I considered a strategy for finding the heir and extracting him without causing panic in his army. I needed to understand what magic he possessed. The enchanters in Ulibon before the conquest had been formidable opponents, but they were not wizards like Legao. They weren't capable of powerful spells, or manipulating the forces of the world. The enchanters of Ulibon were mostly glorified blacksmiths, the forgers of artifacts of power. That would not have been enough to capture Iron Pass and the Clutch so easily. The heir must be more than a mere forger of magic instruments.

I flew over the sprawling rebel army, searching for some sign of its leadership, but there was nothing. It was little more than a boisterous mob, driven by its past victories. Just as I resigned myself to waiting until the morning to try to spot the host's leader, a greater problem emerged out of the deformed hills.

It came fast. This was a fight I'd been dreading since I returned to Rolm.

I had time only to warn Harlan. "Prepare yourself for battle."

"What is it?"

"A dragon comes."

NINE

I didn't want to kill my own kind.

There were too few of us left in the world. But the other dragons of Rolm were slaves, and they would obey their masters.

The other dragon moved quickly. With two blurring beats of its wings, it flew from its hiding place behind one of the Cut Hills through the night sky, then disappeared into the thick clouds. Did the dragon think to ambush me from above? Or did it even recognize me as an enemy? A ryder of Rolm would probably think that I was another of Mendakas' servants, although he might have warned his ryders to be wary of me.

"I could barely see it," Harlan hissed at me.

"Keep quiet."

I accelerated, my wings spread to their full span to catch as much wind as I could without making unnecessary motions to reveal my position. I swung upward into the misty clouds, listening and sniffing. Which of my brethren did I face? The other dragon had moved so quickly through the darkness I hadn't gotten more than a surprised glance. It was on the smaller side. Gandar? No, the color was wrong. This dragon's scales were the color of sand and silver. None of my brethren had mixed coloring, yet there was something familiar about the newcomer. The dragon's ryder had been a slender figure—that was all I saw.

I flew in an arc through the misty low clouds, ever alert, yet I heard nothing, smelled nothing, found nothing. But the other dragon was no phantom. This wasn't the behavior of a friendly cousin. Somewhere nearby, a predator lurked. If I could not find the other dragon, I would bring it to me.

I flapped my wings, deliberately letting my left span shake ever so slightly. Another dragon would hear the sound, however faint. Bait offered, I dove without waiting for a reaction. Even with a head start, I was too slow. The sky whistled. The sweet scent of my kin filled my nostrils. Pain erupted along my rear, just above my hind leg.

Those weren't claws.

My scales had been sliced apart. Not smashed or shattered, but cut through with something sharper than any steel blade. Only *sai* could slice like that. Yet there were no *sai* in Rolm.

I tucked my wings back, accelerating into my dive. I needed to create space. And I needed magic. I dared to shut my eyes as I reached for the Latticework. The air was already thick with power born from the stirring of a building storm. I merely had to hasten the process. My enemy might have *sai*, or something like them, but I had a formidable weapon of my own. I intended to make the first strike count, yet I didn't want to kill the other dragon. Not unless I must. A human ryder was a different matter.

The dragon pursued me even as I raced toward a deep valley that twisted through the Cut Hills. I readied myself to break out of my dive, attempting to simultaneously hold my concentration on the Latticework and not get myself killed as I executed my aerial maneuvers. I expected my pursuer would continue to follow my flight path. I only intended to kill the dragon's ryder, but lightning wasn't easy to direct. I might miss.

I reached out to command the Latticework even as I plunged, directing Chords of Power to do my bidding. Soon, the storm was ready. So was I. My vision of the mundane world returned. A flip of my wings caught the air, changing my trajectory with violent speed. I sensed the smaller dragon behind me mimic my course. *Come down, glorious storm.*

A brilliant, silent flash shattered the night's curtain. A mangled noise of shock and pain followed, something uttered not by a single creature but two distinct ones, with the combined sound being distinctly unsatisfying. Without craning my neck to look, I knew I'd only grazed my target. I'd been too timid with the strike. I'd sacrificed the element of surprise for no advantage.

I swung around, intent on closing with the other dragon. Forget magic. I was bigger and stronger. I could better deal with the ryder in a melee. Maybe Harlan could put one of his daggers in him if I got him close enough. As I came about in a full circle, I expected to find my opponent executing some other maneuver for superior position. Instead, the other dragon seemed intent to close upon me as well. Flames would not stop me. I would have to be wary of Harlan getting scorched, but if a direct confrontation was desired, so be it.

We came at each other. Finally, I got a full, hard look at my fellow dragon. I caught a full whiff of dragon scent on the wind as well. A female horned dragon, which explained the smaller stature, and also made me unafraid of any fire. There was something else I hadn't expected: I had never before seen this particular dragon. None of my sisters on DragonPeak possessed such unique coloring. And how would any slave dragon be fitted with *sai*?

We were close enough to hear the beating of each other's hearts when I realized that the horned dragon didn't actually have mixed scale shades. Her torso was discolored—she'd been horribly maimed, so badly that even a dragon's healing ability hadn't been enough to make her whole again; entire scales had been deformed and destroyed, with plates of metal placed over the gaps. She didn't wear *sai*, but rather parts of her legs and claws had been replaced by forged metal. The revelation shook me, but the workings of my head couldn't match the speed of my body. The dragon was upon me.

"Bayloo!"

It was the ryder's shout.

I swerved, dipping my wing into a sharp turn and pulling my claws toward my body. I twisted into a sharp circle, slowing as I did it. If this was a trick, if I was wrong about this dragon, I'd left myself and Harlan terribly vulnerable. But I wasn't wrong.

Somehow, this maimed dragon was Crema.

I'd seen her fall from the sky, impaled by a griffin. True, I hadn't seen her corpse on the ground, but even Bethy Rann had thought her gone. Rann had told me she couldn't sense the bond between them. But Crema must've survived those wounds and the fall. She must've been near death. Her body had been mended with metal, and possibly magic. The work of a powerful enchanter at the very least. The runes of control had been scraped from her, and a horrible mess of scarring and metal remained.

"Crema?" I asked, speaking with my eyes and my mouth, my emotion thick. Hope surged through me that I wouldn't have to kill a dragon today.

We circled around each other in the air, gliding gently in the wind as we assessed each other. So close, I noticed that one of Crema's eyes had been damaged, and for this there could be no replacement. She was blind in her left eye. With the other eye, she spoke to me, but not as I hoped. There was such a mix of emotion within my fellow dragon. It was like a human trying to speak so many things at once nothing came out clearly. Among Crema's jumbled thoughts was unmistakable confusion.

I tried again. "Crema, it is I, Bayloo. I have returned."

Crema's single functioning eye flashed blue in pleasure, but then faded into a mélange of chaos.

Her ryder, whom I'd ignored until now, spoke instead. "She doesn't remember you. Much of who she was has been lost. Still, she is Crema."

The voice was familiar as well, even though it was muffled by a full-face helm of golden alloy, a single blazing star engraved on its front. The ryder's body was attired in matching armor, a dazzling suit of gold inlaid with silver trimming. Taking one hand from the dragon saddle, she pulled off the helm to reveal herself. I barely saw the woman atop Crema's back, but I did recognize her. The ryder's face was harder than I remembered, with cheekbones as lean as a well-bred horse from Ni-Yota; her hair had been dyed silver since we were last together, and a partially-healed gash marred the bottom of her chin. Yet the eyes were the same, hard and unyielding.

I stared at Bethy Rann.

TEN

I followed Crema toward the western range of the Cut Hills.

Despite her past injuries, the horned dragon moved swiftly through the sky. But as fast as Crema flew, I wished she were faster. I ached for answers.

"You know her?" Harlan marveled as we followed Crema.

"I know them both. Crema is one of my horned cousins. Her ryder is Bethy Rann, my former ryder. Well, not quite a ryder in the Rolman sense, because we were never bonded and we were together only a short time. But she sacrificed herself to save me. I'm not sure how either of them are still alive." And I still owed her. I'd made a promise. I was sure she hadn't forgotten.

Crema set down at the mouth of a scarred cavern that had been chiseled into a hillside by vicious unknown powers. The cavern was easily large enough for two dragons, and it offered protection from prying eyes and cold wind. Too bad there was nothing to eat there.

Bethy Rann climbed off Crema's back with an ease that belied the garish ornamental armor that covered her body. Harlan joined her on the ground. Her eyes appraised him as if he were a bull at auction in Eladrell's marketplace. Her verdict was a frown.

Rann's hand slid down the hilt of a curved blade at her side. "An Islander?" Her tone turned wary as she regarded Harlan. "What trickery is this? Your kind hate dragons."

Harlan executed his most elegant bow, rolling his hand elaborately as he bent from the waist. "Harlan Dor, captain of no particular ship at the moment, at your service. And, while I don't speak for 'my kind,' I like dragons just fine. Most of them anyway."

Rann's hand didn't stray from the hilt. I thought it was time for me to put in a word for Harlan. "Harlan and I have been through a lot together. I carry him on my back willingly." She fixed a questioning look at me. "He is as worthy a ryder as I could ask for. An ally."

Bethy Rann relaxed ever so slightly. "I would like to hear your story, Harlan Dor, and how an Islander found his way to Rolm on the back of a dragon."

I answered before Harlan spewed more flourishing platitudes. "You shall be wrinkled with silver hair growing from your nose and ears if you ask to hear one of Harlan's stories. I pledge he shall do you and Crema no harm."

Rann acknowledged that with a curt nod. "I'm surprised to find you back in Rolm so soon, Bayloo. Did you find your sister?"

"She is well and safe in Ni-Yota, the great land beyond the Wall of Fire."

Rann took half a step closer to me. "You made it across the Wall of Fire, then. Your story of bargaining for information from a ghastray was a bit fantastic, but here you are."

I could tell Rann had many questions, but I desired a more important answer. To Crema, I asked, "How did you survive?" A wave of guilt surged through me. "I saw the griffin that attacked you, but there was nothing I could do ... you fell from the sky. It was so far, even for one of us."

The once-beautiful dragon regarded me with her single functioning eye. I could see the horrific collection of scars, badly reformed scales, and metallic patches that covered her body more clearly now.

It was grisly, but she was alive, and one more dragon in the world was a good thing.

"You are not ... understood," Crema answered in Avian, her words halting and difficult to comprehend. She sounded nothing like the Crema I remembered.

Bethy Rann's face scrunched in pain as if she'd been struck. She replied to me in a voice just above a whisper. "The crash and the wounds ... she should have died." Rann took a hard breath. "After you left, I forced Triton to search for her, my blade at Mendakas' neck. When I finally found Crema, she was shattered and I thought her dead. But, as I came near, I saw a flutter in her chest. When I listened, she had barely a beat left in one of her hearts. Yet she had the will to continue. I did what I could for her." Bethy ran a gentle hand over Crema's damaged scales. "The healing was unlike any other. It was the only way to save her. It took the knowledge of my people, as well as the help of an old friend from ... a lost childhood friend." Rann's lips pursed in hesitation for a moment. "But Crema was saved, even if she isn't whole. In mind, or in body."

I still didn't quite understand. Or I didn't want to understand. "You mean, she ..." I struggled for the words.

"Crema is still in there," Rann assured me. "But confused. Her skull was damaged. She remembers me, but not much else. I can barely make sense of her thoughts." With a deep breath, Rann added, "Perhaps that is not all for ill. She is still bound to me, the runes of control still active, despite the wounds that eased them from her body. Those carvings are far more than markings on scales. If she was whole, I don't know what would happen. We communicate mostly with feelings and images."

"You mean she might not serve you if she knew you fought against Rolm and King Mendakas?"

Bethy Rann barked a singular, triumphant laugh. It was unlike anything I'd heard from Rann before. "You must be newly returned. King Mendakas is dead. How else do you think I am standing here?

Do you think he wished me well after I held him at knife point so you might escape? I have had vengeance, for myself and my kin."

Harlan clicked his tongue in surprise upon hearing this.

Rann looked at the smuggler. "You didn't know quite what your dragon companion got you into?"

Harlan merely shrugged. "I trust the sea to take me where it wills. It appears it has done the same for you."

I reeled from the revelation that Mendakas was dead. I had no love for the human, quite the opposite. But I'd never known a time without him. He was as constant as the glare of the sun. "If King Mendakas is dead, who rules Rolm?"

"Someone of your acquaintance." Rann's voice was almost teasing. "None other than the former Prince of Sapphires himself. Some misfortune related to falling off a tower befell his elder brother. The throne is now held by King Dayne. Or the Sapphire King, as he prefers to be called." She scoffed a laugh again.

If I'd anything left in my stomach, I'd have puked it out. My old ryder, Mendakas' petulant seed, was now king of Rolm. Just as the hateful boy had desired. It was hard to imagine a worse fate for Rolm. Dayne and I had been linked by the control runes, so I knew the contents of his mind nearly as well as I knew my own. Inside that human there was almost nothing of merit. Not even the insatiable desire to rule an empire that drove his father. Within the boy-king there was only blackness. That wasn't what I'd intended when I had spared Dayne. King Mendakas had been Bethy Rann's hostage. Naively, I hadn't expected that she'd kill him in cold blood. But the truth was I hadn't given any thought to Mendakas' fate or even much to Bethy Rann's. I had cared only for myself. There was also another that I had forgotten.

"What of Triton?" I asked.

The flicker of Bethy Rann's eyes to the ground told me all I needed to know even before she spoke. "There was no way to kill King Mendakas and not his bonded dragon. I took no joy in it. There was no other way."

The death of any dragon saddened me, but this outcome shocked me as well. "You killed Triton?"

"You sound so surprised." Rann's voice was cold. "There were a few moments, just after I pulled my blade across Mendakas' throat, while his life poured out of him, that the rune-link rendered Triton near helpless. I did the deed of killing a king without warning, directly in front of Triton's face. The shock of his master's death, the anguish, it paralyzed him. I struck then. Dragon skulls are not invulnerable, and my blade is special." She patted the hilt. "Triton was noble, even if his master was evil. But he would've killed me had I not slain him."

I knew Rann spoke the truth of that. She had found herself in that precarious place by saving my life. I had let this all happen. I could not blame Rann for Triton's death, but I wanted to understand Rann's hate of King Mendakas. "That day, you said Mendakas deserved to die," I remembered.

"I did," Rann confirmed, a sharp gleam in her eye.

"You weren't the first to hate him. He had many enemies. But it was more, wasn't it?"

Bethy Rann flashed a bitter smirk on the left side of her mouth. "Oh yes, it was more to me. The late king's ambition to rule and control all that he could set his greedy eyes upon was an insatiable hunger. He fed his hunger with murders."

"That is the nature of kings, is it not?" Harlan asked. "At least most of them."

"Perhaps you speak the way of things. But Mendakas was not satisfied with mere victories. He didn't want to merely defeat soldiers, or even capture new lands. When he won a victory, he intended it to be forever."

I didn't understand at first, but Harlan did. His voice was quiet when he spoke. "To truly conquer a land, to make it yours utterly and completely, those that might challenge your dynasty would have to be extinguished."

Rann's eyes narrowed in on Harlan. There was a brutal chill in her expression. This was a different Bethy Rann than the person I'd known. "You know something of these matters, do you?" She nodded bitterly at her own words. "He didn't just kill my father. That wasn't enough. He slaughtered my mother and my brother."

My hearts raced. My mind was slower. "Your ... mother ..."

"He was coming for her, for all of us. My mother knew he would kill her and kill my brother. Or worse. But most of all, she feared he would learn her secret."

I flicked my tail as I realized where this was going.

"To save my younger brother and I from Mendakas, my mother sacrificed herself, waiting by the window of her tower with an empty bundle in her arms. When the king's soldiers arrived, she spoke her famous words, that her family would die by her will, not Mendakas', before she jumped. I watched it from a secret bolt-hole behind my mother's wardrobe. I knew, and I remember."

"Your brother is the Heir of Ulibon?" I asked.

"My younger brother is dead." Rann's lips curled. "You should know that better than anyone else, Bayloo. He died to free you."

My insides went cold. "You mean Jona." I gurgled unhappily. "Jona was my ryder. Our minds were bound. Once my mind awoke, I could sense his thoughts. He carried no such hate for King Mendakas, no memory of any of this."

"He was a toddler when it happened. We humans don't retain childhood memories when we are so young. He never knew who he was. To be the Heir of Ulibon meant to be hunted. It meant death. I would've told him when the time was right. There was no reason for him to know, for up until your mother arrived on Maricopa, we had no hope of ever reclaiming our birthright. We were safer blending in with the exiles there."

"You and your brother fled to Maricopa after Ulibon fell?" I asked.

"Yes, that was the only place I knew would be safe. I knew that the people there would keep my secret, because they hid an even bigger one."

It was all so much, but it all fit as well. Except one thing. "Why did no one know about you? In every story, it is always the male heir who survived. I've never heard it spoken that the Highstar had a daughter, much less one that survived the conquest of Ulibon."

"Among my people, there are a precious few who are born with a terrible sign. They emerge from the womb of their mothers blue and still. Dead to the casual observer. But among those tragic births, one in a thousand revive. Those babes are considered cursed—the Returned. To have such a child was a sign of an alliance with the dark, of the displeasure of Haven. Such children are destined to fulfill some evil destiny. They are to be thrown to sea to appease Haven.

"My mother would not allow such a thing; she would not sacrifice the life of her firstborn daughter, and she was a woman of will. So the world was told I died at birth, as was my father. Stillbirths are common and unpleasant enough that they are never spoken of. My birth was soon forgotten, particularly once my mother became pregnant with my brother, the male heir my father and all of Ulibon desired. While Jona was feted and spoiled, I was raised by a trusted servant of my mother's, close to her but always apart. Only in the depths of the night could she come to hold me, to tell me I mattered as much as my brother. Because I was special." Bethy Rann raised her chin. "Always, she loved me. Even if my father never knew me. One day, I swore I would make them both proud. I swore that my mother would know she had made the right decision to save me, and my father would rejoice in the daughter he never knew he had."

A cold wind swept into the cavern. Even I shivered. "It is you."

"Yes, it is me," Bethy Rann confirmed, sweeping an arm toward the Twisted Keep. "My parents are dead, but somewhere I hope they watch and see me avenging them. I am the true Heir of Ulibon."

ELEVEN

"It was you who burned those men."

I said it without judgment, mostly. Dragons burned people all the time. I had taken more lives than I cared to remember. War wasn't pretty. But those burnings didn't seem an action that the Bethy Rann I remembered would condone. This gold-armored dragon ryder was a different person inhabiting a similar body.

Rann looked confused at my question for a moment, before a hard clarity seeped back into her eyes. "Those were Dayne's men at Iron Warden." She said it as if it explained everything. "Neither of you understand what is happening here."

"I'm just a foreigner," Harlan interjected in a mild, near-mocking tone. "I don't understand much."

"Can you not see, then?" Rann's voice screeched. "The fires? The burned fields? The empty villages?"

"We saw them," I assured her.

"Those men in Iron Warden did that. They burned this whole island. People were already short of food, and they burned what was left." Rann's voice trembled with rage. "I gave them back what they dealt. To those who gave the orders to ensure the deaths of thousands of innocents from starvation—those men you saw hanging in their keeps—what I did was not enough. They deserved worse."

I knew Harlan's eyes well enough to know he wasn't convinced by the justification he heard. I chose not to judge Rann now that I knew she was the Heir of Ulibon. She was fighting for her people. "What was their purpose in setting fires in fields and villages?"

Rann sneered with disgust. "They've lost Ulibon and they know it. The Rolman puppet lords tried to make a stand at Iron Warden, and we showed them our power. Crema showed them she could punch through their walls and kill their archers. So the boy-king told his little lords to stop fighting, to run and hide themselves away in the Twisted Keep with their soldiers and most of the island's food stores. In their wake, they burned—fields, villages, fishing boats, anything people might use to keep themselves alive."

"The stomach is a powerful weapon," I said. "Why didn't Dayne send his dragons? You have only Crema." I shot a sheepish glance at my cousin, afraid I'd insulted her, but her good eye remained vacant. This wasn't the same dragon I had once known.

"The Sapphire King has no dragons to spare."

"Why?" I pressed.

Rann's lips tightened. "Oster."

I understood immediately, but Harlan didn't. He shook his head. "For an ignorant foreigner, please explain—"

Rann cut him off. "That is the land of the frightful beasts, of griffin and furies, and whatever else the Pale Wrights cook up in their labyrinth in the Pits of Gargen. But all creatures need to eat, and Oster is experiencing another year of terrible famine. Before Bayloo left, they tried to invade and were soundly defeated, many of their griffins along with their best soldiers slain. When he ascended the throne, King Dayne saw the chance for revenge, to distract from his brother's inexplicable death, and the opportunity to step out of his father's shadow by crushing Rolm's ancient enemy when they were at their weakest. He gathered his fleet, stripped the garrisons of the outlying lords, including those of Ulibon, and sent an armada as well as his dragons to attack Oster and the Shard."

"When was that?" I asked.

"It has been weeks since the fleet departed. Dayne thought his victory would be quick and easy."

"Only a fool would underestimate Oster—a fool who had never seen the Shard."

Rann inclined her head. "As you say. Only a fool. I might add some other words." The corner of her mouth twitched with grim pleasure. "Dayne's arrogance is Ulibon's opportunity."

I didn't share Rann's delight at news of war. "Every dragon is engaged against Oster?"

"King Dayne sent two ryders here, when Iron Warden was besieged. Amos rode Vincible while Joren came with his horned dragon, Killi."

I knew both of my fellow dragons, of course. Vincible was an ash dragon. He was nearly twice my age, slower but still formidable. Killi was only a horned dragon, but together I would've expected they were more than a match for Crema. "You beat two dragons?" I asked, impressed.

"It brought me no pleasure. But, despite her injuries, Crema is in some ways more dangerous now."

"The *sai*," I concluded.

Rann tilted her head in question.

"The metal on your dragon's claws," I explained. "Across the Wall, they are known as *sai*. Or at least something similar to them."

"My people in Ulibon kept alive our unique art—that which the elders brought with them from their home across the Wall of Fire. That same power that made the first Highstar of Ulibon a ruler also forged the metal that patched Crema's wounds." Rann looked at herself. "And this gaudy armor."

"You never told me you were an enchanter," I said, trying not to sound betrayed at the admission.

"I wasn't," Rann said. "As a Returned, it was assumed I would have the gift, but I never had the chance to be trained. On Maricopa, they too knew the magic of enchantment, but the elders of Maricopa never taught me their craft. They took Jona and I in, but they didn't know who we were. They thought us refugees from Ulibon, children of tragically killed parents who had kept to the old ways in the remote seaside village of Durn, where none of them had ever traveled. But that didn't stop me from learning." Rann's voice softened ever so slightly. "The island was a small place, and I had talent. I saw enough to understand the craft, although not the final secret that made it possible to speak to the objects, to infuse them with power. That they kept carefully hidden."

I glanced at Crema. "Then how?"

"It was your mother who gave me the secret to finally unlocking my power. She allowed me to become what I am."

Both my hearts jumped. "My mother?"

"That was part of my price. She showed me the real secret at the heart of enchantment, of magic." She indicated Crema. "My work is crude. Doubtless the elders wouldn't have approved. But what I lacked in precision, I made up for in talent." There was no mistaking the pride in her voice. "Now, the elders of Maricopa and their ways of isolation are dead, and I am alive. I am about to conquer Ulibon and avenge my family by ascending to my father's seat. I need just one more thing."

Rann sounded too pleased for my taste. "What is it that you need, then?"

"I need to take the Twisted Keep before King Dayne and his dragons return from Oster."

I grunted my skepticism. "Why?" Rann's face flashed with annoyance, but I didn't care. "Sooner or later Dayne's slave dragons will return. You will still have to face them. While being inside the citadel is far better than being out in the open, the simple fact is that walls are of far less use against dragons. Your host is large, but apparently ill-disciplined. Dragons took the keep before, and it was more ably defended then."

Rann ground her jaw. "As you know, Bayloo, there are far fewer dragons than there once were. The great horde that once conquered Ulibon is no more. If the rumors are true, the campaign against Oster extracts an ever-greater toll."

My blood heated at Rann's words, even though I knew this was no fault of hers. "Humans waste what is precious because they can. Still, a single ash dragon could reduce this army of yours to dust."

"Vincible would tell you differently. And I do not only count on the reduced numbers of dragons. The fortress is more than walls. It has … advantages that only I can utilize. As to my host, as you see, many are simple folk who are merely angry. But they are desperate. Inside the keep is the largest stockpile of food on the island, perhaps in all of Rolm. And at the core of my force are the original soldiers that formed this rebellion. I can hold the keep, if I first take it." She said the last with such certainty I almost believed her.

I thought back to the battle of the Twisted Keep. Those weren't pleasant memories. "It is a formidable fortress. Impervious to siege, its walls fused together by magic. When Mendakas captured it so many years ago, it took dozens of dragons, both to hold the defenders at bay and to deliver soldiers inside the walls, because destroying the fortification was impossible, even for us."

"You fought against the might of Ulibon. Inside the keep were men desperate to fight for their freedom and identity. You fought enchanters. Inside the Twisted Keep today is the barest of garrisons made up of old men and boys. King Dayne took most of his best soldiers to war with Oster. They will crumble at the sight of two dragons." She gazed at me with intensity. "We will have surprise. They don't know about you."

She might not be wrong about the outcome of the battle. I really had no idea how many soldiers were in the keep or their morale. It didn't matter, though. "Why should I take sides in the wars of men? What does it matter to me who rules Ulibon?"

Rann's eyes widened in surprise before hardening once again. "You owe me. You said you would deliver me anywhere if I killed

Mendakas to allow you to escape. That was our deal. I held up my end. You got out of Rolm. Mendakas is dead at my hand."

"I will indeed carry you anywhere within Rolm you wish to go."

"I want to go inside the Twisted Keep. Aid us now." The hint of a grin played on Rann's lips. "I know what you want." My hearts moved faster. "You want to free your fellow dragons, as always. I can help with that. I will pledge the support of Ulibon to your cause." I waited for her to speak of aurathorn as well, but there was nothing. Did she have it? Did she now play one of Harlan's card games with me?

I growled in displeasure. "That wasn't the bargain. I never promised to take a castle for you or your rebellion. I never promised to kill for you. What you offer is not enough."

Rann's eyes honed in on me. Realization flashed in them. "Of course, you did not come here to find me." She loosed an ugly bark. "You did not come here to help me or check on my well-being. You came for your own quest."

"Yes," I admitted. "Help me free my brothers and sisters. Help me find aurathorn."

I watched her face carefully, but Rann betrayed nothing. "Aid me and I will," she promised readily. "I can help you."

My hearts pumped hard. Did she have aurathorn? Had it been Crema and Rann on Maricopa?

For once, Harlan spoke anxiously. "Do you have aurathorn?"

Bethy Rann's mouth opened ever so slightly, then closed again, her chin hard. She looked at me, then back to Harlan. A mischievous sparkle appeared in her eyes, a new revelation. "You seek the vine as well, Islander?"

Harlan took a step toward her. Crema's functional eye flashed to a wary red when Harlan neared her master. "Maricopa was devastated searching for it. Did you find it when you ripped the island to shreds? Do you have it?"

"Is that what you think?" Rann didn't flinch. "I have no idea what you are talking about. I have not returned to Maricopa since I left it, years ago. I don't have aurathorn with me, Islander. You fools have flown around the world for nothing."

TWELVE

Bethy Rann did not have aurathorn.

She had not destroyed Maricopa looking for it. She didn't even care about that vine. I wondered for a moment if she might be lying, but her heartbeat was steady, her eyes more amused than concerned. Judging by the pained look in Harlan's eyes, he believed her as well. Aurathorn always eluded him, despite his claims it wanted to be found.

"My mother told me she used aurathorn to free me." I recalled the precious last moments with her. She'd hesitated when it came time to tell me of aurathorn. She had been afraid of something. "My mother did not lie."

"Great Dawn would not lie to you," Rann agreed. "I told you that she and the elders traded for the vine. They did something to it."

"So aurathorn was there, on that island?" Harlan pressed, his voice suddenly tinged with hope.

Rann's eyes flicked between us. "It was there. That much I can say. Your mother and the elders attended to the vine more attentively than a mother would a newborn. They did something with it, something to do with magic. I'm not sure what was done, for no one else was allowed near. But I once heard them say, 'Without a fount, the thorns will soon die. The vine alone is not enough.'"

"My mother said something similar." I considered Rann's words. "It was brought to Maricopa. From where?"

Bethy placed her hands together, her lips in a tight line. "I seem to be answering a lot of questions." She pursed her lips before turning to Harlan. "Why does an Islander seek this?"

Harlan's chin twitched unhappily, so I answered for him. "His people believe that it can help them turn back the sea so they can return to their lost island home." Rann squinted at me, as if to see if I jested with her. My eyes made it clear I didn't. I sensed Harlan's displeasure, but he'd eventually learn I did him a favor. Bethy Rann was more stubborn than him. I needed to give her something like the truth to get to the bargain I knew she wanted to offer. She might not care about aurathorn, but she cared about ruling Ulibon.

Rann offered a bitter chuckle. "Is this aurathorn part of the mysterious quest of the Islanders?" She shook her head. "I cannot help you."

To his credit, Harlan kept his body absolutely still instead of allowing the fury I knew was inside him to explode.

Rann wasn't finished. "But Ulibon may be able to help you. If there *is* an Ulibon after all this is done."

Harlan and I both digested the meaning of Rann's words, and her offer. I flicked my tail back and forth across the ground. I could still taste the stink of death from the last time I conquered the Twisted Keep. "I need more than that."

"More than the promise of the true Highstar of Ulibon?" Rann asked, almost mocking now. She knew she had something I desperately wanted, that Harlan wanted.

"Where did the aurathorn on Maricopa come from?" I asked again, knowing I wouldn't get an answer this time either. "Give me what I seek and I shall find a way to aid you."

Rann shrugged. "That is not enough. You will not take my promises as payment. Why should I trust you to keep your word?"

I snorted with derision. "You do not trust me, Bethy Rann?"

"I've never known a free dragon before." Her eyes flicked to Harlan. "There is no telling what company you have kept. You may have picked up some undesirable human habits." She sighed. "More than that, Bayloo, I sense you have changed. Something drives you, but it is not your fellow dragons. What has happened to you?"

Had I changed as much as she said? I didn't like her accusation. "You ride dragons, but that does not mean you understand us. I will do what I must."

Bethy Rann crossed her arms, unmoved.

"Tell us more of aurathorn," Harlan suggested. "Tell us about how you came to your knowledge."

"You want a story, sea captain?" She smirked. "I'm no sailor with yarns to spin."

"Trust must begin somewhere. With us, I had hoped the past was enough." I considered my options and didn't like them. I wanted aurathorn, for my kind, but also because I believed it led to a solution for the rust. "Do as Harlan asks, win the trust of my companion, and I will win your keep."

Rann's eyes widened with pleasure. "Very well, Bayloo." But instead of speaking to us, she turned away and gazed at Crema, running a finger along the dragon's patchwork scales. It was a gesture of affection, but the movement bothered me. It was the behavior of a ryder—someone who thought of dragons affectionately as a pet, not an equal. After an eternity of stroking scales, Rann spoke, her voice distant. "I hadn't fully considered the significance of this strange vine. But your being here ... I now realize it was the reason your mother came to Maricopa. She knew the people there were exiles from Ni-Yota, so they would be receptive to a dragon in their midst in a way natives of Rolm never would; but I think she was ultimately searching for aurathorn."

Harlan hung on every word. "Aurathorn wasn't on Maricopa before Bayloo's mother arrived at the island?"

"No, I lived there for much of my life. I know every speck of that place." Rann rubbed her forehead as she remembered. "As I said, I was an outsider, and the elders confided in no one but themselves, but it was only after speaking to Great Dawn that their behavior changed."

Harlan remained suspicious. "How did it change?"

"The elders huddled for two days, nonstop, which they had never done before, consulting with Great Dawn. And other things ... the more I look back, the more certain I am about what happened." She turned to stare at Harlan with a look that dared him to call her a liar. "I know where your aurathorn came from. I know where it is now."

Harlan wasn't intimidated. "Now you are sure? That is quite convenient."

"The answer has revealed itself, because all other possibilities are impossible. So while I've not gazed upon the source of the precious vine you seek, I know." She huffed at Harlan, looking to me instead. "Enough of this, Bayloo. On my honor, I tell you that I know where this aurathorn came from. I pledge the assistance of Ulibon in obtaining it, for you will not be able to do it on your own, just as your mother could not." Rann drew herself up, purposely not looking at Harlan. "You help us capture the Twisted Keep in exchange for our help finding aurathorn. Do we have a deal?"

I'd gotten better at bluffing in the time I'd known Harlan. The truth was, I would've agreed even without Rann's explanation. I wanted to find aurathorn, but I also had my own reasons to help this rebellion. Foremost, I knew the Sapphire Prince all too well. His malicious mind had been entwined with my own. He was dangerous to his fellow humans, but even more dangerous to my kind. The continued war with Oster—attempting to attack the Shard of Oster— was merely more evidence of his recklessly homicidal tendencies. Dayne had to die. The fall of Ulibon would draw him to me. That alone would have been a sufficient reason to help take the Twisted Keep. Another was that I did owe Bethy Rann. She had saved my life, and I'd made a promise to her. Still, I tried to do what Harlan would've done: I kept playing a game. I answered with fake reluctance.

"I will trust you, Bethy Rann, Highstar of Ulibon." I released a long exhale of hot air through my nostrils. "We have a deal. The Twisted Keep shall fall."

THIRTEEN

The dubious attack started with a meeting.

Worse, it was a meeting with a human, and no drink was served. Not quite what I anticipated from the Heir of Ulibon, but Bethy Rann insisted upon it. Her army had already made camp to give the men time to rest and train. Any notion of surprise had long since been lost. So instead of promptly flying off to devastate the Twisted Keep, I spent the night in a chiseled cave in the Cut Hills, away from the prying eyes of Rolman spies, while Bethy Rann flew back to her army to fetch a human. That part was fine—she sent food to us. Rabbits, some nuts, and hardtack. I offered to share a rabbit with Harlan (insincerely), but fortunately he satisfied himself with a few nuts. We ate and slept. In the morning, Rann and Crema returned with the important human I needed to meet.

The person before me towered over Bethy Rann by a full two human-sized heads. The rest of his body was similarly stretched—his face extended downward like a horse's and his arms grew like tree limbs. I'd have judged his height and reach to be an advantage for a human warrior, except this man had only four fingers on his right hand, and none at all on his left. Despite his missing digits, the stranger dismounted from Crema nimbly enough. I greeted my fellow dragon, but she didn't acknowledge me.

"This is Xedric Gile," Bethy Rann announced of the human, as if the name mattered to me.

The tall man did not bow, nod, or give any other indication that he'd been introduced, which I had thought was a human custom. Perhaps his ears were also mangled. He did have a full head of long hair braided to resemble giant eels. He smelled of something like rotten fish, so I guessed he must be a seaman like Harlan. Perhaps they would get along better than he and Bethy Rann.

"How will Xedric Gile help me take the Twisted Keep?" I asked, trying to be polite despite my skepticism. "It does not even have a moat. I don't need any more sailors."

I didn't understand Rann's puzzled look. Xedric showed me his teeth dragon-style in response, or at least he tried. He had only pinkish gums. I wondered how he ate.

"Without Xedric Gile, there would be no revolt, and I'd likely be dead," Rann declared. Xedric stopped showing his empty gums. "He was a loyal retainer to my father, serving as the commander of the central fortress of the Clutch. When Mendakas and his dragons captured the Twisted Keep, almost all the lords and soldiers of Ulibon surrendered, hoping for mercy, exchanging their lands and castles for their lives. But not Xedric Gile. He, and the few men willing to follow him, stayed loyal."

"Every revolt on Ulibon was smashed by dragons." I tried not to sound proud. The dragons who had periodically burned Ulibon in the years following the conquest had merely been obeying their ryders' commands. But they had been effective.

Gile finally opened his mouth to speak. His words were no prettier than his empty gums. "Only fools try to fight dragons."

This human was smarter than he looked.

Rann took up the narrative again, because speaking obviously wasn't Xedric's primary talent. "Xedric and his men returned to the land, biding their time. When the first wave of doomed revolts subsided, they offered their services to the new lords of Ulibon that had been installed by Mendakas. Using their positions, slowly over time, they stole what a future uprising would need: swords, axes, and armor, at first. Eventually, as their finale neared, they took other supplies, including grain, dried nuts, and hardtack. Years of stockpiles, waiting for the right time. Without their foresight, this host I lead would have neither weapons nor supplies. And it was Gile's men that helped us take our first keep in the south, opening the gates and surprising the garrisons from the inside."

I watched the big human as Rann recounted his exploits. He might as well have been a statue.

"Only when the war with Oster heated and drew the king away did the true revolt reveal itself," Rann explained.

I now understood her gratitude toward this man. "You didn't start the uprising."

"Xedric and his men were fighting well before I returned to Ulibon. But they were betrayed. Xedric was taken alive to be hanged from the walls of Iron Warden. But not before they tortured him before the crowds of onlookers. They took his fingers, one by one. And his teeth. The torture was to stop only once he declared the Heir of Ulibon dead and his revolt a fraud. Only then would his public suffering end—with his death. It went on for weeks, but he never broke." Rann looked at Xedric with admiration. I did as well. "Crema and I had our opportunity in the moment of his last torment. We rescued him, snatching him from the clutches of the Rolman soldiers as hundreds watched." She smiled. "They saw hope. The impossible became probable. The uprising was reborn."

"You couldn't have made a better entrance," Harlan said appreciatively. "The armor is a nice touch as well."

"To inspire farmers to face armored soldiers and the threat of dragons, one needs to capture the heart and the imagination. I needed to look the part. In this, Crema's injuries also served us well. They call her the Reborn. The occupiers had no fight in them without dragons to support them. Only a few of the Rolman lords still fought. But imagination will only take us so far. Of the two thousand men and women—yes, there are women among my fighters—in my host, most of the true soldiers are Xedric's men or late defectors from the Rolman lords, but his men are the only trained warriors that have shown their loyalty. And they are the ones we need to win the Twisted Keep."

"Getting inside the keep isn't difficult," I told them. "One has merely to fly over and land. That is when it becomes difficult. I can carry four, perhaps five soldiers with armor on my back. Perhaps one or two more if I need to fly only a short distance. Crema can carry three at most, yes?"

Bethy Rann nodded. "She is a swift flier, and injuries haven't changed that. Three, with armor and weapons, if one is me."

"Let us say eight humans then, plus Crema and I. Dragons are formidable, but not indestructible. The Twisted Keep was well-equipped with ballistae and other enchanted weapons when I fought there the last time. Do the current occupants have magic artifacts?"

"Unlikely. If any survived the conquest, Mendakas pillaged them for his own use long ago."

That sounded like Mendakas, and it was welcome news. But I still wasn't satisfied. "Two dragons and some humans could wreak havoc. But I don't think we could take and hold a sprawling fortress like the Twisted Keep."

Xedric spat out his awkward words. "You speak as if you face the true warriors of Ulibon once again, dragon. Inside the keep now are only huddling cowards."

"Indeed," Rann assured me. "The Rolmans have spent the past weeks running. They've lost every engagement they've dared to fight. Those men that remain are terrified of the heir, that they will suffer the fate of the others who resisted. This morning I've put my army on the march, but I've also sent a runner ahead to offer amnesty to any soldier that lays down their arms and leaves the keep."

"Your plan is to hope they surrender quickly?" I said it with disapproval, but they might be right. The defenders might be as weak-spirited as Rann and Xedric claimed. The problem was, I had no idea if that was the case, because this was my first time in Ulibon in many years. I didn't like relying on human intuition.

"They will break," Rann said again, apparently believing it. I studied her carefully. She was an able ryder, an adept fighter, but the only thing she'd ever commanded was her slave dragon. I didn't know Xedric Gile at all. I wasn't ready to fly against a thousand soldiers and a hundred ballistae based on the hunch of these two.

"Who leads the defenders?"

"Egan Drehan, Warden of Ulibon," Rann answered in a nasal, contemptuous tone that left no doubt of her feelings toward the man.

I had heard ryders speak of this human, and never fondly. He was a loyal hand of King Mendakas, but known as a schemer rather than a fighter. However, he certainly was not a fool like some of the others.

I flicked my tail about. "Tell me your plans, then."

They did, and it didn't take long. I wasn't impressed, nor was I willing to share with Bethy Rann the full extent of my own power. She knew of ember dragons, but not what I could do with magic. For now, I intended to keep it that way.

"How long will it take your host to reach the keep?" I asked.

"No earlier than midday," Rann conceded. "They move slowly."

"Fetch me then." I had more sleeping to do.

THE BATTLE CAME QUICKER than Rann anticipated.

As I had suspected back in the cave, Egan Drehan was not a fool. He understood the enemy he faced (except me, of course), and he anticipated their weaknesses. One was overconfidence.

Despite my declaration of intent to take a nap, prudence beat out laziness, and I didn't sleep away the morning (in part because the cave was horribly uncomfortable during the day, with dust blowing constantly). Instead, I found a perch on the highest hill with enough cover to conceal myself from any Rolman watchman, while I watched

the advance of Bethy Rann's army—if you wanted to call it an army—
and the reaction of the Twisted Keep's garrison. The march of the
sprawling host bore no resemblance to the movement of a disciplined
Mizu force, except that both involved a lot of feet. Rann's host shuffled along nearly aimlessly, like a parade, except totally devoid of joy
or amusement. A funeral parade, in more ways than one.

Undulating plains of burnt crops and charred grasses extended
from the Cut Hills to the Twisted Keep, with a single well-trodden
road of cobbled stone running the distance. Once, this thoroughfare
had been the major link between the north and south of Ulibon. Now
the feet of two thousand humans shuffling north were its only traffic.
The host mindlessly hugged the road, as if the plains of blackened
grass on either side were the cold sea where they dared not tread for
fear of drowning. Perhaps lured by the flat, open terrain, Rann had
sent out only a few scouts ahead of the main host, thinking an
ambush in such terrain to be impossible. But nothing was impossible.
Bethy Rann thought with an attacker's mindset, a leader who hadn't
yet experienced defeat.

I didn't realize what was happening at first. The activity on the
walls of the Twisted Keep kept my interest as I counted ballistae and
soldiers. Watching humans walk along a road seemed rather useless.
Harlan noticed something was amiss before I did.

"They seem to have slowed," he noted of the army below.

"It's possible for humans to walk even slower?" I wondered. "I
would've thought they had rocks in their shoes, but half aren't even
wearing shoes."

Harlan wasn't amused. "Something's wrong."

The leading elements of the marching host did indeed appear to
have slowed their advance. I saw several humans stop, while others
continued onward. There was some shouting. Crema flew above the
army, scouting the vicinity far more effectively than any human, but
that also meant that Bethy Rann wasn't among her troops. Xedric
Gile had direct command on the ground. A fighter, tough and ruth-

less, that one. But that wasn't the same thing as being an able commander.

Crema broke out of her flight pattern, circling to her left, dropping toward the ground. I thought that perhaps she intended to land, but that wasn't the dragon's intent. My eyes tracked Crema's flight path as she closed rapidly on her target somewhere on the east flank of the marching host. I saw the movement—the rustling of something concealed in the charred underbrush, lying flat on the devastated ground.

I roared a warning, a booming noise that carried across the plains. Crema's wing dipped instinctively, swerving her to the left. An arrow found her hide anyway. A moment of horror followed. She was only a horned dragon, her scales far less sturdy than my own—I didn't want to lose her. Fortunately, the projectile deflected off Crema's scales. Her angry cry answered my own. I was in the air a moment later, Harlan grasping my saddle.

Other Rolman archers arose from their hiding places on the plains. I counted six, wearing only leather jerkins smeared with dirt to match the terrain. They'd buried themselves in the ground of the burnt fields. Neither Crema nor I had spotted them, so they must've been under there since at least the previous night, waiting for the army to march on the road. An ambush against a disorganized host could be devastating. But humans trying to ambush dragons wasn't wise.

I beat my wings, closing the distance to the Rolman archers. I expected more to appear. How many soldiers would Egan Drehan risk outside the protection of his walls?

As I flew to assist, Crema swooped down on a second pass. Bethy Rann had her own bow ready as well. She released an arrow, the tip flying straight and true into the neck of a previously-concealed archer. Crema climbed again, away from any answer from the other archers. But there was none. No one else fired at Crema. Nor did any more attackers appear beyond the original six—now five—I'd seen earlier. That made no sense. What was the point in attacking an army this size with six humans with bows?

Parts of Rann's army began to disperse, moving away from the road. Someone had given an order to get moving, but like everything with the unruly host, there was mostly chaos as humans scattered in multiple directions—some marching, some running. I wondered at the military logic of such an order. Then I saw the arrows.

Three of the five surviving archers had fired their bows. The arrows flew in high arcs. Each had been lit on fire with flint carried by the attackers. The burning arrows plunged toward the army. I didn't have time to do anything about it.

Three arrows should've posed no danger to a host the size of this one. Unless that army had done something really stupid, like march directly into fire oil that had been poured on the road and fields around them. The Rolmans had been burning the whole of this island for weeks. It shouldn't have been a surprise they still had more fire oil and would use it. Except Rann and Xedric hadn't considered that danger. Neither had I.

Bethy Rann's army was about to burn.

FOURTEEN

The flaming arrows dropped out of the sky in a gradual, gentle arc.

The reaction that followed wasn't gentle. After the first arrow hit the ground, nothing happened. I hoped I had been wrong, that Drehan had something else planned. A horrified scream followed the second arrow's impact, and a fearsome inferno followed.

Fire erupted first on the left flank of Bethy Rann's host, then on the road in front of it, and finally in the heart of the army, as the other projectiles fell and ignited. Rann's fighters scrambled in every direction, some fleeing hysterically into even worse flames as the surrounding fields ignited.

Crema was closer than I to the chaos. She dove into the flames at Rann's urging, plucking humans from their doom as best as she was able, but she could carry only one at a time in her claws. I flew faster, but not fast enough. As I neared, I thought I heard Xedric Gile barking in his strange speech. It didn't matter what he said. His army disintegrated around him into a mass of horrific casualties.

I hadn't wanted to further reveal my power to Rann, but there was no longer a choice. My mind went to the Latticework. My need was great, my desire urgent, yet I knew I needed calm to tap my power. I filled my lungs as I shifted my focus to the wind flowing beneath my wings. I sensed the currents of air, the heat of the ground. The Latticework revealed itself easily. I still did not comprehend much of the twisted maze of woven Chords, but I knew enough. I called, rearranging the Chords that connected with and controlled the forces of this world. In response, the sky did my bidding with alacrity.

A wind as cold as that which might be mustered by a storm in the depths of winter howled its presence. Tinged with ice crystals born of the air's moisture and quickly frozen, the unseasonable torrent swept across the plains in violent spasms that threw men from their feet but also saved their lives. The oil-fueled flames bowed to my conjured gusts like a candle flame to a human child's waiting breath, defiantly flickering before being extinguished in a maelstrom of ice. I glided above the storm, my vision fading and returning as my mind entered and returned from directing the Latticework. I maintained the ice gusts until I beat the last of the flames.

I wobbled in the air when my magic was finally done, the mundane world spinning uncontrollably. I willed myself to remain calm, my wings steady. Soon, the tumult in my head subsided. I broke into a gentle arc around the decimated host to survey the damage that Lord Drehan had wrought. Despite my intervention, it was a grim sight.

Rann's army was shattered. Soldiers had scattered in every direction. A group of perhaps a hundred remained clustered together, almost all those on the ground—some on their backs, others on their knees praying to Haven. More humans wandered in confusion. Hundreds of Rann's followers simply ran, heading south, back the way they had come, to their homes or whatever was left of them. I wondered if Xedric was among the survivors. I didn't see him among the tumult.

Crema made a low pass over the chaos, then beat her wings in pursuit of the fleeing archers from the Twisted Keep. I joined the pursuit. I didn't want Lord Drehan to get word of what had happened here. Let him believe this plan worked. At the very least, I didn't want him knowing that magic was at work.

The Rolman archers died easily: I skewered three with my claws, Crema bit the head off another. I took the final one in my jaws. His bow string snapped before I sank my teeth through his torso. The blood dripped into my mouth, hot and fresh, but I spat him out. It wasn't just that humans tasted awful. I also felt guilty about eating one in front of Harlan and Bethy. Never let it be said I wasn't considerate of human feelings.

Once the Rolman archers had been dealt with, Rann urged Crema back toward her army. They landed in the midst of the shattered host, close to the road. Scorched humans littered the ground. Dozens more stood aimlessly, staring at the sky. Rann stayed on Crema's back rather than dismount. She rose to her feet, using the dragon as a great, living podium to address her remaining followers.

"By the grace of Haven, we have been tested," she shouted as loud as a human voice could manage. "We have been tested and found worthy!"

Worthy of what? I wondered. *Worthy of being dinner? Did roasted human taste better than the raw variety?*

I was about to land beside her, but Harlan urged otherwise in an urgent whisper. "A good leader seizes every opportunity, even an opportunity born from a horrible defeat. Let us land well behind Crema, close enough to be seen but not so much as to distract from Rann's words. That is, if you want her to succeed in saving what remains of her army."

I didn't quite get Harlan's point, but he was emphatic. If I intended to assault the Twisted Keep it was better to have an army— any army—to aid me than to not have one, so I did as Harlan suggested, carefully picking a clear spot that was devoid of crisp human flesh. Rann noticed me, but she pretended she hadn't.

"We knew our enemy had a heart as black as the darkest depths of the Abyss. We knew they are desperate as their inevitable defeat draws near. But we didn't anticipate the depth of depraved desperation until this day."

Rann's voice carried well across the plains. Stragglers in all directions stopped to listen at least. They were probably too shocked to realize their leader was wrong. Drehan's tactics had been inspired, a sign of tactical intelligence against a large, mismanaged army. There was nothing desperate about it. Still, I minded my manners, sitting attentively as Bethy Rann shouted and gestured all about.

"Yet, here, they have given us their best, struck at us when we were vulnerable, and what have we shown them instead?"

The true answer: human flesh burns easily. But that wasn't the reply Rann went with.

"We have shown them we cannot be beaten!" She hollered the words, as if making them loud also made them true. "As we stood on the edge of annihilation, we were saved." Rann expanded her arms wide as though they were wings. "This was not a defeat. It was a lesson that so long as we remain true to the cause, we will be protected and guided to victory by the greatest of allies."

Ugh, now she intended to drag me into this. I didn't want her gratitude or that of—

"Haven shines down upon us; divine judgment has declared our cause just! The power of Haven is with us. And underneath its great light, our cause cannot be defeated!"

Ah, so it was Haven that had extinguished the inferno. Not me, but the unseen powers above who favored one bunch of humans over another. Did anyone really believe this stuff?

The ragged host actually mustered a cheer at the drivel. The first shouts of approval were scattered and hesitant, but the next wave had far more enthusiasm. Initially led by a few fervent followers interspersed among the rest, the cheer gained momentum with each repetition. It was charming that the survivors could be happy about what had happened. I still didn't see Xedric Gile.

Not yet satisfied with the adulation shouted at her, Rann whispered to Crema. The horned dragon stood on her hind legs while

Rann adeptly used her dragon saddle to keep on her feet. "To our victory!"

The cries of ecstatic humans shook the ground at this miraculous performance. Stragglers from the distance began to return—some of them, anyway. A few deranged followers even ran toward Crema and their savior, the Heir of Ulibon.

Toasted fools.

I twisted my neck to speak quietly to Harlan. "It seems I wasn't part of her—"

Rann didn't let me finish before she shouted yet again. "Even dragons flock to our cause." She gestured toward me. My eyes turned the color of night. Rann had been a ryder more than long enough to read what I told her. "This is our new ally, Bayloo. A free dragon, to fight by our side. The mightiest dragon in all of Inkra."

I appreciated flattery, but not in this instance.

"Let us regroup and prepare for our final victory!" Rann proclaimed, finally allowing Crema to sink back down out of her humiliating stance. Dragons weren't statues for humans to use to proclaim their own greatness.

Bethy Rann slid out of the saddle, wading immediately into the mass of suffering humanity that surrounded her. She barked orders to various humans I didn't know. Some answered her, some didn't. As a semblance of order gradually returned over the course of the morning, I estimated that half of Bethy Rann's army was dead, injured, or had deserted. Apparently, the host had only a few village healers among them.

Harlan helped as well. "A bad way to die," he said of the burned humans. "Some are worse, but fire is a bad way to die."

"How would you like to die?" I asked him.

He didn't hesitate. "Quickly."

That was a good answer.

Rann split her time among the injured and the able-bodied, trying her best to restore order to the terrible chaos. At least she seemed to care about these people. I hunted for a bit of food for the army, with limited success, and called forth a bit of rain so they might have water. There was nothing else I could do. When she finally approached me, she carried a burnt human in her arms. I recognized him: Xedric Gile.

As she held his barely-recognizable form before me, my eyes confirmed what my nose had already told me. "I cannot heal the dead. Or even the living. That is power denied to dragons, it seems."

Rann didn't answer at first; she merely dropped her head down to look once more at the blackened corpse of the man. "He put this uprising together."

I was weary of the death around me, the death I'd seen so much of since becoming free. My head pounded from the foul fumes, so I may have spoken more harshly to Rann than I intended. "You spin a fine tale for which to cheer."

If Bethy Rann took offense, she didn't show it. "I am the symbol. People need something tangible to fight for, something to inspire them. The Rolmans tortured and mutilated Xedric. His words couldn't inspire the masses, the sight of him stirred no hearts, but his blood was more noble than mine, whatever our lineage."

"That is a failing of your kind. You believe blood confers status."

She jerked her head up sharply. I didn't mean to be cruel. It was merely the truth.

Instead of answering, Rann laid Xedric's body at my feet. "We shall bury him inside the walls of the Twisted Keep."

"You have to take it first," I pointed out.

Rann stared at me with a dragon's gaze. "You have learned magic during your time across the Wall. That storm, the lightning on the night I found you, it was you. Can you not just ..." She smashed one fist into another.

"I have done battle at the Twisted Keep once before. Dozens of dragons unleashed their fire and strength against those gleaming walls, all for nothing. The keep was forged by enchanters, the structure held together by more than limestone mortar." I flicked my tail as I glanced out to the north. "Even if I understood the magic involved,

I'm not sure I could bring down those walls. To stake all of your battle plan on my uncertain magic is unwise."

Rann made a grumbling noise. My nostrils flared.

"All power has a cost, Bethy Rann. I did what I could to save as much of your army as I was able. There is a limit to all things. The walls of the Twisted Keep will not be easily breached." I moved closer. "Believing otherwise leads to disaster."

If the rebuke stung, Rann gave no sign. She bit off each word of her reply. "However it must be done, it will be done. My vengeance is not yet complete."

FIFTEEN

We came at night.

There were a multitude of reasons for choosing the cover of darkness. The most obvious was that we dragons see a lot better than humans in the absence of light, further increasing our combat advantage. Another was that even a battered remnant of an army looked far more fearsome if you were gazing at its camp fires from the walls above. Rann's host might be totally lacking in siege equipment and next to useless against the Twisted Keep's formidable fortifications, but they were noisy, smelly, and still relatively numerous. Their arrival would provide some distraction to the watchmen of the Twisted Keep, although I wasn't relying upon that. If Lord Drehan had been clever enough to plan the ambush that decimated Rann's host, he would also be wary enough to keep a sharp watch for dragons. He knew about Crema. But fighting a single horned dragon was quite a bit different than trying to find a way to deal with me. There wasn't any way to do that.

Crema and I chose a roundabout flightpath to the keep, flying east to the sea, then following Ulibon's coast north. When we neared the keep, we separated. Crema flew directly for the castle, while I took a circuitous route so that I might attack the fortress from the seaward side. The defenders would be watching for Crema, so she went first, carrying Bethy Rann as well as another soldier. I'd drawn on magic to summon more clouds to fill the sky, commanding them to hover thick and low to cover our assault.

I moved through the night at a prowling pace, floating above the dark waves. In addition to Harlan, I had three other humans on my back. It had been many moons since I'd carried such a load. I could handle the weight, but I certainly didn't enjoy it. Worse than their bulk was the unpleasantness of having strangers on my back. Their terror of flying made them sweat—and stink.

Bethy Rann had reluctantly accepted that the gates of the Twisted Keep needed to be opened from the inside, using swords, claws, and wits rather than some imagined magic I might conjure. The humans I carried had their swords, and I knew Rann was adept with a blade. I had claws and magic.

Rann had left a former companion of dead Xedric in charge of the host—a trunk of a human named Gorge. I met him only briefly—he appeared to have been built with no neck but an extra helping of chin. Rann said he was capable. She didn't sound convincing, though. But it wasn't the human army that worried me the most. Crema claimed my angst. Although she was a dragon, and therefore far more capable than a human, her injuries left her fate almost entirely in Bethy Rann's five-fingered hands. My trepidation was prescient.

I watched Crema from afar as she streaked in from the east shoreline, flying high through the cloud cover I'd created before diving toward the twisting spiral of the great citadel. Fires blazed on the three levels of winding walls like tiny infernos, making the fortress look like a burning snake wrapped around its victim. I'd never seen so much light lofted onto the walls of a castle (except when my brothers and sisters set one blaze). The high, dancing flames let off a steady stream of black soot that did more to cloud my vision than any darkness. Being surrounded by the crackling light of so many braziers might have made the defenders feel better in the night, but I doubted it truly improved their vision. It certainly didn't stop Crema.

The horned dragon kept her wings tucked back as she flew in to attack, headed for the lower reaches of the fortress where the main gate beckoned. The defenders must've seen her, but no bells rang, no horns sounded, no ballistae hurled projectiles at her. She crossed over the outer wall, above the ground-level ring wall but beneath the second tier of battlements that were situated on the mountain's jutting cliffs. Heavy smoke clung around the mountain there. When I lost sight of Crema, I didn't panic. Not until I heard the dragon's roaring plea for help.

I pushed hard toward that desperate sound. It took all my self-control not to knock the useless human strangers off my back to gain extra speed. I beat my wing with great thrusts. The keep grew large before me. The smog of black soot was even thicker than it had been moments before, as if a cloud of black had passed over the castle. I could see only the glimmering light of the fires on the other side. Crema roared again, in pain. I went faster.

"It's a fisherman's net!" Harlan hollered, his warning so loud I felt it in my bones.

A fisherman?

Then I got it, belatedly understanding what had happened to Crema. I dipped a wing, twirling into a dangerous turn that I only attempted because my life depended on it. Several humans screamed on my back. One or two might've retched. I snarled at the stink. Never again with the idiot humans.

Harlan shouted again. "From above."

I flicked my eyes upward but couldn't risk moving my neck for a full look. I plunged downward, my direction shifting violently, my angles all wrong for proper flight. In the dark, I finally saw what I should've anticipated—a great spider's web of black netting extending from the upper tier of the fortress down to the lower wall beneath, the soot of the brazier fires cloaking it in blackness. There were dozens of nets hanging, a maze of deadly traps. Crema had been snared in one. I had come within a neck's length of being caught in another. I hadn't, but the price had been a terrible maneuver that forced me to unnaturally contort and finally flip my belly upward. Two desperate beats of my wings righted me, but the force of my maneuvers was too much for one of the human passengers. The makeshift saddle straps that held him gave away, and he fell from my back, his screams lingering until the ground silenced them.

Lighter, I swept back around toward the keep. A hail of ballistae arc-bolts greeted me. Too many to dodge completely. Instead, I tucked my vulnerable wings back against my body and pulled in my neck to make myself as small a target as possible. For all that I did, two projectiles still found me. One hit the hard scales of my belly, leaving a nasty sting but no lasting damage. The other caught me in the foreleg, just above my claw. The tip of the bolt found the crease between my armor plates, wedging itself inside. An angry roar escaped my jaw, echoed by the panicked yelps of the novice passengers on my backside.

The ground raced at me. I risked spreading my wings again, deciding that the danger of more arc-bolts was exceeded by an uncontrolled crash. I caught the air and got a half-flap out of my wings before striking the rocky soil beyond the keep's outer wall. I was in the dangerous zone between the fortress and the army surrounding it. It wasn't the worst crash I ever experienced—not even close. But I landed on my injured foreleg, sending the impaled bolt further through my scales and into my leg. I thrashed my tail at the pain, my eyes white with rage. More humans fell or jumped off my back. I didn't have time to care, since I was certain Harlan would manage to hold on. I hurled myself back into the air as another volley of arc-bolts launched from the keep's battlements. This time I was more prepared, and the operators underestimated my speed; they had probably never fired on a dragon before. Every bolt missed. They'd need to reload. I had an opportunity.

I soared into the air, gaining speed. There was one human still on my back—by his scent, it was Harlan. I was fleetingly relieved.

"Get a solid grip and be prepared for anything."

Harlan acknowledged me with a guttural noise of battle rather than words.

I came directly at the keep, jaws dripping with angry bile. Shouts —some of alarm, but most of utter terror—came from the walls of the Twisted Keep. I surveyed the wall above as well as the battlement below. The giant nets that had ensnared Crema had been hung from the ledge upon which the upper tier of the citadel had been built as it twisted around the central peak. Several tunnels had been cut through the jutting cliff's bottom, from which ballistae could fire downward. Those were the most dangerous. This place had been built by enchanters to withstand even a dragon attack.

As we neared the fortress, my eyes locked on Crema. She'd actually been caught in two different nets. One had snapped off, falling over her, covering her wings. There was no way she could fly, stuck in that entanglement. But the trap hadn't been completely successful. Crema managed to grab onto the rocky wall of the mountain halfway between the ground and the ledge above. This kept her from falling into the massive inner yard at the base of the fortress, and it also made her a difficult target, since the fortress' war machines were mostly designed to fire outward, not toward the mountain spire that served as the keep's spine. Unfortunately, I saw at least one arc-bolt embedded within her torso. Still, I'd expected worse. When I flew over the keep, I'd drawn the fire of the other ballistae, saving her life, but only temporarily.

I had to free Crema. The humans of this place were diabolical. I had no intention of letting them rob the world of another of my kind. My wings propelled me ever faster.

Harlan guessed my intention. "Don't come in directly. The other traps are still dangerous, Bayloo. I'll jump onto the net that holds Crema and Rann. I'm not wearing armor; I can climb and maneuver easily. You keep us safe, keep the ballistae from firing at her."

I didn't change my course. "Too slow."

"You don't have time to try to pull her free with claws. The defenders may have more nets, other surprises. As you said, this place was built by enchanters—"

He didn't get a chance to finish his thought. I appreciated the warning, and it had given me an idea. But I didn't have time to explain myself. I didn't fly to Crema immediately, as badly as I wanted to save her. Instead, I swept down toward the sprawling wall that encircled the citadel, a barrier as tall as twenty humans standing atop one another, with battlements wide enough that four soldiers could march along its length with their shoulders touching. It was littered with ballistae, catapults, soldiers, and smoking braziers emitting blacken soot. The fires were interspersed along the wall walk at regular intervals.

I came in low and fast. A few humans launched arrows, and a single ballista managed to reload and fire, but most of the defenders were too shocked by the nearly-invisible dragon sweeping through the night to do much more than duck. They weren't my targets, though. Instead, I toppled the braziers.

It was almost easy. I just sailed along the wall walk, my hind legs scraping the stone. One after another, the tall braziers fell, spilling the smoky mixture of fire oil and water inside onto the wall. But even that was only the beginning. The burning liquid soon covered the entirety of the eastern portion of the wall walk and began dripping down into the yard below. Like most keeps, many of the inner buildings of the Twisted Keep had been constructed against the great wall to save time and material—and all of them had roofs that burned. Satisfying screams erupted in my wake as I ascended to save Crema. An arc-bolt grazed my neck as I came out of a turn. I was too close to the second tier, an easy target for the ballistae firing from above. Destroying the machines would take too much time. I needed to free Crema.

With a great beat of my wings, I flew to her. The once-beautiful dragon was a bloody, mangled mess. The soldier Crema had carried hung from his neck within the netting that ensnared Crema, but Bethy Rann had kept her head (in all ways), struggling from the saddle to try to cut the bonds that held Crema. Despite the fine metal dagger in her hand, she hadn't had any success.

I attempted to latch myself to the mountainside beside Crema, digging into the rock as best I could with my claws while flapping my wings awkwardly to keep myself from falling. My injured foreclaw was nearly useless, but even my hind claws were failing me. The stone was wickedly firm. I was all too aware how vulnerable I was in this spot even before Harlan shouted, "Bolts from above!"

I twisted my neck around to see a single arc-bolt hurled at me. My eyes narrowed in on the approaching projectile. I pulled up my tail, swiping it into the bolt as it hurtled toward me. I whacked the shaft, sending the projectile into a wild spin that bumped harmlessly into the rock wall. That trick wouldn't work with more than one or two bolts at the most. I didn't have much time.

My hind claws squeezed into the mountain face. Some rock dribbled away. With my foreclaws and teeth I made an awkward grab at the net that held Crema. Once I had a grip, I pushed back off the rock wall, hovering beside Crema as I chewed the net with my teeth and pulled with my claws. The trap's coils didn't break—it wasn't made of rope. This had to be something left over from the enchanters who'd once occupied the Twisted Keep. I could try my own magic, but that would take concentration, and I knew nothing of enchantment. This wasn't my domain.

"The nets are anchored on the rock above," Harlan shouted at me.

I was still wrestling with the net as I answered. "How does that help?"

"Don't break the net. Fly the whole net and her out of here. We'll get it off her elsewhere."

Harlan's idea was the only chance we had. I flew upward immediately, surging toward the ledge above me. It sloped outward from the central mountain with enough girth to support the walls and towers that had been built atop it. The humans had run chains down from the wall on the upper side of the ledge, and then across the rock.

Those chains served as a type of rafter to which the nets had been attached. Unlike the enchanted nets, the chains looked to be castle-forged metal.

I flipped sideways as I flew along the ledge, reaching out to snare the chains with my hind legs. I missed with my left leg, but the claws of my right scraped along the stone surface until they found the links I needed. With the chain secured, I beat my wings, picking up speed, but only for a moment. The metal stiffened, groaned, then snapped.

I twisted in a tight circle back to Crema. "Release your claws from the mountainside, Crema."

Confused and agitated, she didn't move. Being trapped was too much for her damaged mind.

I tried again. "Rann, speak to her! We must leave!"

With Bethy Rann on her back shouting commands, Crema finally released her claws from the mountain just as I grabbed hold of the links of the net that trapped them. "Push off!" I ordered.

Propelled by Crema's shove and the heavy flapping of my wings, I pulled my fellow dragon through the air still wrapped in the net. She was smaller than an ash dragon, but still terrifically heavy. I struggled to keep us aloft. Landing wasn't a choice—not while we were in the range of the castle ballistae. Rann's army was too far for me to reach. Instead, I yanked us out to the sea just beyond the north wall of the keep.

"Where are you going?" It was Bethy Rann shouting at me. She didn't sound very grateful that I saved her life for a second time in a single day, so I didn't reply.

Once over the cold waves, I gave in to my exhaustion, letting the net with Crema and Bethy inside dip into the water. The sea would be cold, but dragons were hearty, and Rann could handle a few splashes. I pulled them the rest of the way on the water until we were well out of the range of the Twisted Keep's war engines. Someone in the high towers would be able to see us, but I didn't care about being seen for now. We were far enough away that they weren't going to run out at night to pursue us.

Grateful to be done with the worst of the evening's events (hopefully), I dragged Crema and Rann from the sea onto a sandy beach. I landed beside her, sniffing at her wounds.

"Pain?" I asked.

Crema answered me with a flash of her eyes. There was such pain in her, I felt her hurt.

"She is weak, near delirious," Bethy Rann told me as she struggled to pull herself from Crema's saddle. She succeeded only in getting further entangled in the enchanted web.

I worried at Crema's condition. She had two bolts lodged in her torso, blood surrounding both. They needed to come out, but I had to free her from the net that imprisoned her first.

Harlan was already at work on the net, pacing around its twisted length with sharp eyes that peered through the night. "It's tricky and tangled, but we'll get it off. A net is no use if you can't get the fish out. It'll just take some patience."

Playing with enchanted nets was a task better suited to human fingers than dragon's teeth. I left Harlan and Bethy Rann to try to cut through the jumbles of coils and suffer the frustrations that went along with that. I focused on Crema's wounds. She had two arc-bolts in her, and I could hear her hearts pounding in her chest as they struggled to keep everything inside working. A normal dragon—even a horned dragon—would recover from these wounds with food and rest once the bolts were out, but Crema wasn't normal. She had already been badly damaged before this latest battle.

Harlan and Rann hacked furiously with their daggers, but the net held. Rann cursed, yanking her sword from its scabbard. The blade glinted with a soft azure hue against the night.

"Get that rock," she told Harlan. He obeyed without comment, helping Rann position the net cord on top of the hard surface. When all was ready, Rann swung her sword. A screech almost akin to a human scream pierced the night as the blade struck and the net's cord broke into two pieces. After that, it was easy. In a few more moments, Harlan's skilled hands freed Crema from the netting. Rann immediately turned her attention to the bolts in the dragon's flesh.

"This one broke through her scale." Rann pointed out what I already saw. "I patched the worst damage in her armor after her near-death fall with enchanted metal, but some of the scales never fully healed." Rann sounded wistful for a moment, but only a moment. "The other bolt cracked a scale and lodged itself inside, but it didn't reach Crema's flesh. I think I can just pull that one out."

I studied the more superficial of Crema's injuries. I had suffered no small number of impalements myself, and as best I could tell, Rann was correct. "Pull out the bolt if you can do so without harming her."

Rann placed a gentle palm on Crema. "Are you ready?"

The horned dragon assured her ryder of her strength with a flash of her good eye. Rann didn't hesitate. She yanked hard. The bolt came away in her hand. Rann flung it toward the sea with a disgusted sneer. There was still the other projectile to deal with.

"You can do nothing for her?" She seemed to plead with me. "You cannot even heal a fellow dragon."

The answer frustrated me as much as it did Bethy Rann. "Healing is a different art, and living beings are infinitely complex in their weavings. I do not even know where to begin. To change something that is alive using the power of Chords is another order of power entirely."

Rann stared at the second bolt, its shaft deep within Crema. "It must come out."

While Rann and I had been talking, Harlan had already torn off his shirt and soaked it in sea water. He held out the damp cloth. "Pull it out and I will cover the wound."

"She will make it through this," I said, but my words were hope, not certainty.

Rann did what we all knew she had to do. At least she was quick. Blood gushed from the wound. Harlan covered it, but his paltry cloth was soon a mass of blood, and the flow continued unabated. Rann's eyes widened. "It's not stopping." She turned to me accusingly. "It should stop. She is a dragon!"

Rann was correct. Dragons didn't bleed that way, certainly not from a mere bolt wound. What had happened to her after she had fallen from the sky near Eladrell? There wasn't time to discuss it. I reached for the Latticework. I could not heal flesh, but perhaps there was still something I could do for Crema.

I gazed at the wounded dragon in the deeper reality of the Latticework. She was magnificent, a dazzling array of forces, weaves, and particles beyond my comprehension. I didn't understand life, and I never would. I narrowed my focus on her wound, to the blood flowing. Within the Latticework, the fluid was a swirling storm of energy, and other forces that I didn't try to sort out. But I could discern that something greater was wrong within Crema than this hole in her flesh. The patchwork of repaired scales was just on the outside. Inside and out, she was no longer like other dragons. Blotches of darkness appeared in the chaotic vortex of her life. She was injured in a manner that went beyond an arc-bolt wound.

I couldn't fix Crema. I needed to do what Bethy Rann had done previously—patch the holes that needed immediate attention. With little to work with, I summoned the cold again, but instead of seeding the clouds, I drew it from the air around us and concentrated it. Then, I summoned the wind, swirling the gust in a tight ring, adding cold until I had a stream of super-chilled air that could turn liquid to ice in a single blast. "Everyone, stand away."

Once the humans obeyed, I sent my magic at Crema's open wound.

The effect was violent. A blast of iced air ripped through the sky, forming itself into a funnel no wider than a human arm. Crema roared as it struck her, more in shock than pain, I hoped. Bethy Rann gasped in horror.

In a moment, it was over. The magic had dissipated and the blood of Crema's wound had frozen. The flow of ugly red had been staunched.

Rann took a step closer, her eyes narrowly focused on the bandage of crimson ice that coated Crema's wound. "Is that what you call healing?"

"That's a patch to keep her alive, so her life's fluid does not leak out. She'll have to do the rest of the healing herself. If she can."

"You mean she may die?"

I grunted unhappily. "Parts of her already are dead, I think. Let us hope we can save the rest of her before Lord Drehan attacks again."

SIXTEEN

I kept vigil for my fellow dragon.

Darkness surrounded us, but at least Crema was not alone. Bethy Rann, too, knelt beside the horned dragon, her hand never breaking contact with Crema's scales. Crema slept, but fitfully. Ordinarily, her wounds would be the equivalent of a human cut, a trifle to be soon forgotten. But something worse than arc-bolts afflicted Crema. It was as if something inside her had died, weakening that which remained. The price of the near-freedom of her mind had been higher than Rann or I suspected.

Harlan interrupted our silent observance, his voice uncharacteristically hesitant. He spoke to Bethy Rann. "Do you not have an army to attend to?"

Rann sucked in a sharp breath, but did not budge from Crema's side. "I left Heffen Gorge in command." Her tone made it unclear if that was a good thing or not. "He had orders to attack only if we were able to capture the gate. Otherwise he would maintain the siege—at a safe distance beyond the range of the Rolman war engines."

"But you do not give orders to Lord Drehan or his garrison, do you?" Harlan prodded. "He does not seem a man to sit idly on his advantage."

The words had their desired effect. Rann pulled her hand from Crema's scales, rising to her feet. She took several hurried steps, peering in the direction of her army, her eyes squinting. We were too far away for her eyes to see anything but darkness.

Harlan kept speaking to her. "I'm just a ship's captain, but if I were Drehan, I think I would risk opening the gates to send out a mounted sortie against my demoralized enemy. Fortunately, he lacks horses. So what does a Rolman commander do in this case?"

"Harriers." Rann whispered the word in the darkness. "Men chosen for the ability to run long distances at speed and still fight effectively." She glanced back at Crema before returning her attention to the darkness. "Bayloo, can you ..."

I had already craned my neck in the direction of the Twisted Keep. "It is too far for me to see at this distance, and there are hills blocking my line of sight." Reluctant to leave Crema, I grudgingly conceded, "I would be able to see more from the air."

"I need to return to my army. I should've done so before now." She sounded guilty. "Crema and I not returning ... they were already on the edge." The tension became thicker in her voice the more she spoke.

It was a long trek on foot in the dark. She knew it and so did I, but there was Crema to think about. She meant far more to me than a thousand humans. If these armies wanted to hack each other to death, should I care?

Rann sensed my reluctance. "I love Crema too."

Love? Did dragons love? The dragons I knew ... whose love I might seek, followed the Way, not the whims of human love. It seemed that Rinxia was not a creature of love. The Way told me to be responsible for Crema. That must be what I felt. Except I wasn't like other dragons. "I must stay with her in case the wound ruptures."

"You have already saved us both this night, Bayloo," Rann said. "I will keep my word to you, but I must beg you, please fly me back to my army. Then return here to be with Crema. It will not take long for you, but in the night ... I don't know if I could make it at all, much less in time to do anything helpful."

I sniffed Crema, studying the strange wound and her labored breathing. If something happened when I was absent, that was a sin I wouldn't forgive myself for, but Rann was correct that it wouldn't take me long to fly her back to her fellow humans—assuming nothing else went wrong.

Harlan stepped into the hesitation. "I will stay with Crema. I'll send a flaming arrow into the air should I need you, Bayloo."

Rann bestowed a grateful look upon Harlan. "You will take me, then?"

"If she could speak, I know Crema would beg me to take you, even at the expense of her own life. And although her will is not entirely her own, I believe her affection for you, and yours for her, to be real." I couldn't bring myself to say love. "For that reason, I will carry you to your army. But that is all. Are we agreed?"

Rann's answer was to hurry over to me. She hesitated for a moment before climbing onto the saddle on my back. She was lighter than Harlan, but kept her seat in the practiced, familiar fashion to which I had become accustomed during much of my life. This was a ryder, and it felt comfortable having her there. That annoyed me.

To Harlan, I said, "Signal if you need me."

I soared into the dark sky. The wind howled and the air stank. Beyond the walls of the keep, where Bethy Rann's army had encamped, there was nothing. Well, almost nothing. As I flew closer, I saw the bodies of the dead, the embers of broken campfires, the remains of what had perhaps been supply wagons and tents. Rann had something uncomfortable in her throat. The noises that squeaked out of her were mere unintelligible sounds of despair.

I went closer, flying lower. The hosts, barely held together after the disaster on the road that morning, had broken apart once again. Humans scattered like sand in the wind in every southerly direction, a trail of dead and injured in their wake.

"Darkness of the Abyss ..." Bethy Rann murmured, her voice nearly breaking.

"At least there is no pursuit. They must've broken the army, then retreated to the keep."

"Drehan is diabolical, but also cautious," Rann said, bitterness in every word. "He wants his precious harriers back behind the great walls of his fortress."

I understood Rann's distress. She had not only lost her army, she had lost a dream at the precipice of achieving it. I understood being denied that which you wanted badly, that which you, deep down, believe you were destined for. Like me, Rann did not relinquish her dreams easily.

"Take me to them," she urged. "I can salvage this once again."

"Twice in a day these men have been routed, Bethy Rann. Defeat is a bitter morsel, but it must be swallowed at times."

"We've lost a battle, that is all. But as you pointed out, that army was mostly useless against the Twisted Keep. It is more about forging a story, the legend that would let me reclaim my rule. With your help, I need only a hundred soldiers to capture the keep. Your presence alone through the night will be enough for me to rally that many."

I grunted unhappily. "I must return to Crema, should I be needed. Although the distance is long on foot, those harriers that smashed your army might dare to march out to her in the morning to finish her if I am not present and vigilant."

My hearing was acute enough to know Rann ground her teeth in frustration. "Ulibon will rise again." She said it with the certainty that the sun would rise in the morning. "I just need a little more help, Bayloo. Once, I helped you."

I wasn't swayed. There were humans scattered, and this wouldn't just be scooping them up. Rann would have to talk to them. That meant I'd have to listen to her. It would all take too much time for a cause that wasn't my own. "This is more than you have a right to ask of me."

My wing dipped as I began an arcing turn back to the north, back to Crema.

"Our arrangement was for your assistance capturing the keep. We cannot do that without some soldiers. I will tell you where to find aurathorn. I'll tell you that and more. But only after we've captured the Twisted Keep."

I hissed with annoyance. "Capture it with what? I see no soldiers, no army, not even that mess of a host you had gathered before. I see only farmers, some dead and the rest terrified. If you will not help us, we shall continue our quest. I will not fail. I might remind you that I already saved your life this night. Any debt I owed you for your help leaving Rolm has been repaid."

"You speak with the arrogance of power. Be careful with something so fleeting," Rann warned, her voice hot with emotion. I kept flying northward.

"A bargain," Rann said hastily. "I will assist this quest you and your companion are on. I promised you the location of aurathorn and that Ulibon will be at your disposal to help get it."

"You already promised that," I agreed. "You can only give that once. Anyway, Ulibon seems like it has other issues."

To my surprise, Rann didn't disagree. "It's true, we are in a desperate place. A precarious remnant against that mighty keep. That is why you should help us. Don't give up on us. We shall be a new nation, forever grateful." She reminded me of her brother Jona when she talked like that—naively hopeful. Jona hadn't deserved to die.

"There is nothing to save," I pointed out.

"Almost nothing!" She said it as if I had proven her point. "Lord Drehan sees all that you do of our defeat. He's in there luxuriating in his own genius, beating an army that outnumbered him, besting not one but two dragons. He is probably toasting his great victory with his soldiers on this night."

Drinking. I missed that. I didn't get the rest of her babble, but I did miss a good drink.

Rann wasn't done. "His arrogance gives us the opening we need. His belief in his utter victory will save us. This can all be salvaged."

She told me her plan. It was utterly reckless, so very human. It also wasn't totally insane. It might even work—if I went along.

It wasn't enough. I kept flying toward Crema.

Rann played her last card. "Within the keep, there are vaults— secret vaults—that I doubt even Mendakas and his pillagers ever found."

"I do not need human riches. Coins cannot be eaten, freedom for dragons cannot be bought."

"I'm not talking about gold. I'm talking about items of enchantment. Artifacts that will help you on your quest. Items impervious to magic, devices to enhance strength. These are things that will help you that you can get nowhere else."

I didn't know whether to believe her or not. "I need nothing from you." It wasn't true, but I enjoyed saying it.

Rann's teeth clenched. "Then let me down at least. Crema and I will do this without you."

"Crema is injured," I pointed out.

"She will recover. When she does, we will attack."

More than any bribe, any bauble of magic, I didn't want Crema attacking the Twisted Keep again. Even once she was healed, a single horned dragon against the keep's enchanted defenses made my stomach feel like I'd swallowed a pot of vegetables. But how could I stop that when Rann was so intent on having her prize? Crema was loyal to Rann. The runes of slavery remained. I knew well the power of the link.

I turned, sweeping into a circular arc that would allow me to return southward if I chose. Rann knew that as well.

"Does this mean you will help me rally my forces?" She sounded hopeful and mistrustful at the same time.

I twisted my neck to gaze through the night at the pitiful, scattered humans. Could Rann really re-form this rabble into an army? I didn't like it. But if I refused, she would most certainly withhold her secrets from me. Crema would heal and Rann would use the horned dragon to raise another army and attack again anyway. This was her quest; it burned inside her as surely as aurathorn did for Harlan and I. Faced with this unhappy choice, I chose the lesser of the unpalatable dishes before me.

"I shall help you capture the Twisted Keep using this plan you have concocted."

"This time, we will not fail," Rann assured me.

"If you betray any of your promises to me, I will crunch your bones in my mouth no matter how awful you taste."

SEVENTEEN

I felt like a dog herding sheep.

Rann used me shamelessly as her prop in cajoling the stragglers of her former army to return, although I had to admit her showmanship was impressive. With my help, Rann chased down any group of survivors numbering over three. There were many such clusters, all headed south. Rann had a story for them all. Resplendent in her gold and silver armor, she was a masterful orator. Having me with her helped a lot.

To the dispirited, she ensured that I would prevail in any battle (probably not true). To those few of her followers that were still dreamers, she whispered that I was a sign from above. To the many skeptics, Rann said they were being tested by Haven, that a victory without cost would lack meaning. To the hopeless (the largest group), she pointed out they had no place left to go. The fields were burned, the ships mostly gone to the south, far away by foot. Only the vast food stores of the Twisted Keep could save them.

Aided by words, lies, and my presence, Rann rallied almost two hundred humans back to her cause. They were a pitiful bunch, braver or stupider than the rest, or maybe both. Three times that number continued south to an even more uncertain future.

Rann gathered her remnant army about her, immediately putting them to work establishing a new camp. She assigned new commanders, seemingly at random. She made sure everyone had something to keep themselves occupied. When dawn broke, I flew off to return to Crema. On my way, I spotted a hill cat stalking a goat up a steep cliff. I snared them both in my claws, but in an act of insane generosity, I left both kills with Rann before flying off to attend to Crema, placing my faith that Harlan had been attentive to Crema and still managed to snare a few fish. He didn't disappoint on either count.

Four huge king fish were waiting, cooked over driftwood collected from the beach that gave the specimens a nice smoky-salt flavor. I ate two, bones and all, and saved the rest for Crema.

"She hasn't opened her eyes," Harlan told me. "She jerked about fitfully through the night, but seems now to have entered a more gentle sleep."

I examined Crema's wound, both with my eyes and then through the lens of the Latticework. My freeze bandage had melted away over the course of the night, but it had achieved its purpose in staunching the bleeding. The damage to Crema's flesh had improved, but the healing was far slower than I would've expected. The strange void within her remained. I didn't understand her injury fully, only that it went deeper than any conventional wound. The core of her existence had been damaged.

"There is little else I can do for her," I said to myself more than my companion. "Except be by her side."

Harlan didn't disagree with me. "Rann's army is smashed, I presume."

I recounted what Bethy Rann and I had done, then I told him the plan.

"Bold." This pleased me. "Dangerous." This didn't bother me. He paused. "Too generous."

That made the spikes of my mane stand on end. "Speak your meaning."

"She will fail without you. But we may still find aurathorn without her information."

"You believe she knows where it is?"

Harlan rubbed his chin. "Aye, she knows something. She isn't a good enough liar to fib all that. But that isn't really why you are helping her, is it?"

I snorted unhappily. "I got her brother killed. It was my fault. I was being foolish with my newfound freewill, picking a fight for no reason."

"Guilt?" Harlan arched a brow. "That is not the Way, I would think."

"I have no Way." I looked away toward Crema. "There are other reasons, as well."

"Your fellow dragon—you stay for her. This, I understand. I had a crew. It isn't the same, but it is a similar idea. But Bethy Rann is a dragon ryder—one who lied to you about her identity and motives in the past. You should be wary."

I hadn't considered that. Had she lied? I'd certainly never asked if she was the Heir of Ulibon, so not exactly a lie. But that wasn't Harlan's point.

"I can think of other, better ways to keep Crema out of combat," he said. "And winning a war will not restore the life of Bethy Rann's brother. He is gone."

"Let me set your mind at ease. It is not out of mere generosity or guilt or fear for Crema that I put my life at risk." Was that true? "I will have need of Bethy Rann and Ulibon before all this is over. I seek to free the dragons of this land as well as defeat the rust. To do that, I may need Ulibon's help."

Harlan looked at me askance, as if I had bunny ears, but only for a moment. He shrugged with fake nonchalance. "As you say. Let us hope she brings us closer to aurathorn as well."

The next morning, Crema opened her eyes. She didn't have the strength to eat for another day after that (I ate her fish so they wouldn't go to waste, but Harlan got us more). I wondered how he lured such large specimens in so close to shore without obvious bait. He waded into the sea barefoot, so I supposed his toes must've been tasty to fish. To my nose, they merely smelled like rotten skunk.

I flew Bethy Rann back and forth to Crema several times under the cover of night, each time bringing some fish and whatever wild game I managed to hunt with me. It wasn't much, but Rann's paltry force had come to rejoice at my arrival, which I didn't mind. It seemed a few former soldiers had survived the earlier rout, and she'd put these to work drilling her remaining farmers in some rudimentary tactics. Rann's concern for Crema was obvious in her eyes and movements, yet I wondered how much of that was triggered by desperation. She needed the dragon. Unfortunately, Crema was equally attached.

By the third day, Crema was well enough to stand, stretch her wings, and speak—such as she did these days. Bethy Rann was able to communicate with her through their rune-link and explain what was required. Crema, as ever, was eager to please and be used as her ryder willed. But she still wasn't strong enough to fly, to the frustration of both dragon and ryder.

"What's wrong with her?" Bethy Rann asked as I flew her back to her camp under the cover of night, hugging the Ulibon coast to ensure we weren't seen from the Twisted Keep.

"I don't really know," I confessed. "It is as if part of her is dead, which also keeps her from healing fully."

"Can someone be part dead?"

"I'm not a healer. I don't know. Perhaps dragons can. We are different than other creatures of this world."

Rann was silent for some time, the rhythm of her breaths revealing tension. Finally, she sighed heavily. "I think I know why." I switched into a glide to hear better. "I gave her my mother's last gift."

"Something enchanted?" I prodded.

"The bracelet. We spoke of it in your cave on DragonPeak, in what seems a different life. You asked what your mother had promised me in exchange for my assistance."

"I remember it." It hadn't looked quite right to me, even back then, before I understood magic. "You said it helped steady your blade. Then evaded my question."

"You were not ready to know about the Heir of Ulibon then," Rann said. "On the eve of her death, my mother told me that every bit of her life beyond that day was infused within that bracelet. But she didn't tell me how to unlock the power before she died—there wasn't time for that. Your mother understood magic—she told me the rest: how the artifact functioned, and how to tap into my own power. She was a wise teacher, and I am grateful to her. Great Dawn told me that by shattering a crystal inlaid within the metal, that power would be released. Enough to save my life, should I ever be in peril. Crema needed it before I did. I placed it on her and shattered the crystal. That melted the metal, but it also made Crema open her eyes." Rann's voice grew thick. "I mixed the remainder of the bracelet's enchanted metal with iron to form the armored scales and false claws you see on her today."

I considered Rann's words, what she had intentionally and unintentionally accomplished. "There is an incomprehensible power in the Chords of life." I tried to sound knowledgeable, but beyond that tidbit I had no idea what I was talking about. I certainly had no idea how such an artifact as Rann described would be forged. "Perhaps that was enough to anchor what remained of Crema's life and bring her back from the Abyss. But not without cost."

"She is alive." Rann said it as if that explained everything.

"You possess her life," I said. "She could not even function without your guidance. You are more than a ryder to her now. Do you ever feel guilty about it?"

"Guilty about what?" Rann asked it as if she had no idea to what sin I referred.

"About commanding Crema to do as you will."

Rann's reply was sharp. "It's not like that!"

My body tensed. "What is it like, then?"

"I share my thoughts with her, we speak. When we take action, she understands."

My reply was more roar than words. "Her will is enslaved by runes. Even damaged as they are, even after what she went through, the link to your mind is one-way. It imposes your will upon her. You saved her life, but for her ends or your own?"

"How dare you!" Rann's words flamed.

"Did you not notice Crema never disagrees with you?"

Rann's retort caught in her throat. "I ... I wouldn't hurt her. I care about her," Rann protested.

"Care? As an equal? An intelligent being? Or as those human hunters care about their hounds?"

"You're distorting this," Rann shouted at me. "I don't want her to be a slave."

"Really?" My eyes glowed hot as I flew through the night. "Would a free dragon help with your plan to take the Twisted Keep? What would she get out of it?"

"Hopefully, a chance to free her kind. Just like you."

"You claim you do this for my kind?" I snorted.

"Look at those people down there, Bayloo. Why do you think they still follow me?"

I really had no idea. I wouldn't have followed Rann after all that had happened. But humans made my head hurt. They had strange minds filled with ridiculous thoughts.

"They want to be free," Rann insisted.

I grunted my disagreement. "They have no runes, no chains around their neck. They are already free."

"Look with more than your eyes. They live under the dominion of the King of Rolm. These people and their families, most are either farmers who barely grow enough to feed their families, or if they have no land to till, they must work mining the metals of Ulibon, venturing into deep tunnels in the mountains. When the mines collapse, or the passages are too small, children are sent to pull out the ore. That which is mined is never used in Ulibon, but instead taken by ship to the smelters at Eladrell, to make weapons for Rolm's wars."

"They can refuse to work," I insisted. "They can go elsewhere."

"Where can they go?" Rann shot back. "What choice do they have? Almost no native man of Ulibon holds his own land. Those that are freeholders can barely subsist. None are lords. None ascend beyond the rank of footman in a village watch. They have no future."

"Their minds are free," I insisted.

"We of Ulibon hunger to control our own destiny, the same thing you want for your fellow dragons. Are we really so different?"

"We are, Bethy Rann. Only when your mind—your entire mind —is subservient to another can you understand. Only when you have been betrayed as my kind was betrayed by humans can you understand." A great gust of wind came in from the east as I spoke, as if Haven gave force to my words. I waited for it to subside before I spoke again. As it blew, a bit of the heat in my blood faded. "But I do understand the desire to control one's own destiny. That, I assure you."

"Help us, Bayloo, and we will help you. That is what we are doing."

"I am helping you," I reminded her. "More than helping."

"Humans may have wronged you, but not these humans. And not I, nor Jona. He risked his life to free you." She cut me with the last reminder. "Perhaps I don't know Crema's true mind. But also allow the possibility that I can see into her hearts as Jona could know yours. She is loyal and brave. I believe she would stand with us even without a rune-link."

The wind gusted again, forcing me to consider my next words before I spoke. "It will be a number of days yet before Crema is healed enough to risk fighting. You had best use the time wisely. Harlan might be of use helping to train your army as well."

"The Islander?" I heard Rann's suspicion.

"He has seen many battles and is decent with a blade."

"I'm pleased to accept any help." There was still reluctance. "But food and water are the more critical needs."

"I can help with water," I told her, knowing I could summon rain. "Game is scarce. I was lucky the first day. I cannot hunt for so many, nor can Harlan catch enough fish on his own."

"We found a few of our supplies. I am sending out foragers. In the south, beyond the Clutch, there are still stores, places to find supplies. I will show you if you carry me."

More work for me. I snorted with displeasure.

Rann took my lack of direct refusal as acquiescence. "Thank you again, Bayloo. My brother was right about your nature. You have kind hearts."

"There is no need to be rude."

We approached the haphazard camp of Rann's rump of an army. "These men will reclaim Ulibon for their children," she declared.

We saw two very different hosts. "Lord Drehan's harriers will come again. Will they stand this time?"

"We'll be ready."

Rann was more confident than I. She still had faith in humans. I only had faith that I would find a way to set dragons free—including Crema. That was going to require killing a lot more humans.

EIGHTEEN

Waiting.

Nights and days passed, until it had been a full week of nursing Crema. She progressed slowly, but it was progress. I knew the humans in the Twisted Keep watched, but they did not dare attack me. The Rolmans thought they were safe behind the enchanted walls of their fortress while the remnant of the rebel army outside starved (which they would have but for my efforts).

Finally came the night when we were ready to put Rann's plan into motion. Crema had almost fully recovered several days earlier, but Harlan insisted on having a few extra days to train Bethy Rann's farmer-soldiers. It turned out the sea captain had a knack for command. Even Bethy Rann was grudgingly impressed between bouts of petulance.

"The men hang on his words like dogs waiting for a treat," she said of Harlan. "They seem to long for more training, but that is because he mostly tells stories instead of making them sweat."

For Harlan's part, he had developed an affection for the farmers among Rann's ranks, and a dislike for her so-called soldiers. "The ones who think they know something are a lot harder to train than those who have never held a sword before. The rest are miners or farmers who know how to keep quiet and use their backs to get things done."

As we gathered around a fire at the edge of the camp on the final night before the attack, Harlan pronounced the men to be barely fit to hold a farmhouse against a flock of angry chickens. "But that's an improvement. When we started, I'd have bet the chickens would've overrun the place."

"We don't need them to storm the walls," Rann pointed out. "These men have stout hearts. All those who stayed despite what we have faced have the bravery to match any Rolman soldier."

"They have bravery," Harlan conceded. "The rest all fled. If we need some rock crushed or shit spread across newly plowed soil, victory would be assured. Unfortunately, their lives depend on using a sword. I've taught them the most rudimentary formations and some basic thrusts. Many don't even have proper weapons, much less armor or shields."

"They will hold," Rann declared with unconcealed annoyance in her voice. "You spin many fine tales—indeed you have my soldiers listening more to your stories than swinging weapons. But they seem to like it. A number of them would sign aboard for your next voyage, I have no doubt. They all admire you. They'll hold the line as long as you do."

Harlan smirked. "Many a sailor will toast your name so loud and so often the gulls start to squawk to you as they fly past, but you don't know if that same seahand will keep steady in a squall until the water is puking in their eyes."

Rann stared at him, confused. "What is your babble about?"

"I'm saying I don't know if those farmers will run away again, and neither do you. They may not even know themselves."

Rann put her hand on the hilt of her blade. For a moment I thought she might pull it out of its scabbard, but instead she pronounced, "We shall find out. I will order them to march tonight."

I could've contradicted her. I could've reminded Bethy Rann that none of this would happen if I didn't want it to happen, but I didn't for two simple reasons: The first was that I've learned that humans get upset when reminded of their obvious need for a dragon's help. The other was I suspected Rann would've attacked without me, now that Crema was sufficiently healed, and she would certainly lose.

I flew back to Crema with Bethy Rann on my back. Harlan stayed with the army. While Rann had left Gorge in ostensible command, Harlan had the ear of the troops. I didn't like Rann on my back, but it was temporary. Not having Harlan with me for the attack would also leave me better able to maneuver when trouble inevitably arose again. I hoped Harlan didn't get himself killed while we were separated.

Harlan and Gorge began to march their troops north in the darkness, using torches to light their path along the main road. It would be a slow, deliberate march, which was fortunate, since that was about all that group could handle. The hard part fell to Crema and me, of course. But I preferred it that way. Better to handle things myself than rely on others.

We waited for the deep depths of the night to arrive, the time when even the second watch in the keep's towers would be numbed by the monotony of staring at the darkness. I'd ensured an appropriate amount of cloud cover, denying the sentries any natural light to ease their task. Many days and nights had come and gone without incident since our last failed attack on the Twisted Keep. The defenders behind the wall of the fortress thought the army sent against them had been annihilated. Based on Crema's lack of movement, they probably thought at least one dragon was dead. Although Lord Drehan had doubtless told his soldiers to remain wary, humans were lazy creatures (not that there was anything wrong with that).

Rann's new plan was daring. I liked that part. I didn't like the part about it relying so much on predicting humans. Still, I'd spent a week trying to come up with a better alternative, and I hadn't, so I flew once again toward the Twisted Keep.

This time there would be no chance to be ensnared in any

enchanted net. The arc-bolts would not fly at us. We were barely even attacking the place. More like an unfriendly visit, made possibly by Bethy Rann and her childhood knowledge of the secrets of the great citadel.

I dipped out of the clouds first, coming down directly above the keep. Crema and Bethy Rann followed my instructions to stay well in my wake. If Lord Drehan had somehow anticipated this tactic, I wanted to be the one to face his defenses, not Crema with her damaged insides. Below me was the central axis of the Twisted Peak, a horribly-mauled carcass of rock that had once been a mountain. On its sloping summit was a lone observation post that was dreadfully inhospitable to human habitation due to wind, temperature, and sheer difficulty to access. There were no fires inside the structure. That was as expected. Even Lord Drehan wouldn't have anticipated what was coming—perhaps because he was too sensible.

I landed atop the peak, the surface of which reminded me of a partially-melted candle, except this place was icy cold. Wind whipped with a fury, constantly shifting directions as if frustrated that the peak still stood. The mountain face below was sheer on all sides, with the only apparent way to access the peak a precarious winding staircase that wrapped around the ever-narrowing mountain. If I were as wingless as a human, I would have found an excuse not to use those stairs.

I searched about for the structures and enchantments that Bethy Rann claimed would exist in this forlorn place, but saw no sign of any man-made devices except the squat stone outpost that barely looked large enough to fit two very friendly humans. Frustrated, I gazed up to look for Crema. The patchwork dragon appeared a moment later. She had more trouble dealing with the shifting winds than she should have. Rann was bundled in several layers of worn rags over her armor for warmth. Crema landed beside me.

"Where is it?" I asked, impatient. Rann relied on her childhood memories for this plan. I didn't like that.

Rann directed Crema to two different spots on the mountain.

The dragon sniffed and clawed at the frosty surface, but didn't find anything.

I growled unhappily. I wanted no more human mistakes. "If you are wrong, let us leave now."

Rann slid from Crema's back, careful to keep a hand on the dragon's leg for balance on the uneven peak. "They are here. Do you notice there is no ice up here despite the temperature? This place collects ice, snow, moisture. But the rocks have shifted after decades of neglect by the Rolman occupiers."

With Crema's help, Rann took a few more uneasy steps, bending over to inspect rocks that she claimed were enchanted to melt snow and ice but just looked like rocks to me.

"See the slope?" Rann pronounced excitedly. "It's a drainage system."

She scraped at the frigid rock with her foot, without moving a stone. I reached out with a claw, clearing a decade of debris.

"That's it!" Rann proclaimed with relief.

It wasn't much to look at—about a dozen metal bars covering a square access shaft that led into the heart of the mountain. If Rann's memories were correct.

"It doesn't seem very large," I observed.

"There are several others, here and further below. But this is the highest shaft, and it is unguarded. They all lead to the same place. We've done it."

She was too excited. "We've done nothing yet besides find some metal on top of a cold mountain that you claim leads to the keep's water cistern."

"It was the only flaw in choosing this location for a fortress," Rann babbled. "They had everything else—an excellent harbor, wide views, bedrock below, this shell of a mountain on which to build—but there wasn't a natural water supply. The designers repurposed some of the shafts used here from the time before the Cataclysm, when this mountain was first mined. They found some tunnels that led to a huge, burrowed-out chamber. It became the great cistern. The rock is enchanted here just enough to ensure that the ice melts, providing a constant flow of water to the citadel." Rann laughed with satisfaction. "Drehan probably doesn't even realize these are up here." She pulled a satchel from around her neck, emptying the powdery contents down the shaft. It drifted down like falling sand, disappearing into the bowels of the mountain.

"That's it?" I asked. "Just some poison sand?"

"That will be enough to foul the keep's water supply. This was all the dried melis we had in camp. The healers use it to treat infections, but if you drink enough, it'll kill you."

"All humans need to drink, eventually," I agreed. "If your poison works, we don't need to go any further. We can just wait."

"I told you, this isn't enough to be lethal—I don't think. The cistern is very large. Enough for a thousand people. But people will get sick—very sick. Lord Drehan will notice and he'll figure out the cistern has been contaminated. There will still be some other water supplies, plus barrels of ale in storage. This won't be enough to defeat the garrison. We must continue."

I already knew that, but I didn't completely trust this plan, so I had prodded one more time.

I stretched my neck to peer down from the summit. The heart of the citadel was beneath us, nestled against the rock of the mountain, ensconced behind the layers of walls and towers. It was an impressive sight, but none of it mattered without food and water.

I thought I detected the faint shimmying of hidden netting around the walls, although it might've been paranoia born of my previous encounter. In any case, I wasn't going to fly near the wall tonight. This plan required a less dignified form of movement. Reluctantly, I began my crawl down the battered mountain, pausing with each step to dig my claws into the mountain face. The rock was coarse and strong. Debris rolled down the peak. Rann hadn't considered that—it might alert those below. Too late now. I pressed on, with Crema behind me. My claws ached after a short distance. I wondered how Crema, with her damaged body, fared against the rock. She was following, but sluggishly.

We worked through much of the remaining night to reach a perch above the uppermost tier of the Twisted Keep, a ring of wall mostly built onto two large ledges on opposite sides of the mountain that were linked by arching stone bridges that spanned the gaps. According to Rann, much of the keep's food supplies were stored in caves within the mountain itself. I doubted even the clever Lord Drehan imagined that we would attack the food supplies as we intended.

There were soldiers on the wall, even in the depth of the night. The towers had fires lit and sentries within. Massive catapults rested silently on the battlements, interspaced at regular intervals with ballistae, but none of the siege engines were attended. As I neared, I detected a bit of commotion among the soldiers—talking and running. It was more activity than I would've expected at this time of the evening. The falling rocks may have given some warning of danger, or at least made the watch concerned. All the more reason to press our attack quickly.

Suppressing a surge of dread, I released my grip on the mountain, allowing myself a fleeting moment of freefall before twisting around and spreading my wings as silently as I could manage. It wasn't quite enough. Several of the soldiers had the sense to look up. There was a stretch of fateful silence on the wall as the human eyes processed what they saw, even though they wished they didn't.

I'm here and I'm real, little crunchies.

Bells rang excitedly as I tossed the first ballista off the wall, sending the contraption plummeting to the ground far below. The noise of the impact would do far more to awaken the keep's defenders than any clanking metal. It didn't matter anymore. The climb to the top tier was a long, hard slog for a biped, and we'd have done what we came to do before any reinforcements arrived.

On my second pass over the battlement, I scooped up a human soldier in my left foreclaw and tore him in half using my right. I threw both pieces onto the wall. That seemed to sap the bravery from the few other fighters who had gathered. They fled, running along the wall, a winding retreat down to the next tier of the keep. They wouldn't be coming back up again. Crema swooped in behind me, landing on the ledge near a great wooden door that was nearly large enough for me to squeeze through comfortably. For Crema's smaller frame, the portal was an easy fit. She bashed down the door with two flicks of her tail. Rann slid down and ran inside, sword drawn, although she had said that she was certain there wouldn't be anyone inside the cavern. I continued my assault on the wall, driving the defenders around the mountain, across the arching stone bridge, toward the next protruding ledge. Authoritative shouts from far below told me that at least one responsible human commander was awake and trying to organize some sort of defense. Still, the defenders retreated, running as fast as their stubby legs would carry them. I could've caught and killed them all, but I didn't see the point. A few more soldiers would make no difference to Rann's plan. I contented myself with being a herder of the terrified.

Rann re-emerged from the cavern. "This is it. The storage cavern. There will be another chamber accessible from the other side of the mountain." She scrambled onto Crema as she shouted at me.

If the defenders were aware they were retreating from critical positions, they showed no sign of it. The short-term human instinct for self-preservation was keen. I hurried them along with several low passes and loud roars. The cries of terror were amusing until an arc-bolt smashed into the mountainside just as I flew past. Several ballistae on the wall beneath me had been readied and crewed. Two more bolts hurled into the air, but I had enough forewarning to soar away, putting myself into an arcing loop that took me far enough away from the keep to get a thorough look at the state of the defense below. I was pretty sure I also got my first gaze at Lord Drehan. I had never seen him before, so I had no idea what he looked like, but I can recognize a pack leader. This particular human was an island walking through a stream of soldiers, the men hurrying to stand aside, then falling into line behind him as he barked unhappy noises. Drehan was also a head taller than the rest of the soldiers. My study of my adversary was cut short by an arc-bolt that came so close it rubbed against my tail spikes.

Crema had reached the next ledge—it was empty of defenders. I flew above her, wary of the situation below. I swung around the mountain, following the path of the citadel's wall. I didn't have to go far before I saw Lord Drehan again. This time he was moving steadily up the keep's wall, a tail of soldiers at his back, all clutching swords and crossbows as if they would help. They saw me, but there wasn't much they could do about it. I flew to the upper tier, yanked the largest catapult I could find, then returned, dropping it in the midst of the advancing soldiers. The machine landed hard, exploding into shards of wood and metal. One soldier was crushed beneath the wreck. I thought that would be enough to halt the advance, but I was wrong. Drehan pressed on, moving as fast as his legs would carry him. A bunch of intrepid soldiers kept pace with him. I fetched another large catapult. This time I swept in lower, intending to drop it directly on Lord Drehan's head.

The soldiers were ready for my attack. A swarm of crossbow bolts greeted me as I swung around the mountain. Unless they were enchanted, the projectiles weren't overly dangerous to any part of me except my eyes. Still, with Drehan, I took no chances. I swerved, throwing off my aim. My catapult bomb hit the wall. A shouted command to retreat echoed in my ears as I went to retrieve another siege machine to drop on the stubborn defenders.

When I returned with a final present for the retreating soldiers, I spotted two large ballistae being pushed up the wall by teams of men with large shields on their backs, their efforts assisted by several unfortunate oxen. The metal of the deadly machines glinted as the first rays of the newly emerging sun climbed above the horizon. I looked to the south as the new daylight spread across the ruined ground that led to the keep. In the distance I could see Harlan and the rest of Bethy Rann's army marching toward us. The defenders could see them as well. Anxious horn blasts followed, one after another, as if blowing ever louder could somehow improve the defenders' increasingly desperate position.

The ballistae stopped moving upwards. I landed on the wall above Drehan's troops, my wings stretched. Lord Drehan gazed up at me. He had long, flowing white hair and eyes like burnt leather. We looked at each other. He would not get past me. The wall could accommodate only four humans standing shoulder-to-shoulder. I could wipe out the little lord's entire army four at a time if he tried to assault my position. Drehan was smart enough to know that. He had probably also realized by now that his enemies controlled most of the keep's food stocks. Drehan snarled as he turned away from me, shouting. His voice echoed through the night, still controlled and confident. He went to rally his troops against the approaching threat on the ground.

It was time to find out if Harlan's pretend soldiers would prove their mettle in battle.

NINETEEN

The Rolmans attacked at midday.

It wasn't a surprise to me or to Harlan. Bethy Rann's host had marched up the single road at a languid pace all through the morning. It was like waiting for a turtle to cross a bridge.

From my vantage point on his wall, I could see Lord Drehan watching Rann's small army approach. The tenuous master of the Twisted Keep surrounded himself with soldiers and every ballista in the keep's arsenal, although none of those would've kept me from killing him had I wanted. But it wasn't time for that. Not yet.

Lord Drehan had to have been hoping that whoever had command of the remaining host was stupid enough to come as close to the wall as they had last time. That would maximize the opportunity for his harriers to reach their lines in a raid, but Harlan wasn't stupid. The host stopped marching well beyond the range of any war machine. The harriers would have to exhaust themselves just to reach those distant lines. This was to be a siege, and Harlan made that obvious. His first orders were to have his troops start digging trenches to protect their new camp. Digging was one of the few activities his army had significant experience performing.

"Drehan is frustrated," Rann said to me as we watched the events unfold below. She was a little too happy with how well her plan had worked out so far. I didn't like seeing her so pleased. Happy humans were reckless.

Drehan took the only course of action available to him. After night fell, he opened the gates of the Twisted Keep, sending out his harriers. He probably knew enough about King Mendakas' dragons to know we had excellent vision—including excellent night vision. I watched the long-legged runners dash out. There were few enough that Harlan's farmers might've been able to fight them off without my help, but I wasn't going to take that chance.

"Stay wary."

I was speaking to Crema, but Rann answered. "We will hold. No matter what comes, we will hold."

She held her bow in her hand as she spoke. I still didn't like it. Crema wasn't herself, and Rann was still a human, even if she shot a fine arrow.

With a huff of breath, I took off to deal with the harriers. They had broken into three groups as soon as they left the gate. I supposed they moved fast for humans, but their legs moved them pathetically slowly compared to me. Once I was in the air, a fourth group of humans departed out of a side gate, taking a circuitous route toward Harlan's men. I ignored them for now. Each group of harriers was just large enough to pose a legitimate threat to a hungry, untrained host that had already suffered two crushing defeats.

Drehan had calculated well. I decided I couldn't afford to ignore any of the attackers. I'd have to kill them all, which, as efficient as I am, would take time. I had no doubt that Drehan would send everything he had at Crema and Rann while I was doing that. I recognized Lord Drehan's plan, but there wasn't any clear way to stop it. My speed, armor, and killing power were superior to Crema's, and my insides weren't part dead, so I was the logical choice to chase the attackers. All she and Bethy Rann had to do was hold the narrow passage through the battlements against a bunch of humans while I was gone. I intended to make my absence short.

Two groups of harriers were well ahead of the others. I picked one of the faster groups at random and dove at them. They expected me, each armed with short bows or crossbows. The humans scattered as I came at them, some diving for the barren ground while others fumbled with their weapons. I impaled one with a claw. When I circled back around, the harriers were back on their feet, running in two different directions—one group back toward the keep, while the others continued toward Bethy Rann's host. I flew at the attacking group, but they split themselves again. I killed two with my claws and a third with my tail, then had to turn to chase the other group. I dealt with them as well, leaving a bloody mess on the ground. I soared back to an observation altitude, surveying the position of the various harrier formations. They had split into eight groupings and were moving across as wide a front as the land allowed. Two formations had turned back toward the keep, then stopped at seemingly random locations out in the open. Too easy, but also too many.

Annoyed, I selected a cluster of about two dozen advancing harriers. I pulled my wings back and dove, intending to make quick work of the group before they hugged the ground like the others. Instead of hiding, this group formed into defensive ranks as soon as they spotted me coming for them. I was unsure if I should be impressed by their courage or appalled at their temerity for thinking they could stop me. These harriers all had short bows. I didn't fear their arrows, but I didn't want to get hit either. I changed my course slightly, taking a less direct approach that would give me more time to maneuver around their arrows.

Unlike the other soldiers I had attacked, these humans held in tight ranks even as I came toward them. They must've been the elite of Drehan's soldiers. Why waste them on what was probably a suicide mission?

A fusillade of arrows came at me. I turned my torso, and with a single beat of my wings, pulled myself out of the projectiles' path. A second wave of arrows came. I turned again, but as I maneuvered, I saw these launches were different than the others. Their tips weren't metal, but some kind of dark material that resembled burnt wood, but wasn't. Several seemed to be leaving a train of ash behind them as they shot through the air toward me, as if turning to ash in flight. I didn't have time to study them further. I just tried to get out of the way. As close as I'd come to the archers, I was still able to mostly avoid their shots.

One whizzed past my nose, its tip crumbling as it traveled. It missed me, but it had come too close for me to avoid its dust trail. I flew through the small cloud. The smell was putrid—something terribly foul and acidic. The smell was also familiar. Another of the strange projectiles collided with my chest, sending a larger, more intense blast of powder into the air. I kept flying, straight and low, or at least I thought that was my course. Some humans were beneath me. I passed them, soaring through the sky, because that was what dragons did. I really didn't know where I was going for a few moments; the world was fuzzy, as were my thoughts. I turned to see a strange, slender mountain in the distance, a great twisting wall scaling its heights. I knew that place. I struggled to remember something else. Something about why I was here. Something I had to do.

A pair of arrows flew across my path. My vision clouded, then cleared. My head cleared enough for me to recall the last place that I'd smelled the scent lingering in my nostrils ... It had been rather hot there, the air so clogged that I could see nothing—just a dark fog. The full memory came suddenly with an unpleasant aftertaste: the Wall of Fire. This was the smell of the gas of the inferno mountains. Maybe the properties in the dust weren't precisely the same, but it was close enough. The substance led to confusion, at least temporarily. Fortunately, whatever Drehan had used to make his arrows was far less potent than the noxious gases constantly pumped out by the infernos that made up the Wall of Fire. Still, I hadn't enjoyed the experience.

I flew into the sky, sucking cold wind to clear my thoughts. My sight returned to its full vigor. Anger came next. Part of my suppressed rage was directed at that devious crunchie, Drehan, but I saved more than a little enmity for myself. I'd assumed his trap would be the obvious one. I should've known better after those nets.

From above, I scanned the terrain around me. My instinct was to dive, to rip the heads off the humans who dared fire the arrows. To kill the rest of the harriers for good measure as well. I made a tight circle, watching, preparing. As I watched, I realized that something else was wrong. The harriers were no longer advancing.

This hadn't been a raid, it had been a ruse.

Drehan had spared only a small group of his best soldiers—probably the ones who'd stood their ground to shoot at me. The rest were throw-away soldiers, not specially trained like the real harriers. They were supposed to make this look like a real assault, to force at least one dragon to come to the aid of the host. That meant Crema and Bethy Rann were taking the brunt of the real attack.

I beat my wings as I dipped into a sharp turn, heading back to the keep at my best speed. The ballistae ringing the main wall were ready for me. The arc-bolts rose at speed, hungry. I soared upward, wary that another dust-like projectile like those possessed by the harriers would come at me, but these arc-bolts appeared to be mundane. The projectiles shot into the sky, but not high enough to reach me. In a moment, I'd passed the initial wave, on my way back to Crema. I dove straight down and found a disaster.

TWENTY

It was the dust.

Lord Drehan had risked a few elite soldiers and some of his inferno dust on me, because he had to delay me. The rest he deployed against Crema.

I hadn't seen it happen. Maybe they used an arrow, maybe the delivery had been as simple as tossing an open sack at her as the soldiers approached. Whatever Drehan and his men had done, it had worked. Crema thrashed about on the keep battlements, her neck twisting wildly in a desperate attempt to find something that wasn't there. She was panicked. I was sure Rann had tried to soothe her, but even with their link, it hadn't been enough. Or maybe Rann never had the chance, because she was fighting for both her life and Crema's.

Before I left, we'd fortified the approach to the upper-tier storage areas using the debris of scattered war engines that I'd gathered from the citadel walls. They weren't much as far as barriers went—Drehan's soldiers could climb over them if their armor wasn't too heavy—but they had slowed the advance. Rann had given ground, but she wasn't beaten yet.

Bethy Rann squatted on the last of the barriers, using its height to help her launch her arrows at the attackers coming at her along the wall. Crema was behind her, useless in the fight, but safe for the time being as long as she didn't fall off the wall. There were at least two dozen dead Rolman soldiers with arrows in their necks, eyes, and chests. Nobody had ever criticized Bethy Rann's aim with a bow. Even with that toll, at least a hundred more Rolman soldiers snaked along the wall, waiting for Rann to kill them as they came at her four at a time. Among the soldiers was Lord Drehan himself. He barked at his men as soon as he spotted me. The soldiers surged forward with renewed urgency as Rann put an arrow in another neck. I wondered how many more arrows she had in her quiver. It couldn't be many.

Drehan should've known when he saw me that his last gambit to retake the bulk of his food supplies had failed. Enough of his men were probably sick from the tainted water cistern that he also knew that his situation was desperate. Rann said any sensible commander would surrender once he realized the situation, but she hadn't counted on a man like Drehan. A human too accustomed to victory found it difficult to admit defeat.

The Rolman attackers came at Bethy Rann with long pikes, their bodies mostly hidden behind high-tipped shields. Rann muttered a battle cry, throwing her bow aside. Her quiver was empty. She met the assault, blade in hand. She had the high ground. The first of Drehan's soldiers stabbed at Rann's feet; she danced away, slashing down at the long pike shaft, shattering it with her sword. The soldier jammed the broken stub at her thigh. Rann rewarded his determination with a well-placed kick to the man's forehead, sending him backward into two other soldiers.

Another fighter used the opportunity to scramble up the pile of overturned catapults on which Rann stood. He jabbed a pike tip at her neck. Rann leaned away, swiping at his weapon, but the attacker jerked backward at the right moment, catching her blade on the jagged head of his pike and turning it aside. More soldiers came at her. While Rann regained her balance, her enemies had a chance to surge forward. She now faced two soldiers atop her hill, both wielding weapons with longer reach than her blade. Rann slashed in a broad arc, then jumped backward, surrendering the high ground as more soldiers surged at her.

I could've entered the melee, killing with my jaws and claws, but I preferred to end this battle more efficiently. Killing foot soldiers took too long. Instead, I released a mighty roar of challenge as I flew directly at Lord Drehan.

He'd been busy shouting at his men, exhorting them to overwhelm Bethy Rann. I imagine in that wonderful moment before he heard my roar, before he turned to see my open jaws shooting toward him, he'd been feeling like his usual clever self. Despite the odds against him, Drehan and his men were on the brink of recapturing at least one of their food storage caves. With those supplies, plus rain water and whatever else they could find to drink, he probably thought he could save his keep. All that might've happened if I had been a little bit slower. Too bad for him.

Drehan's men ducked behind the battlements as I closed. For some reason I didn't understand, the man himself didn't try to run. Perhaps the lord considered cowering to be beneath his station. I'd often heard human lords say things like that—death before dishonor. It was like the Way for dragons, except humans mostly only pretended to be honorable. Or maybe Drehan just knew he was going to die. Standing alone on the battlements, the wily lord had just enough time to turn toward me. Three heartbeats remained in his lifetime. Fear creeped into his eyes at the end, but he started to raise his sword anyway. I bit his head off. All that honor didn't make his skull taste any better.

After spitting out the remains of Lord Drehan, I circled back to deal with the soldiers facing Bethy Rann. I needn't have bothered. They saw their lord die, and they saw how he died. The soldiers retreated, running back down the wall. I buzzed their heads once as they fled, but didn't bother to kill any. I was done for the day. A quick reconnoiter to the south reassured me that Harlan and the host had held to their positions. The harriers had retreated once their ruse failed. I returned to Crema.

With Rann able to devote her full attention to the confused dragon through their rune-link, Crema calmed. Her vision had already returned, although the shifting shade of her eyes told me that she was still disoriented. But she was alive.

"It worked," Rann pronounced triumphantly. "Just as I said it would."

I could've reminded her how close she'd come to being killed. I also could've pointed out that I'd saved her life, again, but what would that get me? It wasn't like I wanted a kiss.

"Is there meat in those caves?" I asked.

"Your first concern is dinner?" Rann pointed to the vast citadel below us. "There are still hundreds of soldiers down there."

"All the more reason to eat now. Crema needs it more than me. If there is salt meat, bring it."

Rann's back stiffened, her chin hard and unhappy. My stomach grumbled. Rann disappeared into the mountainside, shaking her head. She emerged a short time later with an armful of dried, salted meat. It tasted slightly better than beach sand, but that was good enough for me at that moment.

"They had a lot of fight in them," Rann conceded. "Drehan was a stubborn man."

"But not a tasty one, although he died very honorably. And he didn't have time to piss himself. That would make him happy, I suppose."

Rann smiled a cold smile. "The rest won't last much longer. They have no water, little food, and no place to retreat."

"What will you offer them?"

"Nothing."

"Then we should be ready for more fighting."

"No, they'll come to us before nightfall. Only then will I give my terms."

"Nightfall?" I snorted. "Fine. You have first watch. Wake me when the humans start climbing the wall again."

RANN WAS wrong about the timing.

Night came and went, but no human came groveling up to us. Crema had recovered from the strange dust sprayed on her, but I still insisted that she rest while I kept watch. Rann should've slept as well, but instead she spent much of the night pacing about uselessly.

"Any change below?" Rann asked me shortly before dawn. It was the third time she'd asked over the course of the night.

I gave her the same answer as I had the other times she'd spoken. "They are still gathered in the great hall."

Rann pursed her lips in frustration. I knew she wanted to ask more, but she also knew I wasn't going to answer. I didn't know what the Rolman soldiers discussed either. I could make out the occasional shout, but the building's walls were thick stone.

The morning came, but no messenger arrived. Apparently, the defenders had enough to eat and drink for the time being. Rann finally drifted off to sleep in late morning. Shortly afterward, three humans began their trek upward along the wall. I let Rann snooze until they were almost upon us.

I poked her with my tail. Her face contorted into an annoyed scowl but she didn't open her eyes until I said, "They come."

That got her onto her feet.

I've noticed that humans tend to place more clothing and decoration on their body as their insecurity about a particular situation increases. These soldiers had encased themselves in full plate armor complete with face helm. One of them carried a fluttering dragon banner, and one wore a red cape that reminded me of a giant tongue. Rann and I met them on the wall, Crema a short distance behind us.

The human in the center removed his metal helm to reveal an ugly face decorated with a short gray beard with occasional specks of black. Sweat covered his brow and I could hear his lone heart pounding with fear. It was a long walk up in heavy armor.

"We come to speak under the peace of Haven. We shall do you no harm during parley." The soldier had to huff out his words. I hoped he didn't die of natural causes before he had a chance to surrender to us. Not because I cared what happened to him, but because I couldn't endure another night of Rann pacing back and forth while the Rolmans selected another spokesman.

"You couldn't do me any harm if you wanted to," I told him.

Rann shot me an annoyed look. "No harm shall come to you so long as you honor the Truce of Haven. Come forth and speak."

For a moment, none of the humans moved. I smiled encouragingly, showing my teeth, but that only caused the men to glance nervously at each other.

"Speak your words or leave," Rann barked.

The first soldier took a step toward me, then another. His companions reluctantly followed. They stopped at two tail lengths. The others took off their helmets to show me their eyes, as if I cared. I didn't. Both had broken faces—one had a patch instead of a left eye, the other's nose looked like it had been reshaped by a pig's hoof. They were all sweating.

The one with the gray beard spoke first. "I am Utter Horn, Acting Lord of the Rolman Province of Ulibon and Master of the Twisted Keep."

Rann's face went flat. "Your words are lost in the wind, Utter Horn. Ulibon is a nation unto itself. And you are master only of a band of thirsty soldiers in a land that is not your own."

Horn huffed so hard the red of his cheek nearly glowed. "You are a rebel. A renegade. A traitor!"

"I am the Heir to Ulibon." Those words must've tasted sweet on her lips. She had been waiting to deliver that declaration for most of her life.

Acting Lord Horn's jowls trembled. "I didn't come here to listen to insolence!"

"Why did you come here?" Rann asked mildly. "It was a long trek up."

Horn mashed his teeth. Whatever words he had intended to speak, he swallowed them. What came out sounded desperate. "Pigeons were sent when you crossed the Clutch." He looked at me with loathing. "King Dayne knows all that is happening here. You may hold some caves high above the citadel, but even with these pet dragons, you cannot stand against the king and his ryders."

The mention of other dragons did draw my attention. "And where is the King of Rolm and these other dragons?" The whiteness around Horn's pupils grew when I spoke. "My kind move at great speed. They should be here by now, should they not?"

A twitch at the corner of Horn's eye told me I'd hit a sore place, a place of worry. Why had his king not come? Still, he tried to keep his bravado. "He shall come soon, when you least expect it, if you continue with this doomed rebellion."

"Perhaps the war with Oster doesn't go well?" Rann prodded. "I've heard that Rolm is beaten, but too prideful to admit it."

"You lie! Oster is on its knees," Horn insisted. "They are surrounded and starving as the king and his dragons pound the Shard. The Pale Wrights cower in fear in their pits. Soon, the king will return to deal with you."

"Really?" Rann laughed. "That's what you came here to offer? A retreat?"

For the first time, Horn turned to look at the men who had accompanied him. The one-eyed man nodded unhappily, while the one with the bashed nose scowled. "The offer is this: leave the citadel with your dragons—"

"I'm not anyone's dragon," I pointed out.

Lord Horn gaped at being interrupted. This place was so different than Ni-Yota. He swallowed a bit more pride before continuing. "Yes, ah, well ... if this host and all dragons depart, and you swear allegiance to the crown, you would be granted title, and right to govern all the lands south of the Clutch."

Rann's brow rose high. It was a more generous offer than she had expected. "The king sanctions this offer?"

"The notion of this offer came from Lord Drehan ... before he was slain." Horn looked at me as if I'd done something wrong. I smiled my human-style smile at him again. "The offer is made in the name of peace in the kingdom. It is most generous, and will not be made again."

I trusted no offer from a dead lord, who offered that which wasn't his. It didn't matter anyway. I knew Bethy Rann already had made up her mind.

"Your offer is rejected." All three men blinked at the same time. "This is our land and our keep. We built it. You are the trespassers."

Horn's lips puckered as if Rann had shoved a sour lemon down his throat. "You'll ..." He trailed off. He really had nothing else. They probably didn't have many more supplies.

"Here is *my* offer. My only offer." Rann smiled. "There are still ships in the harbor—some of the last on Ulibon. I will give you and your men three. Those among your soldiers who wish to leave in peace may leave their weapons here and depart on tomorrow's tide. Those among your men who wish to declare their allegiance to Ulibon are welcome to do so. I will accept the service of those who pledge their loyalty to me." Horn started an outraged stammer, but Rann held up a hand to silence him. "Those among you who take neither option will stay here to die of thirst, or if it rains in the next few days, you may starve instead."

Horn opened his mouth, but no sound came out. I could hear his heart trying to escape his chest with its angry beats. Finally, he managed to emit a croaking sound vaguely reminiscent of a dog's bark as he turned on his heels so hard that he nearly tripped. Long strides carried him back down the wall. The others left as well, but Smashed Nose dipped his head politely in Rann's direction before he departed.

"At least one of them will tell the other soldiers about my offer.

They'll have a mutiny on their hands soon enough." Rann sounded too confident.

"Not to offend you, but your offer doesn't sound tempting: sail to Eladrell, where they may be hung as traitors, or swear allegiance to a rebel monarch and her ragged army."

Rann pointed behind her, toward the storage caves. "Better than starving. Hard decisions become easier for men with empty bellies."

By late afternoon the human defenders still hadn't given any indication of surrendering. I was impatient. The rust was spreading in Ni-Yota and my brethren could be dying in Oster, despite Horn's claim of impending victory.

"Rann, this must be brought to an end."

She had resumed her pacing already. "One more demonstration may be required."

I didn't like the sound of that. "You have exhausted your favors."

"All you need to do is sit here and continue to look fearsome. Crema and I can deal with the rest."

I liked the idea of sitting, but not of Crema putting herself in danger. But as it turned out, Rann's idea was maliciously practical. She fetched several barrels filled with dried fruit from storage and had Crema begin to fly them out to her army to the south. This served the purpose of getting supplies to her own hungry troops, as well as showing any Rolman holdout that their food supplies were being consumed by others. Seeing a dragon overhead while your own king and his dragon ryders were absent probably damaged morale as well. After Crema's third trip, two humans left the great hall to trek upward to speak again. When they arrived, it was Smashed Nose and a new companion with wide shoulders and stubby legs.

"Where's Horn?" Rann asked.

"He didn't like your offer," Smashed Nose replied as he tossed a canvas bag onto the ground. Horn's head rolled out. The eyes were still open. "Always a suck-up to Drehan, that one." He shrugged.

Rann barely looked at the severed head. "And what are your allegiances?"

An ugly smile of blackened teeth appeared on Smashed Nose's face. "I'm called Rupel, my lady. I mean, Your Highness." He dropped onto one knee. "I'll be the first to be your man, if you'll have me." When Rann hesitated, he added, "I'm the master-at-arms. I'll know the best of the men and who you can trust."

The obvious question seemed to be whether this Rupel could be trusted, as he'd just delivered the head of his previous commander. I was sure Bethy Rann shared my doubts, but she wanted possession of the keep far more than she cared about the sincerity of fleeting allegiances.

"I am grateful for your service." She looked expectantly at Rupel's companion, who also now dropped down in front of us. I snorted louder than I should have.

"Rise, both of you. Carry word to the other soldiers: they must choose quickly." Rann made a fist. "And open the gate."

Bethy Rann's new retainers hurried off to carry out her bidding. I guessed that King Dayne's temper would make the most of the soldiers reluctant to take to the ships. This battle was over, but there were many more perilous engagements left to fight.

"The Twisted Keep has fallen," I reminded Rann.

"Finally." She spoke in a reverent whisper. "Destiny has been fulfilled. My parents are avenged, and my brother can rest in peace."

I was less sentimental. "That's wonderful. Time to pay up, Bethy Rann. Tell me where to find aurathorn."

TWENTY-ONE

Wait and wait some more.

I pretended to have patience while Bethy Rann secured her control of the Twisted Keep, unwilling to get distracted by such trifles as keeping her word to me. She claimed that the story she had to tell me required sufficient time. More likely she feared her long-sought victory evaporating if Harlan and I flew off to get aurathorn while the Rolman soldiers still lurked with their weapons within the keep.

The sun had started to dip toward the horizon when Rann's host of pretend-soldiers marched through the gates, almost as nervous as the Rolman defenders who watched it happen. Discipline within Rann's force broke down quickly as the hungry victors raided the keep's food stores. Water still had to be rationed—it would take time for the great cistern to regenerate after it had been drained. The soldiers didn't care, because there was more than sufficient ale for a lot of humans to get drunk. Harlan struggled to retain some semblance of discipline among the farmer-fighters of Ulibon. Finally, Rann had Crema terrify a few people to get the revelry under control. Almost two days were wasted on such nonsense. At least I got some ale.

After a nearly eternal wait, Bethy Rann's installation as Highstar of Ulibon was set for the next morning. I didn't plan on attending. I wanted her knowledge of aurathorn and I wanted to be gone. There was also the matter of the enchanted items Rann had promised, but that could wait until I knew where to find aurathorn. I summoned a noisy thunder cloud to remind Bethy Rann that she was out of excuses.

As night fell, I carried Harlan with me to the highest tier of the Twisted Keep. Bethy Rann flew on Crema to join us. Shouts and sounds of revelry still emanated from the citadel below, but far less than when victory had been fresh.

Rann slid off Crema with something like a smile on her face. She moved with ease in her motions, free of the tension of the prior days. She had put aside her gaudy costume armor in favor of a cotton robe of unblemished white trimmed with ebony on the edges.

"May the winds be kind to you tomorrow," Harlan said a bit formally as he and Rann eyed each other awkwardly.

"Patience defeats the storm," she replied, a slight twinkle in her eye.

"How many in the garrison will take to ships tomorrow?" Harlan asked.

Rann shrugged. "More than half, which is for the better. It will take time to trust those who chose to swear to me. For now, they are more mouths to feed. I don't dare give their weapons back yet, either."

"There are many fishermen among your own troops. You might outfit them with small craft."

I growled at the banter of these details. Ruling Ulibon was not my problem. "We are here to speak of aurathorn," I reminded everyone. "Where did it come from?"

Rann dipped her head, gathering herself. "The elders traded for it, with your mother's help."

Harlan was quick to reply. "What does one trade for aurathorn? And with who?"

"I don't know the price, but it was high."

"How do you know?" Harlan asked.

"It was obvious by the attitudes of the elders, their looks, their secrecy. Even your mother ... I just got the feeling in the pit of my stomach that something terrible had been done."

This banter was beside the point. It was history. "Enough with the details and speculation. Where did they get it?" I demanded. "Where is the source of aurathorn?"

Rann fixed me with a hard stare, her eyes intense for a reason I didn't quite understand. "Oster. It is in Oster, I'm sure of it."

"Oster," I repeated, not liking the taste of the word.

"Worse than that." Rann crossed her arms. "They traded with the Pale Wrights."

Something I'd eaten earlier turned sour in my stomach. "Why would anyone in Oster—especially the Pale Wrights—trade with a few refugees on Maricopa at all, much less for aurathorn?"

"I believe the trading relationship between Oster and Maricopa wasn't new. The enchantments of the elders required raw materials that weren't readily available on that desolate island, yet they always seemed suspiciously well-supplied." I thought of the barrels and boxes that Brindisi and I had discovered, many stuffed with valuable items. And there was the fine, warm sand from Proving Beach of Oster to consider as well. That had definitely come from Oster.

I thought aloud, not liking the dark places my thoughts led. "Trade with Oster was banned. Those items that your elders possessed hidden in their village were rare and expensive. The exchanges must've been made for precious payment."

"I would think that part is obvious—they must've traded enchanted items. Probably for years, even before I came there. There was one old, odd fisherman who always took particularly long voyages—Hellix was his name. He delivered the goods and likely returned with Osteran supplies."

Parts of what Rann said made sense, but others did not. "I fought Oster many times over the years. Apart from the odd artifact, they

didn't have enchanted weapons. Certainly nothing like the arma-
ments of Ulibon."

"As I said, the elders didn't trade with King Galt of Oster. They
traded directly with the Pale Wrights. There is a big difference. Galt
may not even have known about the illicit trade."

Harlan shuffled with unease. "Who are these Pale Wrights?"

"They are the masters of the beasts of Oster—they bred the
griffins and furies that guard that island, even against dragons."

I flicked my tail unhappily. "But the Pale Wrights serve King
Galt. They are servants of Oster."

Rann moved her head in two directions, as if weighing my declaration. "I have only an outsider's understanding, but from what I
know, Oster is a complicated place. I had the benefit of being raised
in the Twisted Keep and listening to snippets from the powerful. The
Pale Wrights are a power unto themselves, far more so than even the
Sculptors of Rolm. The keepers of DragonPeak spoke of the power of
the Pale Wrights with envy as much as fright or disgust. None had
ever actually seen or met one, of course. No one from Rolm has."

Harlan's gaze bore into Bethy Rann as she spoke. "But you think
that the enchanters on Maricopa traded with these Pale Wrights
without the knowledge of their ruler?"

"Having now had time to consider everything, for several reasons,
I do believe this," Rann told us. "First, as you said, I never saw the
elders produce an enchanted weapon. Not for their own use, and not
for anyone else, either. The few times I spied one of their creations, it
was always some strange device with no obvious purpose—a hand-
sized sphere, a strange leash, gauntlets too thin to be worn by the
hands of an adult. But even more were the words of old Hellix. He
wasn't a talker. In a village of dozens, he kept to himself more than
any other, which is perhaps why the elders relied on him to run their
errands. In all my time on the island, he was either out on his sloop or
walking the barrens of the isle." Rann paused in memory. "He was
never sick ..." She said it as if it was a revelation. "At least I can't
remember a single instance, not in winter, not in summer, not so

much as a cold. Except once—after your mother came, after a voyage that took him away for longer than any other."

"You think that was when he brought the aurathorn back with him?" I asked.

"I'm sure of it."

"There is nothing in the annals of my people to indicate that aurathorn leads to illness," Harlan said too defensively.

"Perhaps meeting the Pale Wrights was what made him sick," Rann replied. "When I brought Hellix a bit of broth that Jilla the herbalist had prepared for him, he had a dark look in his eyes that I'd never seen before. When he gazed at me, he was barely himself for a fleeting moment. Then he told me, 'Beware creatures who cannot abide the light of Haven, child. Nothing that comes from them will bring goodness.'"

Those words felt ominous.

"But they are men, are they not?" Harlan pressed. "The Pale Wrights are still men, like me, if lacking in my particular charms."

Rann shrugged. "The Pale Wrights are whispered about like ghosts in the night, almost the stuff of children's tales. The masters of the mysterious beasts of Oster. It is said their eyes cannot abide the light, because they spend their whole lives underground working their dark arts. Others say their skin will blaze in the day, like fresh tinder in a fire. The stories do not speak to their humanity. Perhaps none ever thought to even ask the question before you. If they are not human, what would they be, Harlan Dor?"

"This world is inhabited by innumerable creations," Harlan replied in his deep storyteller's voice. "Humans are most apt to make their presence felt, dragons among the most visible and majestic, but do not discount the creatures of the darkness. You should not forget about the rest, for that is what they want: to be overlooked. But they exist, and they hunger and want, even as you and I."

Bethy Rann scoffed. "You spin a fine fireside tale. The Pale Wrights are recluses, although maybe not more so than the Sculptors of Rolm. As outsiders and enemies, it stands to reason our tales are darker. In Oster they may be viewed less fearsomely."

"You speak as someone who hasn't yet seen true darkness," Harlan warned.

"Dark or light, if you wish to find aurathorn, you must go to the Pale Wrights. Of that I am certain."

Harlan nodded slowly, determined. We knew where to go. But I wanted something else. "Your elders paid the Wrights with enchanted artifacts, but that was for gold dust, for rare sand, and other precious materials needed for enchantment. What did aurathorn cost them? You must at least have a guess."

Rann's face darkened. "I think we should be grateful that we don't know."

TWENTY-TWO

We ended up staying longer than planned.

It wasn't that I cared about witnessing Bethy Rann become High-star of Ulibon. I stayed because Rann had more promises to deliver—those enchanted items in the hidden vaults of the Twisted Keep. If I was going to fly to Oster in the midst of a war, I needed all the assistance I could get my claws on. While part of me chafed with impatience, the extra night and day of waiting yielded worthwhile benefits.

Bethy Rann had not lied about the storeroom of artifacts, items that had remained hidden since the fall of Ulibon decades ago. The storeroom wasn't within the keep proper. Instead, it was accessible only by following a precarious staircase on the highest reaches of the mountain. The enchantment laid upon the strange steps made them visible only during the last gasps of twilight, when the sun's fading light struck the stone in a particular manner, illuminating a path only for a very careful observer. The way was challenging for a human: the steps led up a daunting slope, then into the mountain itself.

"How do you know about these stairs and this cache of artifacts?" Harlan asked as Bethy Rann led him along the strange path, while I flew nearby. "Even if you grew up here, it's hardly the sort of place someone would bring a supposed servant."

"My mother wanted me to know all the secrets of Ulibon," Rann said, a hint of pride lingering in her voice. "She told me how to get here."

Harlan wasn't satisfied. "You seem to know so much more about it than mere stories or instructions would warrant."

Rann stopped on the precarious steps to look back at Harlan. As a dragon ryder, she had no fear of heights. Her balance was impeccable. "There were others whom my mother trusted who knew about me," she said before resuming the trek. "Not all of them are dead."

That answer seemed to satisfy Harlan for the moment. He shut up until Rann reached the chamber of artifacts. The passage was too small to allow me to enter, so I had to rely on Harlan's description of its precious contents. For himself, he chose a hooded tunic that looked to have been forged of a thin, metal-like cloth.

"It is as light as leather, but nearly as strong as mail, with the hood almost as useful as a battle helm," Rann assured him. "A fine choice for a dragon ryder."

Harlan looked embarrassed at her words. "Or at least someone who is fortunate to be on friendly terms with a dragon."

I wasn't as fortunate as my human companion in terms of selection of treasure. The items within the vault were of no obvious use to a dragon. The weapons and armor had been forged for humans. There were also several of the deadly nets that had been used to snare Crema, as well as other strange baubles with uses that escaped even Bethy Rann's knowledge—or so she claimed. I claimed nothing of the ancient treasure.

"I gave a promise, and I intend to keep it," Rann declared. "Tell me then what would be of use to you?"

There was something I wanted. "I go to Oster, and likely to battle once again. *Sai* would be valuable against those griffins and whatever other horrors the Pale Wrights breed."

Rann looked puzzled. "*Sai?*" Then she remembered our earlier conversation. "Yes, the armored gauntlets for your claws, similar to those of Crema, but you require only coverings."

"Enough for my hind claws would be sufficient."

Bethy Rann pursed her lips. "My people didn't keep dragons, so we will find nothing like your *sai* waiting for us inside the chamber, but there is one who can help. It can be forged."

"Forged?" I asked.

Rann's lips made a satisfied line. "The art of shaping enchanted devices has not been lost. More than just my crude knowledge remains in the world."

I already knew that had to be the case based on the metal that adorned Crema's body. Rann hadn't made all of those fine pieces of armor. "There is someone here who can forge me *sai*?"

"Yes," Rann said, her lips turned downward. "Although she isn't likely to be pleased about it."

Bethy Rann allowed Harlan and I to meet the master forger. She was a crinkled human female with a tightly-wrapped tail of hair the color of weathered steel. When she first arrived at the tower where we stood with Rann, her worn cloth dress made her look like a sack with legs and arms. None of the soldiers and self-important counselors who now clustered around Bethy Rann even noticed the woman. Not until the future Highstar of Ulibon sent the rest of the sycophants away, except the old woman.

"This is Mildred."

I expected a title to follow, because most humans really liked titles, but Mildred appeared to have none.

Harlan introduced himself to Mildred with a flourished bow, as if the title-less old woman were nobility.

Mildred's brows were as wrinkled as the rest of her face, but her eyes were alert, studying Harlan and me while the drooping skin on her face remained absolutely still. After an odd silence, Mildred turned to Bethy Rann. "You have brought some unusual specimens into your service."

Rann didn't correct her servant's misstatement about my status.

"It has been a difficult journey to get here. I needed unusual assistance."

"A long, twisted journey to restore your throne," the old woman agreed. "I've been waiting long years, but the last weeks took the longest. I would've thought a commander with not one but two dragons to aid her could've made faster progress. I've grown weary of washing clothes these many years."

"You served the Rolmans!" Harlan said to Mildred. "That is how Rann knew so much about the keep's provisions and other supplies. Not from childhood memories. You are a spy."

The old woman wasn't flattered. "I am a servant in the keep. No one notices servants, particularly one as old as me."

Rann took in a long breath. "Mildred served my mother, as an advisor and a friend."

The old woman scoffed. "Your mother didn't have friends. She was too clever to trust strangers." The woman named Mildred glared at Harlan as she said the last. "She didn't even trust her husband. That's why you are alive. And it is why Ulibon once again has a high-star on its throne. You would be wise to heed your mother's wisdom."

"A ruler must keep her promises, and I made promises to Bayloo. He saved my life and he saved Ulibon."

Mildred appraised me as if I were a hog and she a chef choosing the choicest cut of meat for a meal. "Your father was never able to recruit dragons into his service. Perhaps you are wise in that."

I understood why Rann hadn't corrected this ill-disposed woman's earlier misstatement about my being a follower, but I was long since done pretending to be anyone's slave, or even their servant. "I owe allegiance to none. A debt is owed."

Rann gritted her teeth as Mildred furrowed her steely brows. "I ... see ... You are a free dragon." She made a clicking sound with her tongue. Apparently, this caused her to repeat herself in an even more morose tone. "A free dragon."

I drew my neck upward, staring down at this strange woman from even higher above. I remembered humans said wine tasted better after it had aged. Was the same true of their own flesh? "I am a free dragon, woman. And this rabble of an army would be scattered or dead had I not lent my aid."

Mildred wasn't impressed. "Indeed. If a dragon says so, it must be so."

Bethy Rann spoke into the tension between us. "Mildred, I have promised Bayloo a set of claw covers similar to those you made for Crema—*sai*, as they are called in the ancient homeland of my ancestors."

The old woman stared at her liege as if she were a talking goat.

I decided to be helpful by lifting a leg so that Mildred could get an accurate sense of the size of my claws. She only looked for a moment before turning back to Bethy Rann. I put my leg down.

"And what are these devices to be forged from? There is no more ore, none alive here can create the *sisolic* primer, unless you, Bethy Rann, have somehow found divine inspiration in the art of enchantment?"

Rann kept her voice steady. "You can melt down blades from the cavern."

"The last artifacts from the time of your father!" she gasped. "They are irreplaceable."

Rann looked at me, then back to her frustrated servant. "The honor of my word is worth even more than an enchanted blade." She spoke with slow-boiling anger. "Do it, Mildred. This is my command."

Mildred grunted at me, as if this were all my fault. "Stick out your claws again, dragon."

I obliged, displaying my magnificent appendages once again. If the old woman was intimidated by me in any way, she hid it well.

"Who do you plan to kill with these, dragon?" she asked casually.

"Any I must."

A skeptical huff followed. "If a dragon wants magical claws, it can only be to pierce dragon scales. You intend to kill your own kind?"

I didn't answer her because I didn't like what I would've had to say, and because it was none of her business.

"I remember when your kind came here the last time," Mildred said as she ran a hand along one of my claws. "Dragons are excellent killers."

"Yes, we are," I said, trying to sound menacing.

Mildred shrugged. "It was not a compliment. Kill away, then. Each time one of Rolm's dragons dies, Ulibon grows stronger. And when your kind are all dead, there will still be Ulibon."

TWENTY-THREE

I sought the Pale Wrights of Oster.

The enchanted *sai* that Mildred had forged from the artifacts of the Twisted Keep fit snugly on the claws of my hind legs. The tips were deadly sharp and the metal deceptively light, but they didn't compare with the originals I had worn in Ni-Yota. True *sai* felt like part of me—these were equipment, like the saddle on my back. Mildred might have been a skilled enchantress (perhaps even the last true enchanter) but she was unaccustomed to making items for dragons. Or she'd intentionally left something lacking in her work. I wouldn't have put it past the crone. We had also rushed her—she'd wanted a week, but I could stay for only an additional two days, during which time I'd watched Bethy Rann get a crown placed on her head by some overdressed humans, babble out speeches, and give people who'd done nothing to help win the war elaborate titles. I slept and ate a lot as well, so time hadn't been completely wasted.

When we departed Ulibon, Harlan and I had supplies and enchanted equipment, as well as the promise from its new ruler that her newborn domain would aid us in our time of need. Rann's victory also helped me in another way: the Sapphire King of Rolm had been humiliated. I knew King Dayne couldn't abide being seen as a fool. Anything that hurt him had to help me.

My regret was leaving Crema. Neither free nor slave, neither healed nor ill, she existed in a middle state. She and I were kin, but she remained linked to Bethy Rann. Before I left, I privately promised Crema that I would return to set her free. Then she could make her own choice to stay or leave. The maimed dragon gave no sign of having understood me, but I felt better.

"Where exactly are we going?" Harlan asked as the Twisted Keep became a memory behind us.

"To Oster, of course. To find the Pale Wrights."

"Aye, that much I gathered, but ... do you even know where to find these Wrights? The way you and Rann spoke, they are almost as much myth as flesh."

"They are real," I assured him. "It is said they live under the ground with the creatures they breed."

Harlan sounded skeptical. "Underground?"

"I don't plan to go into their pits," I assured Harlan. "I think they will come to us."

That wasn't good enough for Harlan, so he made me explain more. I was actually glad when I spotted a Rolman warship plying the waves off the coast of Oster. Better to face the Rolmans than keep talking.

I saw the vessels first, but Harlan knew ships, so I continued to approach, keeping within the cloud cover as best as I could manage.

Harlan impressed me with his vision. "Four large vessels in the open sea, three masts apiece, all flying the Rolman dragon. They move in a tight squadron, daring any other ship to challenge them. Their captain must be confident that he has command of these seas."

"We are well inside Osteran waters, but Oster took heavy losses in their last attack on Rolm before I left. Many of their deadly flying beasts were slain, and I have little doubt that a good number of their warships were destroyed. There isn't anyone else to challenge Rolm on the seas. Even the pirate king wouldn't dare to attack four Rolman warships."

"The ships run heavy in the water," Harlan observed. "Plenty of cargo or soldiers in those holds."

I considered what Dayne would need to conquer Oster that would have to come by sea. "My brothers and sisters can burn castles, but to actually rule all of Oster requires human soldiers. Or they may carry provisions to the soldiers already there, since there will be little else to take from the land. Oster was starving when I left—that's what prompted them to attack Rolm."

"I still see no landmass. How much farther to Oster?"

"It will take those ships at least another day of sailing with the wind at their back to reach the outlying isle. For us, we could be gazing upon the mighty Shard before the sun sets, if I wish it, but it would seem prudent to do a bit of scouting first. I don't want to be detected by my fellow dragons."

"Are you certain the Rolmans will besiege this Shard?" Harlan asked. "You've told me Oster is larger than Ulibon. There must be many castles."

"There are other great fortresses in Oster," I agreed. "But to truly win the isles, one must capture the Shard. The great fortress rises from the sea in the midst of a narrow channel that cuts through the three islands that comprise Oster. When the tide is low, land bridges appear within the Shifting Straits that allow ground travel between the great isles of Oster, but only by passing under the shadow of the mighty Shard. It is the seat of King Galt, and it is there that any battle for Oster will be fought."

I could almost hear the thoughts in Harlan's head clicking as he considered countless additional questions to ask me I knew I wouldn't feel like answering. "It is rather amazing that any fortress could stand against so many dragons for so long."

"You haven't seen the Shard," I assured him. "It is like no other stronghold in all of Inkra. Even in Ni-Yota, nothing compares."

"If we fly to that place, will not both sides see us as a threat?"

Harlan asked. "You are a dangerous renegade dragon to the Rolmans, and an apparent enemy to Osterans."

"Dayne will be at the Shard, his dragons fighting against the remaining might of Oster. The Shard has never fallen. But that isn't where we are going." I beat my wings faster. Better to arrive at Oster sooner than keep answering questions. "We need to go someplace even more dangerous."

TWENTY-FOUR

I awaited twilight.

Dragons can peer through night almost as well as day, but it was during the half-light between, when our sight was deprived of the contrast, that our vision was most limited. At that time, we were merely well-sighted. Twilight would offer the best chance to approach our destination without being seen by Dayne's slave dragons.

Once I reached the barrier islands on the outskirts of Oster's home waters, I swept south, taking a circular course to reach the far side of the island. As I flew, the sun dipped ever lower to the horizon, until finally only the fading vestiges of its light seeped into the sky.

"Once again—where are we going?" Harlan asked, his voice a whisper.

"The Pits of Gargen."

"That sounds ominous."

He wasn't wrong. "The pits are where the beasts of Oster are bred and trained."

"Their beasts are not at the Shard? I would think with a war going on ..."

I grunted my impatience. "The Shard hasn't the space—you'll understand when you see it. The griffins and other creatures there are already trained and grown. The Pits of Gargen are for breeding and rearing and who knows what else. It is a labyrinth of underground tunnels that link the great breeding pits, some so deep and lightless than even a dragon cannot see to the bottom."

"You've been here before?"

"No, no one from Rolm—no human and no dragon—has ever gone into the pits. They are near the Shard, but surrounded by a poisonous waste that is infested with furies and bore worms. The pits themselves are underground, impervious to fire, but more importantly, they have no strategic value. There was never any reason to go there."

Harlan released a low breath. "Then why go now?"

"We know the Shard will be besieged by Rolman dragons. The air around it will be carefully watched by eyes as sharp as mine. I will be seen if I approach, twilight or not. And even if I could get to the Shard, the defenders would think me a slave dragon, and their griffins and furies would try to kill me. Also, going there is unnecessary. We are here for aurathorn, are we not?"

"Yes," Harlan agreed quickly, sounding relieved at my logic. "You believe aurathorn is in these pits?"

"I have no idea where the aurathorn may be, beyond what Rann told us. But she said that they obtained it from the Pale Wrights. The Wrights are masters of Oster's beasts, and legend has it they have an aversion to sunlight. They dwell in the pits, only rarely venturing out. If we wish to speak to them, we must go to the Pits of Gargen."

"I'm in favor of avoiding unnecessary storms. Let us go directly to our objective. How do we get to these pits?"

"They exist in the shadow of the Shard, across the watery causeway, far enough that we might have a chance to slip past both Rolman patrols and Oster's own forces."

"But you said the pits are surrounded by poison lands and fearsome beasts," Harlan reminded me.

"Yes, but at least there won't be dragons to fight."

Harlan groaned, which annoyed me. It was just another example of why I disliked explaining myself to humans. Their moods shifted quicker than the wind and with even less reason. Did Harlan think this was going to be easy?

I bided my time out at sea, beyond the sight of any dragon that might be flying around the Osteran coast, until I judged the light to be most advantageous. When I was satisfied, I dove toward the waves, hugging the water so closely I could taste the salt. Oster's coastline came into view soon afterwards.

This wasn't the first time I'd approached Oster prepared for battle. I flew along the southern tip, where I knew of no great castles or valuable ports, where I hoped there would be less fighting. I beat my wings, increasing my speed. It was the first time I'd noticed the beauty of Oster's coastline. Beaches of fine white sand extended far off the shore, gently dipping into the sea. Small boats were pushed up onto the sand beyond the reach of the highest tides. Small villages clustered together not far from the water. The land rolled gently, mostly uncut by roads or other human works. Even the farms, brown and withered, had an empty, tragic beauty. The slave dragon I once was couldn't see or understand such things. I wasn't sure if it was a good thing these feelings struck me now. With a free mind came complications.

The sights of war weren't absent, of course. Oster was a small place, and the smoke of war hung in the distance. I knew that dragon fire was likely responsible for the burning. The dark clouds clustered to the north, near the heart of Oster, where its three islands were closest. Rising from the narrow channel that bisected Oster stood the Shard, grand with defiance. Lurking in its shadow to the south lay the Pits of Gargen.

To reach the pits, I had to traverse much of southern Oster. I raised my altitude as I flew, skirting the bottom of the clouds. Eventually, I would be seen, but I wanted to postpone that as long as possible. In the chaos of war there was always a chance I would be overlooked by Rolman dragons as long as I didn't fly too close to the Shard itself. Furies protected the pits, but I wondered how many. Surely, the Shard had the greater need for precious furies if the situation was truly desperate. Even Dayne wouldn't dare attack the Pits of Gargen.

The quiet landscape of the southern reaches of Oster faded quickly as I flew. Gone were quiet, seemingly empty villages and fields. In their place was scorched ground and scattered ash. In many places there were fresh burial pits, in others the dead had been left to rot, picked over by scavengers. The few humans living amidst the devastation fled in utter terror as I passed overhead. There was no doubt my kind had done this. I didn't understand why they—or rather, the humans who commanded them—had bothered. Food was already scarce. I saw few keeps or castles on my journey, and certainly none of any military significance.

"I've not seen anything like this before," Harlan said in a whisper. "Even in Ulibon the burning was not so complete."

"King Dayne." I hissed out the name, knowing I was right. The destruction wrought on these lands was vindictive. And no one did vindictive like my former ryder. Even though the link between us was severed, I remembered the twisted, hate-filled mind of Rolm's king. I knew this was done at his command. That he'd forced my kind to do this made it worse still.

"Why?" Harlan wondered.

"Human children lash out at that which they cannot control. I know this child well, and this is how Dayne lashes out." I pushed myself ever faster, because this needed to be dealt with, and because I had no wish to gaze upon scars left by dragon breath longer than necessary.

"In its way, this is worse than the rust," Harlan said. "Here there is no purpose, just destruction."

The landscape turned even more grim as we flew north, drawing closer to the Shard and the pits. There wasn't a single village that had been spared its own inferno. Of the once-proud castles of Oster, I saw not one still intact. Only blackened stones remained. In past wars, Oster's fearsome beasts had kept the worst of Rolm's destruction at bay, the furies contesting our attempt to control the skies. That no longer appeared the case. King Galt's desperate gamble to attack Rolm had failed terribly and his people were paying the price. A tragedy for the inhabitants of Oster, but an opportunity for me. The furies would be needed at the Shard.

Night was almost upon us as the ground below faded from farms and villages on rolling plains to flatlands of gray.

"It's a sea of nothing," Harlan remarked of the bleak land. "Dragons did this?"

"No, this isn't the work of my kind. These are the clay flats of Oster. It is unlike any other place that I know of on Inkra. The ground is hard and smooth, like plaster. Nothing grows here, nothing lives here. In most places, it is like rock. But for a land walker it can be deadly as well. There are places where the surface is as thin as parchment and a single wrong step will send you plummeting into a crevasse or maybe to the Abyss itself. And there are bore worms. We are close to the pits. I must watch for furies—stop distracting me."

We had come so far without being challenged. My eyes scoured the strange gray land below, watching for danger. Any lurking furies would be partially buried, still and waiting. I covered the distance quickly, uneasy at the ease by which we traveled across hostile land.

I knew the peace in the sky could not last, and it didn't. Our position was now close enough to the Shard that I could see it across the dark waters of the Shifting Channel. Surrounding the fortress on its landward sides was the army of Rolm. They were few. Indeed, the host wasn't larger than Bethy Rann's army when I first found it, although these soldiers would be the elite of Dayne's fighting force— the men who merited precious space on a dragon's back or berth on a ship. A large army wasn't necessary when there were dragons. My winged brothers and sisters crowded the peninsula, behind the lines of soldiers and their dirt-walled encampment. My hearts pumped as my eyes focused on them, searching for those I remembered and

trying to count how many were already lost. The dragons were so few
...

My attention was in the wrong place. Harlan spotted the threat
before I did. "They come," was the only warning I got.

Even without seeing the danger, I knew my prior distraction was
potentially deadly. I couldn't do things like that, not when flying over
Oster, not when Dayne lurked nearby. I didn't have time to make my
own decision about how to react. I just heard Harlan's words and
moved. I yanked myself into a sharp turn, twisting my neck and
sweeping my tail with a hint of mad desperation—just hoping that
something I did would save our lives. I needed some luck, but I wasn't
lucky.

I felt my enemy before I saw it. I knew the sensation—pain. But a
particular kind of pain; the distinctive sensation of a fury's stinger
lodging itself into the scales of my rear quarter. Oster may have
sustained heavy losses, but clearly they hadn't been beaten. Not yet.

"By the cook's ass!" Harlan hollered. He was as shocked as I'd
ever heard him. A first encounter with a fury could do that. "What in
the Abyss is that?"

I didn't have time for lessons. I was beating my wings for altitude,
heading into a nearly vertical ascent in case there were others, but
that would also mean a brutally long crash if the fury burrowed deep
enough for its stinger's poison to work. "Can you see it? You must cut
the stinger out of me."

"If I leave this saddle now, I'll be flying without wings."

I leveled my course. Hopefully, I was high and far enough from
ground to avoid any other attacks. Harlan unstrapped himself and
scrambled out of the saddle, grabbing my mane as he crawled along
my spine. "I see nothing."

The fury continued to burrow into me, its saw-like mandibles
making chillingly quick progress through my armor. The poisonous
stinger would follow the instant the creature's jaws found my flesh. I
didn't have much time. "On the left of my tail, just above my hind leg.
The creature cannot be knocked off—its claws are designed to lock

onto things—but the stinger can be severed. Once that happens, it dies."

I assumed Harlan heard me, but he gave no further acknowledgement. I felt him move further along my body. I kept my flight path slow and steady so he could work. I told myself Harlan was handy with his daggers. He'd get the fury off in time. He was close. Then everything got worse.

From the north, flying at speed, came dragons.

TWENTY-FIVE

Two great ash dragons flew at me.

I knew them—Cornethius and Blaris. Of course, those were the names humans had given them. They had no true dragon names.

I remembered each of them, their scent, their roar, the way they moved through the air. I had no doubt they remembered me as well, although their sentiments wouldn't matter. They were slaves, and their ryders came for my blood. I had only moments before they would lay their fire upon Harlan and me.

"Dragons come," I roared. "Fire breathers." Harlan didn't acknowledge me. He was concentrating on trying to reach the fury digging through my armor to poison me.

Neither Cornethius nor Blaris were as large as Gia, but they were large enough. I could sense their thirst for battle, their desire to kill. That was strange to me, for I cared for these dragons. I wanted to save them from their shackles, yet I knew they would show me no such mercy. To them—or rather, to the ryders who controlled them—I was worse than a mere enemy. I was the fear that must lurk somewhere in the recesses of the human mind each time a ryder mounted one of my kin: the fear that the slave would consume its master.

In normal times, I could outfly either Cornethius, with his uneven left wing, or Blaris, with her stubby tail. But to do much more than fly steady risked losing Harlan. The fury still chewed, its stinger ever closer to my vulnerable flesh. Harlan still struggled along my back at his agonizingly slow pace. He had almost reached the fury, but it was too late. Cornethius had arrived. My brother unleashed his fire at my backside.

I rolled in the sky. It was that or let Harlan roast in my brother's flames. Perhaps the enchanted armor would protect him, but I couldn't take that chance. Cornethius' breath struck my underside instead, bathing me in heat. My scales absorbed it. I looked for Harlan's falling body. I saw a dagger fall instead, followed by noise that sounded like a choice sailor's curse.

The burrowing fury's stinger finally reached my soft flesh.

I've never had molten metal poured into my body, but I suspected that the bite of a fury sting was similar—an instant of pain so intense it blinded me. A flood of lesser agony followed the initial shock as the fury's poison pumped into me. The creature itself fell away as soon as its stinger was in place. Its mission was done.

The poison paralyzed me as it moved through my blood. The sensation was uniquely unpleasant—a wave of searing pain that left disconcerting numbness in its wake as it moved up my body. I was large, and the fury had attached to me far away from my hearts, but the stinger would keep pumping, fueling the poison's advance. The real race was now whether I'd die from falling out of the sky due to paralysis, or if the liquid death inside me would stop my hearts first. I preferred the latter. Dying in a splattering crash lacked dignity.

Harlan's voice interrupted my musings on death. "I cut it out!"

The numbness of my hind quarters was such that I couldn't feel the stinger. I could only take his word for it. The poison waves pushing through me seemed to slow, but didn't stop. Maybe I hadn't gotten a lethal dose, but with two dragons pursuing me, it didn't matter.

A mass of scales and claws slammed into me. By her scent, I

knew it was Blaris. She'd hit me at speed, propelling her foreclaws into my exposed chest. Instinctively, I whipped my head around toward the attack. An arrow from Blaris' ryder greeted my careless action, the projectile's tip coming within the length of a human finger from blinding me. Cornethius was already on his way back toward me for another pass. I was in no condition to take on these two dragons.

I let loose a deafening roar as Blaris smacked my chest with her tail, twirling away from me. I beat my wings, intending to flee. I was faster than any dragon except Rinxia, but that was before the fury's poison had found its way into me. I managed to move my wings, but I felt as if I were flying with a couple of horses strapped to me. Still, I pushed on. I didn't see any choice. The pounding in my head matched that of the hearts in my chest. Air swirled behind me as Cornethius cut through the wind. He'd be on me soon.

"I'll have to fight," I warned Harlan. I barely choked the words out. I sucked for air, my body protesting every movement I ordered it to make. There was no chance of using magic. I could barely keep myself in the sky.

"Dive," Harlan shouted at me. He'd almost made it back to his saddle.

I did, because I couldn't think clearly enough to do much else, and dropping was easy. Cornethius' claws passed over me in the near darkness. Like a madman, Harlan stood on my back, holding onto nothing as I barely managed to pull out of my dive and steady myself. A moment later, a blade of metal twirled through the air. A grunt from Cornethius' direction told me that Harlan had somehow managed to hurl one of his daggers into his ryder's back. Impressive and reckless. It wasn't enough.

As Cornethius hollered with rage and concern, Blaris came at me. It was infuriating how easily the slower dragon overtook me in the sky. Back at DragonPeak, she was a slug to my hare, or something like that. Blaris attacked from below, hurling fire as she closed the distance separating us. I think she intended to try to latch onto me, to force me from the air so she and Cornethius could tear me to pieces on the ground. I preferred a different outcome. Blaris expected me to try to maneuver away from her. She probably didn't know about the fury stinger and how badly I'd been hurt. Also, like all the fire breathers, she had contempt for my own lack of breath. I flew directly into Blaris' fire, raising my neck to help protect Harlan from the flames. The heat washed over my face. My nostrils curled, even though I held my breath. In an instant, my jaw was on Blaris' neck. Her fire stopped as the gray-scaled brute twisted her tail to try to strike me. She hit hard, but not hard enough to force me to release her. Blaris stopped beating her wings, and I could barely move mine, so we plummeted toward the ground. Harlan shouted something, but I really didn't have time to focus on him.

I bit harder, cracking some scales. Blaris got a claw on my chest. I dug two into her belly scales, but even with the *sai* fitted on me, I lacked the strength in my legs to do any real damage. Cornethius gave me a bloodthirsty roar as he chased us down toward the ground.

I could've shattered the scales on Blaris' neck. I could've plunged my jaws into her flesh. Even in my crippled condition, I think I could've killed my sister, but I didn't. If I did that, I lost, because I had killed more dragons. And I probably would die in the crash that would have followed. I needed to escape, but I couldn't outfly this pair with a numb hindquarter and poison weakening the rest of my body. I needed another escape route, and there was only one.

I unlatched my jaws from Blaris. "We are meant to fight together as kin. One day you'll understand." I summoned what strength I had in my legs and wings, launching myself away from Blaris.

I overestimated my remaining stamina, as well as the speed of my descent. I got scant push-off from my diminished legs. I gasped for air as I spread my wings. That slowed my fall, but didn't stop it. The ground still came at me, as did Cornethius. I growled as I pushed my wings, forcing them to move. Cornethius adjusted his course, intending to block my retreat to the south. There was no escape in that direction, but I already knew that. I headed north instead, toward the Shard. Cornethius followed, but warily, expecting me to change direction suddenly, as he knew I could. Blaris finally steadied herself and joined her brother in stalking me. They still didn't understand my plan.

I pushed on with everything I had left, catching a fortuitous blast of wind to aid me in my flight. The two dragons pursued, but they couldn't believe where I was going. They thought it had to be a trick of some kind, but it wasn't. I was really that desperate. By the time my pursuers realized my destination, it was too late to catch me, even if they had wanted to continue.

Darkness beckoned, a certain doom that any dragon would be mad to willingly pursue, but that is what I did because I had no choice. I was dying, and I needed what I might find deep below the surface of this world. I located a large gap in the ground. It might have been the final passage to the Abyss for all I could see. My wings failed me just as I turned, sending me into an uncontrolled plunge into the depths of the Pits of Gargen.

TWENTY-SIX

I woke to voices that weren't human.

The noise was too deep, too sharp, and I couldn't understand the words. My body was mostly numb, except for my left foreleg, which burned as my blood seeped out from a gash through my scales. I didn't remember that injury happening. I did remember my wings striking something hard as I fell in a dark tunnel, but nothing after that. Presumably, I hadn't landed well. I didn't know where I was precisely, but I knew I was in trouble.

I opened my eyes reluctantly. I should have kept them shut.

A quartet of oversized wolves stood in the passage, their eyes glowing a sinister amber. Each was easily twice the size of their normal ilk, even bigger than the war wolves Oster deployed in battle. There were other small differences as well—their snouts were shorter and their fur curled like a coarse sheep's wool. Also, they talked.

"En-hanted," the largest of the pack said. The creature sounded like it had consumed a human and the unfortunate fellow was speaking from inside its belly, sans a tongue.

The other wolves emitted more traditionally vicious growls. They were really unhappy about something.

My wit returned slowly. First, I noticed that one of the smaller wolves was leaking blood from the part of its skull where there should have been an ear. Another had an open cut on its nostril. Then I noticed Harlan, a dagger in each hand, looking very distressed. Blood smattered his enchanted tunic armor, but it wasn't his—it was the wolves'.

I realized the pack had probably tried to kill me while I slumbered, but hadn't succeeded. I had Harlan to thank for that, it seemed.

Then, I realized the giant beast had said *enchanted*. Wolf jaws apparently had trouble with certain human sounds, just like dragons.

"It w-akes," another of the wolves said, its speech even rougher than the alpha's.

I intended to tell the pack that I eat wolves (or I would if given the opportunity), but I found my jaw bulky and uncooperative. The unintelligible slobbering that emerged drew a quizzical head tilt from the alpha, followed by a contemptuous bark that I think was a wolf version of a scoff.

"You are bro-ken," the alpha said with satisfaction.

I managed to draw myself up slightly and even move a wing— enough to know there was no chance of flying out of here. My hearts seemed to be working too hard. Even after Harlan had removed the fury stinger, there was still poison in my blood.

"Trapped," the alpha purred.

I was still having trouble getting my jaw to work properly, but I managed a few intelligible words. "No need to fight."

This sent the pack into a tizzy of barking scoffs. They quieted only when the alpha spoke again. "You let us kill you now?" His eyes glinted. "Big meal to end the hunger."

The pack crooned at that idea. Even the wolves were starving.

"I came here to tal ..." I could barely understand myself. I tried again. "Talk, not fight."

The alpha's glowing eyes bulged. "Talk to who, meaty drag-in?"

I took a calculated risk with my reply. "Your masters."

I wondered if these wolves had any self-esteem, or if they accepted their status as slaves willingly. No magic held them. They followed commands that they had been trained to obey since birth.

The alpha gave me a saliva-dripping snarl. "The masters do not bother with the likes of you. The masters say investigate, kill, eat whatever you wish, then report back. Say nothing about talk." The alpha seemed to consider its own words. "Too much talk already. The hunger calls." The wolf sprang toward Harlan, who stood between the pack and me. The alpha was fast, but Harlan was equal to the challenge. In a blur of arms and feet, he repositioned his body sideways to present a narrower target for the alpha, while keeping alert for the inevitable arrival of the rest of the pack.

The alpha pulled up just short of the tip of Harlan's dagger, yanking itself backward, hoping to draw its victim off balance. Two other wolves came at Harlan from his left, while one sulked forward from the other side. Each of the creatures must've weighed more than Harlan; a single bite would mean his death. It was remarkable he'd been able to keep them off of me at all. Maybe that was due to the armor he'd gotten from Bethy Rann. How long had I been unconscious?

The predators first came slowly, then quickly. Harlan spun like a dancer, slicing a wolf's muzzle while elegantly twirling toward the attacking pair's flank side. The alpha jumped forward again, his ugly jaws open to reveal two rows of fang-like teeth the color of steel. Even without feeling a bite, I knew those jaws had been bred to shatter dragon scales. I summoned the last of my fading strength to swing my tail at it. I missed badly, but a large dragon tail was enough to make any wolf wary, no matter how big and bad. My failed attack left the alpha unscathed but allowed Harlan to scamper to a better fighting position. He also backed up closer to me, another wise move. Unfortunately, I was going to be less than helpful in this fight.

"All part of your plan, I suppose," he muttered to me.

I saved my strength rather than struggle with a reply.

The wolves reformed in a semi-circular formation. This time they advanced more warily, each footfall made in unison, their spacing worthy of a well-drilled regiment of Mizu soldiers. I could barely keep my neck up. If the wolves realized the full extent of my weakness, they would slaughter us. I needed to end this melee while there was a chance for an outcome that didn't involve me becoming a meal for a bunch of glorified dogs.

My body was numb, my jaw locked, my head addled, but I knew what I needed to do.

"Get me a moment," I said to Harlan.

He understood what I meant. Before the wolves could react, Harlan slashed to his left before launching a spinning attack to his right. The wolves were shocked at the audacity of their purported victim. They growled at each other. Harlan twirled a dagger in his hand, the wolves' eyes tracking the glinting metal of the blade. They thought he had some purpose. I knew better. Harlan was part genius, part madman, and it wasn't worth trying to decide which was which.

I took the opportunity to close my eyes, plunging myself into darkness as I marshalled my will. I sought the Latticework. It was elusive at first, a mirage forever at the end of the horizon. But I needed it, and somehow that need pushed me where I must go. My grasp of the magic was as tenuous as it had been since I'd first learned what I was, but I didn't need to work any great binding of the Latticework. I merely needed the wind. I called it.

The cavern cooled. The wolves' acute senses noticed immediately. Their fur stood, their eyes searching about for the unexpected.

I spoke my name—my real name. As dragons choose their own names based on their deeds, my own had grown. The wolves might not have understood the meaning, but on an instinctive level they understood that which I wished to convey. "I am He Who Crossed the Wall; I am the Dragon Without Chains."

The wind came at precisely the right moment, the sound of the torrential gust echoing off the walls of the pit, into the cavern into which I lay nearly incapacitated. The fearsome call of wind belied my own dwindling strength. The torrent yanked debris from the ground, pulling it upward in a swirling funnel. It was too weak to do any damage, but it looked impressive. I had certainly captured the attention of the alpha.

"What are you, drag-in?"

The wind ended, with particles falling like heavy rain on the wolves. They scampered about, annoyed, but too wary to do anything about it for the moment.

I clenched my jaw together until it ached. The pain gave me back enough control to say what I needed to say. "I am the answer to your masters' desperate need. All of Oster is about to fall to your enemy, and even if you survive, you face starvation. Take my name to your masters—I can save their lives and yours."

TWENTY-SEVEN

The alpha wolf left us.

His companions remained. I named them Anxious, Pacing, and Dangerous.

I wasn't sure how long passed after the alpha disappeared into the impenetrable darkness of the tunnel behind him. My limbs trembled from fever and my addled mind kept drifting off into hallucinations. I had to keep reminding myself that the three impossibly large wolves, pacing impatiently a short distance away, were real, while the enormous roasted pigs that I saw dancing in the air were not. Reality was desperately unfair.

Harlan paced almost as impatiently as the wolves. He inspected my wound cautiously, trying not to reveal too much concern. He couldn't help me anyway. Harlan's energy was better spent watching the predators hovering nearby. The wolves sniffed at the air constantly, their eyes always on us.

"They suspect," Harlan whispered to me.

I knew what he meant—the wolves sensed my injuries. They just didn't know how badly I had been wounded. Fury poison was intended to kill dragons, but I might live because I hadn't gotten a full dose. And dragons don't die easily.

The wolves made low, growling noises to each other as they paced. Six amber eyes stared, but it was the wolf with the missing ear I'd named Dangerous who took the first step toward me. Then he took another.

Daggers appeared in Harlan's hands. "Keep your distance."

Dangerous didn't listen. He came closer, followed by Anxious and Pacing.

My blood surged. I tested my tail to see if I could even move it. I could, but it was stiff. "Be good pups and wait for your captain to return."

Saliva dripped from the muzzles of each of the beasts. Their lean bellies heaved. Hate filled Dangerous' ugly eyes. The alpha had ordered them to wait, but I supposed there was a limit on how long a wolf held an order inside its furry head.

The pack continued to close, each step deliberate. Harlan spun his daggers dangerously. The wolves didn't care. Their eyes were on me—Harlan was just some meat in the way.

Dangerous sprang forward at Harlan. His trajectory would've put his paws on the human's chest and his jaw on his neck.

"Stop!"

No human voice gave that command. The alpha had returned. Dangerous tried to obey even as he traveled through the air. He twisted his body and snapped his jaw shut.

"Don't kill it," I said to Harlan.

I wasn't sure how much the Pale Wrights cared about their vicious creations, but I doubted killing one now was going to be helpful.

Harlan exhibited remarkable self-control. He couldn't completely avoid the massive projectile of teeth, claw, and fur about to land on him, but he did lower his dagger and turn at the last moment, letting his shoulder absorb most of the weight that struck him. He fell backward, momentarily helpless. The wolf could've torn him to pieces, but it didn't. Harlan scrambled back to his feet faster than a fallen cat, daggers poised but not bloodied.

Dangerous backed away, but not fast enough for the alpha's satisfaction. The pack leader grabbed the top of Dangerous' neck in his jaw, flinging him away from Harlan as I might toss a bone from my jaw. The scolded wolf regained its feet slowly, head hung low. The alpha flashed a teeth-filled growl at the other two complicit wolves who had already sulked back toward the tunnel, both pretending to be interested in the tiny rocks that littered the cavern floor.

The alpha shifted its attention to me. "You follow. You will not be harmed. This is the pledge of the masters."

"You want us to go in there?" Harlan asked. He pointed to the great tunnel behind the wolves. It was large enough that I could fit with my wings folded, but I certainly had no desire to do so. I also wasn't sure if my hind legs were ready to cooperate.

"Not you, hu-man. Drag-in only."

I wasn't anxious to enter the darkness with a wolf. "Tell your masters that we will speak to them here."

The alpha opened its jaw, growled, then closed it again. "These are the masters' orders." It seemed equal parts confused and upset at my reluctance.

"We stay," I repeated.

The alpha's glowing eyes bored into me. He gave a sharp bark, then wheeled himself back into the tunnel at his back. This time the other wolves trailed after. Dangerous flashed a look of hate in our direction before following.

"I guess we'll find out how badly they want to meet you," Harlan muttered when they were gone.

It turned out, the wolves' masters did indeed want something from me, just as I'd hoped. Not long after the wolves disappeared, an ivory-robed human-ish form ambled through the dark tunnel, hood drawn down so far that no part of its face was visible. I doubted a normal human could see in the blackness of that tunnel, but I wasn't expecting to meet a normal human.

The hooded figure stopped at the entrance of the tunnel. The wolf pack hovered around him in a protective cordon. There was no extraneous chafing from the creatures now; they were obedient servants in the presence of their master. I would've felt sorry for them, except they were foul-tempered wolves who had tried to eat me, so I didn't waste my sympathy. I waited for the hooded figure to speak. He stood there for so long, his features hidden, that I was beginning to think he didn't talk. Maybe these things communicated some other way, without words. Or maybe the new arrival wasn't impressed by what he saw. I forced my forelegs to move, pulling myself into a more intimidating position, stretching my neck upward. The effort hurt, but I was also encouraged I could manage it at all.

A sharp intake of breath came from within the layers of thick cloth. It wasn't a sound that a human would make—more like a leviathan sucking air through its blowhole. The voice that followed was a dry whisper that grated like rusted hinges.

"So, it is true. A dragon, unbound by the runes of the Sculptors."

"Indeed," I replied, trying to sound like my usual calm and powerful self, but unfortunately my legs were trembling from the effort of holding my body upright. I was running out of time.

The creature beneath the hood still didn't reveal itself. "You insisted on speaking to us. Say that which you wish to speak."

I didn't have time for idle chatter. A wave of dizziness assaulted me. I think I managed to keep my head steady. "Oster is on the verge of destruction. King Galt can no longer protect his own people."

"This is not the first time Rolm has attacked. Mendakas once thought he could defeat us, but he was wrong. The son will fail. The dragons are much fewer this time."

"Your beasts are decimated. Otherwise, I would never have gotten to this place. Dozens of griffins would've ripped me apart. The Shard is surrounded, while you rely on a few little pups to protect you as you cower in your underground maze."

Four wolves growled, while the human-thing made an intense sucking-breath sound. I'd hit a sore spot or whatever this creature had. "You have no idea what is inside these tunnels, dragon. I assure you that you will not leave here alive unless you offer us something worth sparing your life."

I ignored the threat. I wanted to get this over with. "Even if Galt manages to fend off the dragons of Rolm, your people face famine and starvation worse than anything else they have ever experienced."

"State your point, dragon."

"I can save Oster."

"Oh?" The sound dripped of derision, but it was also forced. "Even if you are free, you are one dragon against many."

"I am an ember dragon. I command the sky, the wind, and much else." I wanted to impress my power upon these creatures, but didn't want to give too much away. "The magic I showed your pup was a minor trick compared with all I could do."

The robed creature was silent again for a discomforting amount of time. I suspected it was communicating with others in some other way.

"What is it that you wish from us?"

This was it. He wanted my offer. I was too weary to be anything but direct. Either these creatures needed me, or they didn't. "I want aurathorn."

The figure's head jerked up as if he'd been poked with a branding iron fresh from the fire. His hood fell back. The face that stared at me wasn't human—at least it wasn't like any human I'd laid eyes upon. Eyes with three pupils apiece stared at me from deep sockets carved into the creature's flesh. The skin of its face was wrinkled like a prune, its pallor that of a corpse. Scant wisps of silver hair clung to the creature's blot-stained skull. I had no doubt I had met my first Pale Wright. It didn't seem pleased.

A mouth devoid of teeth opened ever so slightly, the words chilling but clear: "Kill the dragon."

TWENTY-EIGHT

Four huge wolves bounded forward.

They didn't get far. Not close enough to be within the reach of Harlan's daggers. My numbed body and mind hadn't even reacted when a second voice erupted from the dark tunnel behind the wolves. Another Pale Wright.

"Halt." The second voice was as barren and terrible as the first, but it came with such vehemence that it cut like steel. "Back."

The wolves retreated instantly, as if they'd been yanked on an invisible string. The creature emerged from the impenetrable darkness, where it had somehow managed to remain invisible before that moment. The Wright seemed to form out of melted blackness, advancing without audible footsteps. This new arrival's hood was already pulled back. I could barely tell one Pale Wright from the other. The only discernible difference seemed to be that the new arrival had a narrower face, although it was equally horrible to look upon. It glared at the first Wright and something unspoken passed between them. The original creature walked back into the darkness without a glance back at me. At least they didn't bicker like humans.

"Perhaps a bargain can be made," the remaining Pale Wright said to me, the edge of what had once been its mouth twitching as he spoke. "Only our Conclave can decide. You must come with me. The others cannot come so far into the light as I."

The light? We were at the bottom of the pit and it was night. "You can pass my words onto your Conclave," I told him, still unwilling to venture into the tunnel.

"You do not trust, and that is understandable," the creature said, the corner of its mouth twitching again, as if it didn't quite control its own lips. "Yet come you must. There is no choice. It is clear that you cannot fly out of here even if you wished it. You are suffering from fury poison."

Twitch was right. My legs couldn't hold my body upright much longer. "Dragons heal quickly."

"Not from the stinger of a fury. We made them that way. But I can fix that, because trust must start with one of us if we are each to get what we need." The Wright turned halfway back toward the tunnel behind him, revealing a hand that was more bone than flesh. A single finger flicked up, then he turned back to me. More uncomfortable silence followed, until another creature that looked like a crab appeared. It was no bigger than a human hand, with a green shell and four legs on each side. It scurried toward me.

"This creation secretes a substance that will neutralize the poison in your blood," the Pale Wright claimed. "Allow it onto your body, and you will be mended."

"Why should I believe that?"

"Perhaps you shouldn't. But you really don't have any choice other than to let the poison kill you. You obviously didn't get a full dose from the fury stinger, but you got enough to kill you. Unless I save you. No one else is going to help you here."

Twitch might have been lying about the poison as well, but I didn't think so. I was getting worse, not better.

Harlan turned to me and spoke in a whisper. "They want something badly from you."

I agreed with that. And there really wasn't any other choice.

"Proceed."

The crab-like creature climbed onto me as if it knew exactly where to go, its claws sharp enough to allow it to scale my body without difficulty. It latched onto the area of the stinger wound. I shook as it went to work digging into my exposed flesh first with pincers, then with something wet.

"What's wrong?" Harlan asked.

"It tickles."

A wave of heat surged through me, but it wasn't unpleasant. If this thing intended to finish me off, I assumed it would happen quickly. The Pale Wright stood and stared as its creation worked. Abruptly, the crab-thing stopped moving. It made a short hissing sound before it fell off of me, tumbling to the ground. It didn't move again.

Harlan pushed the crab with his boot. "It's dead."

"It has fulfilled its purpose," the Pale Wright croaked.

More quickly than I dared to hope, feeling was returning to my body. I moved my tail back and forth to test it, then performed a similar exercise with my wings and legs. I wasn't sure if I could fly yet, but I had little doubt that my strength was returning.

The Pale Wright dipped its chin almost imperceptibly downward. "The Conclave awaits." He turned back to the tunnel. The wolves ran ahead of their master. All of them disappeared into a blackness that even my eyes couldn't penetrate.

I exchange a meaningful look with Harlan. His sentiments echoed my own. "I see no other way."

I pulled myself onto my legs. My joints were stiff, but I had no trouble moving now. I still wore the *sai*, which made walking awkward, but I wasn't about to take them off, given where I was about to go. I gave a silent thanks to the little crab who'd died to heal me before I walked into the tunnel, Harlan beside me, his hand touching my side.

The passage was cold, far more so than would've been natural even for a sunless, underground cavern, but apart from that, it seemed innocuous. There were no other creatures within, no apparent threats—just rock. Another dragon could've squeezed beside me, which made me think of Rinxia. Did she still live? Had I made the correct choice leaving her and Kiata behind in Ni-Yota? It wasn't time to dwell on those choices. I just needed to make sure that the chance I had taken proved worth the cost.

We hadn't walked far when we came to a curtain of mist. It dropped from the ceiling, like a waterfall of miniscule droplets. I couldn't see to the other side.

"This explains the impenetrable darkness of the passage," I said.

"Is it water?"

I sniffed at the mist. There was no odor. I didn't know what fell from the ceiling.

"The fluid will not harm you," said a not-very-reassuring voice from the other side of the curtain. I couldn't tell which of the Wrights spoke. "It is for us."

We walked through. The mist—whatever it was—seemed to have no immediate ill effect, but the other side of the curtain was a different world.

It was terribly cold beyond the mist, a deep chill of the ominous. I could handle the temperature better than a human, but that didn't mean I enjoyed it. "Now we are truly in the Pits of Gargen."

"It feels like sailing the northern sea during the short days of the year," Harlan said. "Except in those waters, I know to wear my thickest coat on deck."

The passage opened into a cavern of near impossible size. Ahead of us were the pits. Dozens of them. They were square shafts of darkness, organized into semi-neat rows that spanned the entirety of the massive space, each pit separated by narrow paths of smoothed rock wide enough for two humans to walk side-by-side, but not a dragon. I could've flown over, but the ceiling was too low for flight, and the stalactites would be dangerous to my wings. I didn't like this place at all.

The wolves had disappeared, but the Pale Wright (I assume it was the same one who had brought me here) waited a short distance ahead. "Dragon, if you keep to the edges of the cavern, you may more easily pass through. But stray no further than this cavern, or it is your peril. Human, it is not much further, but be careful with your steps. There will be no return should you fall into one of the pits." With that, the creature turned away from us, moving at a cautious pace toward a doorless passage where another wall of mist shielded whatever lay behind the portal.

I proceeded along the outer edge of the cavern, expecting Harlan to choose that route as well, but he didn't. Instead, he followed in the steps of the Pale Wright, carefully peering into several of the great pits as he walked. I did the same as I made my way across the chamber's edges, but I saw nothing and heard nothing. The smells that assaulted my nostrils told me that many creatures, including griffins, once dwelled here, but at the moment the pits were mostly empty. Across the massive cavern, on the far end from where we traveled, there was a massive archway, as wide as several dragons, silent and ominous. The Wright noticed my noticing.

"Keep to your path," it reminded me. "There is nothing for you down there."

We followed the Pale Wright through another mist barrier, then through a sloping passage that led still deeper into the bowels of the world, until finally we emerged into an elegant chamber of smooth walls of thoroughly polished obsidian stone, upon which disconcerting azure shadows seemed to dance, appearing and disappearing at a frantic pace. It took me a moment to realize the source of the strange light tricks—a pair of large braziers that contained no fire, but rather flickered mysterious, blue-tinged light onto the walls and ceiling. A raised semi-circular platform made of the same polished obsidian as the rest of the chamber dominated the far end of the space. The chamber was cold and empty. The Pale Wright that had led us here had also vanished.

"It certainly isn't the lake palace of Trishan," I noted.

As if upset by my words, the strange, heatless light from the braziers dimmed to almost nothing. That shouldn't have mattered to my dragon eyes, but somehow it did. For a moment, I could barely see anything. When the light returned to its prior (still dim) intensity, the dais was occupied by six Pale Wrights, all attired in identical heavy robes, although none had bothered with their hoods in here. If I were them, I would've stuck with the hood. Eight giant wolves sauntered into the chamber behind us. I didn't like my position if this came to a fight, although I was relatively sure I could kill every one of the Pale Wrights before their wolves could inflict much damage. I hoped it didn't come to that.

The almost-human figures stared at me without expression, their deep-set eyes and pale, wrinkled skin making them appear like upright corpses. I was relatively certain that two of the Pale Wrights were the creatures I'd already met—they were less shriveled than the others, who closely resembled sticks with some old flesh haphazardly attached to the rickety frames.

"We represent the Conclave." I was pretty sure the speaker was Twitch. I wondered if his words meant this was all the Pale Wrights or if there were still more shambling about the dark tunnels.

I wanted to get this over with. I skipped the grand introduction. "You may call me Bayloo."

Another Wright spoke, its mouth shriveled to the size of a big grape. "Bayloo the free dragon, who travels with a human of Farlight. These are unusual times. Desperate times."

"More desperate for some than others," I reminded them. Their island was starving after all, although none of this group looked like they were big eaters.

"Indeed, some are quite desperate." The Wright held out its bony hand toward me. "You have ventured deep into the Pits of Gargen and placed yourself at our mercy to trade for something which you must know can be obtained nowhere else but here. Both of us have great need."

Harlan tensed ever so slightly when the Pale Wright confirmed that they had aurathorn in their possession. It seemed Bethy Rann had spoken true as to where my mother had obtained it. The Pale Wrights were the keepers of this precious secret. But what did they use it for?

"You know what I want," I told the Wrights. "I told you what I offer."

The Pale Wrights all stared at me in disconcerting silence. Those strange eyes of theirs didn't blink. They just stared. On and on. Harlan caught my glance, and I could tell he shared my unease. I grew even more certain that the Wrights were communicating with each other in some way. Finally, a different Pale Wright spoke, one near the center of their line—the most shriveled of them all. That Wright was so gaunt that I suspected a strong fart could've toppled him.

"You were once bound by the control runes, as were the rest of your kind?"

Why did it care? "Yes."

Another pause followed, but not as long as the previous one. "It was another dragon that freed you, using the very same cultivation— that which you call aurathorn—that you now seek."

I wasn't sure if it had asked a question, but I answered anyway. I wanted to get out of this chamber, away from grizzly creatures and strange light. This wasn't a place for dragons, or any being that thrived in the sun. "This is what I was told."

"By your mother?" it pressed.

The spikes of my mane pricked up with discomfort. I didn't understand the reason for these questions, although I supposed it shouldn't have surprised me completely that the Pale Wrights knew exactly whom they had traded with. Once again, I wondered what these creatures had received from my mother the last time they offered aurathorn, but I didn't dare ask.

"Yes," I told it. "Do we have a ... trade?"

"Trade, yes," it said, opening its toothless mouth a bit wider than before. I got the impression that it was ... if not happy, then pleased. It worried me that these creatures agreed so readily.

"We need to see aurathorn, first," Harlan interjected. "It is of no use if it has not been properly cared for."

Was that true? My mother had spoken of a fount, and a vine. I had no idea. Or did Harlan intend to merely try to steal his heart's desire once these Pale Wrights showed it to him?

Any tenuous indication of pleasure vanished from the Pale Wright. "We possess what you seek, human." The creature spoke the last with such contempt that I realized that it did not consider itself part of that race. "The dragon Bayloo is free because of what we exchanged—the cultivation you call aurathorn. We kept our end of that trade."

Harlan shifted anxiously and I decided to trust whatever he had in mind. The smuggler made his desire plain. "I must see the aurathorn with my own eyes. I must know that Bayloo and I do not risk our lives for nothing."

The creatures went silent again, still and terrible, while Harlan and I waited. Finally, the most shriveled one spoke once again. "We will send a white raven with a message for King Galt. He must agree to this bargain as well. If there is to be a trade, then you will be allowed to see that which you covet. We kept our promise before, we shall do so again."

I would've been satisfied with that, but Harlan wasn't. He was the better card player as he liked to say—so I didn't intervene.

"We. Must. See. It," Harlan repeated, his voice as cold as I'd ever heard it. "I must hold it in my hand."

For a moment there was actually some spark in the creature's dead eyes. Anger? "What you seek lies below in the forge, beneath the breeding pits, a dark place, but one that is larger than all the pits combined. It is an ancient place, and it is not a place for humans, or dragons. You cannot venture there." Harlan was about to object, but the Wright kept speaking. "But we shall bring a token of proof. First, though, Galt must be satisfied, and he is not a man easily dealt with. No, not easy at all. But these are desperate times."

Harlan snarled. "Then get on with it."

This time Twitch spoke. He stared at me, then Harlan. His head moved ever so slightly. "We will send word. Galt must come."

TWENTY-NINE

The Pale Wright brought us back to the original pit where I'd crashed.

"We all await King Galt," were its only words before departing.

No food or drink was offered. Food was too precious in Oster, but I wouldn't have eaten anything provided by a Pale Wright in any case —who knew what they fed the creatures in this place? We still had some provisions from Bethy Rann, although it was salt meat and hardtack. Even though he didn't eat much, the salt meat didn't sit well in Harlan's stomach, which meant both of us suffered.

"This is a forsaken place," I said. "It's like sitting on the precipice of the Abyss."

Harlan glanced upward, trying to see the sky. "Aye to that. Once we captured a slave ship sailing toward Ionia. Standing on that deck, knowing what was below ..." He shook his head in disgust. "I didn't even have to see the holds to feel the evil within. This place is like that ship, except worse."

"It is worse on a deeper level than that. I can sense the void within the Latticework. There is something deep below, a blackness. I have sensed something like it only in one other place."

"Where was that?"

"The Forest of Fallen Night."

Harlan frowned unhappily. "Let us hope this King Galt comes sooner rather than later."

I had my doubts. "The Shard is near, but travel will depend on the tides of the Shifting Straits, as ever. But Galt somehow needs to get here without being roasted by my brothers as well. I wonder how that happens."

"It does seem a great risk for a king, but perhaps there is no choice."

It turned out that King Galt did have a choice.

In the darkness just before dawn, a Pale Wright arrived—I think it was Twitch again. I hadn't slept; I couldn't in this place. Harlan had dozed, but was awake with daggers in hand within a moment of Twitch's stepping from the passage.

"Go above," Twitch said. "A man awaits there."

"King Galt?" I asked.

"A man," it repeated, as if they were all the same. "Speak with him as if he is Galt."

"The tunnel is too tight to fly," I observed. "Crashing is easier than taking off."

"You are a dragon. With claws. You can climb until the pit widens."

Twitch looked upward to the surface as if imagining my ascent before fading back into his tunnel.

"I guess we go," I said to Harlan. "Hold fast to the saddle."

"You don't have to carry me. I can climb myself."

That was bravado. "You can't climb these walls unless you've been growing claws. Get into the saddle and strap yourself in."

I managed the ascent. It wasn't nearly as easy as the Pale Wright claimed, particularly because I still hadn't fully recovered from the fury's poison. This pit wasn't intended to be an exit for dragons or any other creature. Only the *sai* made the climb possible. The enchanted metal tore into the rocks, giving my hind legs at least a steady grip all the way up. Eventually, the pit widened enough that I was able to half-leap, half-fly into the air for the remaining distance. I didn't go far, just to the desolate ground beside the opening above. There might have been dragon patrols watching still.

A man waited as the Wright had claimed. He knelt on one knee at the precipice of the pit from which I emerged. My sudden appearance jolted him to his feet, a hand on his golden sword hilt, as if his blade could help him against me.

We stared at each other. The man forced himself to relax his grip on his blade. "So, it is as the message claimed. A dragon has come." Harlan slid from the saddle, causing the man to add unhappily, "And an Islander too."

Harlan flashed his teeth in a mocking smile.

"You are not King Galt," I surmised. I had never met the ruler of Oster, but I knew that kings didn't travel alone through the night as this human must've done to be here. Also, Galt was supposedly a large man with broad shoulders, with a famously thick beard, while this human was built like an arrow, his face all angles, unblemished by any hair except a single red-tinted knot of thin strands tied together at the back of his head.

The man inhaled a sudden breath when I spoke, his eyes widening. "Do you ..." He looked at Harlan. "Does the dragon obey you?"

Harlan's only reply was a sad shake of his head at his fellow human's stupidity.

"You may call me Bayloo," I told the ignorant human.

Galt's man gaped, but only for a moment. He drew himself up straight like the soldier he was. "I meant no offense. Our contact with your kind is limited and one-sided. There is often fire and death involved."

"My contact with your kind has been similarly unhappy," I pointed out.

He nodded his understanding. "To answer your question, I speak with the voice of King Galt. I am Kemet, First Advisor."

"You run swiftly to have arrived from the Shard in such a short time," I observed.

Kemet cringed as he moved a hand almost involuntarily to his neck. Below his square chin was what appeared to be another little crab like the one that had healed the poison of the fury stinger, except this creature had eight pointed tentacles. "The Wrights ... provided this." His tone left no doubt as to how he felt about that necessity. "It gives stamina."

"You did run here," I mused. Kemet didn't confirm that, but he didn't correct me either.

The distance would've been a challenge for the very best harrier in Rolm, and near impossible for an ordinary human. My mind raced. They had bred crab-creatures that could heal poison and offer endurance. The Pale Wrights had been busy indeed. I had fought Oster for much of my life, and the new creations of the Pale Wrights were always something to be dreaded. But a new weapon was rare—it had been many years since the furies started appearing. The Pale Wrights had seemingly become profligate in their breeding programs. Did the desperation of war prompt this new development? Or was it something else?

"I endure what I must for Oster," Kemet declared self-righteously, even as his brows narrowed. "King Galt was promised many things to send me here."

"I made no promises. I offered a trade to obtain what I want."

"The Pale Wrights made the promises," Kemet said. His eyes flicked toward the pits around us, then toward the sky, which had only just begun to suggest the imminent arrival of dawn.

"They didn't seem to want to come out to join our discussion," Harlan said.

"Yes, they dislike the light, as you may know. The first light of dawn is a particular poison, however." By the hint of satisfaction in Kemet's voice, I guessed that his arrival at just the time that would make listening to our conversation most difficult had been a deliberate choice. Quite interesting. "But their beasts are another matter."

I heard the warning: we were probably being spied upon. Why did he care? I sniffed at the air. "No wolves, no humans other than Harlan and you."

Kemet ignored my assurance. "I've been told that you are free ... a rebel who has escaped the magical shackles that enslave other dragons."

"I am free."

"And ... you can ... that is, you ..." Kemet's hands twirled, but he didn't seem to be able to complete his thoughts. "You are a ..." I decided to help him, but answered in my deepest power-dragon tone.

"I can command the greatest forces of the world: the wind, the sky, even the rock. You may call it magic."

"Magic." Kemet rolled his jaw in a circular motion as if tasting the word. Judging by the frown that followed, it tasted sour. "Not sculpting, not even enchantment, but the magic of legend, of commanding the forces of Haven? Forgive me, but a dragon can do this?"

"If I choose, yes, and I do not forgive your ignorance. You know only of the slave dragons of Rolm, but that is not what my kind was meant to be. It is not what I am."

"And you believe that with this ... this strange flower that the Pale Wrights have, you can free the other dragons?" Kemet didn't hide his skepticism. I also thought it interesting that he seemed to know nothing of aurathorn. It was just a flower to him. The Pale Wrights hoarded secrets, keeping them even from their king.

I didn't know how much the Wrights had told him about my mother and the previous trade, but I guessed they hadn't shared the knowledge of their illicit trading so I kept my answer simple. "The flower, as you call it, has unique properties to users of magic, and perhaps to others. I do believe it can be used to free my fellow dragons, thus I am willing to offer my assistance to your liege in exchange for it."

"The other dragons would no longer serve Rolm if they were free?"

I thought about my brothers and sisters. I didn't know their minds, but I wasn't going to show doubt to this man. "They will turn on their former tormentors, just like any slave."

Kemet rubbed his chin, thoughtful. "One dragon cannot defeat many. The boy-king has over a dozen dragons, even if most are the smaller ones that do not breathe fire. Surely you cannot beat them all as well as the Rolman army on your own?"

I'd anticipated that question. "I don't need to defeat my brothers and sisters—indeed, I will not kill a fellow dragon unless there is no other choice. I only need to kill Dayne."

"The boy-king?" Kemet seemed surprised. "Even if you could reach him, that alone will not ensure the departure of his army and the dragons. Nor does it free the other dragons, if I understand correctly. At most, it might buy us time while Rolm is thrown into confusion."

"I know Dayne well. This war was his doing. Others will not be so keen on it, given certain other developments that threaten Eladrell. Rolm and their dragons will leave to protect their homes and fields once the person holding them here is dead."

Kemet's head shook. "I don't understand. How is Eladrell under threat?"

"Because Ulibon will invade." I tried to make it sound like a certainty, even though Bethy Rann's position was still very precarious.

"Ulibon?" The human looked concerned. He might have thought me crazy.

"There was a revolt there."

"Yes, we know. The supposed Heir of Ulibon returned, but ..."

"The Twisted Keep has fallen," I told him, not without a bit of pride. "I did that."

Big eyes looked at me. "Why would you help rebels in Ulibon?"

"I have my reasons. And now they owe me. They have ships—part of the Rolman fleet was captured, and many soldiers of Rolm went over to swear allegiance to the new Highstar."

"Ulibon is no match for Rolm," Kemet declared with the self-importance of a human soldier who fancies himself a fine tactician as well. "An attack on Eladrell would be madness, no matter what they owe you. I don't believe it."

"Ulibon doesn't really need to attack to draw back Rolm's forces from Oster, do they? Rolm's garrisons are stripped bare. They could show their fleet, sail around the harbor of Eladrell, burn a few fields along the coast. That would be enough to draw the dragons back. The Highstar of Ulibon will keep her word to me."

Harlan chimed in, speaking in the tone of a trader with goods on offer. "You are getting the magic of the most powerful dragon on Inkra and the aid of Ulibon in this trade. A rare opportunity. Maybe your last opportunity, I think."

"For a flower?" There was no mistaking Kemet's disbelief.

I made my human-style smile. "It is a very tasty flower."

Kemet tried to stop himself from cringing, but didn't quite succeed.

"King Galt is a cautious man, particularly in matters which seem too good to be true. He does not believe in miracle saviors. Even if you can deliver all you say, Galt will have to commit the last of our reserves for you to have any chance of reaching King Dayne. That would be the last of our surviving griffins and furies, the last of our able-bodied soldiers. Rolm's dragons are on constant patrol, their army at our gates. Even after Dayne is dead, the dragons may retaliate."

"I can kill Dayne, I can help to keep the Rolman dragons at bay, but your beasts and soldiers must fight too," I said.

"This isn't supposed to be easy," Harlan added. "How bad is your situation?"

Kemet's brows furrowed. He didn't answer immediately as he considered how much was safe to say to us. He must've decided it didn't matter or he had little choice. "They probably outnumber us twenty-to-one in fighters. We have only a handful of griffins who can still fly. Barely enough furies to keep contesting the skies for a few more days. Only because of the Shard have we survived this long. We are on the verge of utter defeat—otherwise I wouldn't be here and Galt wouldn't consider such a dangerous plan."

Harlan arched a brow. "What soldier would leave the walls to fight against such odds?"

Kemet's chest puffed. "Oster's soldiers are brave and loyal."

Harlan shrugged. "They are still men."

Kemet gave an unhappy grunt. He placed a hand next to the crab-like creature attached to his neck. "These are new symbionts. The Pale Wrights have bred a hundred or more. With these, one man could fight like three, without tiring. They may even work on griffins."

This was a surprise to me. "Why have you not used them before?"

Kemet's eyes moved ever so slightly toward the pits, to the domain of the Pale Wrights. It was subtle, but I was sure he did it. There was distrust between Galt and his strange servants, I was sure, but Kemet only said, "They are newly bred. New beasts can be ... unpredictable." He touched the creature on his neck, but not with affection. It was how one touched a scab that couldn't be scratched. "Although this one seems to have worked. But they live only a short time before dropping away. We will only have one chance at this."

"Then you should take your chance," I told him. "It sounds as if there is little left to lose. Without my help, Oster will be no more."

Kemet was silent, thinking on this decision I knew he didn't want to make. Yet he really had no other choice. "Perhaps I would recommend this. But Galt ... As I said, he does not believe in miracles. He does not trust easily. He will not believe in a dragon that can do magic. Not unless he sees it."

I snorted my derision, but I had expected no less. I looked at the sky. The sun had risen and the sky was clear. "A beautiful day. How long will it take you to return to the Shard?"

"With this symbiont, I can sprint like a man in his prime all the way there, and make it by midday. Alone, I'm unlikely to be seen by a dragon patrol. The tide will be high, so no land bridge, but I swim quite well."

"Just before nightfall, a single cloud will float through the sky. It shall be alone, coming toward the Shard from where we now stand. My cloud will be unusual in shape, with wings on either side. To a man with imagination it will look like a dragon with its wings extended. When this cloud reaches the sea around the Shard, it will drop thick ice hail, as one may have in winter, onto the mountain, then it shall disappear before it reaches the land to the north of the Shard. Will this be sufficient demonstration that the skies answer to my command?"

"I believe it may be," Kemet admitted, with an almost regretful tone.

I spread my wings, but not because I intended to fly anywhere. I just wanted this human to see the majesty of a dragon up close, to have my shadow fall over him as the sun shone behind me. I wanted him to fear, and despite his best efforts, Kemet's eyes told me that I had succeeded. "Be off, then. Run your fastest. Ulibon already is preparing for this, but it will take days for their fleet to sail once I give the word. Oster has precious little time left from what you have told me, so you had best prepare now."

Kemet took a step backward, then another. "What do you intend to do?"

I let loose a roar—just loud enough to turn Kemet's face to milky white. "Run to the Shard. Tell him there is a battle to be won, a prize to be claimed, and a pitiful little man to kill."

THIRTY

The King of Oster wanted my help.

I had sent my special cloud off to the Shard just as the sun faded. Putting on my magic demonstration wasn't an easy task. The mist had to be woven in just the right way, the moisture timed with precision, the cold hail primed so that it would fall when the cloud reached the sea. I had done it all. Control was becoming easier for me. I was rather pleased with myself. Others were more critical.

"That doesn't look anything like a dragon," Harlan had commented about my cloud. "More like a crooked finger."

The cloud definitely looked like a dragon. Maybe its wings were a bit short and crooked.

Even without the magic cloud, Galt didn't really have a choice. He needed my help. Oster wouldn't survive much longer, even if the symbionts did all that the Pale Wrights promised. Their losses were too great and couldn't be replaced in time.

Word of King Galt's decision arrived at the pits by a white raven messenger later that night. I saw the bird fly into one of the pits. My pale host Twitch appeared not long afterward.

"King Galt prepares his forces." The Wright sounded almost

excited. It was a disconcerting sound. "He orders us to make our preparations. He decrees that, should the Rolmans be driven from Oster, we are to deliver to you aurathorn and whatever else you ask of us."

"I want to see and hold aurathorn first," I reminded him.

"We anticipated that." The words hung between us.

Could it be true?

The Pale Wright raised a bony fist. I could hear Harlan's heart beating. The skeletal fingers unclenched ever so slowly. Somehow, Harlan must've seen it even before I did, because he sucked down a breath like he was a suffocating fish; inside the palm of the Pale Wright's outstretched hand was a single thorn, no bigger than a human's smallest finger, shining like a silver fire had been lit inside. The thorn's light was dim, yet it seemed to distort the darkness around it, like a mirage on a scalding day.

Harlan stepped forward, oblivious to the Wright, his eyes fixed only on the tiny glowing thorn. His voice trembled. "By the seas and stars, it's real."

"Take it in your hand, human," the Wright said. "And know we can deliver what we say."

Harlan snatched the thorn from the palm of the Pale Wright like a greedy child. Its light illuminated Harlan's face. A single, solitary tear fell from his right eye. "Norta, it is here," he whispered to the thorn.

I reached for the Latticework, for I wanted to understand this object, which might look like a thorn, but I doubted could be a mere growth from a mundane plant. What I found when I tried to study it from that deeper reality was ... nothing. Only an impenetrable void. The thorn didn't exist within the Latticework, or I lacked the skill to sense it. The mystery deepened. Then, the light was gone.

As Harlan and I gazed upon the thorn, its glow surged for a precious moment, then faded to blackness, like a firefly on its last flight. In the unexpected darkness, Harlan gazed, crestfallen, at the lightless thorn.

"Separated from the *pisa*—essentially the mother fount—the thorns soon lose their luster. But this one has served its purpose, I trust." The Pale Wright fixed a stare at each of us. "There are many preparations to make, and the days left to us are few."

I tore my gaze from the faded thorn. Some part of me hoped to see it alight once more, although I knew that wouldn't happen. Whatever I had felt while it was alight was gone. It was time to deal with Dayne. "I shall be ready, as promised."

When the Pale Wright had gone, and Harlan and I were as alone as we could be in a pit beside the lair of some of the most terrible creatures on this world, he approached me, coming so close I momentarily feared he intended to plant one of those wet human lip kisses they give to each other on me. Instead, Harlan whispered, his words so quiet only a dragon could hear them.

"Too easy," he told me. "These creatures want something. They want it worse than any gambler, worse than any addict. But I don't think it is the victory you promised that they covet. It's something else."

I vowed to remember Harlan's warning as I prepared for battle once again.

This fight would be different than the ones before it—this time I wished to kill a man. But to do that, I needed my (dubious) allies in Oster.

To prepare for the forthcoming battle, I flew first to Ulibon, returning to the Twisted Keep to meet the newly-installed Highstar. Bethy Rann wasn't glad to see me again, particularly so soon, but she wasn't surprised at my arrival. I had warned her it would happen quickly. The hag, Mildred, was even less pleased by my return than Bethy Rann.

"Do my *sai* not fit?" she asked me bitterly as we stood with Rann on the northernmost tower of the Twisted Keep. "You prefer something softer for your precious claws—wool socks, perhaps?"

"I come to ask the Highstar to fulfill her promises."

Mildred didn't quit and Rann didn't silence her. "Is the Highstar now your servant, to answer the beck and call of a dragon?"

I tried to ignore the old woman's grating complaints, instead staring at Bethy Rann. "In your moment of greatest need, when your human followers scattered to the wind, abandoning you, I stayed true. I am certain you, the Highstar of Ulibon, will do no less for me."

Actually, I wasn't quite certain. Bethy Rann's rule was only days old and she had a nation to rebuild, but she didn't falter. A rare human—perhaps her link with Crema had a positive influence on her.

"I will keep my word. The honor of Ulibon shall never be compromised while I occupy the high seat."

So, I had my fleet, even if they would never actually attack Eladrell. That wasn't necessary. I just needed a credible threat, and the fear of Ulibon raids would provide that. Imagining Dayne's rage when he heard the news almost brought a smile to my eyes.

Mildred grumbled at her liege's promise, but Rann was acting in her own self-interest—which I suspected was the real reason for the ease with which she kept her promise. Tactically, it was always worthwhile to keep your enemy off balance. But even more compelling was the simple fact that Ulibon would never be safe so long as Dayne held the throne and could command slave dragons to attack her. A new king of Rolm might be willing to make peace, but for Ulibon to truly be free, the dragons had to be free as well. I would've liked to believe that Rann's love for Crema swayed her as well. She wanted to help my cause.

I left Rann to prepare her fleet, flying back to the Pits of Gargen that same day. While hardly cozy, the pits were perhaps the only place in Oster that I could be assured of avoiding detection and attack by King Dayne and his dragons. Even if Dayne thought I was still alive in the pits, it would've been madness to risk his remaining dragons to attack this place. In addition to the furies lurking in the clay flats surrounding the pits, dragons were near useless in narrow, underground tunnels.

The Pale Wrights kept away from us, but I heard activity deep in the pits during the night and even when the sun shone. Twice, I saw griffins fly from their deep lair beneath the ground, headed toward the Shard. They always flew at twilight to try to avoid detection. It seemed the last of Oster's beasts were being thrown into this effort, as well as whatever else the Pale Wrights had lurking in their subterranean lair.

Kemet returned twice more before the attack, each time with a new symbiont on his neck. Each time I saw him, his gaze had become more distant, the shading under his eyes darker. It might have been fatigue. On the last of his visits, Kemet finally shared some of the strategic thinking of Oster's commanders. The plan was a bold one. They didn't merely want to defeat the Rolman army—they wanted to crush it. To do that, they intended to destroy the Rolman supply stockpiles. It sounded like a simple idea, except that Rolmans (aside from their king) weren't fools. They knew they fought on a starving land, and so guarded their supplies—most brought by ship from Rolm —with extreme care. Part of the stockpile remained onboard six vessels moored off the coast of Oster. As the Osteran fleet had been almost completely annihilated, the ships were safe from attack, except by griffins, of which the Osterans had only a dozen remaining (no match for even a single ash dragon). The rest of the supplies were held in the ruined keep at Drell, surrounded by the main Rolman host. The castle's broken towers and walls were lined by Rolman war engines, in addition to the dragons who lounged about inside its courtyard. Destroying either stockpile, much less both, had seemed impossible for Oster only days ago. Now they had me.

King Galt might not want to acknowledge the difference a dragon ally made, but without me, they couldn't even have dreamed of achieving such a decisive blow against the enemy. I offered them superior air power, magic, and most of all, hope. Combined with the Pale Wrights' symbionts, Oster now had a chance to survive, even if it was a desperate chance. I, who had once helped try to conquer this land, prepared to save it.

"You are sure the other dragons will pursue you?" Kemet asked me. We had some variation of this conversation on each of his visits.

"If I succeed in killing Dayne, the dragons and ryders will come at me with a vengeance. If I fail to kill him, Dayne will command all his dragons to come at me."

Kemet continued to look uneasy, his lips curled. "You seem convinced of his hatred of you."

"There is no fury equal to that of a child scorned," I assured the human. "I humiliated Dayne like no other in his existence. I know his mind painfully well. His hatred will still be burning. He may also blame me for the death of his father. I am certain he will pursue me if he is able. I've told you this many times."

Kemet dug at the ground with his left foot. He did this frequently when he was uncomfortable, which he usually was when he visited. "We risk everything on your success."

"You are fortunate to even have the chance," Harlan pointed out, not rising from the rock on which he sat. "It has been days, and we've seen nothing from the Rolmans. Is that quiet typical of them?"

Kemet dug his foot deeper. "There have been periods of false calm, usually when the Rolmans were waiting for more troops or supplies. We sank one of their ships two days ago. A griffin caught it alone along the coast. Perhaps that has something to do with it." He didn't sound convinced.

"Dayne isn't patient," I said. "Now is the time to attack."

Kemet's reply was quick. "That is for King Galt to decide."

I shuffled my wings. They got dusty underground. It also made Kemet nervous when I did this. "Galt should speak to me himself."

It wasn't the first time I'd offered to meet, but this time Kemet surprised me with his answer. "It is time for that."

"Does he come here, then?"

Kemet huffed as if I'd made a ridiculous suggestion. "King Galt does not come to the Pits of Gargen."

I wondered why that was, but Kemet made it sound as if everyone, even a foreign dragon, should already know this, so instead of asking, I made a low, threatening growl, which I hoped he understood to mean the conversation was over.

The human kept talking anyway. "Galt requests that you travel to the Shard. Only there will he meet and speak."

I didn't like being ordered around. Or maybe I was grouchy from all the salted meat and tack I'd been forced to eat, to say nothing of the flatulence I'd endured from Harlan. "I am not a subject of King Galt. Even if I had knees, I wouldn't bend them."

Kemet surprised me again. "Please come." My eyes must've betrayed my feelings, for he added, "Galt will not order the attack without looking at you, not without hearing from you directly. As you have said, the Rolmans' unusual hesitation to press their advantage will not last. The Pale Wrights have sent the last of their battle-ready beasts to the Shard. All is prepared to go tomorrow, except for word from Galt. I know you owe me nothing, and you owe Oster nothing. I can only hope that there is a land you love as much as I love Oster, so I beg your help in saving this one. Do that, and you shall always have my gratitude." Inexplicably, Kemet fell to a knee before me. He looked ridiculous.

"Harlan has wretched up his dinner on the very spot on which you kneel several times," I pointed out. "You should get up."

Kemet's hurt expression made it seem like I'd smacked him with my tail.

"Don't worry. I want this over with as well. I love no land, not as you do. But I have come to understand I … love my kin. I understand my place in the fight. I will go to the Shard."

THIRTY-ONE

The Shard.

The greatest fortress on all of Inkra stood like a lynchpin of rock between the three great islands of Oster. With the tides high, it rose straight from the sea, a dazzling island tower that had defied both the sea's relentless waves as well as the hungry ambitions of the kings of Rolm. Even the fire of dragons couldn't bring down the Shard, for it was like no other place on this world.

The Shard was a three-sided mountain of translucent crystal—a giant diamond with a surface harder than rock, its sides mostly sheer, except for the great carved steps that had been chiseled by long-dead humans running upwards to a pair of great mouth-like openings in the southern and western faces of the mountain. Within the diamond peak, the humans of Oster had built their fortress-city. I'd flown inside before, braving arc-bolts, griffins, and furies. Many dragons had perished in battle beneath a bizarre light that passed through the mountain, illuminating the palace-city within. I came this time as a purported ally, escorted by four griffins from the Pits of Gargen. The griffins stank, but it didn't seem like the time to share that observation with them.

The bulk of the Rolman army was encamped in a sprawling arc surrounding the once-formidable keep at Drell, to the west of the Shard. They were too far away for a conventional siege, but the watery defenses of the Shard made normal assault tactics near impossible anyway. A second, smaller Rolman host had been positioned to the north, enabling land attack from two directions when the tides allowed it. But as always, victory would be won by the power of Rolm's dragons rather than the prowess of their land forces.

Despite the distance from Drell to the Shard, I knew that Dayne and his slave dragons would be watching the fortress, so I flew at speed with my escort to the mountain, having judged that strength was preferable to stealth. Inevitably, a dragon rose from the water's edge to challenge us. She was small—one of my horned cousins. I'd always paid less attention to my smaller brethren, but I was fairly certain the humans called her Illias. Her left wing was heavily scarred from a recently-healed wound, and her ryder looked a bit unsteady on her back, making me wonder how long the pair had been joined.

I closed on the Shard along with my feathered escorts. Approaching the mountain was dangerous—the crystalline rock had hidden crevices and tunnels where furies lurked, ready to strike. The Rolman dragons knew that as well. If I could get close enough to the Shard, I hoped to avoid a confrontation.

"Faster, you beasts," I said to the griffins. I had no idea if they understood me—if they did, they gave no sign of it. They had been given instructions—something like 'fly to the Shard with a dragon' and did the best that their limited minds could manage. As near as I could tell, griffins were like super-intelligent dogs. Unfortunately, Illias closed the distance between us quickly, even with her newly-healed wing. The griffins responded to her presence as griffins were bred to—they changed course to attack.

I gave a low growl of frustration, not just for an unnecessary fight but also because of what transpired in the sky behind Illias—ash dragons came in her wake. I needed to deal with this now, preferably without killing Illias.

"Just hold on," I told Harlan as I banked toward Illias. "Keep your daggers tucked into whatever dark places you keep them."

The horned dragon was already maneuvering for position to engage the griffins, gaining altitude as the griffins struggled to match her agility. I beat my wings, overtaking the griffins as I closed on Illias.

The horned dragon kept rising. The griffins made angry snarls behind me as they hungered for combat. Illias' ryder had a bow in hand, an arrow notched. She took aim at me, but didn't fire.

"Begone from these skies," I roared. "I've no wish to harm you."

I was speaking to my fellow dragon, but I suppose her ryder could've decided my warning applied to her as well.

The arrow stayed on the bow's string. "Come back to us, Bayloo," the ryder shouted. It was a woman's voice I didn't recognize. "Come home."

Home? Was she serious?

"Slaves have no homes. The dragon you ride is not yours, the war you fight is not of her choosing. It is you who should go home, and let your dragon's will return to her."

I knew that wasn't possible, but it felt nice to say it. If only the world could be so easy.

"You've fallen prey to spells of the Pale Wrights of Oster!" the ryder shouted back. "Shake free of their taint and return to us."

Was that the story that Dayne was peddling to explain my presence here? I wondered what he'd told my fellow dragons and their ryders. I'd expected something to do with madness, but I supposed the Pale Wrights were an easy tale to weave given that I had initially disappeared during Oster's attack on Eladrell.

Illias didn't change her course as I flew, nor did her ryder fire at me. She whispered to the horned dragon beneath her—another sign of an inexperienced ryder, since the runes permitted far more efficient communication. Still, I was ready to swerve if needed. I flexed my claws, the *sai* ready for action. But I wasn't going to kill Illias. I didn't even want to hurt her badly, so going after her wings was my best option. I needed to take her out of the sky so we could get back to the Shard before the ash dragons arrived.

I beat my wings one final time. I'd be on Illias in moments. I roared another, final warning at the ryder who controlled the horned dragon. "Be gone or be dead."

The ryder stared at me, then lowered her bow.

To my shock, Illias banked sharply, turning away from me. I slowed cautiously, changing my course to take me away from the melee. I suspected a trick, but I was willing to take the risk for the opportunity not to fight. Illias kept turning. The griffins had caught us by then, but Illias was faster if she chose to retreat.

I wondered at the strange behavior. The horned dragon was outmatched, but I'd still expected her to try to engage me long enough for the larger dragons to join the fight. Instead, Illias beat her wings, retreating toward the main Rolman camp at Drell. The ash dragons still closed, but I'd have no trouble reaching the Shard before they arrived.

I seized the opportunity to avoid a fight, even if I wasn't completely sure what it meant. With two quick flaps of my wings, I was headed toward the Shard once again. The griffins still hadn't turned back yet. They wanted to hunt dragon. Somehow, they understood I was off limits, but that didn't change their instinct to kill others of my kind. I needed to remind them of what their masters had told them.

I flew within a hair's length of one of the griffins, yanking its tail with my hind claw to remind it and its fellows to turn around as well. "To the Shard!" I roared.

One griffin turned, its teeth snapping at me, but it followed. The others fell into line shortly afterward. Ahead of us, the massive crystal mountain beckoned, its strange surface glittering with light of a hundred different colors. We were almost safe—if flying into a mortal enemy's fortress could be considered safe.

"Too easy again," Harlan muttered as I circled the crystal

fortress. Massive iron gates blocked access into the mountain. I'd once helped break through those barriers; now I waited for them to open.

"Nothing will be easy tomorrow," I assured Harlan. "Enjoy it today."

The grinding of metal punctuated my statement. The way into the Shard opened for me. I sucked in a deep breath before flying into the great cavern to meet the King of Oster.

THIRTY-TWO

The interior of the Shard dazzled.

Not in the way of other grand palaces or castles. There were no statues of gold, no great towers, no inner and outer courtyards, no great hall. None of these were needed. The only walls were those that guarded the two primary entry points into the mountain, and on those battlements bristled dozens of ballistae meant to keep dragons at bay. Except me. I was permitted to fly inside unmolested by the wary defenders of the Shard.

Instead of a central keep with great spires pointing toward the sky, the surface of the Shard's great cavern had been covered with a thin foundation of rock and soil, on which sat a collection of low-slung wooden structures, all constructed in a similar style, with flat roofs (since it never rained or snowed inside the Shard) and open courtyards at their center. The buildings were connected to each other by a series of wooden plank walkways. The entire north end of the cavern was dedicated to a sprawling garden filled with several ponds—the ultimate luxury within the crystal mountain. The flower and plant species here had been specially bred to grow in depleted soil under the diffuse glittering light that came into the

Shard. It was within this expanse of greenery that I was to meet King Galt.

The cavern interior was expansive, its ceiling soaring like a false sky. Stalactites hung from the upper surface, several so large and sharp they could impale a dragon. As I made my way to the garden, I used the opportunity to do some scouting. The Osterans were obviously preparing their attack. Griffins were lined up in pens near the massive portcullis that protected the eastern entrance to the cavern, while infantry and archers drilled in tight formations nearby. I also spotted a pack of giant war wolves, perhaps the same ones that had pestered me in the Pits of Gargen, although there were more of them here. Beside the pack huddled two hooded figures in distinctive robes of ivory that had to be Pale Wrights. The strange light within the Shard didn't seem to bother them.

I glided onto the soft grass of the gardens near a veranda that Kemet had described to me when he told me where to go to meet his king. I sniffed at my surroundings. Much of the fauna was diminutive versions of trees and plants I'd seen in Rolm, with child-sized trees that should've soared past the roof of the cavern along with bushes on which sprouted tiny roses. Narrow, rock-lined streams snaked through the carefully cultivated greenery, where no other person or creature stirred.

"He'll make us wait a bit," Harlan said as he climbed off my back onto the grass. "It's the nature of kings."

Harlan was wrong for once. Almost immediately, the ruler of Oster revealed himself, emerging from a nondescript hut without ceremony or ostentation. He was accompanied by a lone soldier attired in full mail. Had I not been told to expect King Galt, I'd not have suspected the gaunt human who strolled toward me to be someone of import. This was not the man who had been described to me. The King of Oster was supposedly a giant specimen. This person stared at me with wan copper eyes perched beneath a receding line of dusty gray hair. His shoulders were wide but meatless, causing his silk doublet to hang from him as if the clothes had once belonged to a larger, heavier man. Only a strong, double-barrel chin with the memory of a beard and the circle of gold atop his head marked this human as someone who had once been more than one amongst a crowd. That, and the rocky power of his gaze. Most humans feared dragons up close, but not Galt. He was wary, but not afraid.

Galt wore a sword at his waist, a thin blade with a pommel of what I suspected to be dragon bone. The spikes on my mane stood as I remembered this human was no friend to my kind. Although dragons had given him little reason to call us friend, either.

"You know who I am?" was his greeting. Galt's voice reminded me of two jagged stones being rubbed together.

I decided to be polite. "You are King Adulas Galt of Oster."

"That is what many call me, it is the name given to me. Dragons choose their own names, do they not?"

I wondered how he knew that. Even the other slave dragons of Rolm wouldn't have known that. "We do."

"A fine custom we humans should learn from." Galt spoke to me with ease, as if conversing with dragons was mundane to him. "It might make us more conscious of what we have actually accomplished in our lives, rather than what has been given to us." He touched the thin crown atop his head. "This has been in my family for seven generations. We ruled these islands when the first King of Rolm was just an opportunistic raider mysteriously appearing from the north. This crown came to me through blood—for only my blood can truly rule Oster in these times. But if I was to be able to choose my own name, I would have it be He Who Survived the Tide."

I flashed a dragon smile with my eyes, although I wasn't sure if Galt understood or not. "An apt name for these times. A new wave of enemies rises against you, but I am here as well. There is a chance you may emerge victorious against the wave from Rolm once again."

Galt grunted. He held out a hand indicating that his escort should approach. I belatedly realized the soldier was a human female with thick platinum hair cropped above her ears. "This is my daughter, Jalena."

I wasn't so adept with human ages, but I would've guessed Galt's daughter to be no more than seventeen or eighteen years of age, except for her eyes, which were old and weary like those of her father. And there was something else. On her neck just above the collar of her armor was a splotch of fiery red skin. Humans sometimes had strange conditions on their skin, but this looked more like a barely-healed wound.

"In troubled times, there are few to trust. I trust only my family, and all that remains of that is my daughter. Only my daughter. I cannot trust a dragon who I do not even know. My counselors such as Kemet tell me I must, but that is not so. There is always a choice." Galt's eyes challenged me.

To my surprise, I found myself liking King Galt. "I do not ask you to trust me. I, a dragon, do not trust humans." I saw Harlan's frown. "I do not trust most humans. I certainly do not trust your Pale Wrights, whatever they are. I came here to offer a bargain. I will keep my part of it, because it serves my purpose. Trust in that, if you must."

Jalena looked me up and down, evaluating, although I wasn't sure to what end. "Kemet says that you seek this aurathorn from the Pale Wrights so that you can make a magic to free your fellow dragons." Her voice was almost as graveled as her father's, but there was no mistaking its skepticism.

I willed myself to be patient with these humans. "Is that so hard to believe?"

"For generations we have fought dragons. Never has one done anything but burn and destroy in Oster. Never have we heard a whisper of this aurathorn being able to free your kin from Rolm's slavery."

"My kind are not born slaves. Indeed, the slave dragons of Rolm do not breed. In this part of the world, only on Veralon are dragons still hatched. The Sculptors of Rolm make us slaves when we are newly born. If runes of dark magic can be carved to enslave a creature, is it so hard to believe it can be undone?"

Jalena looked at her father. "And all this time, the Pale Wrights held the secret." Her eyes were angry, but I didn't think it was directed at me, or even her father.

"I know your thoughts, daughter," Galt replied. "I've had them as well. The Wrights say they know no magic, that they had no idea the vine they bred could be used for such a purpose. They claim it was a medicine for beasts. Even more, they claim no one in Oster could use this aurathorn to free dragons." His tone was neutral, but his eyes betrayed disdain. "They say only a dragon can make use of it in that way."

I spoke an obvious truth. "You do not trust the Pale Wrights."

"Slave-keepers." Jalena said her word with such venom, I'd have thought she had known shackles herself, rather than been born the daughter of a king.

Harlan noticed as well. "You hate them so, even though their beasts have helped keep Oster free?"

Something unspoken passed between the royals of Oster. I could only guess at it, although it was likely something involving their supposed ally, the Wrights. No one in Rolm had ever suspected such tension between the great powers of Oster.

Galt took control of the discourse once again. "The Wrights are indeed essential to the survival of Oster. Under constant threat of dragon attack, my family has increasingly relied upon their particular ... talents for breeding griffins and other beasts, without which Oster would've been ground into ash by Rolm long ago." He tightened his eyes, a look that merely highlighted the king's fatigue. "The great beasts they breed have helped us survive, but perhaps in other ways the Pale Wrights are not so different than the Sculptors of Rolm. They are necessary, but not desirable."

I didn't quite understand Jalena's words. Breeding and training those beasts in the pits—with the harshest of methods—could be akin to slavery, I supposed. But I wasn't here to unravel the politics of Oster.

I gave the royals of Oster a snarl and wing stretch. Neither flinched. These were not cowards. "You asked me here to see with your eyes and hear with your ears if you could trust a dragon. My magic does not include spells to make you believe that, and I wouldn't bother with such things even if I could. I came here to get this aurathorn because it may help me free my enslaved kin, and even more. I don't have the breath to explain it all, but Dayne is not the only peril to this land or this world. Still, he must die. I will do as I say. I would not have come to the Shard if it were otherwise. I would not make the offer I make to you if I had a better choice." I refolded my wings. Neither royal had moved as I spoke. "Do you still doubt me?"

Galt met my gaze. "Much like you, if I had any other choice, you would not be here. All my life I have fought dragons, and paid a heavy price for it." He and his daughter exchanged glances. "I brought you here so that I might know if there is another way, that the war with Rolm's dragons need not go on forever. That is the true knowledge I seek. In your plain talk, I believe I have gotten the truth, and thus the answer I needed. And for that chance, I will risk my life, my family's life, and Oster."

"And at the end of this, aurathorn is mine? You swear it?"

"On my blood, and that of my family, I swear it. I shall ensure this aurathorn is delivered to you. Let Oster's victory be yours. We fight a common enemy and seek a common goal."

Somehow, I believed him. I could smell Galt's longing for victory, but also for safety for his people. "When do we go?"

"When the sun rises tomorrow."

That made sense for humans, but not dragons. "Twilight is better. I can get closer without being seen, perhaps. We should go today. Your troops look ready."

"The timing is not my choice, but the choice of the Wrights. It will take time for them to lay their symbionts on the soldiers, and on the griffins. We must attack soon afterward, while the effects last." Galt released a breath. "I take no joy in waiting for what must be done. These gardens are yours till the morning. I will have food sent to you, and bedding for your companion. Kemet, too, will come with more plans. You may accept his words as mine. I must go to be with my soldiers. They deserve that much, at least, for the sacrifice they make this night."

I didn't like the delay, but I understood. I couldn't beat all of the Rolman army and all their dragons by myself. "We shall speak again when Dayne is dead."

Galt left without replying. Jalena lingered for several laden moments, as if she wanted to say something more, but changed her mind before the words came. She hurried after her father.

I wished she had decided to speak.

THIRTY-THREE

We had a plan.

Human, griffin, and dragon, all fighting together. The speed of the symbiont-enhanced humans and griffins would take the Rolman force by surprise. Oster's remaining furies would clear a path for me to the heart of the camp—to King Dayne himself. I would kill Dayne, the Rolman supply depots would be captured or destroyed, and word would arrive from Eladrell of the Ulibon fleet threatening their homeland, sending the remains of the demoralized army to flight (via dragon and ship) back to Rolm, while Harlan and I collected aurathorn. It was more of a dream than an actual plan, but it was a pleasant hope while it lasted.

Evening fell within the Shard, the light fading even as the din bouncing off the great cavern's arching ceiling intensified. Beyond the false tranquility of the garden, the remaining soldiers and beasts of Oster were being fitted with symbionts specially bred by the Pale Wrights.

I rested but I didn't sleep. I couldn't even if I had wanted to, because Harlan paced about with an anxiousness I'd not seen before. I cracked open one eye. "You've danced on the edge of the Abyss enough to know how to balance. It isn't death that troubles you, Harlan Dor. For the sake of this rare grass that grows under the twisted light of the Shard, what is it that keeps you from sitting still for even a few moments?"

"Did I keep you from your sleep?"

"Do you think I'm fool enough to sleep in this place, while armies prepare for battle? I am cautious. Your dancing about the garden is more than caution."

Harlan forced his feet to stop moving. "A good captain can smell a storm coming, even if he doesn't always know the direction."

"You don't think we are the storm?"

Kemet strode into the garden at that moment, cutting off Harlan's answer. His gait was different tonight, his shoulders slouched. For the first time since I'd met him, the soldier wasn't fitted with one of the Wrights' leech symbionts. The space on Kemet's neck where the creature had once attached looked horrific—the skin resembling an infected burn, with capillaries of ugly black expanding like a web from the contaminated center.

Kemet didn't bother with greetings or pleasantries, which I appreciated. "The night slips past too quickly. Galt asked me to attend to you, to share details of his plan for the morning. Soon, our army will be ready. He intends to lead the attack personally."

Harlan spoke before I could. "Does it hurt?"

There was no need to specify the injury. Kemet moved his hand to his neck before stopping just short. "Some, but it is a relief to be without it. I will fight with my own strength and wits tomorrow."

"Oh?"

"Apparently, the creatures become deadly if overused. I'll be slower, but that doesn't mean I'll be less dangerous. A few other soldiers have refused the symbionts as well, much to the consternation of the Pale Wrights." He managed a sickly smile.

"The berserker warriors of Tal consume giant leeches from the swamps near their home before battle. They say it gives them the ability to share their gods' strength. Yet, nothing compares with these symbionts." Harlan sounded concerned, but also impressed.

"The Pale Wrights are unrivaled breeders of the most fantastic beasts." Kemet offered the praise laced with obvious disdain. It occurred to me this was the first time I'd spoken to Kemet away from the Pits of Gargen. Here, he made no effort to hide his feelings for the strange creatures.

Harlan continued to appraise Kemet's lingering scar from the symbiont. "Bayloo has told me that the healing symbionts of the Wrights were known in Rolm, that they were sometimes given to injured soldiers or griffins in prior engagements, but there had never been anything that could strengthen a soldier. Nothing that could grant a man the endurance to run such distance as you ran, at speed and without stopping. These are new."

"It happens like that with the Wrights," Kemet replied. "They lurk underground in their pits, emerging rarely. To speak to them, one must go to their lair, and few wish to dwell in that place. Otherwise, years can pass where those ... *things* seem to accomplish nothing, then all of a sudden, they will breed a beast that changes everything: The furies. An improved griffin breed. The new symbionts."

I decided to take advantage of Kemet's candor. "Where did the Wrights come from?"

Kemet opened his mouth, then closed it again as he thought better of his initial answer. "Only Galt and the royal family know the origins of the Pale Wrights."

"Why trust such creatures?" Harlan pressed.

Kemet shrugged uneasily. "They are connected to the ruling family. More than that I cannot say, but know ... they shall always be together. Like the hilt and blade, one is part of the other, linked as a single whole."

Harlan nodded curtly. "Will Galt keep his promise to us?"

Kemet looked offended. "Galt is many things, and a hard man is one of them. But I have known him all of my life, and I've never known him to break his word. Never. He will do as he says. Of that I am sure."

After that, Kemet told us about Oster's armies. I tried to pay attention, but soldiers' formations and terrain details meant little to me. I knew what I had to do tomorrow. Instead, my mind kept wandering to other matters, to the memories of Dayne that lingered inside me. He was the last human who had tried to command me, an ugly taint that couldn't be fully cleansed.

Eventually, Kemet departed to be with his own men. Harlan stopped walking the garden incessantly for a time. We both pretended to rest in the comparative quiet, although neither of us did. But it was enough of a peaceful lull that ended with the echo of clashing steel ripping through the cavern.

"Not swords," Harlan declared, daggers already in hand, as if they'd sprouted. "Wrong sound. Too heavy. Something bigger."

Bigger indeed. Harlan hadn't been inside the Shard before, but I had. I knew the sound. "It's the gate."

Even from the garden, I could see all the way to the massive portcullis that protected the main portal of the Shard. The eastern gate had lifted suddenly, jerking upwards. Not enough to be completely open, but enough for humans to enter or exit. It could've been opened to permit a scouting party to depart, but that seemed less likely. I knew from past battles that there were other passages out of the Shard, often used by furies, single griffins, or scouts. My suspicion that something was amiss was confirmed by bells of alarm that followed. The din within the great cavern became a chaotic roar. The sound of metal striking metal echoed again. This time it was swords. Shouts followed, but something else was wrong.

Harlan noticed as well. "The area around us is strangely quiet. We are near the heart of this place. Everything is happening near the gate."

I didn't have time to ponder that particular mystery. The huge portcullis moved again, this time with deliberate purpose: it opened. Outside, dawn had not yet broken. Even over the chaos echoing off the cavern's walls, I heard the distinctive sounds of what was coming. I realized I'd been terribly mistaken about the situation I'd placed myself in. Into the Shard flew the consequences of my error.

Emerging from the curtain of black beyond, a massive dragon flew through the open gate.

THIRTY-FOUR

No one had ever conquered the Shard.

King Mendakas had come closest, with the fortress saved only by the unexpected deployment of the never-before-seen furies, as well as a generous heaping of luck. This time, Dayne's dragons entered the Shard without any answer by the defenders who should've been on the wall. I was still missing something vital, even as the battle lurched toward me.

I counted four ash dragons, along with over half a dozen horned dragons. This was likely the last of my enslaved brethren. That meant King Dayne was here as well. I guessed he'd be riding Arutel, the largest of the ash dragons among his dwindling stock. Dayne liked big things.

"If Dayne is here, perhaps there is a chance," I said, as much to myself as Harlan. "I can still kill him." Of course, I would have to contend with many dragons in a confined space.

Harlan watched it unfold. "Why do the Osterans do nothing?"

A partial answer came bounding through the well-manicured shrubbery: war wolves. The protectors of the Pale Wrights. Not just protectors, I realized. Their servants. All the beasts of Oster had been raised by the Wrights. The shivering dread of my grievous mistake swept through me as the giant wolves consumed the distance between us. The alpha was in the lead. There wasn't going to be an opportunity to talk this time. They had come to kill.

The alpha reached us first, but he was also the savviest of the pack. He feigned a leap, flexing his haunches but not putting himself into the air. The wolf I had named Dangerous back at the pits—the beast with the missing ear—was beside him and showed less caution. Dangerous jumped at me, mouth open, as if his teeth could match mine. Harlan put a dagger into the lupine's throat. The creature yelped in pain until I smashed its skull in mid-air with a foreclaw.

The surviving pack surrounded us. They were six, all hungry and ugly. I didn't want to fight them on the ground; unfortunately, the cavern was filling with hostile dragons. I also couldn't leave Harlan here—doing so would mean his death, no matter how many daggers he had hidden in his clothing. I had magic, but its usefulness was limited by the Shard. I could summon no lightning without a sky. There wasn't enough space to use wind effectively as a weapon. The alpha wolf sensed my indecision.

"The pack grows, dragon." Saliva dripped from its mouth. "No one to save you this time."

The giant wolf bounded forward, another feint. I didn't fall for it, but four other wolves came at me. I smacked one back with my tail, but two others managed to get their jaws onto my left foreleg. The teeth were sharp, but their jaws weren't strong enough to penetrate my scales. I hurled them off, sending the beasts spinning through the air. To their credit, they both landed on their legs, dashing back to the fight. I heard dragon wings. I smelled fire.

"Get out of here," Harlan said. "I can handle these."

He really couldn't. Each of the wolves was larger than Harlan, as well as faster and more vicious. I beat my wings just hard enough to send garden debris flying and lift myself off the ground. I didn't go much higher than Harlan's head. Instead of flying away, I came at the alpha, claws twitching. The wolf darted backward so quickly that I ended up with dirt and a few scrubs in my claws. Three wolves jumped on me—one on my tail, two on my rear haunch. That was just stupid. I lifted back into the air, using my tail to smash the wolf riding there into its nearest companion. Both tumbled to the ground with a pair of satisfying yelps.

The last wolf scrambled onto my back, its claws desperate for purchase on my scales. I landed hard on all fours, shaking back and forth like a wet dog. It was an indignity, but it did the trick—the last wolf leapt to the ground, scurrying away to join its chastised fellows. Dragon roars echoed all around me, the cavern amplifying the cries of a few into the sound of a hundred.

Everything was about to get worse, and I had no idea what to do. Saving Harlan and myself was the best place to start.

I feigned another attack, lurching at the alpha, then pulling back quickly, my body pressed close to the ground. Despite Harlan's earlier bravado, he wasn't fool enough to miss the opportunity to climb onto my back. The cavern's tight sky might be filled with hostile dragons, but it was still better than playing with killer wolves in the garden.

The alpha's eyes shifted as he realized we wanted to escape rather than continue the fight. He growled something to his pack as he came at us. I was certain there wouldn't be any feint this time. The alpha wanted a piece of dragon meat, but he'd also seen the failure of his fellow wolves. That made me suspect he'd go for my wings, so I spread them like bait for a hungry fish, beating them as the wolves came again, their leader in the vanguard.

I guessed correctly. As the alpha leaped at my left wing, I swung my neck around, snatching the giant wolf in my jaws mid-flight. His fur was tougher than I expected, as hard as armor, and I almost dropped him as he squirmed in my grip, claws and teeth thrashing. I lifted off the ground before the rest of the pack reached me. They jumped futilely, with only the sound of their howls able to follow me into the air. When I'd reached sufficient height, I dropped my four-legged passenger. There wasn't time to look at what became of him.

Dragons and their ryders closed in on me. The two ash dragons who had chased me into the Pits of Gargen, Cornethius and Blaris, came first, but there were other dragons in the area as well, although most of my brethren seemed busy strafing the ground in support of the Rolman soldiers that the horned dragons had carried inside the Shard. Blaris wagged her stub of a tail like an excited dog as she closed on me, but it was Cornethius who released his fire first.

The gray dragon's fire reached only the fringe of my senses, doing no harm, not even to the fragile human on my back. Blaris saved her breath until she could draw closer. I maneuvered to keep my distance as best I could within the cavern. I couldn't beat every Rolman dragon simultaneously, particularly inside this diamond mountain where much of my magic was blunted. I needed to escape, not fight.

Blaris and Cornethius also expected me to flee, perhaps because that was what they thought I did last time they'd attempted to kill me. To prevent my escape, they spaced themselves generously, cutting off any route to fly around them as they attacked from above. I didn't try to go around them—I accelerated into the gap between them. My wings propelled me upwards with desperate speed while the two dragons dove at me. They didn't expect my speed or my tactic. I was between them before they could react. Neither dragon could unleash its fire while the other dragon was on the far side of me for fear of hitting their precious mind-linked ryder. I sped above my errant kindred, turning immediately toward the Shard's eastern gate. The portal remained open, the glimmers of a new dawn inviting me to escape into the light. I flew as fast as I was able toward my only hope of survival.

Dragon roars ripped through the cavern. My brothers and sisters began breaking off their attacks on the remains of the Osteran loyalists to try to kill me. Ahead, a formation of four clustered horned dragons blocked my path. I sped through the chaotic gauntlet of smaller dragons, colliding with one, which sent me slightly off my intended course. Every dragon and every ryder now turned their attention to me. I had no doubt King Dayne was among those who sought me now. The exit neared, but it was shrinking; the gate was being lowered.

"We aren't going to make it," Harlan warned.

I beat my wings twice more. "We are."

I could see the scratched metal of the portcullis as it descended from a recess in the cavern wall above. Beyond the opening beckoned a new morning. I could see ships in the sea outside. A lot of ships, but I didn't have time to take in any more details. Harlan must've seen them as well.

"May the True Light Shine," he muttered.

There wasn't time to discuss it further. I passed over fighting between human armies just inside the gate. I didn't have time to sort it out. The opening narrowed desperately.

"Bayloo, you can't."

Harlan sounded worried. I didn't want him to be right about our predicament, but he was.

The massive steel gate slammed shut.

THIRTY-FIVE

There was no way out.

Both gates of the Shard were shut. Perhaps, given time and magic, I could've blasted an opening, but Rolm's dragon army closed on me.

My brethren came in waves. At the leading edge were the dragons Blaris and Cornethius, determined as ever to finally catch me. But another had joined them, a larger dragon encased in crimson scales tinged with gold: Arutel. I already knew the ryder before I saw him. The human wore a helm that matched the glittering metallic shade of his dragon, the top ringed by an ebony circle that resembled a painted crown. Among ryders, only Dayne would bother with such a showpiece. I could still feel the touch of my old ryder's mind—dark and twisted. The runes were gone from my chest, but somehow the residual binding of the link was still there. It seemed one of us had to be dead for us to be truly separate. I intended to arrange that.

There was no magic that could defeat so many of my kin, but I didn't have to die right now either. I willed my mind to relax, to find the Latticework. I reached for the Chord that controlled the sky far beyond the diamond walls of the Shard. The mountain surrounding me made it more difficult to manipulate the Latticework, but I still had enough control to call lightning. There was no way to get the bolts into the cavern, but I did the next best thing—I directed the strikes into the mountain itself.

With a suddenness that I hoped caused King Dayne to wet his pants, flashes of brilliant light smashed into the Shard's outer shell. The rumble of thunder echoed, reverberating inside the mountain. The unexpected eruption of light and fury sent blinding flashes cascading along the walls and ceiling of the cavern. The dragons swerved at the unexpected eruption; humans gasped. For a few precious moments, no one focused on me. I made the most of the brief window of confusion: I flew at King Dayne.

I knew his dragon, Arutel. My brother was quick, strong, and temperamental. Even when linked to a poised and experienced ryder, Arutel was prone to erratic actions. With Dayne on his back, he was unpredictable. Ryders were selected for their poise, but Dayne wasn't a true ryder. When the soft gloom of the cavern abruptly transformed to an exploding sun of brightness, Dayne panicked. His emotion fed to Arutel, who instinctively climbed for clouds and safety, but those didn't exist in the confined cavern. The other dragons behaved more sensibly, slowing themselves or taking evasive action that didn't put their ryders at risk. Arutel and Dayne briefly separated themselves from the larger formation. I flexed my *sai* as I closed the distance.

Arutel sensed me coming. I wanted to get above him, to strike at Dayne, but the big dragon reared up and away as I approached. I didn't have enough room to get into position without hitting the stalactites that lined the top of the cavern. Instead, I pressed in ever closer, close enough to get a claw on Dayne. The king shrieked with concerned rage even before I reached him and his dragon. Arutel twisted his neck to block my attack, leaving himself unnecessarily vulnerable to protect his ryder. I could've killed my brother with the *sai* at that moment, but I didn't come here to kill dragons. Unfortunately, leaving Arutel in prime fighting condition while he was linked to Dayne would've been stupidly naive as well. I compromised, sweeping across Arutel, gashing his chest with my tipped hind claws. He roared in fury as the *sai* cut into his scales.

King Dayne had some words as well, his shout as penetrating as a dragon's roar. "Bayloo the traitor! Die, now!"

My former ryder's voice dripped with the arrogance of triumph. I flew past Arutel, my chance for an easy kill gone. Harlan flicked a dagger as we flew, the blade spinning end over end in the air, curving at just the right moment to avoid Arutel's huge form while it sought his ryder. For a precious moment, I had hope, but Arutel saw the danger. The nimble dragon responded by whipping his tail into the dagger's path. Close, but not enough. I was back to avoiding and fleeing.

Dragons came at me once again. I moved too desperately to take note of their identities. I recognized the fire of Cornethius, the claws from Oton, and the ugly snout of a horned dragon I once knew as Ren. I wove and dodged, executing a precarious dance in the restricted sky of the cavern. Soon my body ached with the burn of exhaustion, and a dozen nicks marred my scales. All the time, I was pursued by Dayne's cackling voice, exhorting others to kill me, mutilate me, and engage in other unpleasantries. Eventually, the dragons were going to catch me. I couldn't keep this up.

"By the Guiding Star, there is hope," Harlan shouted at me as the mixed quartet of horned and ash dragons came at us once again. His optimism at this moment grated. I didn't have time to answer. A horned dragon flew up at me, its ryder sending arrows at my belly. I turned in one direction, then spun away from Blaris' fire as she flew past me.

Harlan kept shouting. "Back toward the gate."

I just did it. There wasn't anything to lose. Maybe Harlan had seen something, but I couldn't really fathom how we were going to escape this mess. More dragons came at me. At least one—maybe Oton—got a claw onto one of my wings, but it wasn't enough to slow me down, at least not yet. I dove toward the ground to avoid Cornethius once again. He turned tightly behind me to pursue, two

other horned dragons joining him. I flew over the interior fortifications of the Shard, where there had been fighting earlier, intending to
reach the edge of the cavern and hug its wall back upwards to escape
my current batch of pursuers.

The distinctive sounds of arc-bolts being hurled into the sky
erupted beneath me. I swerved instinctively, but the projectiles
weren't intended for me. A dozen bolts rose simultaneously. A
horned dragon cried out in pain as a projectile hit, while Cornethius
took two direct hits to his armored belly.

It took a moment for my frantic mind to puzzle out what had
happened, but once I spotted Kemet among the ballistae, I understood. It seemed a group of Osteran soldiers had won back control of
a portion of the Shard's fortification. Rolman troops were arrayed
below. There were only thirty or forty human soldiers around Kemet
—hardly enough to hold back the Rolman army, much less all the
dragons.

"Kemet cannot help us," I growled at Harlan.

"We should help him."

He'd urged me here for that?

I twisted my neck around for one more look at Kemet and his
little salient of Osteran loyalists. They had a decent position, seemingly in control of a fortified tower housing several ballistae. The
immediate problem wasn't the Rolman soldiers on both sides of their
position (although that was going to be an issue); more urgent was
Blaris, who was on course to incinerate the Osterans with a belch of
fire. I twisted my body into a sharp turn, heading back toward Kemet.
He'd tried to help me, so I should return the favor, even if we'd both
end up in the Abyss soon enough.

"Bayloo ... back at Maricopa ..." Harlan's words failed him. "I was
wrong. I—"

He didn't finish, and I didn't have time to listen to a story.

Blaris was going to reach Kemet before I did, so I let out a mighty
roar to draw her attention. One glance at me flying directly toward

her was enough to draw the dragon's ire. I'd escaped her claws too many times for Blaris to miss the opportunity.

You're welcome, Kemet.

I'd gotten too close to avoid Blaris. She didn't bother with fire. It was to be jaws and claws. I switched directions at the last moment, feigning a turn, but diving instead. It didn't work. Blaris got a claw on my back, followed by a jaw on my neck. I smashed my tail into Blaris' underbelly. She didn't budge. We were both still using our wings, but our deadly embrace was sending us toward the ground anyway. I whipped my tail again, this time trying to hit Blaris' ryder, but he was too far out of range. Harlan might've thrown a dagger—I couldn't quite see.

The ground was coming. I hoped Harlan had the good sense to hold on. I beat my wings to try to cushion the impact, as did Blaris. The ground called.

We came down atop one of the square wooden buildings. The structure's thin roof collapsed under our weight. Despite my efforts to cushion the fall, Harlan fell from my back at impact, but the crash also enabled me to rip my neck free from the jaws holding me. I swiped a *sai* across Blaris' leg, hit her in the neck with my tail, then jammed another *sai*-tipped claw into her wing, punching a hole that would make flying difficult. Blaris' jaws snatched at me again, but I danced backward and she ate some air instead. I needed to get back into the sky. If I stayed here, all the dragons would be on me.

Where was Harlan?

I saw only debris and Blaris in the vicinity, and I didn't have time to search. He'd be safer on the ground anyway. Maybe a single human could escape in the confusion of the battle. At least he'd have a chance. I beat my wings, but I couldn't get away in time.

A wave of dragons came from both sides, clogging the air above me. There were so many. There was no point. No one could fly through what awaited, not even me.

Dayne flew to the forefront, gazing down at me with malevolence as Arutel circled above. I felt his hate as clearly as I saw it. "You've learned some tricks, but it is not enough. You die with the last defenders of Oster."

I pushed my will at him, a will countless times stronger than when he once tried to master me. "You are a slave keeper with a heart of black. Every ryder here is a slaver. Yet I am more, and they shall all be like me."

The King of Rolm shrieked with rage, inside and out. "Die!"

Harlan chose that inopportune moment to appear, popping up from a pile of rubble, a gash on his head, as if he'd been waiting for just this chance to get himself killed. "Wait!"

The fool was looking right at me, waving his hands in the air as if trying to get my attention. Harlan seemed intent on denying me even a dignified death.

"No, no, no!" Harlan's screams were frantic as he ran in my direction. It occurred to me he might not have been speaking to me, but rather someone behind me.

I turned so that I could see what Harlan was seeing.

It made no sense. A group of humans advanced in tight lines from the eastern gate. It wasn't Kemet or his men. These newcomers had skin of gold-tinted ebony like Harlan, and all held long staffs, the tips pointed toward us. Behind them, the eastern gate was open. What—

Explosions as loud as an erupting inferno mountain ripped through the cavern. The Shard flashed white. Putrid smoke inundated the air. The world stopped in the wake of violent concussions.

Dragons started falling from the sky.

THIRTY-SIX

Inferno staffs weren't just a legend.

Nor were the great ships of the Farlighters, which could ply even the shallowest waters, such as the Shifting Straits of Oster. Nor was the Farlighters' hatred of dragons. It was a lot of truth to learn in a few devastating moments.

The Farlighter fleet must've sailed in from some location off the coast of Oster as the battle began, trailing the Rolman dragons. It would've been easy to spot the assault as dragons swarmed the sky, then to exploit the singularly unique vulnerability of both the Osterans and the Rolman dragons. At no other time could the Farlighters have ambushed all of the dragons together in such a confined space. It was the perfect opportunity for slaughter.

The inferno staffs were devastating weapons, tools of death like no other human creation. Although they looked superficially like a regular iron staff, their innards were hollow. When triggered, the tubes emitted a sharpened metal projectile that flew with such extreme force that it could pass through dragon scale as if our armor were mere cloth. Seeing the weapons' awesome power, I would have assumed they were creations of some powerful enchantment, but the

Latticework told me otherwise—nothing about the inferno staffs had been altered by any magical means I could detect. The terrifying explosions, as well as the deadly force of the staff projectiles, seemed to be the product of human ingenuity. Their so-called dark light might be lost, but the Farlighters still knew how to kill.

The first, shocking fusillade had knocked nearly half of my brethren from the sky, the projectiles blasting holes in their wings and flesh. Those of my brethren still able to fly rallied against the new arrivals. I wanted to join them. I intended to join them. That was my instinct; the Farlighters were slaughtering us. We were all dragons. Harlan restrained me with screams, then by wrapping himself around my hind leg.

"Bayloo, you must not. There is another way. Don't go against them!"

I hesitated, my wings spread, but I stayed on the ground. That saved my life.

The attacking dragons, many of them already wounded by hits from the inferno staffs, flew at the Farlighter formation. I anticipated more explosions, but there were none. Apparently, the inferno staffs needed to be reloaded in some way. It was an opportunity for the dragon ryders. My kin were disorganized from the initial devastation, but it would take only one ash dragon to end the battle. King Dayne still rode Arutel, flying above the fray, shouting to kill, although he himself didn't seem anxious to be in the vanguard.

Cornethius had survived the initial assault. He came in a steep angle at the Farlighter line. Flame erupted from his mouth. The Farlighters scattered. Whatever the power of their weapons, they were humans, and humans burned. But the haphazard dragon counter-attack didn't anticipate that the Farlighters had a reserve. A second line of inferno-armed fighters scrambled into position behind the first line, knelt, then fired their weapons in unison.

The cavern shook from the reverberating explosion. My bones trembled. The scent of fire and poison infested the air. When the smoke cleared, there was still more horror to behold. Never had so many dragons fallen in so short a time. It was an unfathomable tragedy, one that shredded me inside. I couldn't dwell upon the loss. Even faced with such horror, my kin didn't quit.

As he fell from the sky, Cornethius stretched his neck toward the Farlighters, spreading his bloodied wings to direct the path of his fall. He came fast and with fury. A great wave of fire spread across the land beneath him, engulfing dozens of Farlighters in burning death. I had no pity for them. Cornethius hit the ground hard, but I had survived worse falls. That was what I had to tell myself.

Cowardice kept King Dayne unscathed. Arutel was one of only three dragons still in the sky, and the others were horned dragons who couldn't breathe fire (not that there was anything wrong with that). The Farlighters had suffered grievously. Only a handful were still upright. One of them was a woman—a striking one, with shoulders as broad as any male soldier. She had tight, braided hair, highlighted by silver streaks as brilliant as Rinxia's scales. Harlan's eyes fixed upon her. There seemed to be something wrong with him as he gaped, his heart beating erratically. Arutel saw the woman as well— she had a presence that drew eyes toward her, even at a distance, although her own attention was on the carnage of her people. Arutel dipped his wing, his crimson-tinted eyes hungry for vengeance. The Farlighter woman held no weapon that I could see.

"Go!" Harlan spoke in a whisper that was somehow as loud as any dragon's roar in my mind. He was on my back so quickly he might have been there all along. I was in the air a moment later. I came at Dayne. Whatever had happened here, as much as I still didn't understand, I knew that killing Dayne still mattered.

I soared upwards, but it was quicker going down than up, so Arutel had the advantage. Dayne's dragon opened his jaw, the muscles in his chest and neck contracting as he readied his fire. The silver-streaked woman saw the dragon above her. She could've tried to run, or dove out of harm's way—it probably wouldn't have worked, but most humans would've made the effort. She didn't. Instead, she fell onto the ground, placing her body over one of the wounded Farlighters beside her, choosing to be a sacrificial shield.

Harlan saw it too. "Bayloo, save her!"

I did, and it hurt.

With a beat of my wings, I flew right at the human, toward the remaining Farlighters armed with their inferno staffs. That was crazy stupid, but there was something in Harlan's voice that made me do it anyway—desperation. I think I had to do it. Arutel released his fiery spit before I could arrive, but the tiny fraction of time it took for the flames to move from him to his victim was enough for me to insert myself into the fire's path. I took the heat on my head initially, then rolled to let the thicker scales on my belly absorb the rest. My position and Harlan's enchanted cloak protected him.

When Arutel's breath had ended, he roared his displeasure. However, my desperate tactic had put me directly in his flightpath. Arutel had momentum and speed. I tried to yank myself out of the way, but there were limits to even my ability to maneuver. Arutel's hind claws wrapped around my neck as the great dragon accelerated past me. He didn't penetrate my scales, but he didn't need to do that. We both flew at high speeds in different directions, but he had a tight grip around my neck.

In a desperate moment, I tried to slow myself. My partial success was the difference between a snapped bone and mere agony, as my neck was contorted in a most undesirable manner. Arutel dragged me through the cavern. It was a terrible position to be in—if I tried to break free, I would end up severing my own neck; to keep myself alive, I had to use my own wings to keep pace with Arutel, matching every maneuver, every turn and dive, as he flew around the Shard, trying to get me to help kill myself. Dayne cackled like a deranged hyena as we flew our lethal dance.

Arutel had a firm grasp on me, and I couldn't reach him, not with my tail or my foreclaws. Nor could I concentrate sufficiently to reach the Latticework while flying for my life—and I couldn't really think of a way magic could get me out of this in any case. It would've been so easy if I'd been a fire breather. As adept a flier as I was, Arutel was eventually going to kill me. Sooner than that.

Arutel executed a sharp turn. I contorted my body to match both his speed and direction as best I could. Quickly, the other dragon dove toward the ground. Again, I followed. Dayne glanced at me, laughing, as if my death pushed the destruction of much of his army from his memory. My impotence at being unable to end this farce hurt almost as much as my neck. Arutel pulled out of his dive, doubtlessly preparing for another maneuver. For a brief moment, Arutel and Dayne passed beneath me. My hearts thundered. Harlan leapt from my back, falling head first. He dove along my neck line, aiming for the dragon and ryder as they passed below. It was crazy and desperate, but so were we.

Dayne saw him—his head jerked upwards—but I don't think he really believed what he saw. That was understandable, because as a rule, humans don't fly. Dayne didn't react in time, and that allowed Harlan to crash into the King of Rolm. Harlan's strong arms wrapped around Dayne in an unfriendly embrace before the king was able to get a weapon in hand. Harlan twisted Dayne from his saddle, breaking the straps. Dayne cried out, enraged and terrified. With a great heave, Harlan hauled the struggling King of Rolm to the precipice of death.

Arutel felt his master's distress. The dragon released me as we swerved violently, but Harlan kept his balance. Arutel's tail snapped around; the tip reached Harlan's waist, toppling him. The smuggler didn't release Dayne as they fell onto Arutel's backside, but the unexpected attack allowed the boy-king to climb on top of Harlan. With characteristic brutality, Dayne smashed the base of his palm into Harlan's face. It was a solid hit. Harlan was momentarily stunned. Dayne's right hand flashed to his side, to the hilt of a curved dagger at his waist. Glinting steel came out, but by that time I was ready. My neck bones throbbed in agony, but without Arutel's claws on me, I could outfly him or any other dragon (except maybe Rinxia). I'd been accelerating behind Arutel as

Harlan and Dayne fought. As Dayne's dagger moved in his hand, so did my foreclaw.

Just as I was about to skewer the King of Rolm, Arutel sensed the danger and twirled his body. I missed Dayne, and he missed stabbing Harlan. Instead, Arutel's desperate maneuver sent his ryder flying from his back and into a precipitous fall. Somehow, Harlan held onto Arutel's saddle.

Dayne's linked dragon yelped in panic, diving to save his human. I was faster and more ruthless, grabbing Arutel on his back with one *sai*-tipped claw, then two. The enchanted tips dug into him, giving me a firm hold. I could've hurt Arutel, but there was no need. Instead, I used my leg to shove him off course. At the same time, I used his weight to propel myself ahead to reach Dayne, who'd gone unconscious with terror as he fell toward his end. I didn't let the King of Rolm splatter. I wanted something before he died.

I grabbed my former ryder out of the air almost gently, cradling him between my foreclaws. With Dayne secure, I flew upwards, fast enough to keep Arutel from closing the distance between us, Harlan clinging to the hostile dragon's saddle. As I hoped, King Dayne's eyes fluttered open. He was dazed at first, but quickly his eyes bulged as his mind awakened. Fear surged through him, a fever so intense I felt it as well. I let him marinate in his fright as I soared through the air.

"How did you get here?" I asked him. "How did you enter the Shard?"

Dayne's indignity returned, as did his entitlement and the delusion that went along with it. "They wanted me here. They recognized me as a true king, not like that doddering old man, Galt."

"Who wanted you here?" I demanded.

Dayne seemed confused. "All of them. All the people of Oster except those few sycophants around their dying ruler. They wanted me."

Arutel's desperate wings neared. Harlan's shout rang from nearby. Something about destiny. I swept into a tight circle. I wanted more time. "Who told you about the people of Oster's sudden love for you?"

Dayne's jaw hardened. I released my grip on him, allowing him to fall—just a little—before grabbing him again.

He screamed out his answer. "The Pale Wrights. The true power in Oster. They sent an emissary. They told me."

That made more sense. I had what I wanted. This human was useless. "You have brought all of Rolm to ruin. Everything your ancestors built, gone in a day."

King Dayne knew no remorse. "I had the right!"

I dropped him. Arutel roared, diving, desperate to save his master. My brother's cries were so heartfelt that I had pity for him. As fast as he was, Arutel wasn't quick enough. I'd made sure of that. All it took was a thud; King Dayne entered the Abyss and the world was a slightly better place. An uncomfortable splinter in my mind to which I'd become unwittingly accustomed died with Dayne. I was completely free of the runes that once bound me. No creature, no human or dragon, was my master.

I enjoyed that fleeting moment, until the violent percussion of an inferno staff cut through my bliss. Arutel shuddered in flight.

The projectile grazed his ribs, then passed through his wing. The hit might not have been catastrophic if the dragon hadn't already been diving, desperate to try to save his doomed ryder. Wounded, Arutel lost whatever remaining control he still had over his flight path. His low altitude probably saved two lives—his and Harlan's.

Arutel tumbled into the side of a wooden building, taking down a wall in the process. As I flew above him, his flailing tail told me he was alive. Harlan had been thrown, but was blessed with the luck of fools—landing in a small artificial lake located in the interior courtyard of the grand building he'd crashed into. He was already pulling himself ashore when I landed beside the water.

I was relieved to see him. "Fortunately, you swim better than you fly."

Water dripped from his hair, past his eyes. "Bayloo, my people are here. I suspected it might be them back in Maricopa. The signs were there. I just ..." He trailed off as he stared at the new arrivals entering the courtyard. There were five Farlighters with inferno staffs. The woman with the silver-streaked hair was among them. Harlan stared at her and she stared back. It was a heavy, elongated moment of disbelief shared between the pair.

Then, as if an invisible wall collapsed, Harlan galloped out of the water toward her. So many emotions flashed on the woman's face as Harlan dashed toward her, splashing and dripping, that I couldn't begin to discern them all. Certainly there was joy, but also other, more complicated things that I, a non-human, didn't fully under-stand. Maybe sadness.

The pair embraced, breaking the tension. Harlan broke away, stared at the woman's face, then pressed his lips onto hers. It appeared as though he was trying to suck the contents of her skull out through her mouth, but she didn't seem to mind. The woman's companions grinned and hooted with laughter.

When Harlan was finally finished, the woman appeared unharmed, if a bit flushed. He turned to me, then back to the woman.

"Bayloo, this is my wife."

THIRTY-SEVEN

Harlan's wife was named Norta.

She was the leader of the Farlighters. Not just these Farlighters who had come to Oster to kill my kin, but all of them, everywhere. Or at least those who still acknowledged the authority of the so-called First Voice, as they called Norta. And it turned out that Harlan hadn't tried to suck the inside of her skull into his mouth. They had been kissing because they missed each other, or something like that. Harlan told me it was complicated; I was happy to abandon the subject of human mating rituals.

I didn't like Norta. First and foremost, she had intended to kill me. Harlan had stood in front of me, arms extended, swearing every curse a sailor could muster as the Farlighters pointed their inferno staffs at me. As shields went, Harlan was lousy, being far too small and far too soft, but his words temporarily stayed the humans' killing instinct.

"Bayloo is the reason I'm here. He is an ally, true of heart, true of purpose."

"He. Is. A. Dragon," Norta pointed out, as if her husband was bereft of his senses. Harlan's fellow Farlighters showed none of his playful banter, none of his merriment, at least not as far as I could detect. Maybe Norta was more fun at other times, but she took killing dragons very seriously, so I wasn't seeing that better side of her.

"He saved my life many times over. I owe him a life debt."

Norta wasn't swayed. "That is between you and the dragon. I have a duty to our people. Dragons are of the Change. They destroyed our homes, laid a curse on our people. They are our enemies."

I wasn't sure what the Change was, but there was no mistaking the hate in Norta's voice when she proclaimed my kind the enemy of her people.

"Bayloo is different from the others. He is free." No one moved. Harlan tried a different approach. "Without him, you will never get aurathorn."

That got their attention. Norta held up a hand and the warriors at her back relaxed ever so slightly. They didn't lower their weapons, however.

"We took these." Norta reached into a weathered leather satchel she wore across her chest and withdrew two dry needles—pieces of aurathorn that had once glowed, but were now inert like the one the Pale Wright had shown us. "For generations we have searched. Finally, it is *here*." Norta's voice had a fervent tremble that always meant trouble.

My understanding of the situation came frustratingly slowly, but it was coming. The Farlighters had sailed here for aurathorn. That wasn't hard to guess, even before Norta held out her spoiled prize. By now I knew enough of Harlan's people to know the importance they placed on this item. Harlan hadn't been the only captain looking. When it became nearly certain that they had located the source, the Farlighters must have come with their ships. They had been to Maricopa searching for it. We had looked too hard for an alternate explanation.

Like Harlan and I, the Farlighters must have found clues about aurathorn on Maricopa. Those had sent them elsewhere. Maybe to

Ulibon, or Rolm, but eventually those clues led them here to Oster. They had seen the dragons of Rolm, their siege of the Shard. Perhaps they could sense aurathorn in some way. The battle, with all of Rolm's dragons in one confined space, had been the perfect opportunity to achieve a slaughter. Norta was a killer, and I was having my doubts about Harlan as well, even though he seemed to be trying his best to save me. But I wasn't going to rely on him.

"You took those depleted thorns from the Pale Wrights," I told her. The Wrights' must've had some use for them here. "I saw two robed creatures in the Shard earlier."

Norta's lips parted in surprise as I spoke, but only for a moment. "The dragon speaks." She said it mostly to herself. "And what is this you say? Pale Wrights?" She huffed out a single chuckle, as if the creatures were some kind of bitter joke. "Is that what they are called here, then? I suppose it is as good a description as any."

Even if she hadn't wanted to kill me, I would've been annoyed at her snooty, superior tone. I blew some wet drizzle out of my snout as well. "What name would you prefer?"

"If I had to name those creatures, I would call them the dead, for that is what they should be, but they cheated that fate. We know their kind as Shades, but the name does not matter. We didn't know any still existed. Indeed, it is puzzling they still survive ..." Norta's voice trailed off for a moment, before her hard gaze locked again upon me. "In any case, you are correct, dragon. We delivered the creatures the true death they had avoided, and found these. Now, if you want to tell me something useful, you can tell me where the source is? Where are the founts from which these thorns grew?"

I knew where aurathorn was, of course (unless the Wrights had lied, which wasn't impossible, because they had clearly lied about important things like intending to betray their king). Harlan knew as well, but he didn't speak. But he also clearly hadn't told me everything about his people. He told stories, but the hunger in these people to kill dragons and find aurathorn was far more intense than his words conveyed. Giving the Farlighters aurathorn had been such a distant prospect, an ancient quest that seemed to have nothing to do with my own noble goals of freeing my fellow dragons and destroying the rust. Now, having met the Farlighters, who were considerably less pleasant humans than Harlan, I wasn't inclined to let them have it.

"Why do you want aurathorn so badly?" I stretched my neck forward, to see if Norta would flinch as my jaws came closer. She didn't move. Her fellow Farlighters kept pointing their weapons, however. "Why sail across Inkra, why use these weapons that had become distant legends ... all for a flower?"

Norta's face actually softened, although I wondered if that was a deliberate decision on her part. I suspected that she was a far better card player even than Harlan. "I'm surprised my husband has not already told you. He does enjoy telling a story." She smirked, a gesture I thought genuine. "My people hold to a dream that we may one day reclaim our home and lift the curse that afflicts our people. We know that quest may seem silly to others, but it is a dream that unites us, moves us forward. It is at the core of who we are. And, yes, dragon, for that I was willing to sail our last, greatest fleet to this desolate place that is almost unknown to the rest of the world, and use weapons that we would've preferred the world forget."

The inferno staffs.

"Weapons meant to kill dragons," I said. The other Farlighters tensed at my words. I knew Harlan wanted to kick me for making the accusation in this situation, but there was no point in delaying this confrontation. If I was to die (or be forced to kill these people), let it happen now.

"That is not their original purpose. The weapons ... and other items we once possessed, were created to help us survive in the darkest days, when my people were hunted, when Sci-Ance failed, and our existence was threatened. Our ancestors created these things with the last of their strength, so that their children might survive in the twisted world that we came to know as Inkra. We are refugees, a people without a home, who live on ships. These inferno staffs, as they are now called, the legend of them has helped keep our people safe." Norta stared at Harlan for a long moment, and I had no doubt a great deal was communicated in those brief glances. "I, and I alone, gave the order for the remaining inferno staffs to be used. You may hate me for that, dragon. I see that my husband thinks it a grievous mistake. If so, it will not be my first. You may even wish to kill me. But I ask you, was there any other way to defeat the mad king of Rolm and his dragons?"

We both already knew the answer, so I didn't reply.

"My order saved your life, and it saved Harlan's life. Some dragons were killed, yes, but many will live. The inferno staffs fire a powerful projectile called a piercer at high speed that can penetrate armor, or even a dragon's scale. It damages, but by itself, it is not usually lethal, given the healing prowess of your kind. Indeed, as we speak, our time here runs short. Decisions must be made quickly."

She lost me on that. "What do you mean?"

"Even with the death of their king, the Rolman survivors begin to rally, their dragons stir and recover their senses. There are also the beasts bred by the Shades to contend with, and even soldiers of Oster, all within this mountain. My people are comparatively few, our weapons all but exhausted. I have gambled all of our strength to finally get aurathorn, but it is not here, except for a pair of depleted thorns. We must retreat or start killing." In a fleeting instant, Norta dropped her mask of control to show me a deep weariness in her eyes. Or at least she pretended to show me her feelings. "I would see an end to killing, if I can. But I will not leave here without aurathorn."

I mulled Norta's unpleasant words. She was right that there would be casualties among the dragons, and each of those was a wound to my soul, but many would survive. With Dayne dead, someone eventually would take command. Yet, I wasn't ready to help this woman either. Harlan knew me well enough to realize that. He found his voice, although he didn't sound quite himself as he spoke.

"Bayloo, there is much that Norta knows that I do not. She is the keeper of the lore of our people. I can only say this: I married a woman of pure heart. She will not lie to you, and she will always make the decisions that she believes are right."

"You named me a friend, but you are a human of Farlight before everything else," I accused him bitterly.

Harlan sighed heavily with regret. "Bayloo, I am your friend. You have my oath on it. I don't need you to trust me completely. I just need you to trust me enough to give Norta more time."

"How much time?" I demanded.

Norta spoke again. "Let us retreat from this place, this Shard of theirs. The impregnable fortress can also become a prison. We will leave, closing those mighty portcullises behind us, but depart no further. We will hold the gates only, trapping all within this cavern, at least for a time. So that we may decide how best to act."

It was an interesting idea, and one that appealed to me. It would keep the dragons in one place, safe to heal—until I could get to aurathorn. And I intended to get it, one way or another. No human was going to stop me. But there was an obvious flaw in Norta's plan.

"Your few Farlighters can't hold the gates against dragons, against a Rolman army, against whatever else the Osterans have left. Not even for a short time, not if your inferno staffs are as limited as you say."

Norta smiled. "Not just us. I've been offered an alliance. And a tantalizing promise as well."

Galt's daughter Jalena stepped out from the rubble of a building behind the Farlighters. "I rule Oster now. These people have helped us defeat the army of Rolm, even if they did so for their own purposes. Now there is a chance to save Oster as well. My father's promise to you still stands, Bayloo. Help us win this war, and we will get you aurathorn."

THIRTY-EIGHT

Jalena explained what had happened.

We spoke outside the Shard, with the waters of the Shifting Straits around us, our feet and claws planted on one of the tenuous causeways of coarse sea rock upon which humans had laid brick and mortar, so that when the tides cooperated, they could travel by land to and from the Shard. Norta's Farlighter ships, seven in all, hovered on the sea nearby. They were sleek vessels, long and low in the water, with triangular masts and sharp bows that apparently enabled them to traverse great distances and shallow waters at speed. Harlan kept glancing toward the vessels, longing in his eyes. Norta's attention remained fixed upon me, while I kept glancing with trepidation at the closed gates of the Shard, which was now a prison for my fellow dragons.

"The Pale Wrights did it." Jalena spat at the end of her declaration. She stood with her back to the Shard, facing Norta, Harlan, and I. Kemet and his surviving men remained within the Shard, holding the now-closed gates. "They betrayed us. Their marvelous symbionts were a trick. When placed upon our soldiers or our remaining loyal griffins or furies, they didn't enhance anything—they paralyzed us, leaving our army helpless against the Rolmans. The Pale Wrights then arranged to open the gate to allow our enemies inside the fortress."

"The symbiont worked for Kemet," I pointed out.

"That was a demonstration of proof for my father. He never trusted the Pale Wrights. One was real, the rest were false, intended to leave us at the mercy of the Wrights and their new allies from Rolm."

"Why would they betray you to King Dayne?" I wondered. "He is worse than a butcher. Whatever your difference with the Pale Wrights, they assisted you for centuries, since even before I graced this world."

Norta nodded at my words. "Those creatures ... they are loyal to nothing but themselves. They cared for nothing but their own survival. So it has been for centuries."

Jalena rubbed one arm with her hand, making no effort to hide her discomfort. Once again, I was struck at her pallor, despite her youth. "We ... our family, we have that which they most desire. That which they cannot live without." She shuddered. There were dark tidings here. "For those long years, the Wrights were satisfied with the arrangement. But the victories of Rolm, and our own increasing desperation, finally changed their minds."

The chill of dread hung in the air as Jalena spoke. Harlan asked what we were all wondering: "What is it creatures such as those value?"

Jalena pulled down her high collar to reveal ugly red wounds along her neck and upper chest—holes and gashes. She revealed similar markings when she pushed up her sleeves. Some of the wounds were bruised and purple, others angry red with infection. I remembered the marks I'd seen in the garden, and the fatigue that hung about Jalena and her father. "The blood of our family has something special in it. Only our family. It is sustenance for the Pale

Wrights—their only food. It sustains them. As they age, they decay, they grow ever more sensitive to the light of day, but so long as they have our blood, the Pale Wrights endure. Perhaps forever, perhaps not, but at least for many human lifespans. My great-grandfather's diary describes certain of the Wrights whom it seems we still deal with today. As time passes, some of them can't even leave the pits in which they dwell, so sensitive have they become to sunlight. In exchange for our blood, they breed their creatures, raise them, and give them to us. To keep Oster safe. That is the sacrifice of my family, for our people."

Harlan's lips turned downward in disgust. "Those creatures must truly value their pathetic lives if that was all they fed upon."

"Human blood tastes bland and sour," I agreed. Everyone gaped at me.

Norta frowned. "These Wrights, they are doubtless descendants of beings our lore speaks of. Their type is even older than the Cataclysm. Once they were human, like us. Some even dwelled on our island of Farlight for a time, which is how we know them. They were obsessed with one thing: immortality. All of their energies were devoted to it. It was their religion, their god. The Shades, as we call them, lived only to live more, using all manner of devices and powers to achieve this. But when the Cataclysm came, their efforts became useless. The immortality-seekers perished without the great light, without their manufactured implements to sustain their frail bodies." Norta paused, reflecting. "But there were stories that some among them adapted to the new world after the Change, turning to ever-darker methods to keep themselves alive. If you call what they have life. It seems they were not all stories." She peered at Jalena. "Your family must have an interesting history to explain the potency of your blood. Quite interesting."

Jalena's jaw hardened in a manner that made me suspect that there were secrets she wasn't inclined to share, with Norta or anyone else.

"If Rolm won this battle, how did that help the Wrights?" I wondered. "Dayne isn't the type to share his blood, and it sounds as if it would be useless anyway."

Jalena scoffed bitterly. "To keep Oster safe, my family had to offer their blood to the Wrights. With each new threat, the Pale Wrights demanded more. They said more blood meant more creatures. These past weeks, they have been sucking us near dry. Sometimes they came themselves, one who would suck along with minions to carry the blood back for others. Other times, they brought their special leeches to drain us. They were stockpiling, I think. But even that wasn't enough. They must've feared we would lose and die in the battle. So, their attention turned from protecting us as their food source to making a new deal. I surmise that they offered to immobilize our soldiers and our remaining beasts and help deliver the Shard to King Dayne. In exchange, my father and I were to be given to them, to be slaves in their pits. Presumably to be bred like their other creatures, to become a permanent source of sustenance." I was impressed how steady Jalena kept her voice. "Before the battle, my father refused their false symbiont, as did I. That threw off their plans. The Wrights sent their wolves for us. My father died fighting so I might escape." She swallowed hard. "And so that I might avenge him."

Norta seized the sentiment. "The Shades are vile creatures, and the world will be better when the last of them is gone. If they are using aurathorn in some way, perhaps to help themselves to survive, it will be with pleasure that we help you exact your revenge."

Jalena cautioned her. "To even reach the Pits of Gargen is near impossible. The distance is not far, but the land around it is littered with hidden dangers—bottomless chasms, quicksand, and most dangerous of all, the bore worms."

Norta arched a brow. "Bore worms?"

"Bigger than even the greatest eel, the ground of the clay flats surrounding the pits is their water. They can chew through it. We have always suspected they were creatures of the Pale Wrights, guardians they refused to share, even though they denied it. The worms might allow a lone messenger through, but they attack any groups, anything that might be a threat to the Pale Wrights."

I was the solution here. "Easy enough to avoid a worm—for a dragon. And whoever I might choose to carry."

Norta gazed at me unhappily. "My warriors can manage the journey on foot in any case, I'm sure."

They couldn't, but I didn't bother to say it. Let her try if she must.

Jalena shook her head at Norta's misplaced bravado. "Even if you can reach the pits, then what? They are an endless warren of narrow tunnels. They extend forever. Within are the beasts of the Pale Wrights." Jalena sized me up. "Bayloo, some tunnels are large enough for dragons, for they bred many large and powerful beasts there. But if you entered, that would be a difficult place to fight, even for a dragon."

I had spent enough time in the pits to know Jalena spoke the truth.

"Aurathorn shall be mine," Norta declared. "I have crossed this world in search of it. It is the key to the future. There is a way."

"Indeed, there is," Jalena assured us. "Each of you wants this vine more than anything else. I can deliver it. And I want Oster back. There is a deal to be made. But only I can deliver it."

"You have only a few dozen soldiers," Norta said. "How can you find your way through these terrible pits you describe, if we cannot?"

Jalena's lips offered a thin, grim smile. "The Pale Wrights are hungry. My father was no fool. He never trusted the Wrights. They demanded so much blood in the days before the battle. We delivered it, letting their giant leeches suck us till our skin turned near white. But before they came, we each drank a special drink—a tea of luster root, bitter and awful."

"And poisonous," Harlan commented. "If you chew luster root, you die. Painfully."

"When boiled first, it is used by our healers to cure infection. Although the effect can be ... painful. But the pain was worthwhile.

The only blood the Wrights have received recently has been tainted. They have no other food, so they will be getting hungry. Maybe they are already. Certainly, they will be panicking." Jalena held up a disfigured arm covered with the legacy of her dark bargain with the Pale Wrights. "I will offer to feed them."

THIRTY-NINE

I returned to the Pits of Gargen.

Remarkably, I did this of my own free will, carrying Jalena, Norta, and Harlan on my back. I worried about furies, flying as high as I thought my mostly novice passengers could endure, before descending in a series of tight spirals to the pits. The Pale Wrights sent no trouble at us. I hoped that meant that they too wanted to make a deal.

The landscape seemed even more desolate than when I'd been here only a day earlier. Even when we entered the pit where I'd last resided, nothing stirred, not even the wind. My dragon senses could detect no sound from beyond the darkness of the tunnel that I knew led deep into the warrens of the Pits of Gargen.

"We did not have time to fully search the Shard," Norta said. "The Shades could all be dead."

"No." Jalena was adamant as she spoke. "Two and only two Pale Wrights entered the Shard. We watched them carefully. The rest haven't left these catacombs in decades, or maybe even longer. They are here."

Norta looked into the darkness of the tunnel. She didn't seem afraid, even though she should have been. "Do we go deeper, then?"

Jalena shook her head. "To venture into the pits unbidden is death." She pulled a dagger from her belt and sliced her hand. Crimson filled her palm. With nonchalance, Jalena jerked her bleeding hand toward the dark tunnel, sending several droplets flying into the void. "They will know I am here. They will understand the offer. We wait."

Night fell, but the Wrights did not come. That surprised us.

"They know we are here," Jalena insisted. "They are cowards, unsure if this is a trick. Unable to reach a decision. Give them time. Let the hunger grow."

She was proven correct, but only after much of the night had passed. Finally, the disembodied voice of a Pale Wright spoke from the darkness. It carried a simple, unappealing message:

"Enter, Jalena of the House of Geneles. Enter alone."

She laughed as if addressing a wayward pet. "Hungry, are you?"

Silence followed, and I knew that the Wrights were conversing in their strange, soundless manner. The creatures didn't waste time with useless denials. "Name your price."

Jalena looked first to Norta, who answered with a curt dip of her chin. Then she looked to me, more meaningfully. Jalena barely knew me, yet she had to trust her life to me if any of us were to live through this night. I flashed my eyes white in acknowledgement. Jalena accepted my assurance. She had to trust me to save the land her family had sacrificed for so long to protect. "We only demand that which was promised. Deliver to us the founts of aurathorn that were to be given to this dragon and my other companions when Rolm was defeated."

The Pale Wright was ready for that demand. "In exchange, you must stay in the pits, child of Geneles. You will be provided for."

Jalena didn't hesitate. "Without me, there is no Oster. We will resume our past arrangement—send your leeches on every third day and I shall fill the creatures with my blood."

Another pause followed, although I suspected it was for our benefit. They must've anticipated this answer as well. Just as we guessed their next demand.

"It is agreed, but on this night, you must enter. All of the other blood is spoiled. The contamination ... harmed us. We must feed from the source to cleanse ourselves. There is no other way."

"Then come out with what you have promised and I shall deliver my body and blood." She said it more bravely than I would have.

Norta spoke before the Wright could answer again. "The founts of aurathorn must be transported correctly, or they will wither just as the thorns do. The fount must be able to survive a voyage at sea, or it is useless. I have the knowledge. I must transplant it. We demand this."

Jalena's mouth hardened in annoyance at the interruption, but she held her tongue.

Silence followed from the Wrights, but it was a short one. "We cannot leave these pits. Jalena of Geneles must come. You, stranger of Farlight, may come as well. Let the dragon and its companion remain here."

"Bayloo is with us." Jalena demanded this, her voice leaving no hint that negotiation was possible. "I do not trust you. You betrayed my family. The dragon ensures that you will keep your word. I will not enter your lair without him."

There was no pause from the Wrights this time. "We agree."

That was it. The Wrights had their plan, which would be unpleasant for us. They thought we played into their trap. Of course, they had no intention of ever letting Jalena leave this place. But we had our plan as well.

"Follow the wolf," said the ugly voice of the Wright. "It will show you the way."

I sensed the Pale Wright sink further away. In its place plodded a war wolf—an adolescent that was little more than a pup, but still quite large compared to the mundane variety. I took the lone creature as a reassuring sign that much of the Wrights' strength had been expended.

The wolf led us through the winding passage, through the strange mist curtain. I exchanged a quick glance with Harlan, who carried a new satchel provided by his wife. From it he removed an unusual item—one unknown in Rolm, but common enough among the Farlighters. As long as a human forearm and metal, he laid it on the ground as we walked. The wolf paid no mind, too far ahead.

When we exited the tunnel, the first of the great chambers was even more empty than on my last visit, but even in the quiet, the breeding pits below felt ominous. Hidden eyes watched us. I caught movement on the ceiling, but when I turned my head to look closer, I found only dark basalt.

Even stoic Norta showed agitation, her eyes darting about with unease. Only Jalena seemed unbothered. Perhaps she had come to terms with fate. Or maybe she didn't expect to live through this in any case. The certainty of death can bring a certain kind of peace, although not the kind I personally enjoyed.

The voice of a Pale Wright echoed through the darkness. "For what you seek, you must go deep. To the great cavern, that place carved long ago, from a time long forgotten—the great forge."

"Not forgotten by all," Norta whispered under her breath, her tone so low she probably thought no one heard her. She didn't know dragons as well as she thought.

The wolf pup scampered across the row of pits fearlessly, as if this was its playground. It knew no better. Its wiser pack mates were dead.

We were brought to the massive arched portal that I'd seen when we were last in the bowels of the Wrights' lair. Here the young wolf paused for the first time, as if uncertain. A sharp sound from below that reminded me of grating metal ended the wolf's reticence. It pushed through the entryway and we followed.

Beyond was not another passage, but a staircase, or something resembling one. It was huge, wide enough for two dragons to fit

comfortably, with steps meant for giant feet. The stairs spiraled gradually downward without offering any hint at how deep they went.
This most obviously wasn't a natural formation. The walls and stairs
weren't even rock like the rest of the cavern network, but something
closer to ceramic. Despite decades of apparent use, there were no
cracks on the surface. The wolf pup plodded downward, occasionally
looking over its shoulder, as if surprised that we kept following. I
walked in the rear of the group, cautious of my grip on the strange
surface, and wary. Unfamiliar sounds reminiscent of a giant rumbling
belly came from below, but I detected no heat. If we walked toward a
forge, it wasn't of the conventional sort, or it wasn't in use.

The trip down was longer than I expected—worryingly so. The
stairway twisted in three full circles before it ended. My mind drifted
in and out of the Latticework as I assessed this place and what I might
have to do if the worst transpired. I hadn't anticipated stairs.

The wolf brought us to another cavern, not as large or
sprawling as the great chamber above, but a place even more
disconcerting, because it had so obviously been constructed from a
time before the Cataclysm. The chamber was a perfect rectangle,
its angles as precise as any castle wall, every surface perfectly
smooth. The floor looked polished, with unfamiliar symbols inlaid
upon it. The markings came in a variety of colors and shapes, many
of them with unknown symbols that might have been the runes of
the ancients. It reminded me of one of the human churches back in
Eladrell, particularly because at the end of the room, on a raised
dais, stood an assembly of metal and crystal unlike anything crafted
for centuries. The largest section of the creation resembled twelve
interconnected glass cups, each large enough to hold a small human
child. Two were filled with a thick, translucent liquid, while nine
others were cracked and empty. And the very last one held an egg,
suspended in the same thick substance as the other two intact
containers. It was a large egg, too large to belong to any species but
one. Seeing it, my stomach lurched as a black chill whipped
through me. I realized the terrible price my mother had paid to the

Pale Wrights for aurathorn: I gazed upon a dragon egg. My mother's egg.

She followed her Way, I reminded myself. *No price was too high.*

The bizarre cups were held in place by jaws of metal, upon which rested dozens of crystal tubes that fed into large disks of metal attached to the walls of the chamber. Long benches of mundane wood that looked like far more recent constructions lined the floor before the dais, much like pews in a church, except there were several small, empty cages resting atop the benches. All of this would've been remarkable, and the sole focus of our attention, had it not been for the twisting vines that flanked either side of the dais: aurathorn.

The so-called founts of aurathorn resembled tree stumps that seemed to be imbedded into the ground, growing upward through ugly, jagged holes in the otherwise pristine ceramic of the chamber. Tangled lines of interconnected vines twirled along beams that framed either side of the dais, creating an outline of glowing and glittering thorns that grew over the dais itself, like a living roof. The glow of the thorns bathed the metal and glass monstrosity below in its light. I thought it a remarkable sight, impressive in its glory and frightening in its unfamiliarity. The effect on Norta was far more profound.

She ran three strides forward, nearly leaping to reach the dais, while the rest of us hung sensibly back closer to the portal through which we had entered. A Pale Wright appeared before Norta as she advanced, emerging from the shadows that I hadn't even noticed before it appeared. Two more came after it, their features buried within their thick robes. I sniffed the air. Other creatures were near as well. Something unfamiliar, but I had no doubt it would be dangerous. Upon seeing this place, any lingering doubt that the Wrights intended to kill us was banished.

Norta stopped before the creatures, her gaze drawn upward upon the thorns.

"Do you understand what you see, child of Farlight?" asked the first of the Wrights.

For a moment, Norta couldn't speak. Tears streamed down her face as she looked back and forth between the vines of aurathorn. "Mother .. oh, Mother, I found it ..."

I doubted that her mother could hear her down in the depths of the Pits of Gargen. I was less emotional than the human (and certainly wasn't going to cry out water from my eyes), but I too felt something profound. Here was the key to freedom for my kind. All the time, it had been in Oster, hidden even from this land's own king. I slipped into the Latticework to look deeper at my prize. Like with the thorns earlier, I sensed nothing from vines of aurathorn. There was only void. Indeed, all of the dais was a void. An idea crept into my mind about the significance of that void—a hole of black in the Latticework: here was something beyond the reach of magic.

"Yes, the precious aurathorn is here," the Wright confirmed. "Here it thrives, under our care, as ever it has."

Norta pulled herself together. Harlan moved forward to be by his wife's side. Jalena stayed beside me, her hand on the pommel of her blade. She was the wiser. Aurathorn meant nothing to her. It was just a means to an end.

"How ... how is it here after all these centuries?" Norta asked the Pale Wright.

To my surprise, the creature answered. "We brought it here, of course. It has been here since just after the beginning."

Norta looked at the mass of disjointed metal and glass behind the creature. "Shades." She said it to herself, as if it were a curse. "You are truly the Shades."

"So your ancestors named us," the creature replied. It didn't seem offended. "But they have been dust for more than five hundred years. And we remain."

Norta's eyes widened. "You can't be ... you can't be that old."

"No, alas, even the Founders could not survive what was done to the world. We are the first generation, after the Fall," it said. "The Change, as your kind call it."

Norta absorbed all this. Harlan shot me a glance over his

shoulder to let me know he had virtually no idea what his wife and the Wright were talking about.

"This was your machine," Norta said. "This is where you came from. And now you use it to create the beasts you traded to Jalena's family to sustain you. This thing ..." She pointed toward the dais. "It is a creation forge of some kind?"

The Wright had a silent pause. "You are ... knowledgeable. We had not expected so much lore to have survived, even among the descendants of Farlight. You are correct that we survived the Cataclysm within the machine, and it can be used to form other beasts, given time, effort, and proper ... materials." It lifted its head, and the creature's chilling eyes stared meaningfully at me. It was mocking me over the egg.

"You've been down in these catacombs since the Cataclysm with your machine. With aurathorn, to allow it to still function despite the Change. All that time, sucking blood." Norta said it with distaste. It was a relief to know she shared my disgust toward the creatures.

The revelation struck at Jalena as well. With her hand still on her sword, she moved closer to the Wrights. I heard their hidden protectors shift in the shadows as Jalena approached. Something hid within the walls and along the ceiling; perhaps in the stairway behind us, as well. Soon this conversation would end. I, too, moved forward.

"Who was my great ancestor, Abitor Geneles, to you?" Jenela asked. "Our records begin with him, but only a scrap of old writing remains on the stone of his crypt. Why does the blood of my family sustain you?"

All of the Wrights moved their hooded heads toward Jalena as if they were puppets on a common string. One hissed audibly in displeasure. Was this the equivalent of a cow demanding to know why someone ate it?

Yet after a pause, the Pale Wrights answered. Somewhere within these once-human creatures was that same dark place that existed in Dayne—the corner where both superiority and pride resided comfortably.

"We have agreed to share our knowledge with you, Jalena Gene-les," the Wright told her. "A new relationship between us begins today."

A different Wright took up the narrative. "You should know that the ultimate father of your line was one of us—the original generation of immortals from before the Cataclysm. When the Fall happened, his wife was with child. That child survived with unique traits in its blood that are essential to us. It was a boy: Abitor Fredrice Geneles, the founder of your house." With obvious bitterness, the creature added, "A most stubborn and clever man, he turned out to be. But he needed us and we needed him. So, we were left with the arrangement between our kind that you have known, daughter of House Geneles."

Norta didn't care about Oster's history. Her voice trembled. "The machine still functions ..." I knew she cared only about the future of her people, no matter how dark it was for others. "A creation of the old world, of the ancient Sci-Ance, of the Great Light. Yet it still functions. Even after the great Change of the Cataclysm, *it still functions.*"

"Yes," the Wright confirmed with satisfaction. "As your ancestors learned, the last creation of our peoples—those of us that fought against this new, uncivilized age—allows it to work as it once did. Within the dais, the curse of Rima is held at bay by the power of aurathorn. The negation flow is absorbed, allowing the old laws from before the Change to function. Here and only here, these ancient machines of Sci-Ance retain their power."

Norta looked at Harlan, mad joy in her eyes. "That means it can be done. It can actually be done." She wrapped her arms around Harlan, who looked more confused than elated. "Farlight can actu-ally be saved!"

Jalena stared at the two Farlighters, husband and wife, who had only now broken their embrace. "Can you really raise an island that has been swallowed by the sea?"

Norta pretended she didn't hear the question. Instead, she turned back toward the dais, toward aurathorn. I had no doubt that in that moment, Norta could not have cared less about her promises to Jalena. She would deliver the woman to the Wrights tied and gagged if it would get her aurathorn.

The Pale Wright answered Jalena's question when Norta didn't. "They do not intend to raise an island. To 'Return to Farlight' does not mean to go back to a place that has been swallowed by the sea. Not really."

Norta still said nothing.

"What does it mean, then?" Jalena asked.

"Do you even know the answer, Farlighter?" the Wright asked Norta mockingly. "Do the descendants of Farlight even know what their ancestors sought to achieve with their folly?"

Norta glared but didn't speak.

"Tell me," Jalena demanded of her purported ally. "I've offered my blood, the future of my land and my people. Tell me the truth!"

The Wrights made a low-pitched hiss—all of them in unison like a grizzly chorus. It could've been their version of laughter. They were pleased. I already knew the Wrights weren't going to give Norta aurathorn, at least not willingly. This had all been a show for Jalena's benefit.

The Wrights resumed speaking over Norta's shamed silence. "Before the Cataclysm, as the world fought against itself and plagues stalked the land, the people of Farlight considered themselves the most brilliant and most perfect of all beings." The Wright made a sound like a snicker. "They changed their skin so that they could feed from the sun like a plant, they changed their lungs so they could breathe the poisonous air of the old world, they even changed their minds so that they could hear the echo of each other's thoughts. They gathered the world's knowledge and stored it in machines linked to their minds. With all that knowledge and power, but lacking wisdom, they concluded they should rule all of the world."

Norta didn't deny it. "As opposed to your kind, who merely want to live forever. As if dwelling underground and drinking blood is living. Our ancestors wanted to restore order to chaos."

The retort was angry, as if this had all happened yesterday. "A chaos your people helped create. The collapse was caused by the plagues the Farlighters unleashed as they lost control of their own Sci-Ance."

"At least our kind tried to save the world," Norta insisted. "Instead of accepting the end and retreating to live forever in the underground lairs of luxury, as your ancestors intended."

The Wright let its hood fall, revealing its skeletal form. With these revelations I now saw clearly that the Pale Wrights were human —or close to it. They had merely lived far too long.

The Wright fixed its terrible eyes on Jalena, who was the only audience that mattered to it. The rest of us were mere amusement to be had before they killed us. "Daughter of Geneles, the people you have allied yourselves with are far worse than any other creatures on this world. Their ancestors sought to rule the world, but of course, the other humans did not want to be ruled by them and their machines. So the Farlighters used a forge of their own, far larger and more powerful than this machine behind me. With it, they created a plague to end all plagues, a disease so potent and unstoppable it would wipe out those who dared defy their self-declared superiority. They set this horror loose, then retreated to their fortified island to wait while their creation made its havoc upon the rest of the world. While it consumed all life."

Jalena shook her head. "Too much ... I don't understand."

She might not have followed the Wright's explanation, but I did. I, who had been to Ni-Yota, I who had seen the plague of which the Pale Wrights spoke. I knew what Harlan's ancestors had unleashed.

"The Farlighters created the rust."

FORTY

"Is it true?"

There was hurt in Harlan's voice as he asked his wife the question. I believed his pain. Harlan was a fine card player, but he couldn't fake that kind of shock, nor the look in his eyes as he stared at Norta.

"The rust?" she answered, as if searching a memory. "The Mumblers sometimes called the great Cleansing by that name. Others called it the Ravage." Norta noticed Harlan's chin drop as she mused. "Yes, our ancestors wanted to cleanse the world, to unify it. Harlan, it was hundreds of years ago, a decision made by men and women not only dead, but nearly forgotten. And they failed, obviously." Harlan's stare turned angry. His wife noticed. "What does it matter now what they did so long ago? What is done is done."

Harlan's mouth moved, but he didn't actually speak. I answered for him. "Because the rust still exists. It has grown. It is poisoning lands and killing everything in its path. The curse of your ancestors is still with us. Indeed, it threatens to consume us. Their wish to destroy the world may still come to pass, unless I can stop it."

It was Norta's turn to be shocked. She blinked a dozen times before gathering her silky words once again. "It has been so long. You must be mistaken, dragon." She fixed on Harlan. "Surely, this is a sick jest?"

Harlan shook his head. "No jest. Ni-Yota has fought against the rust, with countless deaths. The land once known as Illium has already been consumed. And it spreads."

Norta shivered ever so slightly as she tried to absorb this new revelation. But almost as quickly as the shock had come, she pushed it from her face. Norta's jaw hardened. "It cannot cross the water. Even if it could, there is the Wall of Fire." She held up a finger as her mind rallied. "That this rust still exists makes our mission even more important, Harlan. Once Farlight is restored, everything will once again be possible."

I didn't like her ominous promise. "How does raising an island, or saving it, or whatever you intend, fit into this?"

A new discomfort came into Norta's eyes. I knew I was right to be suspicious of her. But I'd also been painfully naïve before this moment. I'd never considered what raising Farlight truly meant. The Pale Wright made its ugly, pig-like snicker again.

"She does not wish to speak of that to you, dragon, and for good reason."

Norta's unease turned to hatred as her glare bored into the Pale Wright. "You know nothing, Shade."

The creature's mouth twitched. If it were capable of smiling, I think it would've flashed its most contemptuous one in that moment. "It is true we do not know how you intend to do it, but the goal of your people has always been the same. since the time of your fall, your goal has always been to end the Age of Magic. To restore yourselves as gods and to bring back primacy of almighty Sci-Ance, of your great light." Each of the Pale Wrights aimed their strange eyes in my direction. "That, of course, will result in the end of creatures of magic. It will mean the death of all dragons."

It felt like daggers in my heart—Harlan's daggers. He turned his back to his wife and walked to me. "I swear to you, Bayloo, on my honor, on my life, I did not know this was my quest."

Norta spoke harshly to her husband's back. "Your quest was to find aurathorn. To fulfill the destiny of our people. To save the world, to break the curse. Farlight is more than an island, it is an idea. A distant beacon to guide us. If we can save Farlight, we can save the dream of the better world. We do not need the island to rise above the sea for that. The forge on Farlight can fix this world. Everything we have sacrificed has been for that. The curse our people have endured can be fixed once Sci-Ance is restored. We merely need to bring the founts of aurathorn to the site of Farlight. The thorns block out Rima's power, allowing Sci-Ance to function. With that, even submerged beneath the waves, the forge will awaken, and anything we command will be possible." Norta tapped her head. "We still carry the enhancements of our ancestors to command the forge—that is why we do not breed with those not of our kind. We have kept ourselves pure, so that we can once again be what we were intended to be."

Jalena spoke the truth to Norta in a harsh whisper. "You are as mad as the Pale Wrights."

The Wrights gathered closer together, edging back toward the shadow at the edges of the chamber. "Jalena, the Farlighters brought about the Cataclysm. Even now, the taint of their kind remains upon them. They cannot be trusted, nor can the dragons who laid waste to Oster be trusted. Now you see and hear what they are. The world is a better place without these creatures. For generations the House of Geneles has existed symbiotically with us." It sounded pleased, hungry. "We can grow even closer. You have no need of these others."

Despite all she had heard, Jalena didn't flinch, didn't waiver. "I made a promise to them, and my word shall remain my bond. Give to them what you promised, and I shall keep my word to you and yours as well."

"You would still give the aurathorn to beings such as these?" The creature sounded like it was choking. "Knowing that the Farlighters would seek to use it to break the world once again? Knowing that the dragon intends to unleash his kind upon Oster and all the other lands of men, as they once did ages ago?"

"I have heard much on this night. Much of it I still do not understand, but nothing I have heard has been enough to make me surrender my honor." Jalena tugged at her sword's pommel, drawing it ever so slightly. "What of you, Wright?"

It hissed back, "You have much to learn. Much. But there shall be plenty of time to learn it here, with us. And if you do not learn, your offspring shall."

The unseen danger that surrounded us in the darkness moved. Even without seeing them, I knew there would be too many to fight. We were deep in the lair of the Pale Wrights. As weakened as they were, they were the masters of this place. They would never have let us come into their sanctum if they hadn't been supremely confident in their ability to kill us and take Jalena captive. Our only hope was the Latticework. I reached for it, extending my mind into the place of magic that the Farlighters sought to destroy.

As I did, the bore worms came at us. Through dark holes in the ceiling they slithered out. Dozens of them, each with fifty eyes and mouths lined by a thousand spiked teeth. More came from sliding doors in the sides of the room. Jalena had her blade in hand as she advanced on the Wrights, but the worms were quicker. She split the head of one and the front section off another, but it didn't matter. There were a hundred in the chamber, some as long as a human was tall, others smaller than a pup, all hideous. Their numbers grew. Harlan had his daggers and Norta wielded a wicked cutlass. They could slash and kill, but soon they would tire. Two worms dropped on top of me. I whipped them off with my tail, but fighting them was useless. We faced a sea of slithering killers. It would be magic or death.

I regarded the magnificence of the Latticework—a place that I now understood to have been created by long-dead humans to replace the world of Sci-Ance in which the Farlighters had once existed. In that world, Norta's ancestors had wielded supreme power. It was the world that had created the rust. But in this world of magic, ember dragons commanded the greatest of forces. Now, to save myself and my companions, I would need to do something I had never done before. I only vaguely suspected it was possible, and there would be no second chance.

My mind searched outside the darkness of the Pits of Gargen. Above the tunnels and chambers where the Pale Wrights existed, dawn had broken into the sky. I found the light of the sun, bright and powerful. I focused on a ray of daylight newly penetrating the horizon. I studied it, then I commanded it, forcing it to bend downward, into the very same pit I had flown the previous day. The light followed the path I directed, falling downward through the twisting tunnel at angles it never would've traversed without my intervention. From there, I bent it again, drawing light into the tunnel that led into the pit. But within the tunnel was an obstacle that I could not move or avoid: the mist. The strange substance prevented any outside light from entering the catacombs.

It was Harlan who had the idea of how to breach the Wrights' barrier of darkness. He had spoken in the past of his lost spyglass, the device of the Farlighters that brought distant objects near with their magic lenses. Only they weren't magic. It was a secret of Sci-Ance. Like the inferno staffs, they were evidence that the Farlighters still possessed some of the legacy of their ancestors' knowledge. The lens of the spyglass reflected light. Carefully placed, a spyglass could allow the sunlight I'd guided into the pits through the barrier of mist. Norta had supplied the spyglass from one of her ships, Harlan had placed it at the barrier on the way inside, and the Pale Wrights never suspected moving sunlight in this manner was remotely possible, or that we would gamble our lives upon this scheme.

I pushed light toward the floor of the tunnel, drawing it into a concentrated beam that struck one end of the spyglass. Remarkably, it passed through to the other end without difficulty, using the glass as a bridge to bypass the light-consuming mist. Once I'd guided the sunlight inside the pits, the rest was almost easy, except for the spiraling stairs. That took more concentration, more bending, but I did it.

The sunlight arrived. I roared in triumph when the morning's blaze finally shone into the chamber far beneath the pits, where the enigmatic minds of the Pale Wrights had never imagined their doom could reach.

They howled with an agony that sounded all too human. Over the centuries, the Wrights had existed in the dark, feeding on the blood of Jalena's family. During that time, they had become a species apart, losing much of what was decent in humans. But they hadn't completely lost all emotion. The Wrights clung to life like a baby clung to its mother. The moment the sunlight came, they knew it would all end. Their cries were harrowing, echoing through the chamber. The sound was mercifully brief. The blazing light smothered them, setting their pale skin bubbling into boils of mucus. The Wrights collapsed, writhing, dissolving in a stinking mess on the floor.

With their masters annihilated, most of the bore worms left. This hadn't been their fight—they served, ordered by some unseen link bred into them by the Wrights. They were pleased to have nothing to do with swords and dragons. Not all of them, of course. The bore worms were vicious creatures, because that was the way they had been created. So there was still blood to shed, even once the Wrights were gone.

Jalena was a killing machine. I'd never seen a human so adept with a blade. It was part of her, or perhaps she was a part of it. She danced among the worms, slicing, stabbing, and gutting until every part of her body was covered in gore. Norta and Harlan fought as well. They did battle back to back, dispatching their tormentors each time the worms came within range. Part of me envied the trust they had, despite all that had happened. But only a very small part of me felt that way—human bonding seemed very complicated.

I killed the rest of the worms with jaw, claw, and tail—a few dozen worms were no match for me. Mostly, I chafed at the inconvenience of the deed. I was relieved when it was done.

To be sure the extermination of the Pale Wrights was complete, I flooded the rest of the catacombs in glorious light. I sent the sun's rays into every pit and nook and room that I could reach. Soon, it was done. The Pale Wrights had been destroyed, but I dreaded what came next. Some terrible killing remained.

My mother would have done whatever must be done without hesitation. She followed the ancient Way of my kind. It made no room for sentiment or pity, or even love, but I was different. I now recognized and accepted that I wasn't like other dragons. My time as a slave dragon, linked to a human mind during my formative years, had changed me forever. I also realized that I had become who my mother desired. It had been deliberate. She planned for me to be a slave, because that's what she thought the world needed—a dragon with the emotions of a human. The hurt of that ran through me, because I did not share my mother's Way. Also, I liked humans, at least some of them. Although he was a human, Harlan was my friend. I cared about him. I think he felt the same way about me.

I felt terrible that I was going to have to kill his wife.

FORTY-ONE

"You will not take aurathorn."

I said it, but Norta already had an inferno staff in her hand even before I finished speaking. It was smaller than the others I'd seen, not much longer than a dagger, but no less dangerous. I presumed she'd had it concealed up a sleeve for an event such as this. She hadn't used it against the bore worms or the Pale Wrights. She'd saved it, knowing that a confrontation with me was a possibility, because she had known her success meant genocide for my kind. I reminded myself not to underestimate this woman. She led the Farlighters, and she possessed knowledge that few others on this world still retained.

"Stop!" Harlan screamed, as panicked as I'd ever seen him. He put his body between us, as if he could really stop me from doing what I must. I didn't want to see him come to harm, nor could I allow my race to end.

"We had a deal," Norta reminded me, shamelessly. As if I were the one doing the betraying here.

"That was before I knew you intended to use aurathorn to kill me, and every other dragon. That was before I knew your kind created the rust and that its spread pleases you as it once pleased your ancestors."

Norta flicked her free hand with nonchalance, as if the fate of my species and the world were an insect to be batted away. "The Shades are liars, their minds are twisted. The final destruction of Rima will not kill you or anyone else. It will restore the natural laws of the world. Yes, magic will disappear. But you are not magic, you are flesh and blood, even as I. Magic does not allow you to fly—flesh, bone, and muscle do that. In the time before the Cataclysm, countless creatures were created for different uses. Even the special creation forge that made your kind was originally constructed using Sci-Ance."

She was wrong about my kind surviving in a world without magic. Norta couldn't see the Latticework. She didn't understand how dragons were connected by Chords of magic to the new reality and to each other. We were more than flesh, blood, and bone. We were magic. I didn't bother to try to tell her that. It wouldn't make a difference to her calculations. "What of the rust, which even now consumes Ni-Yota, killing countless beings?"

With this, Norta furrowed her face with displeasure. "The rust disappeared hundreds of years ago. Confined to land by the ghastrays, the rust was finally destroyed by the balefire of the dragons —the ultimate power of the magical world. Yet, you claim this rust still exists? I think you are mistaken. There are many other blights. Dig a trench. Burn it."

Norta did not want to face inconvenient facts. "It is the rust. It cannot be burned. The ghastrays sense what it is." I snorted at her feeble excuses. "It spreads across the whole continent. It seeks to build ships and infect other creatures so it can defeat the ghastrays and spread across the sea. It *thinks*. This is no mere blight."

Her frown deepened. "Thinks, you say?"

Harlan found his voice, although it was strained. "The rust adapts, my wife. Each time we found a way to stop it, it changed. And it spawns not just itself, but takes the shells of other creatures to do its bidding. The hollowings, they are called by the inhabitants of Ni-

Yota, for inside there is nothing of their old selves—the things exist only to serve the purpose of the rust."

Something like concern crept slowly into Norta's eyes. "It raises the dead?"

Harlan and I exchanged a glance, but it was I who answered. "I do not know if the hollowings are alive. It seems that their forms are repurposed. There is little left of what they once were. The shell is joined to that strange intellect that drives the rust."

Norta's gaze was so sharp it could've drawn blood. "You are sure?" she demanded of her husband. "With your own eyes you have seen this?"

"With my blood I have faced it. I've flown over it on Bayloo's back. I've seen him nearly lose his life to it on countless occasions. I've seen the rust claim the lives of men and dragon alike. It is a lethal enemy. The most dangerous thing ever created. It is evil, Norta."

For a fleeting instant, I thought we might have gotten through to her, that words would be enough. But that was naïve. She'd been on a quest her whole life—one much deeper and different than Harlan's. Norta was charged with fulfilling the dark dream of a people long since dead. It was not something to be easily relinquished.

"All the more reason to finish what we have begun," Norta proclaimed at last. "This was not what our ancestors intended. Perhaps after its first near-annihilation, the rust adapted in unforeseen ways. But once Sci-Ance has been restored, our people can deal with it. Even submerged for hundreds of years, the great forge at Farlight survives. We can use it to beat this rust. Your magic has failed. Let us try now to save the world in a different way."

"Your Sci-Ance failed long ago," I reminded her. "That is why those who created my kind had to change the world. Because there was no other way to save the world from the rust, except to change it."

"The rust will end itself," Norta snapped. "When it has nothing left to consume, it will die out, leaving the world for us to re-populate. The energy of everything that it has absorbed will be left behind after its termination for those who inherit the world. That was always the plan. On Farlight, we will survive, just as our ancestors intended. There are great storage facilities at Farlight; within them is everything the new world needs. Sci-Ance can bring them back." She must've seen the look of horror in Harlan's eyes, for she added quickly to me, "Join us there with your fellow dragons, Bayloo. There is room in the new world for all. You don't need magic anymore, once the rust is gone. Dragons and humans can find a way to live together."

I drew myself up. We were reaching the limits of words and discussion. "You wish virtually every human on this world to die? Every horse or pig, every bird, perhaps even the ghastrays and other creatures. All so you can take a chance that the rust may just disappear and allow you to remake the world in the image of a people who died hundreds of years ago, and left you with their mission and their curse. To this I say: never."

Norta had not become the leader of her people by accident. She knew that a confrontation was inevitable. Her finger twitched on the inferno staff. I expected that. She aimed at my neck. I yanked myself to the side. Unfortunately, Norta was also a cunning warrior. She'd baited me. I moved, but she didn't fire. Not until I'd shown her my maneuver. I was exposed; a large, relatively easy target in this confined space.

She fired the weapon.

FORTY-TWO

Harlan struck his wife's arm.

That was something she hadn't expected. Even after years apart, she must've thought their trust ran deeper. Harlan had known me for only a few months. I didn't have time to be flattered, but I was glad that my caring for Harlan was reciprocated. My mother would not have forged such a bond. The Way was not always the answer.

Harlan's blow disrupted Norta's aim just enough to send the projectile off course. The iron slug hissed angrily as it shot past my neck. I whipped my tail at Norta's head. It would've been a lethal blow, but Harlan jumped in front of her. That surprised me. Humans were just so fickle. I pulled my strike as best I could, but I still struck with enough force to send Harlan and his wife to ground, but better there than into the Abyss (at least for Harlan).

I advanced to stand over them, my head craning forward. I let the saliva from my open jaw rain onto Norta. I had offered her a choice and she had made it: she tried to kill me. The rest was easy. Except for Harlan interfering again.

"Bayloo, don't do this." Harlan was still on his back, his body mostly on top of his wife, but it would still be easy for me to put a claw into her without harming him.

"I can kill her. I will kill her. I am sorry for that, my friend."

"Do as you must, then, dragon." Norta's voice betrayed no fear of death. "I did as I must. This is the right path for my people, and eventually, all peoples. Your kind was created to be a tool, nothing more. I don't expect you to understand. You were made without true emotion. You were made to destroy."

"A very convenient belief."

"But know that with my death, your fellow dragons die too."

My nostrils flared. "What fresh betrayal do you plot now?"

"If I do not return, my seahands will turn their inferno staffs on the remaining dragons. You have not seen all our weapons. There is more in our arsenal. Enough for one last task."

Jalena came closer to us, bloody sword still in her grip. "I swear I know nothing of this, Bayloo. On my honor. If there is a betrayal, it shall not be from Oster."

I didn't move my eyes from the treacherous Norta. Harlan really had terrible taste in mates. Norta might be lying, but I didn't think she was. "Will your Osteran soldiers fight to protect my kind if the Farlighters go to slaughter them?"

Jalena's heavy sigh confirmed my fears even before she spoke. "There is no love for Rolman dragons among my soldiers. I doubt they would intervene without an order from me. Perhaps Kemet ..."

Perhaps, but perhaps wasn't enough.

"Bayloo, there is another way," Harlan promised.

I wasn't in the mood for compromises. I placed a claw next to Norta's neck. "As you say, I was made to destroy."

Harlan put a hand on my claw and shoved it away. "You know that to be untrue. Both of you stop this." Harlan scrambled to his feet even as I kept Norta pressed on the ground. He kept staring at my claw. "Bayloo, I need a truce for you to hear what must be heard by you and Norta both."

I didn't let his wife up, but I didn't kill her either.

Harlan put a hand on my side. "Is it agreed?"

I still wasn't in the mood for anything but a clean kill. "Harlan, in this battle you must choose a side. You have tried to choose both sides, and this will not do."

Harlan surprised me with his reply. "I chose the side of saving this world, my friend. There is no other choice that can be made. Norta will soon see that as well. And she will help us. Let her up."

Norta's fierce eyes told me she didn't agree with anything that her husband had just said. Nevertheless, I released a long, reluctant snarl, then moved my claw away from her so that she might drag herself from the ground.

"Norta, for six years I have plied the seas, traveling from place to place, visiting nearly every surviving land within reach of the great seas that cover this world. I've met kings and princes, farmers and beggars, whores and holy men, children and the nearly-immortal, and everything in between. I've even spoken to ghastrays and dragons." Norta's face was hard, but Harlan's eyes were soft. "Some of these meetings were joyous, others tragic. I've known evil and shocking kindness. Through it all, I stayed true to you and the mission I had been set upon. I will tell you the simple truth: This world that exists is flawed, but it does not deserve to die for a fever dream of the past."

"It's more than some ancient dream," Norta shot back, the fury in her eyes flowing into her voice. "It's about our people surviving. The curse can only be ended by restoring Farlight. Sci-Ance can cure us. Other mothers and fathers don't need to end up like us, with lost children. Ana and Hora will not have died for nothing."

A quiet, heavy with emotion, followed. Harlan's eyes stared downward as if he'd been kicked in the heart. Perhaps he had. He had told me he had escaped the curse of his people, the curse of losing one of his twins; Harlan had told me he was without children. I now realized the terrible truth of his words and what he had really meant: He and Norta had lost both their offspring before he'd left on his long voyage, rather than just one. The comfortable solitude of an endless quest made sense now.

Harlan forced his head up, forced himself to meet his wife's trembling eyes. "The curse of our people will not be broken by Sci-Ance. We have the power to end it now."

Norta hissed with anger. "What are you talking about?"

"We can mix with the other peoples of this world. We can marry any who we desire! We can give up our existence as nomads of the sea. We can find a place to settle, invite others. The curse afflicts us because we have children only with each other, on pain of exile or death. All for a dark quest. End that custom and we can end the curse."

I waited for Norta to explode with anger, but she didn't. Instead, she deflated. "And end ourselves as a people. We are so few. It would be extinction for us in two generations. I won't be the leader that ends us."

"You don't have to. I will."

"You?" She huffed angrily. "You're a ship's captain ..." But even as she said it, her voice hitched with doubt.

"I'm Lord Fish." There was self-mockery in Harlan's voice, but it was tinged with something harder. "Every captain knows my name. More importantly, every seahand knows it. What they don't know is that the great secret of the Mumblers and the First Voice is some quest, not to save our old home but to help unmake the only world they have ever known. The ships are already rife with discontent. Our people tire of only the sea and of always being alone. Most of all, they are weary of knowing that finding love also means the curse of a dead child. How many captains or crew went rogue in the past year? Three? Four? Before that, even more. Every new dawn is the same."

Norta didn't answer, but her silence was enough confirmation.

With reluctance, Harlan added a final verbal dagger. "It will be easy to end this, Norta. Particularly with a dragon to help me spread the word among the remaining ships. You will be First Voice of no one but a few fervent stragglers who will be gone in less than a generation."

Norta knew Harlan spoke the truth. She had lost, but she was also a leader. She wanted to salvage what she could, wanted to save as much of Farlight as she could. I understood that. "What do you want me to do?"

They were painful words to speak. Harlan knew it as well. I could feel him inching to embrace the woman who he still loved. But he restrained himself. Harlan, too, was a leader in his own, unique way. He looked toward me. "What must be done, Bayloo?"

The sun knew how to shine, and Harlan knew humans. I was grateful for his help and his friendship. "Show me how to cut down the aurathorn without killing it. It is finally time for all dragons to be free."

FORTY-THREE

Aurathorn.

I finally had it. My mother had given one of her eggs for this. In exchange for her horrific sacrifice, she'd obtained a single cut vine of the thorns, but without the precious fount from which it grew. It had been a brilliant and desperate idea—using the unique thorns to disrupt the magic runes that enslaved my mind. That's what aurathorn was—a magic blocker. Or more precisely, as Norta explained it, aurathorn absorbed residual energy using the fount, concentrated it within the thorns, which used that stored energy to negate the all-encompassing blanket of force that Rima continually rained down upon the world, canceling Sci-Ance and replacing it with the magic of the Latticework. My mother probably hadn't understood all that, and she hadn't known enough to obtain the fount that kept the thorns' power alive. But she knew enough. She had only a vine of aurathorn, which wouldn't survive on its own. Maybe the Pale Wrights had tricked her with that. In the end, she'd used enchantment to try to coax the vine to work, then she'd had to use Jona to get the thorns to me, to ingest them, hoping that the residual power would still be enough to break my invisible chains.

I wondered when my mother had first devised her plan. When she had allowed me to become a slave, had she already known the price for freeing me? I told myself it didn't matter. She had done it, although the price had been high for both of us. At least now I understood why she had thought it had been necessary. My mother understood magic. She knew the Latticework was damaged. For her plan, she needed me to be a slave. She needed me to be linked with a human, my mind forever altered by that experience. She needed me to have emotion, which was why she had told me the Way wasn't for me. A human would say she was cold and heartless, but she merely followed the Way of our kind. My dragon mind understood why she had done all these things. My human-like emotions ached at the betrayal.

For all my mother's brilliance, she understood less of the nature of aurathorn than I. She also did not command the Latticework as I could. No one did. My mother had given me that. Through my passage from enslavement to freedom I had earned that power. I was a dragon mage like no other. I intended to use my power. There would be no need to coax my fellow dragons into drinking some concoction against the will of their linked ryders. I didn't have the time for that anyway.

Norta showed us how to safely cut on the aurathorn founts without killing them. The key was dirt. Aurathorn had to be connected with the ground from which it drew its particular form of sustenance at all times, or the unseen force of Rima that surrounded us would quickly destroy its nemesis. For that, we brought in dirt and gravel from the pits and the area outside, using one of the thick robes of the eternally-departed Pale Wrights to hold it all. Soon we had a small, moveable vineyard. We left one fount in place.

"I shall ensure this place is well protected," Jalena promised. "After this is done, I hope we shall have no more need of the breeding pits. But, should the world need aurathorn again, it shall be here. I pledge it."

I liked Jalena. She was young enough to still believe that she would always be able to hold true to the words she spoke. The world would eventually teach her differently, but for now, I enjoyed the effort she made.

"The Shades created aurathorn?" I asked Norta when we finally returned to the surface with our prize.

"Yes, with the help of my people, as we both searched for a way to continue to use Sci-Ance." I had noticed that the glittering thorns continuously drew Norta's gaze. She was a moth to its flame. "We thought it lost forever when Farlight was destroyed. But there was always a hope that the Shades or someone still had it hidden somewhere, which is why we had to search for it."

"You should know that when this is done, if there is a way that magic can help the curse of your people, I offer it to you." I caught Harlan looking approvingly at me as I offered my peace to his wife.

Norta took in a long breath. I expected a refusal, but Norta managed to croak out something a bit more pleasant: "Thank you for the offer, Bayloo."

At least she didn't call me "dragon." I still didn't trust her at all, but it's nicer when someone remembers to use your name.

Together we flew back to the Shard. Norta offered to go by herself, on foot. Maybe she was wary of climbing onto my back after having tried to kill me. Harlan insisted she accompany us, and so did I, although for different reasons. I had no intention of letting Norta out of my sight until I had what I needed from her. Some of what I wanted from the Farlighter ruler included helping with aurathorn and not trying to kill any dragons (including me), but not all. She still had knowledge I needed. My offer to help her people hadn't been benevolence. I could play games too.

While still beneath the Pits of Gargen, I had spent considerable effort trying to glean more about the mysterious aurathorn, its properties, how it interacted with the Latticework. I got nowhere. Knowing that aurathorn negated magic, that outcome made sense. I was trying to gaze into a void. I had also done some brief tests on myself to help me determine the intensity and duration of the thorns' magic suppression. This was as simple as holding and dropping thorns as I attempted to work magic. I learned that aurathorn acted instantly, and its effect dissipated with the same alacrity once out of the vicinity of the thorns. That gave me a stupid idea. Harlan confirmed the stupidity of the idea, but time was scarce, and we didn't have a better plan.

In a rare demonstration that fate was not at all times against us, we arrived back at the Shard before my fellow dragons had counter-attacked to destroy the gates of their impromptu prison. I had feared we'd been too long in the pits, but with King Dayne dead, the surviving ryders had acted with prudence, giving their dragons a chance to heal and the human soldiers an opportunity to regroup before the inevitable assault to try to free themselves from the Shard. The shocking appearance of the Farlighters and their inferno staffs probably played a significant role in that reticence. Still, I was grateful to find no fatalities among my brethren beyond what had been suffered in the initial surprise attack.

"I know better than to try to persuade you to reconsider," Harlan said to me when all was ready. "But I wish there was a less risky way to do this."

"We always wish that."

"What of the Rolman soldiers?" Jalena asked.

I wanted to be generous. "I would ask you to do all you can to avoid a fight with them for as long as you can."

The ruler of Oster didn't hide her surprise at the sentiment. "They serve the same king that enslaved you. They would kill you if given the chance. They have killed thousands of Osterans."

"They outnumber you, but your soldiers have vastly better positions. If I am successful, I hope to broker a peace."

Jalena's face stiffened at that. I guessed Kemet and the other Osterans would share those hard feelings toward their ancient foes. There had been too much blood spilled for this to be easy.

"It is not for me to solve every human conflict," I said wearily. "If you want to have a lasting peace with Rolm, I suggest you start here.

And send a message to Ulibon, for they may be of some use to you, whichever path you choose. You may tell the Highstar that I vouch for your unparalleled honor."

Jalena didn't smile, but I still think she was pleased by my praise. I was getting better at this.

There wasn't any more time to dwell in the moment, however. "Time to open the gate."

With everything as ready as it could be, Jalena gave the order to her soldiers to raise the portcullis that protected the eastern portal of the Shard. The heavy metal of the gate scratched and groaned as it moved, pulled upwards by teams of humans who pushed two huge wheels attached to an elaborate pulley system. After the rumbling of the gate opening, I knew every dragon and every ryder inside the Shard would be alert, ready for battle. I flew inside the mountain the moment the opening was large enough to accommodate me. The gate would open no further than it must—at least as long as Jalena's Osteran soldiers held the passage.

I pushed my wings for speed, but ventured no further into the giant cavern than necessary to make my presence obvious to all within. Dragons roared and humans shouted. I roared back, loud enough to be heard by every creature within the Shard.

"Today shall be the last day the dragons are slaves. From this day forward, we shall all be free!"

The dragons wouldn't believe me—they couldn't. The human ryders would be angered. Still, it felt good to say it. The Farlighters had held onto their dark dream for generations; my hope was a mere babe in those terms, but the intensity of my mission was greater, clearer. I could make it happen. My mother knew I could—I was an ember dragon. We had been made to lead our kind.

The dragons and their ryders came for me. I counted them as they rose. Each of my brethren came to do me harm, but I silently rejoiced in their flight. Even Blaris coming at me was a welcome sight, for it confirmed she lived. Arutel, too, took to the air—ryderless, vengeance in his eyes. I had worried for him. The horned dragons came as well. I counted seven in all. I circled the formation, trying to keep away from my pursuers as long as I could. I knew I needed to leave. But I didn't see Cornethius yet. My eyes scoured the ground. I found him quickly, his crumpled form alone beside a building. His ryder wasn't with him. I risked a low pass over him, but it only confirmed that he was dead. As was another of the horned dragons. The inferno staffs had taken their toll.

With my hearts like lead in my chest, I turned to do what I had to do. I beat my wings, flying hard and fast for the lone open portal—the narrow opening to the sky that I'd entered through. I'd intended to stay close to my escape route, but I'd gone further into the cavern to check on Cornethius. Somehow, Arutel had guessed I'd try to fly back through the open portcullis. He was flying toward it even before my course was obvious. I tried to increase my speed, but it was no use. Arutel would get there first. But he had no interest in escaping this place. Ryderless, and driven by his own twisted memories of Dayne, Arutel swept around in front of the gate and came at me.

With Harlan and Jalena's assistance, I had re-fitted myself with only a single set of *sai* on my left foreclaw, and I didn't wear it for the purposes of hurting my brother. I'd come to save dragons, not slice them to pieces, but I was tempted to use it against Arutel. He was vicious, with a strong, thick neck. Still, I restrained myself. I came within range of his fire, but Arutel didn't bother with flame—he wanted to kill me with tooth and claw. I kept on course toward him, still coming at my best speed. Arutel probably expected me to try to pull some maneuver at the last instant, because that's what I ordinarily would've done. He knew there were too many other dragons chasing me to risk getting trapped in close combat where I'd lose the advantage of superior flying abilities. So, I did the opposite of what Arutel expected; I rammed him.

It wasn't until my claws were almost on him that Arutel fully accepted that I meant to give him what he wanted. Only at the very last moment did he focus fully on positioning himself for the melee that would ensue once our bodies were locked. Arutel twisted his neck away from my advancing jaws, attempting to lift himself above my foreclaws. I was faster.

My outstretched claws found the scales of Arutel's underbelly, even as he beat his wings to avoid my grasp. The base of his neck also came into reach of my jaws as I extended myself fully. But locking myself onto Arutel wasn't my intention. I needed to be close, but I had no desire to engage in a deadly sky dance. Instead, I pushed him eastward. Normally, pushing doesn't work well when two dragons are flying, but in this case, Arutel was trying to change his direction to avoid me. He'd lost most of his momentum in the interim, while I was moving with speedy purpose. Surprised by my tactic, Arutel was forced toward the Shard's metal portcullis.

I flew with too much speed and force for Arutel to stop us, no matter how hard he beat his wings. He released a desperate roar. A moment later, I slammed him into the thick metal bars of the Shard's gate, wings hitting the metal barrier first. The collision probably hurt him, but that wasn't my intention, either. I pressed Arutel against the metal. Just above him, on a ledge that the Osterans used to control the gate mechanism, stood Harlan. In his hand he held glowing thorns that had been dipped in sticky sap. He sprinkled them on Arutel, as if pouring grains of sand on the beach. The dragon didn't notice—aurathorn didn't hurt. Once that was done, I shoved Arutel away from me, toward the ground. Suddenly, he was free of my attack. That surprised him as well. If I'd intended to kill him, I had surrendered a decisive advantage, but of course I wasn't going to kill him. I escaped out the narrow opening that had been left in the Shard's gate.

As I expected, Arutel chased me, as did the rest of the dragons and their ryders. As each passed through the narrow gap, tiny thorns fell onto their heads, wings, and bodies. The debris was tiny, near invisible, seemingly harmless, and very sticky. I suspected that the ryders would sense something was wrong with their link to their dragon's mind, but they wouldn't know why or what to do about it.

The dragons departed the Shard into the densest patch of fog ever to grace the surface of Inkra. I'd conjured it just for my brethren. The air was just a touch less thick than soup, inundated with misty rain and unnatural waves of intermittent wind. The idea was to disrupt sight as well as hearing and smell. I suffered from those same hindrances, but I had the advantage of my link to the Latticework to guide me. It was enough to give me the advantage of surprise, which was what I needed.

I pounced on Blaris first. I'd always had a feeling about her, some innate sense that, more than any other dragon on the Peak, she resented her ryder. Concealed by the fog and rain, I was able to strike at her without any initial resistance. By the time Blaris knew another dragon was near, it was too late for her to do anything about it. I was on her, a foreclaw holding the base of her neck, while I swiped at her chest with my other, *sai*-tipped claw. I struck her as gently as I could, telling myself I was acting like a healer rather than an enemy. With two quick, decisive swipes, I brutally defaced the sickening runes that had been carved onto my sister's body since she was a hatchling. Owing to the aurathorn, her link to her ryder was severed, and the magic of the rune rendered powerless. For good measure, I had now destroyed it.

"You are free, sister," I told her, still holding onto Blaris. "Your chain is gone. You have merely to shake off the last of the yolk within you, and you shall be free like me."

Blaris' answer was to smash her jaw into my foreclaw. I'd feared this. It was one thing to destroy the magic of the link. It was another for my sister to realize her mind was free. If she even wanted to be free. Slavery was a poison that lingered.

"I know you, Blaris. You want this. You always have. Don't be afraid." Then I smashed her in the head with my tail.

I returned to the cover of the fog, flying on a twisting, erratic course, in case Blaris intended to follow. She'd work things out. I had more to do before my fog dissipated. I went for Arutel next. He sensed my coming somehow, and bathed me in a blanket of fire. It hurt, and I cut his chest scales more deeply than I intended, drawing blood. I could feel his anger as I escaped back into my conjured mist.

"When you are free, you shall realize our bond is far stronger than the rune that the Sculptors carved into your mind, brother."

I turned my attention to the horned dragons. They were easier, because I didn't need to worry about fire, and I was far stronger than my smaller cousins. I defaced the runes of two more dragons before Blaris found me. The fog had thinned, and I was distracted. She grabbed a hindleg in her jaws. Before I could fully react, a tail smashed into my underside. Blaris was damnably strong—it felt like the contents of my torso were forced involuntarily through my neck and out my mouth in a single instant. Besides that, her bite hurt. A foreclaw gripped onto my scales, followed by an arrow from Blaris' pesty ryder. There was an embarrassing lack of gratitude here.

I answered the attack with an embrace of my own. I grabbed at Blaris with my foreclaws (and the one with *sai* probably stung when it sank through her scales), and answered her with several strikes from my tail. I roared at her as we twisted and tumbled through the air. The mist dissipated. More dragons would be coming.

"Look inside yourself, sister. I am not your enemy."

Her answer was to try to rip out a portion of my neck with her teeth.

I tried to reach out to her another way—the dragon way—through the Chords of the Latticework that connected us all. I sent my power into her, hoping she could sense my consciousness as well, that I was with her.

It didn't seem to have any effect. Blaris writhed and attacked with the vigor of a slave dragon instructed to kill. We were falling toward the Shifting Straits rapidly. She beat her wings harder to stay aloft— she could survive a fall into the sea, but her precious ryder might not. I didn't really care about the human, though. I pushed our flightpath downward even as Blaris turned more and more of her effort into keeping us aloft. She tried to separate, but I held firm.

I kept trying. "That human in your head isn't you. Find yourself, sister."

The sea didn't care about our struggle. We crashed into the waves, the cold of the water surging through me. I kept my hold on Blaris—dragons didn't swim. Luckily, the tide was low and we dragons were large. My legs touched the sand bottom of the waters near the Shard. I felt some of the fight leave my sister. Perhaps she was searching for the human who had ridden on her back. I pulled Blaris toward the nearest shore. We were close. The crash could've been far worse. Dragons roared furiously at me from above. I looked up to see Arutel coming at us. I left Blaris in the shallows, leaping toward the shore. I couldn't fight Arutel while I was in the water. I needed to get back into the sky.

I reached the rocky shore just as Arutel reached me. His claws raked across my head. One of them sunk deep, tearing a scale. Blood poured into my right eye. I needed to get out of this position or he was going to tear me to pieces. I spread my wings to fly as Arutel made a tight circle in the sky. He'd be back in a moment, but my wings were soaked in salt water. I shook them, but it wasn't going to be enough. I was stuck on the beach. Arutel dove at me. He opened his mouth. Fire came forth, leading the attack. He'd follow with claw and jaw, tearing my wings if he could.

I crouched low to the ground, bracing for more hurt.

Another blast of fire came, but it wasn't aimed at me. These flames rose from the ground, answering Arutel's fire. The new blaze was thick, strong, and unexpected—enough to keep any dragon from flying directly into the inferno. Arutel broke off his dive, turning into an arc in the sky as he circled around. Blaris was at my side. Her words were sweeter than biting into the flesh of a newly-roasted black pig (probably).

"I am with you," my newfound kin told me. "I can finally see, and I am with you."

FORTY-FOUR

Once Blaris was free, I knew the rest would follow.

Arutel broke out next. I think the shock of seeing another dragon turn against him did it. After Blaris came to my aid, Arutel's anger melted away. Confused, he disengaged, flying off into the clouds.

Blaris intended to fly after him, but I counseled otherwise. "Give him time. You were chafing to be free. The others may need time to find their will." I didn't mention that we didn't have the luxury of time. I wanted to give my sister a chance to revel in her new identity —I'd save explanations about the forthcoming end of the world for the morning. We could afford that, I hoped, although I knew that each day that I delayed meant another day of peril for Rinxia and Kiata.

The horned dragons broke free almost as one after Blaris joined me. They had been made to follow the lead of the ash dragons. It wasn't all roars of celebration. Revolutions weren't pretty. Many ryders died—some in the jaws of their former slave dragons, others because they refused to accept what had happened. Those who surrendered, I allowed to go free. With Dayne dead and the dragons free, my fight was no longer with Rolm.

Arutel came back to us as the sun began to fall into the horizon, just as the rest of us were flying back to the Shard. I was exhausted, but elated. Arutel came to us from the north, darting out of the clouds like an apparition. His eyes set me at ease even before he flew to me.

"I'm sorry, my brother," were the first words he said to me.

"There is nothing to be sorry for. It was not you I fought. It was the poison of Dayne in your mind."

Arutel grunted. "I knew what he was. I was ... in that fog, I didn't care. I just wanted to ..." He searched for the words for a moment, before roaring in frustration instead.

"That particular nightmare is over."

My newly-freed kin followed me without question. This was all new to them, and I was the one who'd freed them. To be surrounded by so many dragons, all of them flying together by choice, seemed unreal. I wished my mother could have seen it. Even more, I hoped what I'd done would be enough to save the rest of us, and this world, as she intended.

An armada of dragons delivered quick victories. After Arutel burned half a dozen Rolman warships, the Rolman army surrendered and agreed to leave Oster, abandoning their supplies, save what they needed for the journey back to Rolm. Every Rolman soldier in the Shard quickly surrendered as well. Still, that left the Farlighters.

Despite the gratitude of my fellow dragons, it took all of my efforts of persuasion to keep my kin from killing every Farlighter (and possibly the Rolmans and Osterans as well) when we returned to the Shard. Arutel was particularly keen on blood vengeance. Perhaps it was a legacy of Dayne's influence, perhaps he was still furious about almost being killed himself. Either would be understandable.

"The war between humans and dragons must end," I told him.

There were many unhappy dragons, but my authority held. We had returned to the Shard for a higher purpose—to find those who had not flown out to pursue me. While I searched the Shard with Arutel, Blaris and the horned dragons remained outside—I still didn't trust Norta or her people. We found only one of our kin still alive inside the Shard—a horned dragon known as Arla. I freed her mind, but she was in too much pain to notice. She had holes in her wing and her body—too much for even dragon healing to easily overcome.

"Our healers will do all they can for her," Jalena assured me. "When she is ready, she will be free to go, I swear it."

"More human promises," Arutel sneered.

"Our kind killed thousands of hers," I reminded my brother. "And you would still be a slave without her help."

Arutel made an unhappy rumble in his throat. "What now?"

"Tonight, we feast as free dragons. We shall take our pick of the Rolman food stores, and much more. You really need to try ale." Arutel's eyes glowed with approval. "And then I must tell you of the history of our race. Afterwards, we must save this world."

There was considerably less approval in his eyes after that last bit.

I WISHED their first meal as free dragons could've been more impressive.

There was no fresh meat in the captured camps of the Rolman soldiers, but there was plenty of the dried variety. Blaris and the horned dragon, Saba, brought back some small game from Oster's arid plains to liven things up. But what we lacked in fine food, we made up for in camaraderie. There was also ale. I realized after the first barrel was consumed that I needed to ration the supply, or no one was going to remember anything I said.

We chose an open landscape within sight of the Shard for our first-ever dragon council. We numbered ten. It was both a remarkable number, and a tragedy. There were but two fire-breathing ash dragons. I worried if that was enough to beat the rust, even with Rinxia and Kiata to help.

My kin had questions, but fewer than I expected given the momentous change in our collective circumstances. I think that was due to the particularly diabolical nature of the control runes—they enslaved us without our truly realizing we were slaves. The mind-slavery provided a kind of false contentment, because pleasing our masters was our single overriding concern. It would take some time for my brothers and sisters to fully realize that. Better to let them get there on their own. Also, I didn't want to talk that much. It turned out that chatting with too many dragons was exhausting. Mostly, they were concerned with the war and the fate of Rolm, because that was what had mattered to them before this day.

"Will Oster attack Eladrell?" Saba wondered.

"It no longer matters to us," was the answer of Arutel.

"Is Oster now our friend?" Blaris wanted to know.

I told my kin about my favorable opinions of Jalena, and that she had risked her life to help me obtain aurathorn, the strange vine that had helped to free them all. That seemed to have the desired effect. Linked dragons all understood the human concept of gratitude well enough. The consensus was that the Osterans themselves would decide their future relationship with our kind. Dragons were far less bloodthirsty with full bellies and a barrel of ale.

"Why shouldn't we punish the humans?" asked Arutel, who was one of the few who hadn't touched the drink. "They took us from our nests and made us slaves."

Dragon eyes flashed with approval. Arutel spoke like he would be willing to burn Eladrell that very night. I didn't want that. I had changed.

"The Sculptors of Eladrell should indeed be dealt with. And they will be," I assured him.

"Let us do it now, while they are unaware of what has happened here," Arutel pressed. "I will burn their temple and watch them scream as they turn to ash."

Most of my brethren seemed to think that was an excellent plan. The burden of being an ember dragon had revealed itself already. I didn't relish the role or what I must now do. I had given this moment considerable thought, but I still didn't feel ready. "There will be time for everything, but we have a higher calling. There is something we, as a race, must now do."

A lot of surprised dragons looked at me. At least one snorted with derision—I think it was Arutel.

I had to tell them more, but how much? I glanced longingly at the ale barrels before returning my attention to the inevitable. "Long ago, we dragons came into being when the world was in peril. We destroyed the threat, but it has now returned. Our enemy is stronger than ever before, while we are depleted and robbed of much of our power as well as the lore of our race. But we are dragons, and we have been through worse."

Blaris captured the mood of the gathering. "What are you talking about?"

"Our true enemy is known as the rust."

I spoke deep into the night. I spoke about our history, at least what I knew about it. The notion that humans, even long-dead ones, had created us, wasn't popular. I moved on, telling my kin to believe whatever they wished for now, that there was much I still didn't know. I told them of the rust, and the past, when dragons had cleansed the land with the power of balefire. Then I told them about Ni-Yota, the land beyond the Wall of Fire, a vast land of plenty, ruled until recently by dragons.

"There are others of our kind beyond the Wall of Fire?" asked Saba in wonderment, even though I had just told her and the others exactly that. I understood her reaction. It was a comfort to know we weren't alone, even though few dragons remained in Ni-Yota. And I desperately missed and worried about those same dragons. I wanted to be there, not here in a jabberfest.

"In Ni-Yota, our kind once thrived," I told them, trying to muster some of Harlan's dramatic flair. He used his voice, his face, and his hand to create mood and images. I compensated with the emotion in my eyes, but also by trying to push imagery from my memory into my brethren's severed rune-links. I could manage only the roughest communication for the moment, but I knew the potential was there.

"Few of us now remain in Ni-Yota. Those that do are fighting desperately in an impossible battle against the rust ... and other enemies. It falls to us to put things right, as our ancestors did centuries ago."

That got them. Harlan would've been proud, I think. The idea of saving the land of dragons, even if lots of humans also happened to live there, struck at the newly-awakened imaginations of my brethren. Also, the legacy of what we were remained in these dragons. We had been created to destroy the rust, and that instinct returned easily.

"We still have plenty of fire," Arutel declared naively.

"Fire is not enough, as our ancestors learned. Only the balefire can cleanse the world of the rust."

"But you said balefire was lost to us when Rima cracked," Blaris pointed out. I was grateful someone had been listening.

"There is a way to bring it back. My mother found that path, and she died to give us the chance. But her death was not in vain. We can do this, but it shall not be easy. The rust is not some passive growth waiting for us to find a way to destroy it. It adapts, and it and its minions will doubtless be ready for battle. Only once the rust is defeated can we be truly free."

"What can possibly stand against the might of all of us?" Arutel boasted.

If ignorant confidence could deliver our salvation, we would be victorious with Arutel alone, but I knew it would be harder than that. At every turn, with every stratagem, the rust and its hollowings had found some way to answer. It had survived the centuries; it had somehow survived balefire once in the past. I needed to find a way to destroy it completely this time, or there would be no more dragons left. And I still didn't know quite how. Still, there was no need to share my fears on this night. Let them think victory was certain. At least my brothers and sisters would get some sleep—I would not.

FORTY-FIVE

While the others slumbered, I prepared to fly.

I walked as silently as I could, moving away from the thicket of sleeping dragons so that I might lift myself into the sky without waking any of my kin. It turned out that dragons do, in fact, snore. Also, I didn't move as quietly as I thought, or else not all my brethren slept.

Blaris hurried to my side. "Where are you off to, my brother?"

I didn't want to tell her but I didn't want to lie either. "Veralon. To see if there are any more of us."

Blaris' eyes darkened to near black. She had something to tell me, but couldn't bring herself to say it.

"On Veralon ... we did things." She hung her head as words failed.

"You were not in control of yourself. Tell me."

"When Dayne became king ... he wanted more dragons. He was warned adult dragons cannot be taken, that the dragons on Veralon were without sound minds anyway. He would not listen." Blaris looked away from me, as if ashamed. "You will not like what you find there."

"Still, I will go," I told her.

Blaris forced herself to look at me again. "I will fly with you. We should face that place together."

I loved my sister for the offer. Already, she showed remorse and kindness. I hoped we would be a better kind of dragon. Yet, I didn't want any company.

"I must go alone. I will be back in the early morning for our journey." She seemed on the verge of protesting, so I added, "Watch over the others while I am gone."

Before Blaris could change her mind, I lifted myself into the air, headed for the once-forbidden island of Veralon.

Its precise location in the shoal-infested Dagger Sea northwest of Rolm was the most closely-held secret of Rolm, whose warships plied the waters for intruders while (before today) dragon patrols ensured the exclusivity of Rolm's most prized asset.

Since my mind had been freed, Veralon had held a special allure, but I didn't undertake this journey for curiosity's sake. I heard Blaris' bitter words, but I still hadn't abandoned all hope. I couldn't, because I feared that three ash dragons would not be enough against the nemesis we faced. Supposedly, there were no more ash dragons on Veralon anyway, but Kiata's father as well as mine had been of that island, based on what my mother had told me before she died. I pressed onward, and dread flew with me.

Despite its reputation for security and secrecy, I encountered few difficulties on my journey. I saw no sign of Rolman warships, nor of any dragon patrols. The last of Rolm's strength had been committed to the Osteran campaign. I found Veralon quickly enough.

At a distance, the island appeared smaller than I expected. Shaped like a cracked egg, it was many times the size of Maricopa, but still a speck compared with the vastness of Ni-Yota. The island was dotted with teeth-like peaks that seemed to rise from nowhere. The stories told of a lush place, filled with jungle beneath its peaks, the sea lanes leading to its stony beaches made perilous by hidden shoals in the water on every side. The island I gazed upon was so different than what I expected that I hoped I had come to the wrong place.

I hadn't. Veralon had been burned to cinders.

I made a long, slow arc over the devastated island, disgusted at the petty rage of the man who had ordered this—and I had no doubt it had been Dayne. There was not a tree still standing. Even the rocks of mountains were scorched. It was so senseless. What had happened here?

My knowledge of Dayne made the fate of Veralon obvious. The dragons that still remained here must've defied King Dayne's wishes. My mother had told me they were a lost offshoot of our kind, driven from their senses by the shattering of Rima. Yet, my mother had still come here to mate. Surely, that meant the dragons retained something of their former selves. I felt sure that one of my mother's hopes had been that I'd find a way to bring the dragons of this place back to their rightful place. I had hoped that too. It seemed I had failed before I had even started.

I landed on Veralon, even though I already knew there would be nothing to find, no dragon to save. There was only one last thing I could do for my dead brothers and sisters, and that was to mourn their passing.

I let loose a grievous roar, letting it turn into a desperate howl of mourning, just as I'd done for my mother. I didn't know these dragons, but they were my kin. My father might well lie dead on this forsaken island. I bid them all a last farewell, but I dared not tarry for long. The sun would return soon.

I headed back to Oster, not to my dragon encampment, though. First, I needed to collect Harlan. Bringing a human with us wouldn't be popular with Arutel and the others, but they would have to learn sooner or later that we were stuck with the humans. They had knowledge that we dragons needed if we were going to save this world.

I arrived back at the Shard in the back half of the night. I was expected. The gate of the diamond mountain was open, although there were plenty of Osteran guards inside and the ballistae were ready. Harlan waited dressed in his enchanted armor, pacing in the same garden where we'd first met Jalena. Norta was with him, as I'd asked.

"Do dragons not sleep?" Norta asked as I set down on the grass.

"Not on nights when fate is deciding which way it will fall."

"My husband has told me much about you." She flashed a cross glance at Harlan, implying his status as her mate was very much in doubt. "Even allowing for his embellishment, his stories about you are remarkable. Far different than any dragon known in our history."

I wondered what about me Harlan had thought important enough to share with this woman. "Do your people keep records of many dragons?"

"Oh, yes. Your kind were created to thwart the designs of our ancestors. They tried to learn all they could about you."

This wasn't what I'd come to discuss, but the knowledge of Norta's people was important. Indeed, they might know well more about my own race than I did. "And what do the ancestors of Farlight have to say about us?"

"That you are a warrior race, created to defeat the rust, then die. The humans that made you intended to create fierce fighters, so they imbued into your race the traits to further those ends: strength, fearlessness, loyalty to each other, a sense of duty, and a hunger to accomplish your goals. But they didn't intend for your race to survive forever. They didn't bother with other traits that humans consider essential—compassion, friendship, the ability to love. The dragons we have a record of are consistent with all that."

"That was centuries ago. No matter how we were once created, we have grown."

Norta allowed herself a slight nod. "You have, at least. But you are not like the others, are you?" She held her chin as she looked at me. "You've done more than grow."

"I was a slave to a human mind. I understand your kind."

"From what Harlan has said, it is more than understanding. You are more human than the rest of your kind."

I showed her my very large teeth. "I did not come here to eat insults."

Harlan interrupted. "Bayloo, it was a compliment."

Norta didn't care about my implied threats anyway. She was curious ... and more. She smelled opportunity. "You need more from me," she surmised, looking at me and then Harlan. "What is it that you are missing?"

"You recognized that ... thing that the Pale Wrights possessed. Those glass cups, the dragon egg ... you know what it is. How it works?"

"It is a machine ... a creation forge, as I told you. The ancestors used them to create things. There were many different forges. It is not surprising that the Shades had one. Some forges were used to create specialized beings—living creatures that performed tasks that people needed: worms to fertilize soil, fish that bred ten thousand of their kind in a single spawning, birds that spoke. Other forges existed for different purposes. Some even created other machines."

"Your people had one of these forges as well," I surmised. "It can be used as a weapon as well, I would think. Is that how Rima was almost destroyed?"

"Farlight has ... had many treasures. Yes, a forge was among them, one that could create fabulous things. But our forges stopped functioning when Rima became active in the sky. We did not damage Rima. We lacked that power. Your own creators did that, as they fought against your kind."

"Rima, too, was made in a forge, then?"

"Indeed, but we didn't make Rima," Norta reminded me unnecessarily. "Its power undoes all we strove for."

"But you understand the process of forge-creation. You possess more of the history of the Cataclysm than any other person on this world, or so it seems."

Norta sighed, as if resigned, but I didn't believe she was conceding anything. She was still searching for my true purpose, and to understand if she could use my need to her advantage. Our creators were wise to not make dragons like humans. "Rima was created in a forge, and lifted above the world to do its work."

To even say such a thing seemed incredible. I understood the lure of Sci-Ance if it could do such a thing. "Rima blocks your Sci-Ance, and replaces it with different laws, a different order."

"That is essentially correct."

"We dragons were created in one of these forges as well?"

Norta nodded slowly. "I wasn't there, but that is how things were done before the Cataclysm. Hundreds or thousands of dragons were created at the same time Rima was sent into the sky. As I understand it, the rust had been running rampant for decades, unstoppable, its roots in the ground deep. It took the balefire of many dragons to finally defeat it everywhere."

That worried me. We dragons were so few now. "Where was this special forge that created dragons located?"

Norta shrugged. "Your progenitors were understandably secretive. If the other ancients of their time knew how or where they worked, your creators would've been destroyed long before you came to exist. The utter destruction of Sci-Ance was not a popular event."

"Was it in Ni-Yota? Is that why the Wall of Fire existed? Is it the legacy of a protection of some kind for that land?"

"I honestly don't know. As much as we Farlighters still know, we too only have fragments of history."

"How did the Archivists—that is what I've come to call the humans that created us—when we refused to meekly die, how did they fight against dragons without their Sci-Ance?"

"They turned to the weapon that was available, of course. They created magic, they knew how to use it, even if that wasn't the original intent. Your war with your creators was a battle of magic. They did their best, but you know the result."

I thought of the Grafts that Legao used to command the Latticework—dull things, not properly of the Latticework. They were more like a hastily constructed repair—like a slab of wood placed on a wagon axle at the last moment to keep it running. Human magic was rough. Brutal. The Ar-Shadow was merely a distorted reflection of the actual Latticework, created to allow their limited senses to manipulate magic. Human power lacked the elegance of dragon magic, but that made sense if it had been born out of necessity, during war. This was what the Archivists had created so that they might defeat the dragons they had created. "Even with magic, how could something such as Rima be damaged?"

"I don't know that. Your creators ... the Archivists, as you call them, were a resourceful people. Maybe even more so than my own." I saw a glimmer of something sinister in Norta's eye. "Why are you so curious about this bit of history? About forges and Sci-Ance?"

There was no way I was going to tell her the truth, but I was afraid she might guess anyway. "So much has been lost. We need to understand how we came to be if we are to avoid our past mistakes."

It wasn't enough of an answer. I could see Norta's mind racing behind her dark eyes. Finally, she laughed a triumphant laugh. "You don't know how to destroy it. You were bluffing like my dear husband. You can't destroy the rust."

I huffed. "I am an ember dragon. I understand the hidden secrets of the Latticework."

Norta wasn't impressed. "Fire and magic weren't enough against the rust. Only balefire finally destroyed it the first time. But that was before you turned on your creators and killed them. That was before Rima was shattered in the war that followed." Finally, she understood. "Balefire is lost to you. And you are so few now, anyway. You cannot win. The Archivists are dead, as are their secrets. Your kind ensured that."

"My ancestors protected themselves, protected their right to live," I said defensively. "And I do indeed know the secret of balefire." I hoped I wasn't bluffing.

"Then why are we talking" Norta asked. "What do you need me for?"

I had grown too weary to lie, and I think she already knew anyway. "Because you are correct that balefire has not been summoned to this world since Rima was shattered. Because it is not enough to understand how balefire is created. I also need to be sure that I can summon it with enough power to destroy the rust once and for all. Our balefire must be even greater than that used by my ancestors. The rust adapts. There will not be another chance."

Norta's gaze was hard and determined. "The ancient Farlighters may indeed have underestimated their creation when they made the rust. Certainly, they didn't anticipate the lengths other humans would go to avoid the fate my ancestors intended for them. But your creators made the same mistake. Dragons became far more than they imagined, adapting, and yes, stealing power that your creators never meant for you to have. The dragons themselves became rulers, as happened in Ni-Yota. You destroyed the humans, then you took over their land." Norta stared at her husband. "Humans are prone to making terrible mistakes."

I let a low, rumbling roar echo through my throat. "Dragons do not seek to destroy all life. We kill when we must. We do not lust for more than we need—we are not like you and your rust. We shall not repeat the hubris of the humans and become slaves to our own power."

"There may yet come a time when you need humans, Bayloo. You may even need the Farlighters." Norta stretched her lips into something that was supposed to be a smile, but brought chills rather than warmth. "I shall be waiting for that day."

I WAS anxious to return to Ni-Yota.

I spent the morning with my fellow dragons eating Rolman supplies and discussing the hollowings. It was difficult to describe the enemy to them, for I didn't know precisely what we would find when we returned to Ni-Yota. When I left, the rust was advancing, while the tigris still fought a brutal campaign in the east. A human wizard had taken command of Ni-Yota, perhaps with the intent of raising an army of fellow magi. But whatever my feelings toward Legao, she was powerful, and she had Rinxia and Kiata with her. I hoped that they had managed to hold the worst of the threat at bay. Perhaps they had even come up with a plan to worked. I was anxious for Arutel and Blaris to meet Rinxia as well. Together, their fire would have to cleanse the world. Three ash dragons assisted by two ember dragons to do a task that had once been accomplished by hundreds of my kind, and that had been before Rima had been damaged.

"How do you know that the balefire will come to us?" Blaris asked me for the third time that morning.

I gave her the same answer again. "I know it. The Latticework is part of me, just as the balefire is part of you, even if you don't realize it. Rima has been damaged, but the power is still there. I know it can be done. Trust me in this."

"Should we not attempt to call balefire now, before we cross the Wall of Fire?"

"The magic necessary is … difficult. I fear I will be able to do it only once and I need my sister as well. We do not have the time. But I know it can be done."

That was all a lie, which pained me to tell, but I couldn't share my true reasons for not wanting to bring forth the balefire. Not yet.

After everyone had eaten and I'd silenced all the grumbling about the human I carried on my back, we took to the air—all the remaining dragons. I tried to enjoy the moment, but could not. There was too much that could go wrong.

"You did not need to come," I said to Harlan. "You can be with your people."

"I made my choice, Bayloo."

"You turned against them. Against your own mate. Back in the Shard … her eyes had no kindness for you." Then I added some additional words because Harlan had earned them. "I am sorry for what has happened to you. Your bond of friendship has great meaning to me. You are my first and only friend."

He looked at me, pain and resignation in his features. "Aye, dragon, we've been chosen for each other, it seems. I've been too long away from the rest of my people ... I've seen too much, and I know what is in your hearts. My people's beliefs about dragons were wrong. Once I understood that, I knew that other things could be wrong as well. As for my wife ... well, that's complicated. Women are complicated."

I thought of Rinxia. "Indeed, they are."

"But we are a part of something, we two friends. Your quest is now mine. Our bond will see us through this. I will not abandon you, just as I know you would do the same for me."

Something clogged in my throat for a moment. Some stray meat? I thought it best to stop talking.

I flew soon after that. The great armada of dragons first went to Ulibon. The arrival of a swarm of dragons set off more than a minor panic in the Twisted Keep, but the tidings we brought about the defeat of the Rolman army quickly improved the mood. I tried to coax another set of *sai* out of Bethy Rann and her enchantress, but she was having none of it. I had brought a bit of aurathorn for Crema, severing what remained of her rune-link. It didn't seem to make any difference to her damaged mind, though. The injury that had been done to Crema wasn't easily cured. Some of what she had once been was lost, apparently forever. I mourned for her, but at least she was alive. Crema would be safer in Ulibon than any dragon who flew with me to Ni-Yota.

After taxing the Twisted Keep's food stores, we flew again, this time passing over the open seas until we finally reached the smoldering mountains of the Wall of Fire.

"Follow my route," I told them all as we neared and a putrid odor began to permeate the air. "Do not falter. Do not slow."

I flew for the secret mountain that Vengeance had told me about months ago—months that now seemed like an eternity. I wondered how the strange ghastray and his kind had fared against the hollowing leviathans. Somehow, I was certain the ghastrays would find a way to deal with any threat in their domain, just as they had done since the

Cataclysm. If we could stop the rust in Ni-Yota, we could be rid of the hollowings everywhere. But first came the Wall of Fire.

It wasn't pleasant. Even though it was my third time flying this route, there was still that moment of panic, when I feared the disorientation of the fog. For a dragon, to lose our sense of direction and place was among the most disconcerting experiences. I worried for my fellow dragons. I willed them through, roaring encouragement and giving them a beacon that I had never had. With the sound to guide them, they knew they were not lost and they weren't alone. On the other side would be Ni-Yota, and Rinxia and Kiata. It would be a relief to be back, to see them again, and let them know that I had a plan to defeat the rust. I returned to Ni-Yota with hope.

I passed through the smoke of the mountain, relieved as the air sweetened and the sky began to brighten. Then it stopped. It should've been shining daylight on the other side of the wall, but it wasn't. Something terrible had happened here.

My hearts thundered as I struggled to understand the strange sights around me, but it was already too late. A curtain of black came for me.

FORTY-SIX

Swirling darkness surged toward me.

The black sheet in the sky was large and dense enough to blot out the light behind it, casting a dark shadow over everything. As my initial surprise passed, I recognized the threat: blood raptors. Thousands of them. The rust had replenished its forces. But how did the rust know I'd be here? All the possible answers were ominous.

My immediate problem was that the birds were going to tear Harlan to shreds in moments, and my fellow dragons were flying into a storm of harm they were totally unprepared to confront. I dove, heading nearly straight to the sea, intending to get below the black wave coming at me. As expected, the birds adjusted course. I turned swiftly, beating my wings. I moved quickly, but not at my best speed. I wanted to draw the raptors off before the next dragon came through. It didn't work.

I roared a warning to Arutel as he struggled through the Wall of Fire, disoriented. The raptors had closed the distance to the smoking mountains, and my fellow dragons had even less time to react than I to a threat they had not faced before.

"Those birds serve the rust. Protect your eyes." I knew Harlan would do the same. He had his enchanted covering to protect him as well.

Arutel responded to my warning with fire—the first instinct of an ash dragon. He roasted dozens of birds even as he flew directly into the feathery wave. Hundreds more blood raptors latched onto him, but my brother didn't panic. He executed a sharp turn, holding his pace, spraying more fire as he tried to clear a path for our fellow dragons as they emerged from the inferno smoke. His courage attracted even more ravens to me. I called upon the Latticework, summoning wind and cold, even as I kept enough speed to elude the hundreds of blood raptors trailing me. I ascended higher into the sky, letting the birds draw closer, then I dove again, sweeping beneath the swarm.

My conjured mist of cold was ready. I pushed it at the great mass of birds that harried the sky around Arutel and my other kin. A satisfying sound distinctly similar to glass shattering followed as raven feathers froze into brittle icicles, then snapped as the birds attempted to use their wings. As dragon fire erupted across the sky, the heat rapidly reversed the birds' temperature change, with deadly effect. Soon, a rain of avian parts tumbled into the sea. Still, hundreds of hollowing birds remained. The sheer numbers were such that I couldn't see clearly enough to be sure all my kin had made it through the Wall of Fire. Dragon roars shook the sky; chaos reigned among us. For that I was responsible—I had brought them here, and I was the ember dragon, meant to lead.

"To me!" I roared.

They came, with the blood raptors following. Many of my kin had birds clinging to their bodies, while the raptors' razor beaks pecked at their dragon scales.

"Fly strong, I will cleanse you," I told them.

Once we had put sufficient distance between us and the larger bird horde, I sent another blast of freezing mist at my brethren. Unlike blood raptors, dragon blood flows hot, and we're made of sturdier stuff than any little bird. The cold wouldn't damage a dragon wing the way it froze raptor feathers.

Arutel and Blaris assisted my cleaning efforts with carefully calibrated blasts of fire. Those efforts rid us of the vast majority of raptors, although a few tenacious stragglers had to be removed with claws.

We had overcome our first obstacle. When I finally slowed the pace of our flight, I knew that every dragon shared my fatigue. Even with the stop in Ulibon, it had been a long flight to the Wall of Fire. Another daunting journey lay ahead to Ni-Yota itself. I'd rested at the floating waystation the last time I was here, but there was no chance of rest now, not with the blood raptors still in pursuit.

"We make for land at speed," I told my brethren.

For a large ash dragon, the flight to Ni-Yota was long and hard, but doable. For our smaller kin, I feared the distance was too great after the trauma they had just traversed. While the occasional atoll poking out of the sea could have provided a respite for some, I didn't want to stop with the blood raptors trailing us. If we left one of our number behind—particularly a horned dragon—they would be swarmed and killed. That wasn't an option.

I summoned a mighty wind from behind us, bringing the gust down from above and directing it at our tails. The gales weren't enough to let us glide the whole distance to Ni-Yota, but they provided additional speed, as well as a respite from constant use of our wings. As the day wore on, several of the horned dragons neared exhaustion despite the helping wind, but Arutel, Blaris, and I alternated essentially carrying our kin through the air for brief intervals to give them a respite. Together, we flew to within sight of the coast of Ni-Yota without the loss of a single one of our number. The blood raptors had disappeared behind us. Hollowings didn't need sleep or sustenance like living creatures, nor did they have unlimited stamina. The bodies of their captured hosts broke just like ours did. We had made it. But the sight of land offered no glad tidings; Ni-Yota burned.

As far as my dragon eyes could see, there was smoke. Villages and fields, castles and cities, everywhere some kind of fire either seemed to rage or had showed signs of being recently extinguished. A thick smog hung low across the landscape, like a roof catching the sooty refuse of the flames raging beneath it.

"Who did this?" Blaris asked me. "Not those vicious birds. They are not fire breathers, at least."

I didn't know the source of the mayhem, but I had a decent guess. "When I left, battles still raged in the eastern domain of Ni-Yota, the embers of a rebellion led by giant cat-like creature known as the tigris, along with some opportunistic human allies."

Blaris was surprised. "Purring felines did this? The ones that vomit hairballs?"

"The tigris aren't cute. They are giant cat-like monsters that talk and deceive as well as any human," I said. "Perhaps it was them, but it could be more, for the damage is so widespread. Clearly, things have not gone well for Ni-Yota since I have been gone."

"Where are the other dragons you spoke of?"

I wanted to know that too. Given the devastation in the far east, they must be occupied with even greater crises elsewhere, or they would be here. "This land is vast—a hundred times the size of Rolm. It is likely they fight against the rust in the far west, across the mountains that divide Ni-Yota, but I do not know. We will find them quickly enough."

Arutel snorted with impatience. "We came here to destroy this rust, to exhale balefire like our ancestors. Shall we burn these giant cats—the tigris—instead?"

"If only it would be so easy. I shall go closer."

"I will accompany you."

I didn't relish having Arutel along for any task that didn't involve burning or killing, but I didn't have time for a battle for primacy now. "Let Blaris stay with the horned dragons, then, keeping high above the land. Seeing so many of us will scare the locals."

"I thought you said dragons ruled here, that we were revered."

"That was before we started fighting each other. Before we

started acting like humans."

I flew to Ni-Yota with Arutel in my wake. I could sense my companion's fascination with what he was seeing—this vast land which seemed to go on forever, a place where dragons were never slaves. That had been me once. How quickly things change. Now, this was a place that sat on the precipice of doom, where dragons plotted for power just like humans had before the Cataclysm.

My brother and I landed in a fishing village. It hadn't burned— barns and simple dwellings still stood. Small boats lined the rocky beach. It smelled of dead fish, but there was no living creature to be found. Harlan slid from my back to investigate the dwellings. He too found nothing.

"The humans have left," Arutel said unnecessarily.

"They took their livestock and supplies. From the look of this place, they left quickly, but not in a panic," Harlan said.

Finding no answers in the empty village, we soon departed. I led us next to the nearest plume of smoke, which turned out to be the remains of a town consisting of perhaps half of a hundred buildings built around two rutted roads and a ruined palisade. I didn't like what I found there.

The north side of the town's wall had been badly burned, as had most of the structures inside the wall. It was the pattern of the fire that disturbed me: the tops of buildings had been charred and there were no other signs of fighting. Several of the largest wooden structures still had a slow smolder. If the tigris or their allies had attacked, I would've expected more obvious signs of fighting—bodies, broken weapons, spent arrows. There were none here.

"Just more burning," Arutel said, sniffing the air. "Although there is meat nearby."

I saw more than my brother in the wreckage. "A dragon did this. The buildings have all been scorched from above."

Arutel wasn't concerned. "Perhaps they deserved their fate, then."

My brother didn't know Ni-Yota, but I did. The only fire breather that survived in Ni-Yota was Rinxia. Why would she burn an insignificant town in the east? Harlan probably had his guesses, but he kept his silence, reluctant to discuss anything while Arutel was near. I didn't press him.

As I contemplated my dark thoughts on what had happened here, Arutel spoke more practically. "We have been flying non-stop. Our brothers and sisters need rest. There is food here as well. Not fresh, perhaps, but I hunger."

I gazed westward, where the Pillar Mountains stood high in the distance, separating the great domains of Ni-Yota. Despite the ache in my wings and the emptiness in my stomach, I wanted to fly now, but Arutel had the right of this. "Gather our brethren. Let them eat and sleep. It is another long flight tomorrow, even if we have the wind to aid us."

It's never difficult to get dragons to eat. The meat that Arutel located was partially-roasted cattle and chickens that had been dead or dying for too many days to tempt me. It didn't dissuade my kin, who were still accustomed to human scraps far worse than this. Life hadn't always been easy since I'd become me, but I had gotten to taste some of the finer things in life. Fortunately for me, some of the livestock of the town had fled when the human inhabitants ran away, but they still stuck close to the area where they had been raised. It just took a bit more effort to hunt them. Of course, it turned out to be chickens on the prowl. I was cursed. Still, I forced two birds down my throat, feathers and all, then I managed to sleep, for I'd had none the previous night. With the dawn, I awoke with my brethren to fly.

Mostly, we kept above the clouds, traversing the great landscape of Ni-Yota. I called upon the wind at several instances to speed our journey. The speed at which we traveled made conversation uncomfortable, though not impossible. Arutel and Blaris worried about balefire.

"How will we breathe that which we have never commanded before?" they wanted to know. "We know fire."

"It is within us when we work together; the breath of ash dragons and the magic of ember dragons," I told them with more confidence than I felt. "We are linked by the Latticework. Its energy makes us more, together. We were born to destroy the rust, and we shall."

They were brave words. I hope they gave the other dragons some comfort as we flew over burnt keeps and blackened fields. Not all the land had been scorched, certainly—Ni-Yota was far too vast a place for that. But the damage was extensive, and there was no sign of marching armies. By the end of a day of flying, I had no doubt a dragon had done this. The Pillar Mountains loomed ahead.

My brothers and sisters slept in an open field, each pressed up against the other, although the night was warm. I stayed apart. Even among my own kind, I was different, and I carried a heavier burden. Harlan understood some of that.

"Your mind is on Rinxia."

Rima had crept into the sky, her strange light shining upon us as we spoke, adding the feeling of fate in the night.

I didn't bother to deny Harlan's guess. "She is the only fire breather in Ni-Yota."

There were plenty of reassurances or platitudes that Harlan could have offered me in the night. He chose none. He merely looked at me through the eerie light. There was nothing more to be said. It would be worthwhile to rest, not to worry.

The dying echo of a distant roar woke me before dawn. None of my brethren stirred. Even Harlan still slept, curled in a ball nearby, still wearing his enchanted cloak from Ulibon in his sleep. I struggled to remember the sound I'd heard when half-awake, but its memory was faint and unfamiliar. I listened carefully for any other sounds. I expected to hear more, perhaps the beating of wings, but I did not. There was nothing. Not even the chirping of birds that would usually accompany the approach of morning. I pulled myself to my feet. That brought Harlan out of his slumber. He crawled over to me.

"What is it?"

"A dragon awaits us in the mountains. A dragon I have never met before."

FORTY-SEVEN

I could wait no longer.

I had waited for dawn to come. I had waited for my brothers and sisters to bestir themselves. I had waited as my fellow dragons plied the sky at their languid pace. I wanted to be at the mountains. What I had heard had been no dream. A dragon was there—or had been there.

As the great peaks neared, I pushed further ahead of the rest of my kin. Even Blaris and Arutel couldn't match my speed. I needed to be at the mountains.

"Have a care," Harlan cautioned.

I knew he was correct, but I didn't slow. It was a relief to move through the air, to push myself for speed. It kept the anxious fear that had been building up inside me at bay, at least temporarily. From high above, I spotted the keep at Hundra Pass. At least it hadn't been burned. Its banners still flew, pushed eastward by the winds whipping through the canyon it guarded. Yet, I saw no life there, no soldiers on its walls; no heat or smoke rose from its bakeries or hearths. I could think of no reason why a fortress of such strategic value would be abandoned. The mountains came closer, until finally

I passed over the foothills. I circled the mouth of the Hundra Pass from high above. In that moment, the horror revealed itself: the rust had come.

The western wall of the keep was infested, as were the mountains of the pass itself. I understood why the occupants had fled. Swords and arrows were useless against the rust. Only balefire could turn it back. That was why I had come, bringing Arutel and Blaris. Soon it would be time for us to discover if the great plague could be destroyed. Except the rust wasn't the worst of it.

Even as my eyes fixated on the spreading contamination, a dragon rose from hiding in one of the valleys to the northwest. The morning sun reflected off of its scales, the glint nearly blinding. The form was familiar yet foreign, the movement of its wings strangely halting, but it came with power and speed. I turned about, cautious at first, until I recognized the silvery scales and elegant mane. My hearts screamed for my wings to move faster, and they did. It was Rinxia. Finally, she was here. Alive. She was alive. The rest I would fix.

"Bayloo ..." Part of me heard the cold dread in Harlan's voice, but I didn't want to acknowledge it.

I could see the elegant curves of Rinxia's form as she cut through the air. My eyes locked on hers. I glowed with excitement. In return, she stared back from an empty void.

I recognized what I faced, but I couldn't bring myself to turn, to stop. I couldn't accept it. This was one horror too many, one loss that I couldn't bear.

Harlan told me what I already knew. "She's a hollowing."

I roared with a mad rage. My body trembled with anguish. A single thought dominated my mind: save her. There had to be a way to save her. That was the reason I kept flying toward her. The hollowing-Rinxia was almost as fast as the living one. She came at me, bathing me in her flames. My face, my neck, and Harlan too.

He screamed in pain, writhing on my back as he desperately hid beneath his enchanted cloak of magic. That may have saved his life, but it didn't protect my vision. The flames had seared one of my eyes;

the soft fluid inside bubbled and burned. I was half-blind. Rinxia would be on me again in a moment. I had no idea where she was, but I knew what she was: a hollowing. She would sink her claws into me, her teeth. I had come so close to ending this, but the rust must've known that. Somehow, it knew whatever Rinxia had known.

I sensed her a moment before she struck. She came from my blind side, rising from below, her jaws already open. There was no roar, no sound, no pity. I prepared to absorb the blow as best I could. I was numb to the peril. Part of me wanted Rinxia to come, to kill me. There was nothing to do. I accepted death, until magic intervened. But not my magic.

Lightning flashed—the bolt appeared so close to me that the spikes on my mane curled in the heat. Rinxia was hit, but she didn't cry out. Only the cracking of her scales confirmed that the summoned strike had struck its target. She still reached for me—a foreclaw stretched out in malice even as Rinxia's strength failed her. She fell toward the ground as I looked away, searching the sky for my savior with my one functioning eye.

Kiata flew toward us out of the west. As painful as it was to confront Rinxia, my relief at seeing my sister whole in her flesh took half the weight of a mountain off my wings. She had grown, not just in size but in strength. That bolt had both power and precision. My sister had come into her legacy as an ember dragon—just as our mother had hoped and planned. I hoped she understood control as well.

"Don't kill her!" I roared to Kiata. "We can save her."

Kiata flew close. The flashes of her eyes told a saga of emotion in moments. There was too much even for a fellow dragon to absorb, but one message came through clear. Just so there was no mistake, Kiata spoke it as well. "She is gone. She is hollow."

There wasn't time for any more discussion. Rinxia was climbing back into the sky toward us. The black hole in her neck scale would've been agony for a regular dragon, but a hollowing felt no pain. What was left of Rinxia would fight until her body failed her.

She did not return alone. A flood of blood raptors rose up from mountain valleys and down from high peaks. They swarmed up from the Hundra Pass and even from hidden crags in the rocky mountainside. They flew at Kiata and I, but also at the wave of dragons who had followed me here from the east. I had no doubt that the intellect of the rust knew why I had returned. It mustered all of its forces to stop us. I roared a warning to my brethren, but trusted that Blaris and Arutel would be ready with their fire. I had to deal with Rinxia.

She came again, flying at me like an arrow with all that remained of her speed. There was no subtlety in the attack—not Rinxia's style at all. This was the rust, its urgency driving her shell.

The rust knows I am key, because Rinxia knew.

I needed to immobilize her; wound her, stop her, but not kill her. No hollowing had ever been saved or healed, but did that mean it was impossible?

I had enough time to call upon the sky's fury. So did Kiata. "Don't, sister. Please."

Kiata growled her displeasure. "Your hearts rule your head like a human."

I had a lot of human in me. That would help me beat the rust, in the end. But it also meant I needed to find a way to save Rinxia, even if that wasn't the Way for other dragons. I called the cold, rather than the flashing fire. Streams of hail formed, coming toward us from the north and east. I flew upward, knowing Rinxia would follow. I beat my wings, creating distance to give my conjuring time to increase in power. Despite her injuries, Rinxia somehow quickened in the air. I turned and dove, but she matched my maneuvers, closing.

"Rinxia, stop this."

Dead eyes fixed on me without reaction.

The hailstorm I called from the Latticework struck her, twin funnels of hard ice battering Rinxia's scales and wings. She struggled, beating her wings, twisting at the unexpected obstacle. I called upon more power. *I need to slow her, to exhaust her.* The icy particles directed at Rinxia would have frozen and cracked a human's skin.

They barely slowed Rinxia. I called more wind, urging a vortex into existence. I twisted into another sharp turn, diving and climbing desperately through the sky to get more time. The shell of Rinxia knew my tactic. It knew me, and sensed my maneuvers.

I put more of my will into my summoning, creating a concentrated whirlwind to yank at every creature in the sky. The blood raptors were caught first, their wings too weak to keep them away once caught in the grip of the vortex. I directed the force of my creation at Rinxia, willing it to pull her into its embrace. She slowed, her strength finally dwindling. I forced even more of my energy into the summoning, directing the glowing Chords of the Latticework like a master musician plucking strings. Rinxia still came toward me, but slower. There was a chance.

"Rinxia, quit now. Enough. I shall bring you back."

Black eyes from the Abyss stared at me. Rinxia's head tilted, in a gesture that almost reminded me of her. Meanwhile, her wings continued to move. I was so close to succeeding. Or that was the illusion the creature let me believe.

"It's not her!" Harlan shouted at me.

With a burst of strength I did not suspect she still possessed, Rinxia broke from the vortex's grasp. In that singular, terrifying moment, I realized my magic summoning had never really held her. It had all been a ruse. To get closer. To tire me. I beat my wings, but Rinxia had bided her time until just the right moment, catching me in a turn. She had also been hoarding her strength. Her wings moved unnaturally fast, all of her energy directed at catching me. She did, first with a foreclaw, then with her tail. Her grip was cold, so unlike Rinxia. Because this wasn't Rinxia.

The hollowing creature went for my throat with desperate jaws. I got a foreclaw in front of her at the last moment. Her claws grappled onto me mid-flight. We tumbled as she scratched and snapped at me. Her tail struck my body, then hit the foreclaw I used to protect my throat, batting it away. Rinxia had a clear opening at my neck. She took it.

The sky screamed. The world flashed. A searing heat passed through me, scorching me.

Rinxia's claws dropped away, and so did the rest of her. Limp, she fell toward the sharp mountain rocks below.

I went for her, diving with all my speed. Harlan grasped onto me desperately, the saddle straps straining, but in that moment I didn't care. Rinxia had a smoking hole in her back, but I could still save her, if I was fast enough. I beat my wings, my trajectory nearly straight down. Rinxia's inert form spun as it fell. With strength and angle, I gained. The rocks closed faster. Pulling out of this dive with her weight was going to be ugly. I didn't care. My claws reached for Rinxia. I almost had her; then, I didn't.

Kiata slammed herself into me, knocking Rinxia from my grasp. Another claw grabbed at me, yanking, even as wind surged from beneath me. The jagged rocks faded away from me, but not from Rinxia.

She smashed into a peak. She was gone.

FORTY-EIGHT

"You killed her."

Pain I couldn't control bubbled to the surface, transforming my words to accusation. This was one loss too many. It couldn't be real. It couldn't be over.

My sister's hard eyes softened ever so slightly. "I did not kill Rinxia. The rust killed her, three days ago. I gave her peace."

We perched on the ledge of a peak, Rinxia's remains scattered below us. A great host of blood raptors swirled around my brethren in the distance, but the incoming birds had not yet reached us. I couldn't look away from the body, even though the sight churned the void of hurt inside me.

"I could've saved her," I growled with a mix of anger and agony.

Kiata spoke with neither compassion nor cruelty, as a normal dragon would. "Not unless you have become the master of the Abyss while you were away; nothing could have saved her. That thing was a shell that looked like Rinxia, but it was part of the rust."

My sister's truth was still too painful to endure. I didn't want to face this. The sorrow inside me grew, so I reached for my anger to quell it. I would have revenge for this. Inside, my agony fueled a burning desire to kill that was worthy of the late King Dayne himself. Kiata knew me well enough to see that emotion in me. I knew she didn't approve. I was different than other dragons.

"Rinxia is a great loss for us all," Kiata said. "I know that you cared for her. She knew it as well."

I merely growled. I didn't need to be told what I already knew.

"There is little time for mourning now, my brother. The hollowings and the rust went berserk, five days ago. The pestilence began to spread differently, directing itself in narrow pincers jutting deep into Ni-Yota, while its hollowing servants marshalled. Legao and her acolytes called her human magic to tear the ground asunder, to bring forth rain and water from the bay, using all of their magic to try to protect Trishan and the millions of souls huddled inside. But time is short. She may have failed already. Did you find what you sought?"

I forced my mind to refocus. Rinxia had died for this; to fail would be to fail her as well. "I can destroy the rust."

"Let us do it, then," Kiata replied, turning her head toward the hideous spread through the mountains. "This is what Rinxia would want from us. Let us act while there are still people and lands to save. But how?"

"As our ancestors did: balefire."

Kiata deflated with disappointment. "It is a legend of the past. No dragon can produce balefire."

"No dragon can do it alone. That is what our creators intended. We ember dragons are the bridge to make it. We can shift the power of the Latticework to our brethren, restoring the power of balefire to them."

Kiata's eyes told me she doubted me. Maybe she doubted my sanity. Perhaps she thought the pain of losing Rinxia addled my mind. Perhaps she was partially correct. "Brother, even I don't know how this might be done, and I feel all of the Latticework."

"You cannot feel the Gap," I reminded her. "That damaged place, the place of the eternal void. The Gap is where the power of balefire is to be found."

"There is nothing in the Gap," Kiata insisted, speaking as a dragon who relied on instinct for magic. "In that place, the Latticework is gone, destroyed."

"The destruction of Rima damaged the Latticework, robbing us of part of both its function and its power. That was when balefire was lost. But it can come back. I will make it come back."

"How?" Kiata asked. "There is nothing to manipulate in that place. The Chords are gone or useless. It would be like a human wielding a sword with no pommel."

"But what you cannot see—what no other ember dragon could ever see—is that there is a way to bridge across the Gap. To go through it, to access the Latticework and the power of balefire once again. Human magic is the key. Their Grafts are not part of the Latticework. Humans can create new connections, while we dragons must rely on those Chords that flow from the original Latticework as it was created. The Grafts created by the humans can cross the breach."

"Human magic?" Kiata said with contempt. "It is a brutal thing that eventually drives them mad. It is nothing like our power."

"Human and dragon magic are two sides of the Latticework. We sense the Chords as the Latticework's creators originally intended. But later, to fight us, the Archivists also created another mechanism of control for the Latticework—the Graft, as I call it. This is the human magic."

"So, humans must help us?"

"Humans can cross the Gap, but no human can command the dragon Chords that are also necessary for balefire. They are not linked to our fellow dragons as we are. Certainly, I would never trust Legao enough to ask. But I too can use the human Grafts. I finally understand that is why mother sent me into slavery. It was deliberate." I still had trouble saying it. Kiata didn't understand my pain. She knew the Way of dragons, like our mother. I carried the burden of being different, and I carried the burden of losing Rinxia. "To make me what I am, our mother did this. Only a mind like a human mind, an emotional mind of love and hate and passion, can access the Grafts as they do. The only way to make a dragon feel human emotion was through prolonged mingling with a human mind—slavery. But now I can use both instruments of magic. That is how I will call the magic that will grant balefire to our fellow dragons. But I will need your help as well."

"Somehow the rust knows what you can do," Kiata concluded. "That is the reason it has done what it has done. More will be coming. We know its cunning. If balefire can be summoned, let us do it now. The blood raptors have descended upon the few ash dragons that accompanied you. I will handle the birds. Do what you must."

"I cannot—not yet." I felt Kiata's disappointment flash at me. "I told you that Rima—the source of magic—was damaged. Magic itself was damaged. There isn't enough magic—enough power within the Latticework—to produce balefire as we need it. The last time we had hundreds of dragons, now we have only two firebreathers. We cannot use balefire the way our ancestors once did. But there may be another way. There is another creation forge in this land that still functions."

"A what?" Kiata was impatient. "Bayloo, much of what you say makes no sense."

"It is a machine of unimaginable power. I don't have the time to explain now. You merely need to trust me. There is one last thing that must be done, Kiata. I must do it. Our creators left one last legacy behind. That which they used to attempt to destroy us may help save us. It is you who must guide our remaining brothers. You must transfer the magic of balefire to them, as is your destiny as an ember dragon."

"What will you do?"

"I shall give you the power to do it. You must channel that magic to them. We are all connected."

I spread my wings.

"Where are you going?"

"I fly to the place where we dragons were created. The place where the last forge on this world exists—the one that created us, and there our creators used it to try to destroy us. A place hidden from the eyes of the ancient world of humans, and all the beings of this new world as well."

"Tell me where you are going," Kiata demanded.

"I fly to the Forest of Fallen Night."

"HOW DO you know it will be there?" Harlan asked as I flew, drawing upon a magical tailwind for more speed. "A working creation forge?"

"Your wife all but revealed it, although she could not know the value of her lore to me or she wouldn't have said it."

Harlan was briefly quiet as he thought. "She merely told you that your creators had to hide their work."

I spotted a formation of black coming from the east. The rust knew what I sought. I turned, headed southwest, accelerating even further. No bird would catch me. The forest was well-protected, against birds and dragons and whatever else the rust had to send against me. I merely needed to reach it without getting killed trying to get inside.

"Oracle told us the Archivists had a creation forge. It makes sense that dragons rose to dominance in the land of our creation. The stories of the Forest of Fallen Night tell of an oasis, or some call it a lake, where a being could drink and become immortal. Supposedly, this elixir turned men into the tigris, who became its guardians. But it turns out the tigris are real. They were creations of the humans who once lived there, as are dragons. All these stories lead back to the Forest of Fallen Night."

"Those are mostly stories," Harlan protested. "I could tell you better ones."

"The rust never made it to the Forest of Fallen Night. Consider that astounding thing. Nor could any dragon venture there. Only a few even desire to try to reach that place, which may be a function of the immense power that protects that place. You don't want to go there, or remember what you saw if you attempt the journey. Think of the power necessary to accomplish all that."

"Why do you believe this forge is still there? And that you can somehow use it after all this time?"

"I have no idea how to operate the machines of the ancients. Nor were they meant for dragons. But we know that the Archivists tried to destroy all the dragons. They tried to undo their creation. In desperation, they even tried to undo the magic world they'd forged by shattering Rima. But how? Rima's power blocks all Sci-Ance, all of the old dark light, even theirs. Except, I do not believe Rima was their sole source of power. They kept something for themselves. The so-called last ember within the void—a last source of power unaffected by Rima. Enough to bring balefire back into the world in a form even greater than that once wielded by my ancestors."

"May all your guesses be true," Harlan wished.

I flew until darkness fell and then flew more, aided by the winds of magic. Rima appeared and disappeared several times throughout my journey, as if trying to speak to me. If it did, I had no idea what the mysterious machine-moon wanted. Did it wish my quest good or ill?

I wanted to fly through without stopping, but that would've been foolish. The Forest of Fallen Night had protected its secret from all comers for centuries. Even though I had some idea of what protected it, I was equally certain that I didn't know everything. I finally set down on a hilltop during the late night to rest. I think Harlan slept as well, but I wasn't certain. I wasn't awake long enough to find out. The next day I flew again, resting only a portion of the night. Until, finally, I saw the forest once again.

The world had changed since I'd followed Elasu to the edge of this place, but the island forest had not. The rust had advanced to the far shores, but it had not crossed the black river water that flowed around the Forest of Fallen Night—it could not. The trees of the island were as dense, impenetrable, and forbidding as ever. The canopy was dark despite the sun's light battering it from above. The leaves shifted—perhaps from wind—but the movements were unlike any other trees I'd seen. The massive boles linked their branches and pushed at each other like an unruly mob. Sharp edges glistened on the leaves. I had no doubt those edges would be laced with poison.

"It makes the Pits of Gargen seem welcoming," Harlan remarked.

He wasn't wrong. Only this time I better understood the place upon which I gazed. Through the Latticework, I recognized the work of master craftsmen of magic. *The master craftsmen.* The creators of Rima, the creators of dragons. The people who had somehow created the Latticework and magic itself. They built this place as a sanctuary, for themselves and their secrets. This was where my kind had been created, but the creators did not want their children to visit. The vegetation had been made unwelcoming to us—poisonous. They set the tigris to guard it. Yet Elasu had entered, because that suited the tigris, I suspected. The malevolent cats might still be within.

I examined the sentinel trees through the Latticework. There was no question that the massive boles had been set in this place to keep away prying eyes and undesirable visitors—these were creations of magic, like dragons. Chords of the Latticework wove through the forest—a magical shield against light, and perhaps other things as well. Nowhere else on Inkra was there a weaving like that which protected the island. I pushed at the sentinels, probing the strength of the magical defense. The shield tightened as it sensed me. Dragons came here at their peril—unless invited by the tigris.

Using dragon Chords would avail me nothing here. This sanctuary had withstood the great war between men and dragons. But I was unlike any ember dragon that had come before. I looked inside myself, releasing that part of my mind that had been linked to humans. Indeed, in a way, my mind *was* human—it was filled with conflict, guilt, and heavy with sorrow. That part of me could see the magic of humans. I plucked at the Grafts that humans had forged in the distant past when the made the Ar-Shadow, which I now knew to be a reflection of the Latticework. I spoke to the living barrier as a human magi would, as those long-dead humans who had created this place must've once done. I asked the sentinel trees to part as humans would have, and they did, the branches moving as if a hundred arms unclasped. I flew inside the opening, descending into a clearing completely concealed until that moment. The passage downward was surprisingly long—the trees were as tall as a small mountain.

Within the hidden valley of the forest there was a gloom, but not darkness. Apparently, the canopy did also allow some filtered light through. The air smelled and felt no different than that beyond the tree shield, yet I found myself sucking in a deep breath as soon as I passed the forest perimeter, as if fatigued.

A small village, remarkably similar in design to the buildings within the Shard, stood on the ground below, silent and seemingly frozen in time. The fired clay roof tiles looked as though they had been recently cleaned, the lacquered exterior walls of the buildings shone as if they had been newly raised. Manicured gardens grew in the courtyards around ponds of clear water. Only the inhabitants were missing—I saw neither humans nor tigris as I cautiously descended. Beside the pristine village was a great lake, its shores perfectly circular, as if someone had used a giant cup to trace its boundaries. The water within was so clear it might as well have been polished glass, but when I peered into the depths, I could see no bottom, just an eternity of water. In the center of the lake, like a glittering pupil in the perfect watery eye, was a dome-shaped hole, its surface made of some kind of enamel that glowed softly with azure light.

I put us onto the ground beside the village, on the shore of the lake of strange water. It was a relief to land, even though the distance hadn't been great. I sucked in more huge breaths. What was wrong with me?

"This is the home of the humans who created dragons?" Harlan asked in wonder as he looked around, staring from lake to village to the spire-like trees that surrounded it all.

"Those buildings seem fit for humans," I said, forcing my fatigue aside. "Indeed, they are not so different than homes of humans of Ni-Yota and elsewhere."

"Perhaps they expected to be here a long time," Harlan suggested. "A long journey is made easier with something familiar close by. Although those structures do not look hundreds of years old."

"The creators could do many things. Or perhaps some of the tigris are still here, maintaining the buildings of their creators." I sniffed the air. "Although I can neither hear nor smell them."

"And what about that lake?" Harlan asked as he slid off my back to stand at the shore. "I've never seen water so clear."

I focused my mind, returning my perception to the Latticework and its near-infinite connections. I expected this place to explode with Chords of Making. If the Latticework had been created here, surely it must have a special place in the fabric of the unseen world. But the opposite was true. Within the boundary of the forest canopy, the Latticework stopped. No Chords, no Grafts, not even the mundane connections between physical objects, existed here. I suddenly became aware that my own connection to my fellow dragons had been severed. I realized why I was finding it hard to breathe inside the canopy. Magic didn't function inside the forest as it did elsewhere, and dragons were creatures of magic, at least in part.

"Bayloo, what is wrong?" Harlan asked. "You look as if you are about to topple over."

I hadn't realized I was swaying. I continued to suck in air, but that wasn't the problem. My body needed something that it was no longer getting.

"There is no magic in this place," I managed to say. "No Chords connect me with anything. This place is like the world your wife wanted to create."

I was a fish out of water, except the water was my connection to the magic of the Latticework. It didn't matter how much air I got.

"I don't understand," Harlan replied, with rising concern. "Isn't that why we came? Because there was magic in this place to aid us?"

I didn't answer. It wasn't worth using the last of my strength to explain. It wasn't just that I couldn't survive in this place—I'd come here for a magic source sufficient to summon balefire. But the forest was an island in more ways than one. It was cut off from the rest of the Latticework, and I'd lost the connections to my fellow dragons. Without Chords linking me to my brethren, there could be no balefire.

"Bayloo, the lake!" Harlan shouted. "The lake isn't water."

Did he really think I cared?

"A regular hot forge of a smith would have its fuel nearby, to keep the fire going. If the parallel holds for these so-called creation forges, the makers would've kept whatever it was that ran them near as well. That dome in the center of the lake is the forge. The lake is the fuel—the energy for the forge. Bayloo, I think we are next to the source of magic you seek."

If I'd been able to breathe better, I would've been more excited about the revelation. I forced myself to focus on the strange lake. It was just as devoid of Chord connections as everyplace else within the forest. At least connections leading outward. I probed deeper into the water-that-wasn't-water. Finally, I understood. The liquid was a Chord. All of it. Whatever this substance was, it was the material of the Latticework itself. The lake was the storehouse of magic that I sought. This was the material that had created dragons and later created the Ar-Shadow and the Grafts of human magic. I couldn't focus enough to use it. I could barely keep my eyes open.

I did the only thing I could: I fell into the lake of magic.

There was no splash. It was like falling into mud. Except this mud was magical energy. Almost instantly, my faculties returned. Power like I'd never experienced before surged through me. It was sweeter than honey, a nectar that called to me. I indulged too much, and pain shot through the whole of my body. I grabbed the shore with a foreleg, pulling myself out of the reservoir.

"With this, I can bring forth balefire. A balefire like none the world has ever seen. With this I can destroy the rust. Or anything else. It is the ultimate power of making or unmaking."

At least my delirious mind thought that I could do it.

The magic in the reservoir coursed through me. It was elation like no other. If I combined the best of my nights with Rinxia and the giddy buzz of guzzling a barrel of fine shaojiu, raw magic felt a bit better than that. The fog that had clung to my mind disappeared. I sensed the connection between the Chords with utter clarity for the first time. At the edge of my consciousness, there was even some understanding of the larger design that had gone into creating the Latticework. I luxuriated in the power, until the pain came again like a claw inside my body, the sharp ends grasping at me. I clamped my jaws together.

We were not meant for such power.

I realized that I could not continue to tap the reservoir. It had not been intended for dragons or any single creature. This was the raw power of a creation forge. I needed to act before it tore me apart.

With nearly unlimited energy surging through me, I commanded a new series of Chords to form. From me, these new veins of energy grew, expanding upwards, past the canopy of trees that surrounded this forest, back into the world where the Latticework dominated. Once there, I sought Kiata. My sister was the lodestone, her links to me stronger than any other dragon. It was to her I channeled the reservoir of magical energy. Carefully.

Blaris and Arutel were near as well. I connected all of us, pulling together the elements necessary for balefire. From each part of the world I drew part of what would make this possible. I breached the Gap with the Grafts of the humans, temporarily repairing the Latticework links to allow for balefire to be summoned. Through these repaired channels came a power that had no place in the natural world. It was the force of unmaking. That was the true nature of balefire—it was chaos itself. The primal substance from which all else sprang. For these precious moments, it was mine to direct. I gave it to Kiata, and through her, to my kin.

"Brothers and Sisters, it goes to you now. Call forth your fire and cleanse the world."

I felt my fellow dragons as they flew, Blaris and Arutel at the lead, Kiata a short distance behind, directing the power I sent to her. My brethren had already crossed the Pillar Mountains. They awaited on the peaks, watching as the rust spread below.

Arutel unleashed his breath first, a silver and black blast that resembled flame on the outside, but within it was the power of pure chaos. The balefire struck the rust, subjecting it to the supreme power of unmaking. Against this, there would be no adaptation, no clever strategy of survival. The rust unformed, breaking into the pieces that had once made it what it was. Once begun, the inferno of unmaking spread, the complex structure of the rust providing kindling to the spreading flame. It was a chaos fire. For so long as Kiata fed the balefire energy, it would continue to grow. I sensed the rust reacting. It had no fear, but it had will. It wanted to survive. It broke itself into pieces. It pulled power from the ground to maintain its structure. It tried to hide. I would allow none of that to succeed.

I channeled power to Kiata and she kept feeding it to my kin. Blaris joined the attack, adding to the pockets of dazzling destruction spreading across the land. My brethren flew quickly, igniting new infernos of balefire across Ni-Yota. Kiata urged them westward. The effect spread rapidly, cleansing the land wherever it touched. It was an inferno of chaos and the rust was the fuel.

For much of the day and into the night, Kiata and our brother and sister flew, spreading the blaze. It spread more rapidly than any fire, unmaking the rust. I lost myself in the process. I was a conduit of power, but a necessary consequence was that I was constantly flooded with magical energy. So long as I didn't absorb too much at any one time, the pain remained manageable. As my brother and sisters flew across Ni-Yota and into Illium, I lost all sense of time, and eventually I lost all sense of myself.

At some point, reality became a dream, and the dream was rather pleasant. There was a period when I had no desire to leave the strange world of the Latticework. That was followed by not even knowing that there was any place other than an eternal void of power, where I could sense everything but I was nothing ...

If this was death, I would take it.

FORTY-NINE

Reality returned suddenly and unpleasantly.

It began with pain, because what better way to signify life? The sensation of fire, of muscles torn and insides shredded, assaulted me at once, reminding me that I did possess a physical body and it would retaliate if mistreated. This particular punishment was singularly brutal. I whirled and bucked, and I might even have roared out in pain. That was just the start.

There was another level to the pain. A deeper level, provided by the emotional part of my being. It was that part of me that had helped me turn aside the rust, but it also was traitorous. Memories stalked me, thoughts of my mother. I re-lived her death, this time with a better understanding of the things she had done. She was a follower of the Way. To her, giving her offspring to slavery, sacrificing an egg to the Pale Wrights, enduring exile and finally a painful death, would've all been on her path. To me, many of those same actions hurt. I had been part of duty to her. Yet, the ache of my mother's passing was distant compared with the stabbing wound of losing Rinxia. She was as close as I had ever come to another dragon. I had hoped for so much more from her. The future I fought to create had been for her as much as anyone else. She would never share it. Worse, she died not understanding the depth of what I felt.

I opened my eyes, filled with pain.

Kiata was there, as was Harlan, Arutel, Blaris, and Saba. More dragons flew overhead or hovered behind the rest. I lay on a grassy field. The sky was clear, the sun no longer new in the sky. In the distance were trees.

Trees. Normal trees.

And I lay on grass.

I drew a long breath into my nostrils. On it was the scent of blooms and flowers and my companions.

"You all smell horrible," I told them.

Harlan graced me with a warm smile even though he did indeed smell worse than usual. "You did it."

His words didn't quite register.

"The rust has been eradicated," Kiata told me. "The balefire worked."

"More than worked!" Arutel proclaimed. "Never before has there been a fire such as that—more golden than the sun and dark as the night, blinding, but without heat. It traveled like light itself, not even burning. It was something else."

"Cleansing," Kiata offered. "The land has been cleansed. The grass and trees and birds and weeds return. It has been only a few days, but from the ruins of destroyed rust, true life again reveals itself as that which was stolen is released. When you are strong enough to fly, you shall see it for yourself. Once again, dragons have saved the land."

I should have been more pleased at that news than how I felt. "Where is this place?"

"The southwestern tip of Ni-Yota," Harlan told me. "You fell into some kind of trance within the forest. I couldn't wake you, no matter what I did. Eventually, the lake drained and the liquid that remained became clouded. After that, the canopy of trees parted. Kiata and the other dragons came and lifted you out."

Somehow, his words were another blow to me, although I didn't quite understand the reason. "The lake ... the reservoir of magic ... is it gone?"

"It is certainly less." Harlan's brows furrowed. "You wish to return?"

The truth was, I did—not to the forest, but to the dreaming void where I was part of the Latticework, when I was power. A place without the pain of this world. But that wasn't what these people who had gathered about me wanted to hear. "No, but perhaps it might be needed again. Once before, the rust came back. It could happen again."

Arutel gave a low roar. "We burned every bit of it. Kiata had us fly from one end of this continent to another. We scoured mountains and valleys, islands and fields. I am told that the rust grew, always attached to the greater whole. It killed itself, except on a few scattered islands in the far west where the sea separated it. There we burned relentlessly. It is gone."

"It was the creators themselves who saved it the last time, I think," Harlan said.

"How do you know that?" I wondered.

"You were in your trance for a long time—days." Harlan shrugged. "I could not merely stare at you all that time and do nothing. I searched the forest village for something to help you. The buildings contained both the mundane items of everyday life—bed and baths, paintings and wash clothes—as well as the fantastic: devices of metal, globes of light, as well as items I do not even have the words to describe. But in one room, a place ... well, it seemed larger on the inside than the outside. In that place were walls and walls of plants and flowers contained in spheres of crystal. The flowers looked alive, as if they had just been picked, the plants green and thriving, although they all were frozen, like the village itself. I walked that room for all of a morning and the afternoon that followed. Not a single sphere was empty, not a single one out of order, except one. There was one that had been shattered, and its contents removed."

"You think some of the rust was in there," I concluded. "Why would they do that? It was they who created dragons to destroy the rust."

Harlan rubbed his chin. "Humans are curious creatures. One of the oddities of our kind is that the more we know, the more we yearn to know even more. It is the more learned among us who collect countless volumes of books, it is the scholars who spend their whole lives at study. My ancestors tried to accumulate all the knowledge of this world on their island, but always they wanted more. Well, this lot of humans who created that forest and the Archive at Silla, they were as knowledgeable as any. The rust must've fascinated them. They would've wanted to learn more, to study more. And if I know humans, they were probably arrogant enough to think they could control it."

"But somehow it got free?" Kiata asked.

"Perhaps they released it in spite, when the war against the dragons seemed lost," Harlan offered. "That pettiness can be found in humans too."

Harlan's theory was possible, but I had another. One I had suspected since I'd learned that Jinu had sent expeditions to the Forest of Fallen Night. "I think it was the tigris. Those griffins that attacked Trishan may have come from this place as well. More guardians of the vanished Archivists that served the tigris."

Kiata snorted with indignation. "The giant cats have fled. Even before the first of balefire, they went silent. Their raids stopped. They abandoned their allies, slipping into the night from which they came. They are cowards. It would not surprise me if the rust was their weapon, as well as the griffins."

"Hundreds of years passed between the time of the first rust and when it appeared once again. All that time, the tigris merely waited?"

"Their human masters died or disappeared. Or dragons killed them. I think the tigris, too, slumbered during those long years.

Perhaps they, too, were held in spheres of glass, frozen in time. Maybe in the village somewhere, maybe elsewhere in the Forest of Fallen Night. Until something disturbed them, awaking them from their long slumber. It could have been Jinu and his meddling. He came here, with Aragor, if the stories are to be believed."

"And they somehow awakened the tigris, who decided to kill everyone once they were again aware of the world?" Harlan asked. "You really don't like cats, do you?"

"The tigris were close to their human masters. They would've fought in the war against the dragons. They would've shared the vision of their creators. When the tigris emerged from the forest, they found Ni-Yota, a land ruled by the dragons, the enemy who had vanquished their masters. They would have thought it their duty to continue to fight. The machinations of humans ... and dragons, provided them every opportunity to do so." My blood heated as I thought again of the selfishness that had brought the world to the edge of ruin. There was plenty of blame to go around for all the races. "Jinu the spymaster, he said none who ventured to this place returned, but is he a man to be believed? Here was the repository of human power. Jinu hungers for it, I have no doubt. Aragor longed to be Skyking. Perhaps a deal was made with Jinu that enabled Aragor to defeat his sister to become ruler of Ni-Yota. But there was a dark price to the bargain. The tigris were devious. Elasu was, by all accounts, as ambitious as any human. Somehow, she was enslaved by the tigris, used by them to sow rebellion in Ni-Yota, while all the time the rust grew and gained strength in the west."

"Then we shall hunt them," Kiata promised. "Without the rust to contend with, there is nothing to stop us."

"And what of Legao?" I asked. "What has the Protector to say about all this?"

Arutel's eyes flashed with displeasure at the mention of Ni-Yota's human protector. If Kiata noticed his reaction, she chose to ignore it. "Legao fought bravely against the rust. Her magic saved Trishan—she carved a great chasm and filled it with water from the bay as the rust surrounded the city. One of her own magi died building it. That was the battle where Rinxia fell as well, contending with a behemoth. Legao tried to save her. The wizard collapsed and nearly died from the effort; she was lying unconscious for a full day afterward. Legao has acted as a Protector should. At least for now."

Hearing of Rinxia only opened my wound again. Arutel had never known her, so he didn't care. But he knew how to hate humans.

"This Legao is a human, a wielder of magic like the Sculptors of Rolm," Arutel said. "Such humans are dangerous."

I snorted with displeasure, even if I didn't disagree. My body ached as well as my head. Already, conflict smoldered between human and dragon.

Harlan held out two open palms. "Let us not search for dangerous shoals when we are already in a storm." Everyone stared at him. "That means there is no need to look for new enemies when we have plenty already. The tigris remain dangerous. They came from the Forest of Fallen Night, and doubtless possess tremendous knowledge. We should not underestimate them." More quietly, he added, "Or the other dangers to this land. Peace is fragile."

I suspected Harlan's thoughts lingered on Norta and the remains of the Farlighters as well as the tigris threat. Despite their losses, there were still Farlighter ships out plying the seas, some of them with captains who shared Norta's vision of a world without magic or dragons. We had won the great battle, but there were still enemies among us, within and without. But that was not an issue that I could deal with on this day.

If I had to live in this world, I might as well make the best of it. "It has been many days since my stomach was filled. Please tell me you had the foresight to bring food and drink with you."

Finally, those humans got something right. They brought plenty of shaojiu. I drank it all, hoping to forget.

FIFTY

Eventually, I returned to Trishan.

There, Legao awaited. The palace was still a ruined hulk. The area around the city was even worse. It was as if the ground itself had erupted, but I knew that was the result of the chasm Legao had created to save the city from the approaching rust. The remains of her magic summoning were a mud-streaked canyon collapsing in on itself as I flew overhead, and a battlefield still littered with pyres for the dead. But the city and its inhabitants had survived. Legao had done well.

The cost of her magic was obvious the moment I saw her. I barely recognized the wizard. Deep lines of age had carved themselves into her face, while loose skin seemed to drip from her throat. We met in the gardens, just the two of us. She walked slowly, as if struggling for balance.

"Tell me about Rinxia," I asked.

Legao turned her head slowly, her eyes haunted. "Rinxia." She said the name with pursed lips. My hearts ached at the memory still. "The chasm I managed to make was too narrow. The hollowings tried to cross by filling it with their own bodies, along with whatever debris they could muster. The battle was a horrid quagmire of blood and mud. We concentrated on stopping the behemoths, but one breached our lines. Orli, of my own guard, died there, as did Ega, my most promising pupil, who drained herself trying to stop the onslaught. In the end, Rinxia saved us with fire and claw and bravery. She saved hundreds of thousands who live in Trishan, but at a terrible cost. I am sorry to have failed her. And you." Legao did sound genuinely remorseful, although she could've also just been exhausted.

"You did well to save the city," I offered, but the words were hollow. They were what I was supposed to say. I wanted Rinxia back. I would have traded all of Trishan for her, although I knew that was unworthy of me. Rinxia would not have approved.

"It seems I was wrong about your mother's quest, and balefire," Legao admitted. "Such power. I never could have imagined." Her last words animated her—the prospect of such magic reawakened a fire inside her. Suddenly, she sounded like her old, dangerous self.

I replied cautiously. "Only the unimaginable could defeat the rust. All else would have failed."

"Can balefire be brought forth again, whenever you wish it?" Legao asked pointedly.

"If the rust survives, we will be ready."

"How is it done?" Legao pressed. I appreciated her bluntness at least. She understood and desired power. "No ember dragon in five centuries could unlock this secret. Many did not believe that balefire ever existed."

I could've been coy about this great conjuring, but letting Legao know the truth served my purpose better. "I can command the magic of both the Latticework and the Ar-Shadow, Legao. I can use the Chords and create Grafts. All magic is mine to command." Legao's face went pale, as if she'd eaten some bad fish. I got closer to her as my words sank in. "And I can sever any magic binding. No wizard, no ember dragon, can match my power. I am the master of the Latticework."

It wasn't quite truth, but I wanted Legao to understand that she could never be my equal.

Legao's jaw pulsed, her supposed fatigue vanishing. "You brought more dragons here. Former slaves from Rolm who will hate humans. I did not wish that."

I thought of Arutel. Already the tension between dragon and human grew. "They came to destroy the rust."

"They will leave now?"

I didn't know. "You are the Protector of Ni-Yota. I suppose that is your decision to make. But you would be wise to allow them to help you should the tigris reappear."

Legao's eyes narrowed on me. "Do you insist on that?"

Her question was not an easy one. I did not want to become Protector. I did not envy Legao's place. Nor was her authority going to be absolute. I would not tolerate a new Conclave of human wizards that would make war on the remaining dragons. I hoped she took the lesson to heart. "I do not know," was my answer. "You would be wise not to force me to make such a decision."

Legao stared at me for a long time before dipping her chin in acknowledgement. Legao was too smart to fight a battle she could not win. "I have named Kiata as head of my council of advisors."

That gave me a bit of hope. "What of Jinu?"

"He disappeared as the rust closed in on the city. It seems he doubted me." Legao gave a wry grin. "I am not blind to what Jinu is, you should know. I will be no one's puppet."

"That is a relief to hear. I hope you will hear Kiata's counsel as well. She is young, but she has a desire to protect this place. It is her Way."

Legao's eyes managed to show a bit of warmth. Whatever her feelings toward me and the other dragons, I did believe she had a genuine respect for Kiata after their shared experiences.

"What are your plans?" Legao asked me.

"The chefs of Changsha prepared an excellent black pig, a variety bred from Elasu's stock. I have a hankering for it."

Legao made a noise from her throat that resembled a laugh. "Then what?"

"After that, I shall be watching. Even if you do not see me, I will be watching."

I left Legao alone in the garden after that. I wasn't joking about the meal, but it was not my reason for departing Trishan. On my way to Changsha, my journey took me back to the place where Rinxia had died, but there was no sign of her remains. The wind or scavengers or something else had wiped the mountain clear in the days I had been away. Still, I hoped her *jing* lingered.

I circled the sky, roaring another farewell at Haven, my hearts heavy. Rinxia would've said her death was merely part of the Way. She wouldn't have approved of my sadness at her loss, but I hoped she would have understood, at least.

Soon after I reached Changsha, I received a glasswing from Harlan to inform me that Legao had offered him the charge of supervising rebuilding the fleet of Ni-Yota—this time without waveships. The Protector had been listening to Harlan's stories, it seemed. Already she planned great trading expeditions to the far-off isles of Harlan's memory. My friend had committed only to building ships, with the promise that one of the new craft would be his own. I was glad for him, even though I would miss him.

After I had eaten my fill in Changsha, I spent several days flying across Ni-Yota, traveling across the vast rice fields of the east toward the fishing villages that lined the far coast. The land healed quickly. The roads were bustling, fields were again being tilled.

There was no sign of the tigris. Like the rust centuries ago, they seemed to have vanished. I had hope to find at least one of them, not to kill but to speak with. I had to settle for speaking to the human lords—those who had once fought alongside them. They all claimed to know nothing of the whereabouts of their allies. They all claimed to have been deceived. They all professed their undying loyalty to the current Protector. I had no idea what Legao planned to do with these, but I still gave them all the same message.

"Tell the tigris that this is their world, too."

I hoped the tigris would get the message, if not from the lips of these lords then the whispers of the courtiers who overheard me deliver it to them. For once, let the whispers carry an offer of peace.

After that, I returned to the sky. I flew east, back toward the Wall of Fire, toward the land of my birth. I flew knowing that my fellow dragons were free, and the world was safe from the rust. I told myself that I had done my part in this. Let Legao and Kiata deal with the problems of Ni-Yota. Let Blaris and Arutel help nurture our race back from the brink of extinction. Finally, I could do as I wished. Or so I wanted to believe.

I knew that somewhere in Trishan, Harlan was laughing at me. If he were here, I knew what he would tell me: The wind chooses your destination—you merely decide how long it is going to take to get there.

I beat my wings, letting the wind take me.

HERE ENDS BOOK 5. My gratitude to you for coming along on this adventure with Bayloo and me is beyond words. Thank you. If you haven't already done so, please sign up for my newsletter where I will announce new releases among other news (and you get *A Dragon's Doom*, a free prequel novella too!). Join at www.robertvanenovels.com. All is not done, either. Even greater stories await, and you'll hear about them first if you sign up! My one final plea is that if you have enjoyed these books, please tell a friend. Doing so bestows upon me the opportunity to tell more stories. I am in your debt, dear reader.

We are all dragons.

--RGV